Casilda had led he... ...the spare room upstairs. As I entered he was kneeling with his face pressed against her stomach. She sat, naked to the waist, with an arm around his bull neck, twisting his dark curls. They were too absorbed in each other to take any notice of me.

He had evidently set about his business without a second's hesitation. With his head sunk in her lap, blindly, with both brown, hairy paws upstretched, he mauled, rather than fondled, Casilda's breasts. The way the fellow manhandled those sumptuous tits struck me as exceedingly uncouth for a Latin lover. Nevertheless, there was no sign of objection on her part, just the fast, heavy breathing that shook her magnificent body violently from within . . .

– *A Gallery of Nudes*

Also available from Headline:

Eros in the Country
Eros in the Town
Eros on the Grand Tour
Eros in the New World
Eros in the Far East
Eros in High Places

Erotic omnibus collections
The Complete Eveline
Lascivious Ladies
The Power of Lust
Follies of the Flesh
Forbidden Escapades

Venus in Paris
A Lady of Quality
The Love Pagoda
The Education of a Maiden
Maid's Night In
Lena's Story
Cremorne Gardens
The Lusts of the Borgias
States of Ecstasy
Wanton Pleasures
The Secret Diary of Mata Hari
The Pleasures of Women
The Secrets of Women
Sweet Sins
The Carefree Courtesan
Love Italian Style
Ecstasy Italian Style
Body and Soul
Sweet Sensations
Amorous Liaisons
Hidden Rapture
Learning Curves

Wanton Excesses

Anonymous

HEADLINE

Copyright © 1992 HEADLINE BOOK PUBLISHING PLC

First published in 1992
by HEADLINE BOOK PUBLISHING PLC

10 9 8 7 6 5 4 3 2 1

All rights reserved. No part of this publication may be
reproduced, stored in a retrieval system, or transmitted,
in any form or by any means without the prior written
permission of the publisher, nor be otherwise circulated
in any form of binding or cover other than that in which
it is published and without a similar condition being
imposed on the subsequent purchaser.

All characters in this publication are fictitious
and any resemblance to real persons, living or dead,
is purely coincidental.

ISBN 0 7472 3718 2

Phototypeset by Intype, London

Printed and bound by
HarperCollins Manufacturing, Glasgow

HEADLINE BOOK PUBLISHING PLC
Headline House
79 Great Titchfield Street
London W1P 7FN

Contents

A Gallery of Nudes	3
The Town Bull	195
Blanche	269
Madge	359

A Gallery of Nudes

I

It was not a big dinner party that night at the Delavignes'. There were eight of us, all told – an awkward number to seat. Disliking Lucien as I do, I might easily not have accepted Helen's invitation. As a rule it was an honour that I made a habit of declining, although I did a fair amount of business with the Baron Delavigne. On this occasion I believe there were a couple of pictures which I hoped to persuade him to buy – a Guardi and a Zubarán, if I am not mistaken. Probably that was why I came to be dining at his house in Regent's Park. Only the year before last – and yet how immensely long ago it seems!

The fare itself was excellent, I must admit. And the wines too, as usual. Lucien has supremely good taste in everything. Helen, for instance, is a show-piece: one of his finest possessions. Although he had tired of her long since, and made no secret of it, even his exorbitant pride must have revelled in the thought that he owned such a dazzling beauty for a wife. Helen is not exactly my type – but she was looking wonderful that evening, and no two ways about it. Dark, pale, fragile, superbly *soignée*, she had that genuinely cultured yet peculiarly humourless mentality of the extremely well-bred American. Perhaps she would have appeared more admirable in Boston than in London.

Despite Lucien's arrant cynicism and physical coarseness, in many respects they were a well-matched couple. Taut and distraught as she was beneath that elegant surface, I feel sure that Helen still derived the utmost satisfaction from her successful marriage to a member of the French aristocracy. She enjoyed his title, their smart town house, their distinguished guests, her socially eminent position in the art world – for she had a foot firmly planted in both camps, and more than anything she resembled the graceful equestrienne daintily straddling the broad backs of a pair of stolid horses at the circus. By the matriarchal instinct of her American upbringing, as a good hostess and a convinced feminist, she had not relinquished her lawful place at the head of Lucien's table. I was on her left, with her handsome young friend Casilda Vandersluys between me and some dismal diplomat, a wealthy Argentine or Venezuelan, I vaguely remember.

At the corner diagonally across from mine, where Lucien sat, the conversation sparkled with that bright banality which one expects at politely convivial gatherings of this sort. It toyed with topics ancient or up-to-date, yet neither truly wise nor gay. Helen's splendid diamonds outshone a famous Italian soprano's broken shafts of wit. For myself, partly in desperation but largely from habit, I endeavoured to draw out the personality of my quiet, attractive neighbour – the American girl with the fair complexion and the exotic looks, whose place in the household I suspected of being more than simply that of an intimate friend of the family. I had met her briefly once before – that is to say. I had been introduced to her, wearing ballet tights, some weeks previously, when I had called round there one evening to talk business with Lucien. She had spectacles on her nose then, and seemed strangely aloof. Tonight she struck me as a good deal less forbidding.

Lucien had said: 'You know Casilda, don't you? A great friend of my wife's. She lives with us.' I noticed at the time that there was the hint of a leer in his voice, as though what he really meant was: 'They live together.'

But one could never tell with Lucien. He often employed that sly tone when referring to Helen, as if to nudge you and confide: 'All the money is here, I suppose you realise. I married a very rich heiress.' So I thought nothing of it. We shook hands, and I went with Lucien into his study.

I had the impression now, that Casilda and I were hitting it off pretty well, and this rather surprised me, although, of course, there was no earthly reason why we should fail to get on. Admittedly I was twice her age, I reckoned – wrongly, for she was over twenty-five (in fact she was two years older than I guessed). Anyhow, what did that matter? Probably she was just as bored with these people as I was. My cherished reputation as an insatiable *roué* and expert ladykiller was not likely to worry her, for she seemed a sensible young woman, and must have realised that I took no particular interest in her from the mating point of view. Besides, if she did happen to belong to the rival persuasion (which I could scarcely credit; you never would have taken her for a lesbian – or at least not an authentic one), what difference could it make? Might we not be all the more agreeably at ease together? I for one would certainly not hold any queer little foible of that sort against her. As I worship and adore women, and every single lovely woman, on principle, if two of these heavenly creatures find delight in each other, I, a professed and eager sensualist can only wish them joy. Alas, I cannot myself fornicate with them all – not even with a tenth as many as I still could wish. Why then should I be so churlishly narrow-minded as to resent what some members of my sex deplore as a wicked waste of ecstasies which they consider they should be called upon to share? On the contrary, I would be the last to deny the ladies their innocent pleasure, while merely regretting that it is of necessity both limited and negative. Good luck to them! By all means let them solace their unfulfilled cravings as best they may, since my fellow men have lamentably neglected to satisfy their natural feminine desire.

Not just one wench in heat, but a pair, a couple of women's bodies locked in the throes of passion – the very thought of it excites and fascinates me (providing of course that neither partner in the frolic is old, ugly or too masculine to arouse my lecherous envy). Each of them kneels at the same shrine as I, and as a spectacle it always thrills me, for the multiplication of their charms doubles my lustful impulse to give the crazy bitches a taste of the real thing. If I set my mind to it, I am confident that I can wean them away from their pointless preference – or at any rate I can usually break up the affair by enticing the one I want back to normal. Fortunately, genuine, dyed-in-the-wool lesbians are rare, for they tend to appeal to the natural instincts of a proper man as laughably little as either type of male pervert – the murky-eyed bugger or the simpering bumboy. Sappho, in that setup, wears the trousers. She is an even greater menace than the ordinary husband she apes and would give a good few years of her life to be. Husbands, after all, have been known to see reason, nobly overcoming the cruelest pangs of jealousy. But not the female homosexual. Scorned, she is, as ever, deadlier than the male. Beware of her vengeful claws – but lure her dreamy little wife away from her just the same. It can be done with patience, skill and care – like prising certain spiky kinds of seafood off a rock.

This train of thought did not enter the crowded, smut-begrimed station of my mind – nor even flash through it, I swear – during that dull, yet eventful dinner at the Delavignes'. In the whole of an existence devoted mainly to the keen pursuit of pleasure, I have seldom been less conscious of an intriguing opportunity. The brain and the heart, no less than the flesh itself, frequently let one down in such cases, I have discovered. Be that as it may, I can truthfully assert that I was not, at the time, in the least concerned or curious about any amorous relationship that our handsome hostess might have established with her dear friend on my left.

Helen I admired for her good looks, her social gifts, her poise; but she meant almost as little to me, I confess, as the plump and merry Mme Gomez-Garriga across the table. And if I went out of my way to be affable with Casilda Vandersluys, it was chiefly in order to pass the time of night as congenially as possible. I had no designs on her person. My only ulterior motive, if any, was of a more sordid kind: there is never much harm in acquiring an extra ally at court. By the beginning of the third course I had contrived to glean several essential facts about my charming neighbour.

She had lived with the Delavignes, on and off, for the best part of ten years – ever since her mother, a school friend of Helen's in Baltimore, had abandoned Casilda's father for a series of disreputable lovers. Or perhaps he had already left her by then. He was a Dutchman and a wastrel called Vandersluys, who had vanished without a trace at this stage, when Casilda was finishing her education at Lausanne. Her mother, a hopeless alcoholic now, was seldom out of an inebriates' home. She herself had undergone two brief marriages, and after the second divorce had reverted to her maiden name. 'Aunt' Helen, as she then was to Casilda, and Lucien, the soul of kindness, had adopted her, so to speak, at the age of seventeen, when her parents separated on the brink of murder; and she had returned to them at intervals, whenever her life threatened to become unbearable. Not that she had ever sunk so low as to go crawling back to them for comfort, she was at some pains to assure me – but Helen 'just naturally seemed to be there, on hand when needed' (as I could well imagine) 'like a lifeboat in constant readiness to anticipate any signal of distress.' She received a small sum of alimony from her second husband, whom she had dismissed for 'persistent cruelty,' and her old Dutch grandfather, an East Indian planter who adored 'his little girl' (she shuddered at the phrase, as though accusing him by implication of incestuous tamperings with a minor), had left her a dwindling legacy which she scornfully described as 'conscience money.' She wrote fairly regularly for the fashion magazines and had done 'quite a bit of modelling' in her time (as also I could well believe).

'Mother is American-born,' she added, 'like me. She's of Hungarian, Irish and Scots extraction. So I suppose you'd say I'm a thorough mongrel. My paternal grandmother was slightly Eurasian – I think a quarter Javanese.' At this point the watchful Helen intervened. I had monopolised Casilda too long, evidently. As a guest I was not pulling my weight – and I had hardly addressed a single remark to my hostess. I assume it was etiquette, rather than jealousy, that prompted her to cut in:

'I was just pointing out to Count Zwieburst that we're a perfect cocktail here tonight – if you go back a generation, I mean. Between us there are as many as nineteen nationalities represented around this table. Isn't that interesting? Lucien has some Polish blood, you know. Mr Grey is the only one of us – except, of course, Wagstaff – who is pure and unmixed. You *are* entirely English, aren't you, Anthony? And even he has lived most of his life abroad, I understand. Really you and Lucien ought to have switched birthplaces!' She ended with a gay, reproving little laugh.

'Yes, my home,' I said, 'if I had one, would be Paris.'

'But you were born in England, surely?' Helen inquired. 'I would describe you as more of a cosmopolitan than an expatriate.'

A Gallery of Nudes

'I'd like to think so myself,' I answered. 'There was a time when you would have called me an exile. That's what I was. I fled the country – let me see – thirty years ago; and waited out of harm's way until any troublesome consequences were bound to have blown over.'

I was aware, as I spoke, that it was stupid and ill-mannered of me to tease Helen with this facetious reply. I have no idea what made me do it. But her air of superiority annoyed me, I wanted to ruffle her smug, grand-ladylike composure. And she should have had the sense to leave it at that, without provoking me to further indiscretions. Her butler and I were clodhoppers, were we? We were the only two dumb Englishmen in the company of her high-born foreign guests. Then why didn't she go on chatting with her wretched Count and leave me in peace? He was heavily engaged with half a partridge on his plate; perhaps he was a trifle deaf: he paid no attention to us. I had been quite happy talking to Casilda. That was just it, I expect. Foolishly, Helen chose to pursue the conversation.

'You make it sound as if you were wanted by the police for some terrible crime!' she exclaimed. 'But how thrilling!'

'I was. For indecent assault – with violence.' I informed her. (I was gilding the lily a bit; there had been no actual violence.) 'But in later years I've come to doubt whether they would ever have managed to pin it on me. The offence was committed by stealth. The circumstances were peculiar. Probably I'd have been safe enough, had I stayed. And yet – who knows? Somebody might have identified me, if the victim herself couldn't.'

Helen recoiled indignantly, as though I had leaned over and pinched her thigh. She glared at me for a second in utter amazement before plunging into small talk with the blissfully impervious Count. I could see her thinking: 'Anthony is drunk!' At that same moment I was conscious of Casilda's gaze, fixed inquisitively upon me from the side. I turned and smiled at her in apology – but whether it appeared a sardonic or a sheepish apology, I cannot say. Her hazel eyes were twinkling and brimful of amusement.

'Explain the mystery to me, please,' she requested, so softly that it was almost a whisper. 'I simply don't follow. Did you blindfold the poor girl? Or strangle her with her stocking? No, I see – you bashed her on the head and knocked her out, is that it?'

I tried to talk of something else, I forget what.

'Tell me,' she insisted. 'I'm consumed with curiosity.'

'Come, I was only joking,' I said. 'And curiosity is both unhealthy and dangerous at your tender age.'

'Never mind. I am going to know. You can't refuse to answer – or I shall drag Helen into it again.'

'But you have already heard. As I told Helen, it was a – well, rather too great a liberty perpetrated on impulse. A case not of malice aforethought, you might say, but precisely the reverse. A stab in the dark.'

'How tiresome you're being! I still don't see what you mean.'

'No – I didn't intend you to. Let's drop the subject. Personally I'm entirely in favour of mixed marriages. I've known –'

But Casilda by now was hobnobbing intently with the gentleman on her left, the swarthy diplomat from Ecuador or Peru. We had been served a delectable cheese savoury. Lucien was a stickler for observing the customs of the country, oddly enough. He even subscribed to our ceremonial segregation of the sexes at the end of dinner: his guests had to linger over their port or brandy in the approved style. He had not gone so far as to emulate the Englishman's longing to dispense with the company of womenfolk entirely, although he had acquired the habit of brightening visibly as soon as the opposite sex were out of earshot. I meanwhile was cursing myself for having succumbed to the temptation of shocking Helen. What were they discussing now in their domains, I wondered? Surely Casilda would never be so tactless as to taunt our mutual friend about my piece of atrocious bad taste a moment ago? Ah, to hell with them. What did I care, anyhow. Lucien was not one to let his wife's dislikes interfere with a business deal that happened to take his fancy.

When we finally joined the ladies I was granted the privilege of exchanging platitudes with the highly scented Mme Gomez-Garriga. Casilda, I was glad to note, ignored me completely. It was time, I felt, to end this happy evening, I rose to my feet. 'Don't go yet,' Lucien protested. 'Cassy, give Grey some whisky.' We met and hovered by the tray of drinks at the far side of the room. She was almost as tall as I. I saw her suddenly for the first time – the slender, supple body in the low-cut, shimmering, powder-blue sheath of an evening dress that seemed so cold and metallic, though it moulded her hips like a bathing suit and barely, precariously shielded her arrogant bosom; the plain, chilly platinum band at her throat; the rich tawny glint on each loose chestnut curl. She was appetising in the extreme, it now dawned on me. If this was Helen's playmate, then Helen was lucky. A sleek young beast, full of surprise: an amalgamation of contrasts.

'Mostly soda,' I said. 'And plenty of ice.'
'Say when.'
'Tomorrow.'
'What's that? I don't get you.'
'An invitation.'

There was a loud splash, a clinking of ice against glass, and silence. She did not look up.

'To luncheon or dinner,' I repeated. 'As you wish.'

Damn the girl – still not a word. She might have been stone deaf.

At last 'Is that how you like it?' she asked, without interest.

'Yes, fine thanks,' I answered, sipping my drink.

Casilda shrugged her naked shoulders. 'I'll settle for that one story,' she said. 'Tell me now. Nobody's listening. Or do I have to accept your hospitable suggestion and hear the whole saga of your life?'

'Heaven forbid.'

'But you prefer to make it a bedtime story apparently, Mr Grey?'

I laughed. 'Certainly not,' I assured her. 'I've never mentioned it to a soul until tonight.'

'I'll think it over – if I may.'

'By all means. I will telephone you one of these days to learn your decision.'

Her tone abruptly changed. 'No – please don't do that,' she begged. 'I would rather you didn't call me here. I will ring you.'

'Very well. But I won't promise to obey unless you contact me within the next week.'

'That's quite likely. I'm dying to hear this unrepeatable tale. I simply can't wait.' She grinned, to my astonishment, as though delighted to have pulled my leg. 'Goodnight, Mr Grey.'

It was too much, that twist. The mischievous, deceitful slut! What the devil was she playing at? I had not had the very slightest intention of seeing her again or taking her out to lunch – not seriously, anyway. I can't imagine what got into me. I didn't want the woman. Yet for the second time that evening I had made an ass of myself – a youthful, callow, incautious ass. At my age I ought to have known better. Bewildered and embarrassed, I watched Casilda walk away from where I stood, finishing my whisky. In that tight, shining prison of a gown her buttocks moved like a pair of wild animals pacing steadily back and forth across a cage. My, but how they stood up to the most searching scrutiny! They jutted out at you in marvellous, mocking challenge under your very nose. Hers was a body, not a 'figure'; it was built for the beach, the bath or the bed, not for clothes. The majestic action, the impudent, visible shape of her backside, its taut, inviting contours, the deep, dividing crack, the firm-fleshed, rolling spheres, sweeter than water-melons – you missed none of it. Too sallow for a blonde, her dark-brown hair of too light a tint to rate her a brunette, with those clear, perplexing hazel eyes that seemed to take on different shades as you gazed into them, she was – as she herself so rightly said – a thorough mixture. But by no stretch of the imagination was this the fluffy, soft, fey, feminine type that is most often apt to inspire a lesbian love.

Zwieburst offered me a lift home, but I insisted that it would be taking him out of his way and hailed a taxi, which I stopped in Belgrave Square for the pleasure of strolling through the mild September night to my small place in Chelsea. The fresh air would do me good. 'You're flushed with wine,' I told myself, wishing that the remonstrance were true. The fact was that Casilda disturbed and puzzled me. Not for many more years than I cared to remember had I experienced this unmistakable, obsessive, overwhelming tyranny. I had given up all hope – or fear – of succumbing yet again to the sexual infatuations of early manhood. Tonight I had gone to the Delavignes' in a mood of the purest innocence and boredom – but here I was now, suddenly trapped and ensnared. Only momentarily, I swore to that: I must put her right out of my mind by the morning.

I struck down to the Embankment. Not far from there – a couple of miles up river – was the scene of the crime, the huge office block where that lapse had occurred in my young days, when I had recently arrived in London. I was just over twenty. It was midsummer. I went to fetch a former college friend of mine out to lunch. His office was on the top floor of a tall modern building that overlooks the Thames. He had forgotten our appointment, I discovered, for there was nobody in. His door was ajar, as he must have left it. I was scribbling a note for him at his desk when I heard strange sounds from the next room, where his secretary worked. I listened, and made out muffled cries for help. I went to look and an extraordinary sight met my eyes. At first I was at a loss to know what was happening. Miss Morley – Beryl, as I think he called her – was leaning on tiptoe, far out of the window. Both her shoes were off. Her feet hardly touched the ground. She may have been feeding crumbs to the birds or watering some potted plants on the ledge. But she was a prisoner, caught and held fast by the heavy frame, which had fallen across the small of her back. The sash-cord must have snapped. There she was, half-in and half-out of the room, pinned at the middle on the window-sill, unable to move.

No one was about. The other couple of offices on the same floor were empty; everybody else had gone out to eat. And the noise of the traffic below drowned her piteous calls for assistance. She would have to wait for an hour at least, until someone returned – and rushed to set her free. I glanced at my watch: 12:55. My first impulse was to spring to Beryl's rescue. But those hideous short, tight skirts of the period presented me with a vista so startling that I stopped dead in my tracks. I knew the girl to be a plain, unromantic specimen – young but mousy, with a shiny pink complexion and ginger hair. Seen from this angle, however, Miss Morley showed a marked, a most striking improvement. As stretch of stockinged leg, topped by garters, and a glimpse of bare thigh revealed to me hidden charms which I could never have suspected, but for this

A Gallery of Nudes 15

fortuitous and surprising encounter. In a position that was both provocative and comically undignified, she presented, in utter ignorance, an irresistible target. She was none other than Venus Calliope in person! Bless her beautiful bottom! I stood there for a moment, transfixed, enjoying the view to the full – and a full, firm, pleasant prospect it was: the great round moon veiled by clouds. Quickly and quietly I went back and shut all three doors, bolting the outer one. She had no idea, not an inkling, poor sweet, that there was somebody there. It gave her a start – what a start! – when I touched her. She jumped – though she could not budge, her backside leapt in the air, like a porpoise – when I slid my hand gently between her soft, fat thighs. She struggled violently, trying to turn her head, to see who it was that dared to caress her so intimately, so brazenly, and yet anonymously . . . I was quite safe: there was no chance of her recognising her unknown, unwanted (and perhaps unwarrantable) but far from unfriendly assailant.

Her response to my prying fingers was anything but calm, resigned or generous. She fought a fierce rearguard action, kicking out at me viciously with her heels. It was all she could do, though absurdly ineffective. With her tail tilted up towards me at that angle, her frantic attempts to press her legs together were quite useless, and however hard she strained, shrinking and closing her buttocks in a kind of frown, I would not remove my hand, so she might as well have abandoned any hope of dislodging it. I merely stepped aside and continued stroking her at my leisure. She was waving her arms wildly, like a signaller, and I suppose she redoubled her anguished shouts, but I did not bother to listen. I was much too intent on the task at hand. I myself made no sound; I scarcely breathed. With great difficulty I managed to tug her narrow, almost skintight skirt over her hips and roll it up neatly out of the way, exposing the smooth, ample panorama of her luscious behind, clad only vaguely in that unbecoming, silly garment known as cami-knickers, which women wore at the time. It was an obstacle all too easy to displace; that is the best you could say for it.

Now I could see what I was doing – and the sight of those rosy, rounded, twin spheres, that beauteous, broad map of the world, those glorious private bastions at the gates to inner joy, was as pleasing to the eye as was the satin-sleek feel of the pure flesh, the warm, furry cleft, the tender, chubby lips, to the touch of my exploring hands. But her savage efforts at self-defence continued. Her silken heels hacked ferociously though vainly, at my shins. There was nothing else for it: a ruler lay within reach on her desk, unluckily for Beryl's rump. She could not aim her furious kicks, whereas it was impossible for me to miss. Half a dozen peremptory strokes – not too hard, just by way of warning – were enough to quiet her down, after she had danced a lively little jig, with brightly blushing cheeks, for my exclusive benefit.

As soon as order had been restored by this brisk though not vindictive chastisement, I changed weapons, discarding the inflexible ruler for a more personal instrument of correction, specially designed for the purpose, as the bayonet is the arm to use when it comes to attacking at close quarters. Naturally, by this time, I was so eager for the fray I could restrain myself no longer. My aggressive instincts had been roused, for minutes on end, to the fullest pitch of enthusiasm – and in those far-off, happy days of bounding, abundant youth I was equipped with instantaneous and imperious reflexes that would brook no delay; the very last thing I could muster was patience or pity. Time was short; one o'clock had struck some while ago. I had a couple of open targets at my disposal. I reconnoitred them both for a moment or two with the tip of my sturdy thermometer – still in absolute silence, without a word or so much as a sound, not even a grunt. I spread the girl's protuberant buttocks apart with both hands and examined each orifice carefully, at some length – as also in depth – until I could stand this tantalising choice of objectives not another second, but at once lunged forward all the way into the further redoubt, lifting her up by her strong, wide hips as I did so, thrusting inwards with my palms to cushion the impact of my belly as it collided sharply with her pierced and battered fanny from below, while I rammed home my unfair advantage to its swift, speechless climax of convulsive rapture.

Raised in that position, like a wheelbarrow, with her feet off the floor, as though flying, yet gripped in midair and clamped on to me, almost sailing through space – but saved by the weight of the heavy wooden frame across her waist at the back – the mingled sensations and emotions that ran riot through her brain and body were not easy for a heartless male to fathom. All I know is that my own bliss was complete, though soon over. I was also greatly relieved, let me add, to find that she had not in fact been a virgin when I so rudely forced my attentions upon her. I thanked her for that, too, in my fashion – by kissing her fondly on both cheeks, and giving them a friendly pat, before I adjusted her dress, and fled. It was the least I could do to show my profound gratitude.

Perhaps there was no real need to worry – but something told me that I had been recognised, by the hall porter or an office boy, I could not be certain who it was exactly, as I hurried out of the building. This vague but alarming impression preyed on my mind; I took fright, as I admitted to Helen, and went abroad within the next thirty-six hours.

How could I have dreamed of recounting this singularly unedifying tale to a stranger? Whether it shocked or amused her made no difference. I would be asking for trouble if I let myself get mixed up with Casilda. Fortunately, the question was unlikely to arise, however. Curiosity is a powerful snare, it's true, and Helen's handsome inamorata seemed to have swallowed the bait of my saucy story. That by itself was surely enough to indicate that she was not addicted to tribadism by nature but merely as a hobby. Still, we both had sound reasons for fighting shy of each other, I argued. There was precious little chance of my contriving to seduce Miss Vandersluys.

Yes, maybe so. I knew that I was right – yet the idea of wresting her from Helen excited me. I had sensed a challenge and, whatever the consequences, I already knew that I could not resist it. She had thrown down the gauntlet, and I must brace myself once again to give battle. I would defend my honour as a chartered libertine at all costs – and take a manly tilt at hers. Confound the haughty half-caste houri! I was still capable of humbling her wanton's pride. We would see by what right she put on such superior sexual airs and graces.

The fresh night breeze blew cool in my face as I walked beside the river, but it did not clear the fevered confusion of my brain. Let me be strictly honest with myself, since I am writing this frank record of my private life for one person, above all, who knows me intimately. I was torn between two moods – exhilaration and despondency, self-assurance and fearful anxiety, optimism and a nagging presentiment of defeat. I strove to overcome the secret admission in my heart that Anthony Grey was not the man – the potent male, the rake, the wolf, the stallion – that he had been until very lately. Don Juan's flamboyant, cocksure attitude was a bluff, a grinning, youthful mask to hide the wrinkled look of worry verging on despair. His boasts lacked conviction, as his limbs now had begun to lack vigour. His virility was approaching exhaustion. It was a sham – or at best, a matter of luck.

The change was recent, and I fought against it. Only a few months before I would have had no cause for alarm at the prospect of pitting my wits against Casilda's wiles; I would have popped her into bed without any of this miserable hesitation, I would have put her straightaway on her back and taught her a lesson, serving her as she deserved. But there had been too many failures – sad, shaming, inexplicable failures – since my previous birthday. I did not care to dwell on them. I was 'pushing fifty,' as the saying is. Muscles once supple were hardening, what had been stiff had grown limp; my body no longer obeyed me promptly and precisely at will. I could not, I dared not, rely on its performance. All too often it let me down at the crucial moment, giving rise only to mutual, meagre disappointment.

The memory of Mireille, for instance, was mortifying – and also the humiliation I suffered with little Joan. Veronica H. F. had been patient but puzzled, that ravishing redhead picked up on the Rome flight had insulted me, and sweet, darling What-was-her-name burst into tears. She was only nineteen. There were others, too – though I had scored some partial successes. It was not all over with me yet; I was certain of that. I had the proof in an occasional, wholly satisfactory response on their part. The slim, brandy-freckled maid at the hotel in Zurich had evidently enjoyed herself with a vengeance when I lugged her on top of me in my room; she came back for more, but the next time there wasn't any at first, until she had earned her fun. A willing worker. And the plump Danish trollop I met at a stifling cocktail scrum: she was too drunk to notice how little she amused me until later, after she had slept it off; then I could not get rid of her, she hollered for a repeat, sober, which of course was ineffectual, and called me a lot of rude names. . . .

I was not going to run the risk of any such disastrous scene with the sophisticated, derisive, intensely desirable Casilda. Slouched in my big armchair at home, clasping a tall glass of whisky that was the colour of her glowing, deep-golden skin, I brooded over this painfully personal problem far into the night. It was impossible – but I must have her. Peace would elude me until I had altered that faint smile on her lips to a different grimace. Could I still do this to a woman, as, and how, I wished? I had put a match to the logs in the grate, but already my fire was out. Too soon.

II

Days passed without a sign from Casilda Vandersluys. I felt offended, relieved, angry and glad by turns. It was just as well that my silly gaffe should be forgotten, and anyhow I had never expected her to ring me up, I told myself. She was really not in the least interested, for a start. There was nothing brazen about that young woman in either appearance or behaviour, so far as I could see – and obviously she was not so unwary a player as to lay herself open to a crushing snub or a lecherous pounce on the fully justified assumption that she was asking for it. I should have had to be a thousand times more courteous and more subtle if I was going to get anywhere with her. But since it had never been my intention to try my hand as a poacher on Helen's preserves, why was I now so acutely hurt and disappointed by Casilda's indifference? Surely I must remain equally aloof. It was a completely trivial incident, and it was closed.

A week went by, and still I could not banish that haunting, attractive ghost from my thoughts. She flitted through my dreams like an elusive nymph, whose image I was constantly remodelling in my mind's eye, as one always does in such cases. I longed to see her again, if only for a moment, to fix my changing impressions of the girl. I recalled her features and certain isolated details of her figure and expression, her walk, her unusual colouring, the sound of her voice, the serenely forceful impact of her calm personality.

Yet she escaped my groping recollection of her portrait on the mental screen which we employ to recapture absent scenes and people, just as in reality she denied me the favour of her physical presence. It was not a blurred picture that I carried with me, but a reflection on the still waters of a lake, which a tossed pebble or a light gust of wind was enough to shatter.

I decided, against my better judgment, to disobey her strict injunction. I would telephone her at the Delavignes' – not immediately, but within the next few days. The effect of this decision was magical. It was as though I had rubbed Aladdin's lamp, summoning a genie on the line. The bell tinkled, and Casilda spoke. She had half an hour to spare that evening, thanks to a cancelled engagement. She supposed I would not be free, but if by any chance I was, and cared to receive a social call, she would drop by for a drink, towards 7:30. I asked if she knew my address before it occurred to me to put her off with some patently false excuse. That perhaps would have been the proper course, but I did not think of it until later. She said yes, she would be visiting friends in the Fulham Road beforehand. I wondered if she regarded it as slumming.

I took careful stock of Casilda in the flesh as she sat curled on the broad, comfortable sofa. She was wearing a dark plum hopsack suit, smartly cut, with a velvet collar to match, a huge topaz brooch, several gold bracelets, and shoes of a simple elegance that was worth the large sum she must have paid for them. Her slender legs were surprisingly long and seemed perfectly shaped in fine nylon from the slim ankles to the crossed, rounded knees and the strong, amply curved thighs that swelled into smooth, solid hips below the narrow, neat waist and fairly wide shoulders. The bosom, which had appeared to me generously full and opulent in evening dress, now, clothed but by no means concealed by a good tailor, was distinctly less obtrusive. Certainly I did not suspect Casilda of those crafty and eminently feminine deceptions that can be guaranteed by the manufacturers to take most men in with commendable regularity; but no rule of thumb so truthfully applies to a woman's tits as that seeing is believing. She was wearing no shirt under her jacket, by the harsh decree of fashion, and I looked forward with interest to a first-hand investigation of the evidence.

While she chatted with habitual ease of this and that, I studied her face more closely than her body. There would be time, I promised myself, for everything. Besides, I already knew the obvious facts of her physique: she was tall but not thin, she was supple and lithe but sturdy rather than lissome, lean or muscular. Her limbs and her whole bearing had kept the energetic, fresh appeal of youth, unspoiled but ripened with the steadier strength, the more harmonious balance of maturity. She had the poise, the power, the sleekness of a big, beautiful, tawny jungle cat, with all the cat's languor, dignity, control and grace in action. Her head, too, was catlike, for the large, widely-set eyes and the high cheek-bones seemed to fill the broad face, except for the flash of white teeth in her great red mouth when she smiled, as she frequently did. The somewhat flat features, the bronzed yellow tinge to the skin, unlined and glowing, and the slant of the eyes themselves, despite their open shape and hazel hue, gave her an exotic look that might well have been inherited from a faint, distant touch of East Indian blood. 'Javanese or not,' I thought to myself, 'they must have rolled her in saffron as a baby.'

Casilda gave me an entertaining account of the visit she had just paid to her friends, the artistic couple, in their Chelsea studio. I was not very astonished to learn that they were women, both of them – and, of course, lesbians. But their marriage, it appeared, had gone on the rocks and was cracking up fast. Summoned by distress signals, Casilda had listened with sympathy to their joint and separate tales of woe. While vainly attempting to effect a reconciliation between the bedraggled lovebirds, she found herself suddenly courted from either side. These fervent and unexpected overtures had amused her at first by their sheer absurdity, as she put it. 'I'd do almost anything to help the old monsters,' she said, 'and I'm not easily shocked – but really what a nerve! Who can they have taken me for? By now, I suppose they'll have made it up and at this very moment are busy consoling each other in a flood of remorseful tears! It's too disgusting. I hate to think what Helen would say if she knew.'

'But doesn't she?' I asked. 'Surely you don't hide anything from Helen? I should imagine that she has a terribly jealous temperament, and that you could never risk her digging up such secrets on her own.'

Casilda laughed. 'I am my own mistress,' she said. 'As well as Helen's.' She swallowed the rest of her martini, and handed me the empty glass. 'But I didn't come here to talk about myself,' she added. 'I came to get a new angle on the seamy side of a gentleman's life.'

'From one seamy side to the other?' I inquired, adding hastily: 'Sex in Fulham Road, I mean – won't that do, as a revelation, for one afternoon?'

'Oh, there was nothing new there, I'm afraid.' She sighed, with boredom rather than regret, 'Anyhow, the afternoon is over, it's evening already and I have, as you know, an insatiable appetite.'

'You will dine with me? But I would say it was a bit early still. . . .'

'Thank you, I can't. Helen is expecting me back to dinner. Also, my appetite is not so easily satisfied. We will go out some other night perhaps, if you'll ask me again. Right now I am holding you to your word in a different connection. You promised to tell me a story,

A Gallery of Nudes

which I'm quite sure is fascinating. Unless you made it all up on the spur of the moment to annoy Helen. In that case you got me here under false pretences. I told you that I am curious by nature. I adore to hear other people's sexual experiences. It's a hobby of mine, an obsession, and I confess to it freely. Don't please pretend that I'm shocking you. From what Helen says I supposed that you were unshockable. Like me. Everyone assures me – my men friends included – that I have an entirely masculine outlook on such matters – meaning Sex with a big snaky capital S. Maybe they are right, at that. I can't have enough of the subject – in conversation at least. Most dirty stories leave me cold, mind you – if they're not extremely witty, they're just wishful thinking, like masturbation. No adult person should stoop to self-abuse, in my opinion. I'm sure you agree. But a true story can be shared. It imparts a genuine emotion. Whether you know the people involved or not makes no difference. Eavesdropping has its own special charm – and I personally get immense pleasure, a particular kick, as an onlooker. Either figuratively or literally, give me a ringside seat and I'll be happy. More than happy – enchanted. I would rather have Peeping Tom's role than Lady Godiva's, any day. Few women understand my attitude – and I see their point. But that is how I am made. I am counting on you to excite me with a wealth of lurid details from your past. You are the first intelligent and cultured rapist I ever met. They are usually even more to be pitied than their wretched victims, I imagine. Probably you, on the contrary, are to be envied. You're practically a professional seducer, they tell me – or have warned me. But that's nothing. Because, as we all know, two can play at the game. It takes two to play it properly, in fact. There is only one thing that you can do, as a man, that I cannot. Other sensations I, as a woman, am allowed by nature to share, to enjoy in my own way, or even, with artificial aids, to imitate. Forgive me for being so frank, I may entice a man, and use him, if I will, to a greater advantage than he could ever guess. And yet I cannot claim to have him without his having me. I must grant him the chance to boast – or at any rate to gloat on the idea – of taking, of possessing me, however briefly or incompetently or indecisively. My sole recourse, my one prerogative is to deny him that chance by rejecting his advances and withholding my favours – which is often nothing better than a form of cutting off my nose to spite his face. Not that I would change my sex – Lord forbid! I'm delighted to be a woman, and ask for no more of life than contentment in the female condition. Ours is the richer part. But rape – the actual, physical forcing of oneself upon another human being, without her consent or desire, with no need for cajoling, persuasion or surrender, merely by the instinct of lust for its own sake – that is an act which I can only imagine. And the masculine side of my mentality relishes the thought of it, I am bound to admit.'

There was a pause. Then she said: 'After that long speech, I'm dying for another martini.'

I walked across the room and busied myself with the shaker. Meanwhile I embarked upon the tale that she wished to hear. A few moments before, I had been firmly resolved not to let her wheedle one word out of me. I was embarrassed, I refuse to be bullied or patronised, and – damn it – why should she always get things her own way? I wondered, as I talked, whether crass middle-aged vanity had not clouded my fitting tactical sense of this peculiar situation – but I believe the simple truth was that her frankness disarmed me. I had never met a woman who spoke and thought in this fashion. There was no doubt that she was a freak – an engaging, beguiling freak, a sort of hermaphrodite, combining the magnetic appeal of a gloriously feminine anatomy with the admirable, essentially male qualities of candour, intelligence, companionship and plain sensuality. Her direct approach to sex, led and governed by an inquiring emotion and sentiment captivated me, filling my nostrils with the bright, sharp tang of an early morning landscape, newly hosed streets, or a breeze off the sea. Her calm, clear voice swept away the shabby garbage, the mounds of conventional refuse that clog the corridors linking impulse to idea, instinct to action, body to brain. She was a strange creature, but a creature after my own heart.

Casilda leaned back against the cushions, a faint smile playing about the corners of her mouth. As I finished my story, sparing no details, she finished her drink to the last drop. I fetched her another.

'That's very kind of you,' she said. 'A perfect host. You mix excellent martinis and tell an enthralling story, with equal skill. Excuse me, won't you, if I don't blush for shame? Both the potions – alcoholic and pornographic – elated me, though I suppose I ought to rebuke you, on behalf of your sex, for your treatment of that poor, defenceless girl. Still, she probably enjoyed it in spite of herself, if we only knew. But you were a cad not to make any amends or send her some form of reward.'

'She sued the company and got damages out of them, I gather. No bastard offspring was the result on that occasion. I am not so deeply sorry for my crime. It is a woman's privilege, of course, that she can conceal her pleasure in the act, whereas no man can hope to fool his partner on that score. His orgasm is a secret that will out. All the same I got the definite impression that Miss Morley felt herself not wholly unrequited for her pains.'

'Perhaps not,' mused Casilda. 'The incident might have started a lasting friendship. I would love to have seen her face throughout the performance, from the rise to the fall of the curtain.'

'Her tail end, I assure you, was far prettier – and, I bet, no less expressive.'

Casilda gave me her gay, light, bubbling laugh, pulled on a glove, and sat up straight, as if to go.

'You baffle me,' I remarked. 'I simply cannot picture you as a lesbian. It's not convincing. You have so few hallmarks. Yet you remain faithful to Helen. You rush back to her whenever she calls or expects you. How long has that affair been going on?'

Casilda relaxed with a slight shrug of her shoulders, and examined her pink-gloved fingertips with care.

'Oh,' she answered, and was silent. 'Well . . . it's a matter of habit – an agreeable one, and no trouble. I'm devoted to Helen. She has been kind, and she is sweet. I won't pretend that I don't love her – and I like what we do together. I dote on being adored. But you're wrong to imagine I'm faithful to her. Far from it. She forgives me my lapses, poor darling – when she catches me out. She has to. So I try to deceive her on the quiet – because she can't exist without me, or not for long, and jealousy sickens her. It makes her ill. But in this whole thing the passion – or no, the emotion – is a little one-sided, really. She doesn't see that. She will never understand me – not if it lasts forever. But I don't mind. No, I'm not homosexual. Most certainly I am not. I would hate to miss so much . . . it is just that I would as soon go to bed with a woman as a man. Sometimes. Not always – but as often as not. Women's bodies attract me more, usually – and satisfy me less. There are different degrees, different kinds of desire for us. A man may arouse them all; and a woman can't – that's the sad part of it – though I may want her as much, and often her need for me is twice as intense as male lust, so I find it harder to reject or resist; it flatters me more. Still, there is no valid comparison – if you like, it's rather the same as wines and spirits. I prefer a good wine. I can drink any quantity I am offered; but I need my hard liquor too, from time to time, like everyone else – unless I happen to have gone on the wagon, as I do occasionally. Helen is my staple vintage, for regular consumption – not as regular as she could wish, I'm afraid. I would hesitate to call her a *vin ordinaire*, though. She's superb in bed. I'd be a fool to give her up.'

'Both of you were unhappily married when you took to each other,' I insinuated.

'Maybe,' Casilda replied. 'She's much nearer to being a true lez than I am. The instinct was there, deeply buried, long before Lucien began to neglect her – which he very soon did, almost completely. But she didn't seduce me. I mean, it wasn't the first time in my case – though it was in hers. Helen's a terribly moral person, according to her lights. She has rigidly strict principles, and insists on living up to them. I had the devil of a time getting her to make love to me, although she was in love with me, desperately, and had been for years. Neither of us has ever regretted it since, I don't think – but that is perhaps the main reason for my tremendous hold on her: I led her astray. She is the lover mostly, and I am the loved – but it is I who am the wicked one, in her view of things. She won't let me forget it. Still, what do I care? It salves her conscience – and there is nothing worse than a conscience in bed, don't you find?'

I nodded. 'When did you discover that?'

'Oh, I've always known it. I'm a healthy girl, I hate hypocrisy – or any other trumped-up complication. It was like that with me from the very start. I took Helen in my stride, you might say.' She smiled. 'She came a good way down the list. I had seduced myself, to all intents, as a schoolgirl, right at the beginning. With the games mistress. So, you see, I couldn't be more normal. It was the classic gambit.'

'What age were you?'

'Oh, I was a senior. A prefect. Rising sixteen.'

'And a virgin?'

'Yes – that all happened at about the same time. A couple of weeks later, in the holidays. It seems a century ago. I'm over twenty-seven. My romp with the games mistress was fine and dandy in its way, as an eye-opener – but it left me in an even more inquisitive mood than before. I am horribly inquisitive by nature, as you know – and always was. I made a ghastly mistake – which is also quite normal, I gather.'

'You mean you were let down, and that is why you prefer your own sex to mine?'

'I've told you I don't *au fond*. It didn't put me off men for long. But I chose badly – as I guessed, or half-realised, at the time. He was much more of a virgin than I was, though he struck me then as wonderfully grown-up, almost old. A boy of about twenty-two. The clumsy lout! God knows I made it easy enough for him. But he hurt me like hell. In a punt one night on the river at Cambridge. I must have screamed like a stuck pig. It was shameful, messy and revolting. How I bled, and how I loathed him! The brute – he didn't even do the job properly. I found that out afterwards, though for the moment I felt sure he had killed me. In my next incarnation I shall plump for the bank. Never deflower a girl in a punt, Tony.'

'Very good, I'll remember your advice,' I said. 'It explains your profound fellow-feeling for Miss Morley.'

'Ah now, that was done without her consent. I've never been raped in that sense. Sometimes it has been rather the other way about; there's a certain added zest for me in a quick, animal encounter of that kind with a total stranger. It's the masculine side of me again, I suppose, that grabs what it wants, with no questions asked, no strings attached, and no preliminaries. They're so often a bore – all those tiresome *hors d'oeu-*

vres – if one's just hungry and in a hurry for a snack . . . I'll never buy myself a gigolo if I live to be ninety. But a hither look and your latchkey will work the trick as neatly as a dive into the nearest thicket for cover. I'm considered good-looking, I know, but it seldom presents any difficulty to get oneself laid – even for the Miss Morleys of this world – if that's what one is after. They take you for a cheap whore, not unreasonably – and treat you as such. That is partly the attraction for me. But because you're a free gift they won't turn rough on you – not too rough. I picked up a gorgeous Swede in a hotel lift once – just took him by the hand and led him to my room. I believe that's the common practice in Sweden – whereas a man followed me in Harrods the other day, so I pushed the stuttering idiot ahead of me into a taxi and we drove to his flat in Kew for a tumble. I remember similar incidents occurring more or less on the dance floor, on a park bench in Italy during my second honeymoon, and against some very hard and grimy railings in the blackout. But who doesn't? Helen, for one, of course. No – maybe I'm wrong, at that. Most girls wait to be introduced to a man before he can touch them. But there are some men I want that I don't want to see again. I'm glad to save them the bother. Frequently, then, they pester you to tell them your name. I still keep the cards of two gentlemen who expected me to follow up what was indeed a pleasant if passing introduction. One of them I often see around in the West End, he is always trying to get to meet me socially. I sold myself to him for ten minutes – at a whacking high price – in an upstairs room over a restaurant. He's a stockbroker. It was a flag day. Fearfully hot. I gave him all the flags I had left, for fifty pounds. At least he swore that he got his money's worth, after accusing me of scandalous dumping. But the fleeting adventure I most enjoyed at the time was a whale of a set-to I had with a Mexican – Lieutenant-General

Arcadio Jesus Maria Quintana Zunzunegui, on his card – in a crowded compartment all one night on the train journey across France from Lausanne. He began it as soon as I settled behind my newspaper and magazines in the seat facing his. He put a rug over my knees and a well-manicured hand between them. We were by the window, but there were six other passengers packed in with us. It was agonisingly difficult not to squirm, and almost as hard not to laugh. He leaned far forward from the edge of his seat and never took his eyes off the cover of the *Vogue* I pretended to be reading. He was a funny little fellow, but absolutely indefatigable. I didn't get a single wink of sleep; he never let up for a moment. I could not make him stop, and it would have been too risky to move the rug and try to escape into the corridor. His caresses were incredibly artful. He was adept at delaying and prolonging the most exquisite sensations in me to the sheerest brink of ecstasy. I bit my lips till they bled. I was literally crying for mercy – for some final respite, either way. It wasn't that I couldn't reach the climax – I did, again and again. But it was never quite over, it went on still, the whole time . . . if only I could have come! But coming I was, continually, without a pause, except for infinite variations in the degree of my torment and delight. Whenever I got to the very end of my tether and was almost on the point of screaming, when I could bear it not another instant, this diabolical Mexican would withdraw his hands for a while, to stroke my thighs or tickle my short hairs and gently pinch my belly. I was young, not yet seventeen, though I looked older. I was terrified, too, that we were being watched. That may have been the cause of it. But I have never had the same sensations since, I promise you.'

'What happened in the end?'

'I scrambled out into the passage, and lurched along to the lavatory. It was no good: he followed close on my heels, opened the door for me – and shut it behind us.'

'Didn't anybody see you?'

'There was no one about – that time. But he led me back there again in the morning and two people were waiting in line by the door when we came out. It was awful.'

'And possibly a bit cramped inside?'

'Yes – but we didn't even notice. It was over in a flash, as you can imagine.'

'How?'

'He sat down and pulled me on to his – er – lap. I must say the General was magnificently armed.'

'Which way did you face?'

'Towards each other, as we had been in the compartment. I straddled him, on the first occasion. The next time, just before daybreak, he spun me around and skewered me from the rear. It took slightly longer. I think the men outside must have heard us. Not a word had passed between us until then. I still didn't speak – but he poured out a whole flood of endearments, and I expect I contributed a fair amount to the din.'

'You have a deliciously vivid memory. I admire you for that. It's marvellous. Vicarious pleasures are almost all that's left to me, at my advanced age. Like you, I revel in sex even at second or third hand. I could listen to such tales for hours at a stretch. No, no, don't go – for heaven's sake! Let me fix you a drink. I'm fascinated. Tell me, how on earth did you get rid of him?'

'Eventually I shook him off in Paris. I was determined to keep my distance – which didn't make sense to him. He was going home to run a revolution, and implored me to string along with him and see it through. I like prying and spying into the sexual habits of my fellow men and women, especially if they are the friends of my most intimate friends – or complete strangers. But nine times out of ten I don't, myself, wish to become involved. Mine isn't the typically feminine kind of curiosity. I may have their shamelessness, but women, I've found, are only drawn to sex for love of the emotion they can get or give with the body. A man, though more selfish, more importunate, far more clumsy and eager, is generally not so personal, so limited, so romantic. Of course he doesn't live for sex, as we do; he just wants it handy. His attitude to the business may be scientific, literary or merely biological. Yet men don't like a girl to look on sex in the same way as they do. You have to enjoy it for their sakes, not as a vital private experience on its own. Your interest in sex is something that they demand from you as an exclusive gift, a sort of fulfilment of their personality. They say they want you to share it with them – but it has got to be all theirs, when you get down to it.'

'That's only natural, while they're in love with you.'

'I don't agree. Look – my second husband was an Englishman, but not of the common-or-garden variety. He taught me a great deal. I cannot think of any caress, any method of love, that he did not practise to perfection and lavish on me. I needn't go into details, or even you would consider the story long-winded. He brought tarts to the house, he urged pals of his to make passes at me, he stripped me naked and fondled me in these chaps' presence, he used ropes, gadgets and fetishes galore, there was nothing he would not do in front of me or induce me to play at for his amusement. I didn't object. Most of his whims were peculiar but highly exciting. I'm not one to hang back at any invitation, however novel or laborious. But the fellow, frankly, was depraved. He was downright degenerate. I left him after a few months of incessant orgies. Do you know why? Because he hated me to enjoy any part of it. For a time I made a pretence of being cold, horrified, nauseated. That was what he wanted – once we were married. Until then he had seemed normal. An ingenious, exhausting, unquenchable lecher, who vented his ruttish passion on me a dozen times a day – but I could take it. His enthusiasm flattered me at first, then it frightened me; finally I was disgusted. He was Priapus, and all his extravagant lunacies were devised to prove it to me, for his own joy and glory.'

'Well?' Casilda had fallen silent, frowning over her cocktail.

'We went on our honeymoon to the South of France. Motoring back, we stayed at a quiet country hotel. And he was shocked – imagine! – violently shocked and furiously angry, because I listened, with my ear pressed against a thin partition, to the couple next door. They were probably on their honeymoon also. We had seen them that evening at dinner. He was an earnest, nondescript young man, who wore glasses. She was rather sweet – in a well-brought-up way, pale, pretty, and unpainted. But, my word, how they shagged, those two! I didn't hear him at first, or guess it was her. I thought someone was sick, mortally sick, at their last gasp. She moaned, she mumbled, she called upon her Maker, panting, letting out sudden shrill yelps of anguish. Then I recognised a male's hoarse, strained, heavy breathing and the regular creaking crescendo of springs. I was in our bathroom, which adjoined theirs, with one wall evidently running alongside the bed itself. From the way she carried on, really he might have been throttling her! Such a little innocent to look at, but she had taken to the game like any ugly duckling to water. I listened . . . by stopping up my other ear, with one cheek flat against the wall, I got every sound. I was pleasurably tired myself, mark you – not to say groggy from fornication and praying for a snatch of sleep. But this intimate symphony next door, the grunting of the two-backed beast in heat, like a human locomotive in action, was wildly exciting. I sprang up from the bidet and rushed to fetch Rupert – he ought not to miss it. I, an eavesdropper of long standing, so to speak, had never heard such a grand, full-throated performance. Talk of ballet or opera! This had words, music, movement – the lot. Her monologue was neither inarticulate nor obscene enough for my taste, to tell you the truth – but I may be hypercritical. Blasphemy repels me at any time, but particularly from a woman in the throes of coition, and more so if she's a convent-bred bride unconsciously babbling her bliss in religious terms. Leave that to the man, as his right. It is *his* act of creation, after all; ours comes later. I prefer the poetry of the good dirty words; they are sublime, too. Anyway, Rupert wasn't interested. He lost his temper and shouted like a maniac, cursing me for a foul-minded slut and asking how *I* would like *my* privacy invaded by lurking, cowardly neurotics who had nothing better to do than to frig themselves with lascivious, cerebral impotence at the signs overheard of my innermost rapture. I was flabbergasted – but there was no arguing with him. I dashed back to my coign of vantage – just in time for the finale. Rupert was utterly incensed; he sulked for days afterwards. And he never forgave me. He kept throwing it in my face when his weird notions revolted me, or when I fell in with some complicated, salacious scheme of his – which was always supposed to be for our mutual enjoyment. "You love the part of the passive spectator, don't you?" he would say. "Then watch this!" Or he'd put a garish, shop-worn floozy to work on me with her mercenary, mechanical cunning and exclaim: "Now you know what fun it is to do the belly dance in public." The last straw that broke our marriage was one of these frolics, when he had a reeling-drunk Irishman in tow, who was actually an old jilted suitor of mine, and tugged the brassy bitch off me as soon as she was through, so that Mick should "go ahead, my dear fellah, and finish the job properly" while he and his hireling held me down, before ordering us to "shift over there, and we'll show you how to poke." I had realised by that time what his sadistic kink was – but at this early stage in France I didn't have a clue. And it wasn't as if I had jumped from his arms and fled to the bathroom at the wrong physiological moment. On the contrary, even he was satiated – but awake, not actually aching for a rest, as I was. No, he was jealous of my independence, mad with the morbid envy of inverted puritanism. Later on I learned that he had been warped in adolescence by semi-incestuous idolisation of his mother, a famous Edwardian beauty who was as naughty as they come. I was to be his ideal, as pure as the driven snow – and he would do the driving. What he craved was a fallen angel who is not common property but a private pupil, wide-eyed and pleading to be debauched in the headmaster's study. Up to a point I indulged his fancy. But he failed to break my spirit – my personal freedom, my sensual idiosyncrasies, my choice of pet vices, my detachment, which he deplored as selfishness, greed and cynicism.'

I was standing behind Casilda as she ceased talking and glanced at her watch. I bent over the sofa, lifted up her wrist, and kissed it. I peeled off the one pink glove, then ran my fingers round her neck and stroked her nape and shoulders. To do this I unbuttoned the jacket, lest I should spoil its line, while tipping her chin towards me. Her breasts remained covered under the open lapels, for they were set far apart, like a prancing chariot team linked by a frail lace halter. We gazed at each other searchingly, in silence, during those slow, timeless minutes that stir and start the blood in languid motion through the veins. Casilda closed her eyes and smiled. She, who was no enigma when she talked, seemed faintly mysterious to me now. Here we paused, lingering on this familiar threshold that is always new. Would she bid me a gentle goodnight and turn away?

Calmly my mind pondered on acceptance of the thought. I resolved to let her alone if she wished. Everything was changed between us, as one's whole being changes at the crucial moment when the decision is already taken, and tacitly agreed, but still may be withdrawn, before the bond is sealed. We were no longer as we had been a single sudden second ago. There was the contact, the touch on the lever, the spark that hung upon a command, to be born or denied at one quick motion, one last irrevocable gesture.

'No, Tony, not now,' Casilda murmured. 'I must leave you.'

By then it was too late. My clear intention of a flickering instant since was gone. I could not now bow to defeat. The warm, creeping tingle of desire was in my body, glowing in my loins, rousing my manhood, pulsing through me, clamouring for battle. Ah, what delirious happiness to feel again this thrilling call to action! I rejoiced in these first symptoms of a glad state which nowadays, under the threat of enforced chastity, was all too seldom vouchsafed to my waning constitution. They mustn't be neglected; I could not afford to ignore them wastefully when the raised finger of opportunity beckoned. Seizing the ripe fruit within my grasp. I plunged my clutching hands into Casilda's undefended bosom, releasing its twin splendours from their flimsy imprisonment, as I crushed my mouth on the soft, intoxicating treasure of her parted, pouting lips. Thirstily I absorbed their sweet, refreshing fire, while baring her firm breasts to receive an awaited steady shower of ardent kisses. Well might she be proud of their young arrogance, I reflected, as I weighed, fondled and tested them like a gardener or greengrocer examining his wares – holding them in my palms and lightly pinching the small nipples – the model for a luscious masterpiece which Mother Nature chose to copy in alternate versions, as the raspberry or the wild strawberry. With head thrown back and arms spread wide, Casilda arched herself in my embrace as I tore my mouth away at last and sprawled beside her, sampling her tits, devouring them, whipping their stiff, perky little points with my tongue. I pictured Helen relishing this amorous task. . . .

Tense but abandoned, Casilda stayed in that position, reclining on the prop of my encircling arms, while my other hand groped beneath her skirt, up thighs as smooth as silk, towards the warm, wet, tender gash that shrank and shut instinctively, like a sea anemone, at my approach, but then surrendered, clammy and afire with yearning for the delicate homage that my avid fingers would pay to the most sensitive and secret fibre of her anatomy. Her clitoris also was not large in size. For a big gal she was fashioned with a disproportionate neatness of detail. Her breasts, as I now knew, were not the apple, the orange or the pear, but slightly flattened and more heavily rounded, solid, firm and golden, like the grapefruit – yet her nipples and the hidden bud of her sex were small.

The response to my touch upon it was immediate. Her short, strong torso heaved and shuddered, her long legs stretched straight out, and for the first time since we kissed she made some slight, incoherent sound. It was a faint, plaintive sigh. Her breathing grew louder and faster. She tossed and turned her head from side to side. But this was nothing yet. I was going to teach our young Sappho a lesson. I started to undress her. I wanted her stripped. Naked she must be, at my mercy, and I too would shed all this decent covering that marred attempted intimacy, keeping us as dummies and strangers at arm's length. I'd show this voluptuous, misguided slut what she was missing since she took up with Helen. . . .

'No, no,' she whispered. I was trying to unfasten her skirt.

With a hand on my forehead she thrust me gently away.

'I despise making love with one's clothes on,' I complained.

'So do I – but you won't,' she remarked with a smile. 'I mean, we aren't going to. I'm not giving in to you now. Not tonight. Ssh – be quiet! Because I say so.'

As she spoke, she ran her fingers through my hair and kissed me lightly on the cheek, while the other hand darted down to a lower level and found what it was searching for. Ah, but damnation and hell, the traitor did me less than justice! She clasped my member in a fond, sure, gentle grip, as if to soothe an aching pain. A moment ago he had made his defiant presence felt against her flank, but no sooner did she greet him in this courteous manner, trotting him out into the open, than some blight of inexplicable shyness overcame him, and he appeared, hanging his swollen head with surly embarrassment and blushing deeply. It was obvious that he lacked all zeal and appetite for combat. His brief enthusiasm had quickly dwindled. What was the point of entering on such a venture at half-cock? I cursed him bitterly under my breath, and in my turn drew back sharply from Casilda's arms.

I noticed then that her face still wore a charitable smile, as if to pardon the grievous incivility of my physical indifference. There was nothing for it? All hope of gallantly displaying my male authority over her had crumpled. But she herself was not the kind that gives up easily. She slipped to the floor on her knees, and studied the matter in hand at close range – with loving care and a good deal of amusement. I was powerless to stop her doing what I now saw she intended. She cupped my testicles in a softly squeezing grasp and tickled the stem of my penis, from the knob to the root, with her tongue. It was unbelievably deft, her tongue – it rang all the changes and executed every tune of my flute, so that even that woebegone, overworked instrument could scarcely endure the ordeal. She led it a dance that began as a stately pavane and developed, through a succession of varying rhythms, from a merry hornpipe, a wild fandango and lilting waltz, into a riotous can-can and a frenzied highland fling. She rubbed it and pressed it between her lips, which were like moist, warm rose-petals drenched in sunshine and summer showers – and finally, as the night filled with stars before my eyes, she swallowed it whole. She ate me alive – and left me limp, blind and gasping, faint, trembling, weary and drained to the dregs. Never before had I known what it was to be gamahouched in this way – to the hilt of extinction, as it were. The joke was on me.

I picked myself up off the sofa when she returned, in a moment or two, from the bathroom. She blew me a kiss from the doorway.

'I must rush,' she said. 'I'm frightfully late. Helen will be as sour as mud.'

'I'm sorry. My car's out of order, but –'

'Never mind. She'll forgive me.' Casilda gave a happy, expectant chuckle of laughter in her throat. 'And it's you that she will have to thank – for putting me in such a fine frisky mood. There, think of that – you wicked man!'

'Run along now – you mustn't keep her waiting. That would be too bad. But please,' I begged, 'don't tantalise me! Don't – damn you – tantalise me!'

'Why?' She gazed at me with great big open eyes that now looked dewily innocent and blue. 'Surely you're not jealous of Helen?'

'Oh, stop it!' I cried. 'Shut up, get out! What wouldn't I give to watch, to see you both, to be there. . . .'

'Would you, now?' She laughed again. 'Then so you shall – if I can arrange it. I'll think. I'll try to find a way. Goodbye. Goodnight.'

The pink glove turned the handle of the door, and she was gone.

III

Once or twice in the course of the next weeks – though we met all too seldom for my liking – I tried to remind Casilda of her promise, which had left me on tenterhooks of anticipation. I found her constrained and awkward about it, however. Each time I broached the subject she would frown, give a short nod, and with a hasty 'Yes, yes, we'll see,' whisk off at a tangent, like a billiard ball. It was clear that she regretted ever having made the offer to let me in on her amorous entanglements with Helen. Or else she was quite stumped for a means of bidding me to the feast without Helen's knowledge. Obviously one ruled out any chance of her talking Helen into a threesome; the very idea was fantastic, preposterous. For all Casilda's hold over Helen, coax, cajole, bully or blackmail her as she might, the mere suggestion of such indecency would have put an abrupt and bitter end to their affair forever. Imagine profaning their sacred, sisterly love with a *man* in the room – and me of all men! But the alternative – to smuggle me into the wings somehow, or hide me under the bed as a stowaway – was almost equally difficult. I had an excellent pair of binoculars in my possession, as I told Casilda jokingly – yet, even if they had done for this purpose, at long range half the beauty of the spectacle would have been lost on me, naturally. As a voyeur, I hate to miss the sounds and the atmosphere that are complementary to the actual thrill of seeing the players in motion – especially when one cannot or must not touch, so that ultimate satisfaction, come what may, is impossible.

I did not dare to insist or appear too keen on the giddy treat that Casilda had pledged herself to provide for me, since it had begun to fade into thin air like a mirage. She had thought better of it, and my reverting to the topic would only jeopardise the cheerful affection she showed towards me on the rare occasions when we were able to meet. Far from giving any indication that her first visit *chez moi* had left an ugly taste in her mouth, the dear girl was most friendly and obliging. In a subtle way, without either reticence or obscenity, she managed to combine the best of both worlds for she was sensitive but never sentimental, wholly uninhibited but quiet and sensible, frankly sensual, even lascivious, but neither neurotic nor depraved. Sex did not defile or cheapen her with any taint of that rabid nymphomania which compels the sufferer to seek frequent, impatient, vain relief for the aching void of her vagina. In Casilda's case the mean was truly happy.

'Flippancy or whimsy I can stand,' she confessed, 'but coyness and facetious persiflage are the devil.' I christened her Messalina Incorporated – or Sappho II, like a yacht – and my appreciation of her 'androgynous attitude to love' made her smile. She could abandon all control in the total surrender of her typical self without upsetting her mental balance in the slightest degree. Her poise bore no trace of pose. She would celebrate the sacred carnal rites of the altars of the oldest mystery with none of the pious mumbo jumbo that mars the cooperation of many an addicted and accomplished votaress in the ineffably simple frenzy of the sexual act.

Or so I believed. I could not have sworn that it was true, for lack of proof. Some unconscious restraint kept us in check. We did not choose to copulate. I had not taken Casilda, and she did not give herself to me. Looking back on that time, under two years ago, I am at a loss to explain exactly what retarded the normal development of our intimate acquaintance to its foregone conclusion. We saw each other only in secret, when Helen's social engagements permitted; there was no hope of our sleeping together in the full meaning of the phrase – but even so we had plenty of opportunities to cuckold her thoroughly and time enough, surely to 'leap into bed,' as the silly saying goes, for a hurried 'roll in the hay.'

I wonder still why we dallied so long on the brink. Casilda has since assured me – and she is the soul of honesty – that it was not for my sake, to spare me embarrassment, that she steadfastly refused to consummate our mutual desires, but preferred to appease them by other methods. I glumly suspected that she had assumed I must be impotent – or physically incapable of proper intercourse. The idea that she might have gained this unflattering impression from my deplorably feeble showing at our first skirmish worried me to distraction. I was determined to prove her wrong. I would vindicate myself up to the hilt at the earliest possible juncture. Yet somehow that juncture never occurred, the supreme moment never came, the situation did not arise. I grew desperately alarmed – to the point where I would have failed ignominiously, I am convinced, if Casilda had not used the utmost tact in avoiding the issue. I suppose she realised that, caught up as I was in a welter of wounded pride, expectations, lecherous vanity and doubt, we were treading on dangerous ground. One false move on her part might bring our budding romance to instant and final catastrophe, she may have felt. Perhaps it is not surprising that she diagnosed and sought to treat me as a pathological case. I, in my anxiety, was acquiring a serious complex about the problem in possessing her – utterly at last, in complete fulfilment, without further thwarting delays. I was becoming frantically tired of this prolonged beating about the bush. Yet – almost literally – she slipped through my fingers. Whenever I tried to clinch the argument, she employed the same evasive tactics with absolute success.

Why did I let her get away with it? Was I, at my age, a greenhorn so gullible and guileless that I must succumb to the crafty but rudimentary stratagems of any plain tart's amorous technique? Not even the most innocent duellist, in the first flush of youth, would have sat back contentedly, as I did, and allowed a slut to fob him off in such a one-sided fashion, however great might be the artistry she applied to the task or the pleasure he derived from her skilful ministrations. And yet with me the trick worked, more than once. The scene on the sofa was repeated at least a couple of times when Casilda came to call. She would spend a happy half-hour browsing among my books or pouring over my fine collection of photographs and sketches – the pick of my library. I refer, of course, not to my regular stock in trade as an art dealer but to the various shelves and portfolios crammed with erotic treasures. Of these, though I say it myself, I have many magnificent specimens, gathered and stored through the years; Casilda, as I had guessed, took a typically masculine interest in such curios. She would examine each detail, in spellbound silence, with grave and meticulous care, never biting off more than she could chew at one session, but concentrating her attention on a single set of illustrations at a time. When her curiosity was slaked – and her senses inflamed – she would beckon smilingly to me and, with an almost jaunty little sigh, exchange the lickerish images of venery in two dimensions for the tangible, stirring, more colourful reality within her grasp. She wanted to be made love to. I seized her in my arms, and caressed her from top to toe with all the mingled tenderness and vehemence of pent-up, famished passion.

I ought to have laid her then and there, pounding the anvil while the iron was hot. Something prevented me. I had no wish to rape her. The ordinary slow process of seduction by degrees was going to suffice. She must demand it, she must want to have me herself, summoned, needed, welcomed within her. Not that I belong to the effeminate breed of lover who has to be carried across the threshold like some trembling bride. But my courage deserted me. I did not even manage to strip her naked on these occasions. Always before I could snatch the last wisp of clothing from her body, to reveal the living sculpture, the statue of flesh that I was about to enter, to impale and penetrate, to strangle, invade and use as my own property by right of conquest, she would contrive to escape, eluding my embrace as swiftly and smoothly as a snake slithering away into the grass or a stately schooner casting off her moorings. She gave me no time to complain. Only sheer force would have stopped her. I had to let her have her head, after it was too late. 'No, darling,' she murmured. 'No – not just yet, not now.' That was her invariable plea, the same urgent whisper that had defeated my purpose, unmanning me, at every previous attempt. And it was all she could say for a while, because then her lips closed greedily upon the beautiful big lollipop which she was licking and tickling with her tongue, as she observed me quizzically from the point of vantage where she had now installed herself, squatting on the floor between my knees, her elbows across my thighs.

She won; she did as she liked with me. I was a fool to submit. This anteroom prologue suited her low plan; I should have ordered her through to the bed next door. She hoodwinked me disgracefully – but so enjoyably that I soon forgot my anger and indignation against her. A younger man would have rebelled at her taking matters into her own hands with such bareface aplomb.

I could only chide her and protest when it was over. A cockteaser I called her.

'At heart that's all you are – just a slick little cockteaser. You're a dodger, a shirker, a cheat – a charming one, but vicious. And peculiarly unemancipated – in spite of your brave claims.'

She simply scoffed at my sour look of frustration, which may not have been very convincing.

'Why, you beast!' she retorted. 'I think you're horribly ungrateful. Didn't I do it nicely? I've been highly complimented on my special talents in that line. It's one of my specialities, I'd have you know. Gold medals and recommendations galore. In great favour with tired businessmen.'

'And pampered elderly ladies,' I added.

'Oh, there you go again! You're incorrigible.'

Sometimes we were content to behave like old friends in each other's company: sex did not come into it. We would lunch or dine together at small restaurants where there was hardly any danger of being seen by someone we knew, or we would hide ourselves in a local cinema. She always declined to go for a drive in the country. 'No time,' she said, 'and I would rather wait until we can spend a weekend miles away, when Helen's out of town.'

It is an extraordinary admission to make – and I am loath to acknowledge the possibility – but it may be that by instinct, subconsciously, at the back of my mind I was glad not to be put to the test . . . just yet. I pretended, for appearances sake, that I was chagrined and deeply vexed – but that was only to protect my self-esteem. Already Casilda meant far too much to me – though I would stoutly have denied her importance in my life – to run so big a risk of disappointing her. I was inwardly afraid, terribly afraid, of failure. I could not bear to envisage any outcome to our present emotional impasse short of a memorable and tremendous tri-

A Gallery of Nudes

umph. She must be forced to avow her ludicrous error in underrating my virility. Afterwards I might be prepared to cast her aside. I could drop her then, if I wished, like a dirty shirt. I wasn't hunting just now for a regular bedfellow, and didn't require one. But first she would have to learn in the flesh, beyond any measure of doubt, once and for all, that I was still my body's own master and able to impose its will or its whims on others.

In the circumstances the passive role of onlooker, which Casilda had dangled under my nose, was the ideal solution. I will make no bones about it, as I did at the time with her, out of some queer, involved, ambitious scruple: the very thought, the mere prospect of seeing those two in bed together was an obsession which I could not banish from my tortured brain; it stayed with me night and day, filling my dreams and every waking hour with the turbulent, crazy fancies of a forlorn hope. What a contrast they would offer, the pair of them, what a stupendous show to watch! I could picture no spectacle, no orgy, nothing to match it. Ah, if only such a blessed bath of beauty, such a heavenly bonanza were possible! I felt I should die happy if this miracle of excitement, this private vision could be achieved – for me alone. But I knew that was too much to ask. . . .

And then one autumn evening, weeks later, it happened. I was on the point of going out to dinner with an old flame of mine and her newly-wedded husband. I had one foot in the street when the telephone's shrill semaphore lassoed me, dragging me back with an oath to answer its call. A voice spoke in tones so low and conspiratorial that at first I did not recognise Casilda on the line. 'Listen,' said the voice. 'Tony, are you there? Hold on a minute.' After a maddening pause, as I was about to hang up, my loud 'hullos' unheeded, Casilda babbled: 'Sorry. Wanted to be on the safe side . . . it's all right now. Look, I've booked you a single seat – in the front row of the stalls – for tonight. Don't get here much after eleven. Put off whatever you're doing – and come round by taxi. But only as far as the corner. . . .'

'What on earth are you talking about?' I inquired downright gruffly.

'Charity performance,' she replied. 'As You Like It – with a reduced cast of two. Sort of gala duet. Your cup of tea. I think – or so you've kept telling me for weeks, pretty well *ad nauseam*. Call beforehand, though. If anyone else answers, hang up – it'll mean the party's off. Okay?'

'Darling,' I exclaimed as the receiver clicked.

Never shall I forget the ordeal I underwent that evening, dining at Janet's. For the best part of an hour we tippled sherry while she cooked an elaborate meal. The other guests – a married couple – were in no hurry. I breathed into Janet's ear: 'I have a date, my sweet. . . .'

'Oh, I thought you were going to kiss me!' I did.

'Of course, Tony dear – but don't show off so. You always have somebody waiting for you. Still, I'll forgive you this time,' Janet agreed. 'You may be excused on important business as soon as I've served the coffee – if that's soon enough.'

I made my escape on the stroke of eleven.

'Good Heavens, Helen,' Casilda said loudly, when I got through from the nearest call-box. 'Have you forgotten your key? I'll sit up for you, to let you in. Don't be long, honey.' Then she added: 'Yes, that's all thank you, Smithers – goodnight,' and rang off.

Smithers, I knew, was Helen's elderly maid.

As I approached the flight of steps to the large Regency mansion after dismissing my taxi at the entrance to the Park, the Delavignes' front door swung open, hiding Casilda, who winked at me like a schoolgirl with a finger to her lips, and silently led the way, from rug to rug, across the hall. She was wearing an ankle-length housecoat of jade-green taffeta, and once again, as she walked ahead of me, I was lost in admiration of her back view under the billowing folds that rippled and rustled darkly, like a tropic sea. The ample hips, the slender waist, the fully rounded buttocks that swayed to a rolling, majestic cadence as she sailed upstairs, their rich contours and appetising bulk presented at eye-level to my riveted gaze – this was the rear prospect that had first appeared to me on that night in September when the sight of Casilda's bottom, sheathed in clinging silk, aroused my sudden lust with a shock as swift and cruel as the lash of a whip.

Just as it was from behind that I fell for Casilda then, so now the magnetic attraction of these plump, protruding nates sent such a violent tremor tingling through my veins that I was dizzily tempted to renounce the great adventure on which we were embarked and immediately lay rough hands on this almost sitting bird that was so obviously worth two in the bush. I had a damned good mind to fling the girl face down across the nearest bed – or anywhere, on the landing if need be – and settle our old debt at once, right away, without more ado, before Helen got home.

I cannot say whether Casilda's sharp wits told her what was brewing in her wake, but she effectively balked my barnyard intentions by hissing a rigmarole of advice to me over her shoulder as we crossed Helen's room into hers.

'Be frightfully careful, darling – don't make a sound,' she implored. 'It's Wagstaff's night out – but he'll use the back door. Smithers and Cook are asleep at the top of the house. Lucien has gone to Scotland. Anyhow, I expect you've had lots of practice in creeping about on boudoir manoeuvres of this sort. You can hide in my clothes closet meanwhile – until Helen gets in. She'll be back any minute. I shall leave our door open – though she's sure to shut it. If she does, step out on to the balcony, and sneak along there, through her window. Look – it's quite safe. The next one is Lucien's – that's your line of retreat, downstairs and straight ahead . . . I greased all the hinges myself.'

She guided me around on a rapid reconnaissance and pressed a wee pencil torch into my hand. It was a cloudy night, not raining or actually cold. The balcony overlooked a strip of gloomy garden behind the house. The stage within was nicely set: it might have been devised especially for some intricate bedroom farce. Casilda threw her arms about my neck and kissed me gaily. 'Be good,' she enjoined again in earnest. 'And you won't hate me, will you, whatever you do?'

I laughed. 'Whatever *I* do?' I asked. 'That's hardly the question. It's to be all your doing, I trust, from now on – or mostly. I shall stay quieter than a mouse in the panelling, so long as you do your stuff. But I warn you I'll roar like a lion if I find you're a fake.'

'Cas-seeel-dah!' Helen's yodel echoed up from the hall – refined but imperious, and alarmingly close. We had not heard her arrive.

Her protegée pushed me into a tunnel festooned with soft, scented frocks and furs, like lianas smothering a jungle trail, and dashed away to greet Milady Delavigne, the distinguished madame of this high-class house. For what seemed eternity I remained cooped there, condemned to languish in a dark, all too fragrant padded cell, while they presumably lingered, chatting over a nightcap below. . . . Emboldened finally by boredom, I peeped out from my cubby-hole. The coast was clear. I slunk on to the balcony. There was a faint glimmer of light showing downstairs, but it was switched off after a moment, while I waited, leaning back against the wall, and then it came on behind me, shining through the thick curtains, as both their voices in animated dialogue entered the room. Casilda's, pitched loud and distinctly, approached the window saying: 'Oh yes, Cyril would, of course, he's such an idiot . . . but you must be dog-tired, my poppet. I'll see if we're getting any air in here – isn't it a leetle bit stuffy? Tell me more about that arrant hussy Flo. . . .'

Gliding through the heavily draped curtains like a ghost – a warm, benevolent ghost – she signalled me in by the French window, which she left slightly ajar at my back as she sat down on a convenient leather pouf in the ample recess, a veritable stage box, and was gone with a parting pat on the cheek. There was nothing to see straight in front, through a chink the width of a razor's edge, except the huge, high-canopied, empty nuptial couch – but by squinting sideways round the rim of the curtains to the far end of the room I espied Helen at her dressing table, swathed in a shimmering white satin gown, with Casilda lolling in a tall chair beyond, brandy balloon aswirl in one hand, neck comfortably propped, eyelids lowered. Helen was busy transferring a tidy fortune from her person to a jewel casket the size of a pirate's chest. She stood up, and her friend helped to extract the neat, slim, marvellous torso from its costly covers, as Helen wriggled free, like a mermaid shedding her fishtail, to become a pocket Venus risen from the foam, an alabaster nymph springing to life from the pedestal of discarded trappings coiled about her ankles. With leisurely deliberation for my benefit, Casilda fetched the diaphanous negligee that was chastely to envelope the perfect proportions of an exquisite small figure clad incongruously in skintight nylon briefs and a strapless bra. To my sincere amazement the vision, while it lasted, was of breathtaking purity. Helen was – how old was she? Forty-four? Forty-two, if a day. But she was not, as I had imagined her, remarkably well preserved for her age: she was lovely in her own right, a priceless Tanagra statuette, delicate, dainty, at first glance almost girlish, and yet ideally formed, on shapely classic lines, with every curve and facet of the trunk and limbs impeccably drawn, trimly contrived, firmly, admirably modelled. It was a miniature, fashioned on a tiny scale, but certainly not starved or skimped in any detail, nor distressingly fragile or puny. Nothing indeed was lacking to lend all natural enchantment to this delicious little body, save only the sheer, inimitable bloom of youth itself. Charm it had, and harmony . . . but sexual energy, stamina, strength?

Helen, who had retired to the bathroom, belonged by rights in a museum. Although no doubt we would shortly see this pale porcelain shepherdess converted, under Casilda's tender care, into a raving maenad, I could scarcely conceive of her as a creature of flesh and blood, or recognise the haughty hostess whom I knew, loaded with diamonds. The transformation in any event should be worth witnessing.

Casilda was too efficient, a producer to let the attention of her audience flag in Helen's absence. She took advantage of this interval to display herself before me, stark and entirely naked at last. Floating into focus with the mannequin's slinky, calculated grace, very slowly she disrobed in a comical parody of a striptease act, divesting herself in one continuous movement of the long green wrap, a gossamer slip, a black lace brassiere, and transparent frilly panties to match. As though unleashed, rather than merely relieved of her clothes, she glided airily, imperviously, without a stitch on, to lay these flimsy trifles over a settee, and returned to face in my direction across the bed's broad, low expanse, that well-sprung wrestling ring, which cut her off at the shins. As languidly as a cat, she stretched, arching her back and raising her ribs in a voluptuous gesture that lifted the fine pectoral muscles, the gleaming provocative swell of her breasts, which she cupped in both hands and squeezed; before pressing her palms against her haunches, belly and flanks, like some immoral masseuse. Then she drained the rest of her brandy and subsided onto the quilt, not under it, to lie there encamped, her long legs crossed, wearing a surreptitious smile, relaxed but expectant.

Helen played the opening scene as prettily as if she were an actress out to woo recalcitrant critics. She could not know that she had already melted my initial indifference. Mute and motionless for a while she hovered at the foot of the bed, absorbed in pensive contemplation of a family vista – the sunny hills and shadowed dales of a beloved anatomy, which she surveyed with the same fond longing as the traveller, homeward bound, who scours the horizon for a glimpse of his native land. When Casilda sat up to offer her the happy haven of her outheld arms, Helen responded only with a grave, mysterious nod of rapt appraisal. Thereafter the tempo changed, gradually gathering speed, increasing in fervour, rising and falling, recovering by imperceptible degrees to gain fresh impetus, drifting, dwindling into the distance but always ready to revive and renew its dominant themes in a succession of varied movements like a symphony. I in my corner drank them in, one after the other. Enthralled, breathless, carried away, I watched the drama unfold its destined course of action, quivering with excitement, gasping and panting no less loudly, I feel sure, than the lovers themselves as they strained and yearned and struggled on the soft, spotlit stage under my staring eyes that were glued to the resplendent nudity of their flailing limbs and troubled, tense, bliss-ridden bodies. I confess that the swift, intoxicating, endless sequence of events dazzled and confused me, as sometimes at the theatre there is too much to observe and retain in one's glutted, grasping memory, which jumbles up a flood of vivid fragments in the wrong order. I remember how the play began, I recall every fleeting incident and episode, I can recapture each ravishing moment with precise clarity – but if I try to string these loose impressions together, it is just a tiresome, doleful waste of effort.

The curtain went up when Helen's filmy garment came off. Casilda deftly removed it as Helen sank onto the bed beside her and nestled in the bosom which leaned out above her, as she snuggled under the lofty throat and tilted chin, like the jutting, painted bubs on the figurehead of a full-rigged vessel. Gently they rocked, clutched tightly in an almost maternal embrace, until Helen's feather-weight prevailed and she bore her opponent down, willingly overwhelmed, her shoulders square against the sheets. Helen's small, hungry mouth had fastened upon the summit of a generous tit, which she clasped firmly in one hand, while the other roamed over all the wide, smooth surfaces of Casilda's body and probed its every crease and hollow. Sprawling with a glad air of lassitude beneath this onslaught, while Helen crouched across her stomach like a sleek black panther, Casilda lay supine yet alert in the idleness of temporary surrender, a country defeated but unbowed under occupation. In time, however, as her flesh was stirred, she started to twitch and squirm a little, until at last, her resistance sapped, she turned an expressive face towards me that I might read on its contorted features an eloquent record of Helen's work in progress. I was thankful for this kindly gesture, and with good cause, for round by round thereafter, through each successive phase of their ding-dong combat, Casilda exerted considerable ingenuity to show herself and Helen to me, if not always in the most dignified or flattering light, at least from every possible angle and to the onlooker's best advantage. It was an exhibition match, and evidently, she wanted me to get my money's worth. I did in fact receive my fill of her friend's charms, as well as all her own finer points, and no mistake. When Helen's lips skimmed her belly, when her fingers combed the curly clump of fern adorning the lush Olympian mount of no-man's-land, which is no woman's either, nor anyone's private property, since it is the universal seat of love and belongs, so its name implies, solely to Venus; when Helen's eager snout went burrowing between her thighs and nuzzled the shy rose that blooms there only at a lover's touch, Casilda slewed around on the bed, lifting Helen by the hips and setting them up, as it were on an easel, for me to scan, so that I should miss no aspect of what we both regarded – fixedly – as the most entrancing view in all the world. Like the lady of the house arranging the flowers for a party, Casilda opened the bouquet presented to her by her devoted admirer as soon as the donor's back was turned. She studied, patted and stroked each precious bud and petal, displaying the whole sweet cluster of blossom as a garden of delights centred on a diminutive patch of dewy moss.

A picture of neatness it was, to be sure, Helen's quaint, cute little quim: deep, raw, red gash and all, amidst the raven's nest of her luxuriant short hairs, one felt it ought to be filled by anything but envy of even its choicest rivals. It was so smart and tidy a job as the owner herself. Casilda certainly was unable to resist the temptation of biting into this ripe black fig, so succulently split and set there between the milk-white nates as on a luscious dish of clotted cream, asking to be devoured. Casilda's chestnut mane obscured my sight. All I could see now was Helen's butting, upturned rump that leapt and bounced like a bucking bronco endeavouring vainly with wild gyrations to dislodge the stubborn rider from her tail. The effect was as droll as the antics of a tethered goat exasperated by a swarm of wasps. She could bear it no more – and I beheld her parts again, fully exposed, when she broke away suddenly and swung right about, like the mad mare she was, rearing up and hurling herself into position against

Casilda's groin, which she heaved into cunning, interlocked contact with her crotch, so that their juicy, drooling slits were grafted, crushed, jammed together as though they sought by this ravenous kiss to soothe and close a single gaping wound. Hers Helen held open while she twisted and strove to entwine their lower limbs, drawing one of the other's supple legs around her waist to tie a sort of profligate lovers' knot which should seal their nether lips and join their tiny tongues, dissolving all their pain in the hot, salt taste of that one mingled mouth's saliva.

How long they continued to grapple and clash, slipping and weaving and sparring like a couple of boxers, I cannot say. It was a futile equation of minus quantities which, however well matched, could only exacerbate but never finally quench their lesbian lust that crumbled and clicked like fiery coals sputtering in the grate for want of a poker. But it rubbed me up the right way, this lurid scene of friction, I have to admit. I could barely contain myself in my hiding place behind the curtains. I held my breath, for fear of betraying my presence in the offing – and that was not all, to tell the truth, that I had to take a strong grip on, though I am no more an onanist at heart than Casilda is genuinely homosexual. Yet I did not really masturbate; it was they, the pair of them, who abused me by their shameless, pernicious example. I would instantly have extended my unsolicited compliments and most assiduous service to either of these poor fornicating females – or both, if I had been given the chance.

The naked contrast between them was as divine as I had supposed; but what I could not have guessed was that Helen's body would please me more, to some extent, than Casilda's. Even allowing for the joyous shock of its discovery a moment ago, strictly speaking, as a nude, it enchanted and fascinated me still more profoundly by reason of its pure artistic values – which were superlative – than its opposite number, which I already knew. Casilda's physique was brimful of sexual attraction; Helen's was somehow more seductive, not so exciting but – that was the word – more enticing. It was the wonderful symmetry of her shape, first of all, and then that particular quality of a radiant, fastidious elegance about her whole person that I found so moving. The frailty of this prim China doll, belied by an adorable, pneumatic bottom, the definite, impertinent, pretty little tits, even that ugly thing, her twat – a livid pink parting in the glossy mesh of jet-black pubic hair – was at once so absurd and so fetching as to kindle and captivate one's incredulous interest. Perhaps, if you searched for faults, carping exception might be taken to the big brown aureoles that seemed to smear too large a dub of cinnamon around the twin cherries topping the bosom's glistening goblets of ice cream. Ah, but how jauntily they danced, above the narrow hips as she bestrode the rolling roads of pleasure! She had a nearly grown-up daughter, I reflected. What must the child be like, compared to a mother whose beauty in middle age was such a paragon, a source of such frank astonishment to the most exacting student of feminine form? Here these two specimens were striking enough in partnership – the tall, fair girl with the glowing golden skin, the long lean curves, the tawny tuft, the solid build, and, lording it over her, the slight small dark older woman, carved out of ivory, polished, delicate and hard, a pagan goddess, a camellia, a fairy queen, and yet . . . Casilda's abject slave. The sweetness of the honeycomb had dizzied, vanquished, overcome the bee.

But it was a linked sweetness infinitely sustained, as the romantic poet wrote and the dreams of my waking memory confirm. I recollect a host of sights and sounds, a plethora of visions in so short a space of time. . . . I see Casilda crucified, her gritted teeth bared and choking back a noiseless scream as Helen's voracious maw sucks out, her innards. I see her fingers clutch a crumpled pillow, or hooked in Helen's hair, tugging the harpy's drowned, dishevelled head into her throbbing fork, thrusting her pelvis in an acrobatic arc against those thirsty lips, that darting adder's tongue, which will not release its lacerated prey until the fainting victim has reached her stormy climax twice.... I see Casilda's quick recovery and prompt, pitiless revenge. Now it is Helen's turn to whimper and cry out, blurting the lovesick vows, the rasped commands that interrupt the murmurous monotone of goading, gloating exhortation, ecstasy, delirium, gratitude – all things utterable – as though she were plotting aloud the soaring graph of frantic folly, from the first flicker of libidinous instinct to the last blind paroxysm that is in solemn truth the seventh heaven....

The dim grey light of a November dawn, invisible as yet, but imminent, was at my heels when I, at home, like Helen and her love, clasped in each other's arms, a hundred streets away dropped off into exhausted sleep.

IV

Three months, I thought to myself, upon my soul, that's just about enough. Everything comes to him who waits – but I damn well wasn't going to wait for Casilda much longer. It would have to be now, at once or never, I decided, and if she could not bring herself to sleep with me after all this time, then to hell with her; we had better part. I had been far too mild and patient; her shilly-shallying would have to stop, or else I'd send her packing, and not mince my words, either – that would be that. If she thought there could be any more of this tomfoolery, I'd show her how wrong she was. The worm would turn – and really I would be quite happy to see the end of Miss Vandersluys, I had begun to think.

Actually, I was waiting for her at that moment, in a Mayfair bar – an unusual place for us to meet, and not one of my most favourite haunts at the best of times. She was late. I had been pole-sitting on a high stool, drowning my sorrows – or mulling over my bitter grievance against her – for the past half hour. But she was looking even gloomier than I when finally, with a frowning absence of the slightest apology, she turned up and ordered herself a gimlet. So far as I can remember, this was our fourth rendezvous in over three weeks since Casilda had staged her special charades for me that night at Helen's.

'What's the matter?' I inquired. 'You appear extremely aggrieved or depressed.'

'I am both,' she replied in a low, angry tone. 'But who cares? It's my own fault. I've just lost myself a job.'

'Oh?'

'Yes, and I'm through with women. Horrid, vicious, gnat-brained strumpets – ugh, they're worse than men! Even more of a nuisance. . . .'

'Why? What's happened? Don't tell me you've turned over a new leaf! Has Helen been making jealous scenes? Did she catch you out once too often? Or is she deceiving you now, for a change? Perhaps I'm at the bottom of it – does she know about us?'

Casilda glowered at me in disgruntled silence. 'Don't you be an idiot, too,' she said. 'I couldn't bear it.'

'I keep asking you to explain what the trouble is,' I suggested sympathetically.

'Oh, it's only that boring Social Editress of *Chic* . . . they're a fine magazine to work for, they pay well . . . I was afraid of this, I could see it coming. She was always half on the point of pawing me – you know what I mean. She asked me at every turn to model lingeries – 'just slip these on, darling, you'd look lovely in 'em' – as though she, and not Mrs Knoblaugh, had charge of fashion. She wanted me to pose – in the raw, of course – for a photographer pal of hers, such a talented chap, who is absolutely on the verge of becoming famous. Whenever I went to see old Knobbly she'd waylay me with a cup of tea, theatre tickets, the present of some cute little trifle that would match my eyes or go so nicely with what I was wearing. She was dying to help me, my dear, she has heaps of influence. It's true, too – especially on the paper. Now she'll do me all the dirt she can, I expect. I've lost my *Chic*, you can bet your life on that.'

'Hm, rather a pity. Couldn't you have choked her off without hurting her feelings?'

'I had kept her at arm's length up to now. All innocence I was, I smiled like an imbecile. She has never dared pop the question, I looked too horribly sweet and dumb. But today it was different. Blast the bitch – she'd been out to some very grand, important luncheon, and tottered back to the office as tiddly as an owl. There was no holding her. I didn't stand a chance. If I weren't a hefty girl, with a good right hook, I would never have got away with it . . . practically unscathed.'

'Rough stuff on those plush premises – the incident has a certain novelty value at least.'

'Rough! You should have seen the pass she made at me – and the cut I gave her over one eye. Naturally I cleaned her up a bit before I left – there was blood dripping onto the carpet – but we didn't part friends, even so. She had sobered up slightly by then, but she was still rather groggy – and starting to go all maudlin with remorse. A dreadful mess.'

Casilda ruminated glumly for long enough to swallow three gins in a row, like nips of medicine.

'Pretty funny, it was, really, I guess,' she conceded with a wan smile, 'the silly nitwit tried to rape me. There was a lot of sentimental talk at first about natural attraction, and how she always had this devastating thing for me. Then she grabbed and kissed me, full on the mouth, in her own office! I was so taken aback – literally, I mean – that I fell with a thump on the desk and sat there on her blotting-pad, gaping at her blankly. Damn me, though, if her hands weren't up my skirts in a flash! She huddled down to it in her swivel-chair, frigging me for all she was worth. As happy as a sandgirl, what's more, with an ear pressed hard against my tummy, as if auscultating that area to note my reaction.'

'Didn't you stop her.'

'My sweet, how could I? I was laughing too much inside – and maybe the gurgling in my guts encouraged her. But it was utterly crazy. Her secretary might have pranced in any minute – or one of that bunch of pansies who flourish on *Chic*.'

'They'd have knocked, surely?'

'Yes, but only to sweep straight ahead without pausing for a second. She wouldn't even have lifted her nose from the grindstone. She was past caring. And anyway I was powerless. She had got me pinned on the edge of the desk, with an arm round each of my legs, from underneath, holding them apart and me fixed in place, astride her lap, leaning back on my elbows . . . watching the door. This is how she had me.' Casilda swung backwards on the barstool, in a discreet demonstration of a defenceless, semirecumbent position.

'I see,' said I, reflectively. 'So that was how she had you.'

'What do you mean? Well, almost.' Casilda laughed.

'Only I picked up this great big expensive silver cigarette box, when things began to get serious, and I clocked her – pretty hard, harder than I meant – on the forehead. I suppose it was rather ungracious of me. . . .'

'But honour was saved?'

'She let go, at any rate. I put a foot against her chair, and shoved. It was on casters, so she went spinning halfway across the room. 'Please, please,' she implored, even then. 'It'll only take a minute, and I promise you'll enjoy it – oh, my God, blood!' she shrieked. So I mopped her up as best I might – and here I am. I must say I feel awful about it. All sticky and beastly and hot. . . .'

'I'm not surprised,' I remarked sourly.

At my jaundiced expression Casilda laughed again. 'I wish I wasn't so squeamish, that's all,' she explained, and then added: 'I could dine with you tonight, if you like. Helen has gone away to the country. I deserve a really swell, slap-up dinner, don't you think, after what

I've been through? Only I'm not a bit hungry . . . or let's just go to a movie. I'd quite as soon skip food. Oh, I've no idea *what* I want. That foul old bag ruined everything.'

'Try to forget all about it,' I said soothingly.

But Casilda had sunk into a reverie. She even ignored her tepid little drink, and sat bemused, staring into space. I mentioned half a dozen restaurants by name, and pushed the evening paper, with the list of cinemas, in front of her eyes. But they were fixed, vacantly, on a point past my right shoulder, and when at last she spoke, I could barely catch the words, they were uttered so softly, under her breath.

'Yes, I do, too – I know what I'd like. It's over there in the corner. Daddy, buy me that.'

I followed her gaze the length of the bar. At the other end, facing towards us with an evidently keen interest in Casilda, sat a hulking, swarthy young dago in a flamboyant brown suit, with vastly padded shoulders and an air of almost insolent admiration. Casilda, I am sorry to say, was giving him very much the same look in return.

'You can't mean that seriously,' I exclaimed – as a statement of fact, not a question. For one thing, he sported the sort of moustache that might have been drawn with an eyebrow-pencil an inch below his nostrils.

Casilda merely nodded, but as an affirmative gesture it was all too definite. Any doubt in my mind was pure wishful thinking.

'I thought you said you didn't go in for gigolos,' I protested.

The girl gave a snort of mirth, 'Nor do I,' she agreed. 'But I can have this one for free, I assure you – if you'll let me. And you could watch,' she added in the same quiet tone, scarcely above a whisper. 'Wouldn't that excite you?' Her face was set, almost sullen.

There was silence between us for a moment. I needed time to think, to ponder this startling proposition. Without a word I paid the bill, kissed her cheek and walked out, bowing stiffly to the baffled foreigner, who hastily returned my salute with joyful bewilderment.

Was he any less puzzled on the back seat of the car, after an unceremonious introduction as 'My toreador,' while we drove towards Chelsea, with Casilda, happy and tense, nestling against my shoulder, her hand on my knee? He had a smattering of English – enough to gargle polite assent when Casilda asked him if this was his first visit to London, but her next question – 'Have you ever been kidnapped before?' – virtually drew a blank. 'Very pretty,' he assured us.

'Isn't he, though?' Casilda murmured, hugging my arm. 'He's a matador, you know,' she insisted.

'More like a picador, to judge by his looks,' I retorted. 'What are you going to do with this tough when you get him home?'

'The best he can,' said Casilda.

He chose whisky and accepted with alacrity an invitation from Casilda in French to be shown the house. I poured myself a big dollop of brandy, and settled down to read a couple of letters that the postman had brought. To this day I could not tell you what was in them. A few agonising minutes' wait was as much as I could bear.

They were not next door. She had led him off to the spare room upstairs – which was very considerate of her. He was kneeling with his back to me as I entered, his face pressed against her navel. She sat, naked to the waist, on the high four-poster, with an arm around his bull neck, twisting his greasy curls. She took no notice of me whatsoever, and her conquest, oblivious of all else but the free gift of this magnificent body, did not even hear me come in. I lit the fire for them, and slip-

A Gallery of Nudes

ped into an easy chair near by to contemplate the scene.

He had evidently set about his business without a second's hesitation. The square, exaggeratedly masculine shoulders obscured her lower half from view, while his bent head was sunk in the hollow of her lap, and blindly, with both brown, hairy paws upstretched, he mauled, rather than fondled, Casilda's breasts. The way the fellow manhandled those sumptuous tits struck me as exceedingly rough and uncouth for a Latin lover: he plucked and tweaked and tugged at them, like some famished urchin snatching oranges from a tree. Nevertheless there was no sign of objection or complaint on her part; she kept her mouth shut tight and made not a sound, except for the fast, heavy breathing that shook her whole frame more violently from within, it seemed, than the harsh treatment to which this clumsy lout was subjecting her shapely facade.

She did not budge or flicker an eyelid. Yet if she, in rigid submission, might have withstood his bold assault indefinitely, it was clear that the hot-blooded Spaniard could brook no further delay. Muttering with impatience, the coarse creature sprang to his feet and started to tear the rest of her clothes off. She helped him then at once, promptly raising a docile backside to facilitate the complete removal of her rumpled dress and skintight panties, while she herself took off her fetching little suspender belt and stockings. As she leaned forward to do so, she suddenly, as I saw, undid his fly – and I too had the same impulse of unrestrainable curiosity, though for a different reason. What intrigued me was not Don Juan's credentials, but the effect they would produce on her. By craning my neck I caught a glimpse of her face, which revealed an expression of such sad and obvious disappointment that I probably let out a delighted guffaw. He spun round on me like a tiger, with eyes blazing fury at my intrusion. But his beautiful big dark eyes did not interest me; his erection did. It was rather short; not small, exactly, but a funny, fat, stubby instrument – a replica of the cocky young masher himself. His spitting image, I thought. Thick, I'll grant you – exceptionally thick, and to all appearance hard as marble.

Personally I am fairly large, even now, and though of course comparisons are odious, I could sympathise with Casilda for taking such a dim view of his singularly unimpressive member. Certainly this was not the doughty Toledo blade by which she had expected to be smitten to the quick. It was stiff enough to fit her sheath, and stout enough to fill it adequately, but surely not long enough to pierce her very heart, as she had hoped.

In any case, this queer little blunderbuss was the last alarming weapon that our swashbuckling Spanish guest could brandish at me as he advanced in threatening fashion. I stood my ground, and watched him with some amusement.

'Go away from here!' he shouted, pointing towards the door. 'Madame and I will be alone.'

But Casilda rose up at that moment, like some vengeful goddess clad in the imposing plenitude of her pagan nudity, and summoned the hound to heel. She clung to the sleeve of his chocolate suit, restraining him. 'No, no!' she cried. 'Quiet, Carlos!' It was an order, rapped out sharply in the tone you would employ to subdue a ferocious mastiff, and she accompanied it with vehement shakes of the head, which he could not fail to understand. He hesitated, scowling in my direction, but she gripped him firmly by the convenient handle she found within reach and clamped her mouth on his, silencing his ugly splutters of rage. Barefoot, she was considerably the taller of the two, though no match for him in strength. He flung her back against the bed – but she held on to his penis firmly, so that he fell sprawling across her where she lay.

'No, no!' she cried once more. 'Not like that – naked like me. Hurry – take all this stuff off, quick!'

Hastily he obeyed her, stripping at full speed. He was as hairy as an ape. With a shock of surprise, I noticed that his shoulders were in fact immensely broad – no less broad than his natty suiting had made them out to be. Like Casilda herself, the brute looked better out of clothes. He was admirably built, I have to admit – as strong as an ox, evidently, and well shaped, with a deep chest and narrow hips, although too hirsute and too short of stature to qualify as an Adonis. But the general impression was of good, young male muscle beneath the thick coat of black fur which covered him like a rug from his neck to his ankles. It was only his genitals that were not up to much, by contrast, with the rest of his sturdy physique.

Casilda eagerly scrutinised this classical virile type while he undressed. Reclining between the pair of carved, slender posts at the foot of the bed, where he had thrown her, for all the world like a goalkeeper alertly awaiting the next exultant forward rush, and with her eyes still riveted on him, it was then that she made the lewdest gesture I ever beheld in a lifetime of debauchery. Slowly, deliberately she stretched her long, lovely legs as far apart as she could spread them, doing the splits in that lolling position, so that we both – he and I – were confronted with a medical diagram of the vulva, highly coloured and fully extended, as in a textbook for students of gynaeocology. Not content with this obtrusive exhibition of her secret flesh, she turned exposure into invitation by offering him the target of her parted lips which she held open with two fingers in an inverted V for victory – or vagina.

For him it was an explorer's survey of the promised land, a preliminary viewing for his approval of the savoury dish that he had ordered. For me it was a blow across the face, a sudden, stinging shock of jealous horror. Until then my emotions had been mixed, uncertain, mostly dormant, as though by dint of will I had contrived to keep my feelings, if not under complete control, at least in abeyance. Curiosity and a shameful, vicarious excitement had usurped my normal faculties, numbing the spirit of revolt in my brain like a narcotic. Now, realisation of the vile role that I had assumed, both as pimp and cuckold, seeped over me, and a sweat of anguish broke out upon my brow. I was enveloped in some foul nightmare when I heard Casilda cry in the same urgent, raucous tone of imperative, intemperate desire:

'Come on now, man – take me! Give it to me! I want you.'

Before the words were out of her mouth he was inside her. He hurled himself forward into the open breach that was presented to him, as a battering ram of old must have crushed triumphantly through the weakened ramparts of an enemy citadel, vanquished and abandoned under siege. The impact winded her, and she uttered a loud gasp as the weight of the gorilla's vigorous onslaught knocked the breath from her body. His grappling hands dragged at her hips, pulling her half off the end of the bed, as he clambered upward, thrusting and jolting against her, jabbing and jerking, but at the same time holding her pelvis suspended in midair, as though to prevent the force of his attack from carrying her backwards, lest he should lose the prize he had seized or risk diminishing the violent contact of their private parts. I studied Casilda's face at this juncture, as she was lugged bolt upright into a sitting position by her arms, which were clasped behind his neck. She looked stunned, bereft, flabbergasted. Her eyes and mouth were as wide open as her legs, and fixed in a dazed expression. Rocked and pummelled amidships, she was beginning now to pant and strain in a wild attempt to draw the man down on top of her, so that she might herself enjoy the act in comfort, prone beneath his lunging bulk but solidly supported by the bed and able therefore to reply on even terms and keep her end up. He had gained the initiative; with his feet firmly planted on the floor, he seemed solely concerned to take his pleasure of her surrendered sex without scruple for his amorous partner's physical need, but seeking only to press home his own advantage over an all too easy victim.

My heart leaped for joy when I saw what was happening: this brash little dago was manhandling Casilda with the utmost rigour, he had roused her erotic instinct to fever pitch, he tupped her as savagely as a beast of the field – yet he could not satisfy her. He was using her merely as an object suited to his lustful purpose; but his very success in this selfish aim would prove a bitter blow to her – and she had asked for it. I was delighted to think that she was doomed to experience the direst disenchantment in my presence. Already I toyed with the idea of how I would upbraid her for this sordid and disgraceful display when it was over. If she was so wanton and so immoral as to hope that I might take the satyr's place, after he had finished with her, and carry on from where he left off, she would soon discover that she had made a big mistake. This was the end – I realised the fact with meridian clarity as I watched her lascivious antics in the arms of another man. I was through with Casilda Vandersluys for good and all. Directly after the fellow had gone, I would kick her out of the house. Or she could buzz off with him on her own if she liked – I didn't care.

Alas, how wrong I was! The mistake was entirely mine. I underestimated the dirty bastard – and the harlot who had picked him up, frankly preferring him to me, as casually as I might choose a whore in a brothel. She could not have guessed beforehand that he possessed such a small, stumpy tool which would scarcely fill the bill; but then neither could I foresee, at this initial stage of events, what stalwart use he would make of it, what fantastic feats of endurance the monster was capable of performing, how complete his victory would be, or what a shattering effect his persistence would have on so doughty an opponent as Casilda. She, I knew, was a tough nut to crack. I had marvelled at her reserves of energy and enthusiasm when she lasted through round after gruelling round with Helen. Keen as she was for the fray, Helen had not stood the pace to the finish with half so much in hand as the younger woman, who seemed wholly inexhaustible, ever ready to renew the engagement, gallantly impervious to fatigue. Casilda met more than her match in Carlos. His staying powers were incredible. Again and again he outlasted her, checking his own orgasm but making the randy bitch spend with increasing ecstasy each time, with longer, more profound, more exquisite spasms, by a delaying technique of extraordinary resilience which I never would have credited from hearsay.

Unfortunately for my peace of mind, it was not from hearsay that I learned the grim, incontrovertible truth of that young orangutan's sexual proficiency. To my chagrin and disgust I was obliged to witness the revolting demonstration of his prowess untiringly exercised on Casilda's wracked but willing frame, as it appeared to me, for hours on end . . . I was in agony throughout, yet powerless to prevent it. The experiment was conducted under my nauseated gaze – but there was nothing that I could do to stop the unspeakable cad from screwing my girl to distraction . . . and at her own request.

He started by his sliding both hands under her thighs and tearing them apart still further; then, when he had wrenched her open like an oyster, he pushed her knees back, bending them outwards as supplely as a frog's, so that he mounted her as if to probe her guts upon the operating table. She protested feebly, but her long legs were crossed high around his loins while he gradually ploughed his way deeper into her and farther up onto the bed. Eventually he had her flat on it, and she got a chance to retaliate in kind, battling against him hammer and tongs, as he crushed her under his weight and pounded her with his stiff, stout, chugging piston. For a time, as though moved by clockwork, he stuck to the same steady, regular, relentless rhythm, which was neither fast nor slow but evenly stressed, a succession of short, sharp stabs for many minutes at a time – until, not heeding Casilda's cries but of his own volition, to please himself, he would alter the tempo and shift the angle and the manner of his strokes. These tactical changes, occurring at odd intervals, swept all before him and soon reduced Casilda to an abject state of unassuaged, amazed submission. All tract of restraint, dignity or pride was gone. She had what she wanted – a surfeit of it, lashings of cock, almost more of the sweet physic than she could stomach. Well and truly was she getting laid; he poked her, decidedly, as she had never been poked before. The devil's pitiless prong sparked the molten red volcanic fires that consumed her burning crater and licked her entrails like subterranean tongues of flame. Tied to the stake, she wilted in the searing heat while he kept her there dangling upon the brink of an eruption, yielding to the protracted torture which she craved, yet yearning for the coup de grace to snap the unbearable tension of her nerves.

What the occupying force lacked in size, its seasoned spearhead, diligently employed, irrevocably entrenched, made up by aggressiveness. He humbled her twice, without succumbing himself, without the slightest sign of exhaustion. Indeed he seemed annoyed by the readiness of her response, for on each occasion, as she neared the inevitable climax, he growled 'No, no, wait – not now, not yet!' when plainly she was incapable of obeying his command. Otherwise he seldom spoke, but uttered only a continuous series of guttural grunts while she, fainting in his arms, loose-limbed, tossing and floundering like a spiked fish, raved and moaned incessantly, repeatedly, through gritted teeth:

'Yes, oh yes, that's it, that's it, go on, yes, like that, go on, don't stop – ah, yes, my God, dear God, don't stop, don't stop – you mustn't, oh Christ, now – ah – go on – more, more, oh please, no, don't stop, that's it – come on, you brute – oh God, yes, like that, damn you – ah, Jesus – you're killing me – go on, more – now, now, my God – I'm coming – I can't bear it – aah – now!'

They lay quiet, scarcely stirring for a while, but he did not withdraw. Hatred of them both sickened me; my knees were weak, escape or interference would be equally impossible, pointless; stricken with misery, anger and resentment, I retreated to my corner and slumped there, dosing my distress with brandy. The minutes slipped by. This disgusting farce had gone on long enough. Even Casilda must have had her fill by now, and more, by the sound of it. I must tell her southern stallion that time was up, that he would have to leave, he need not think I had invited him to spend the night.

I was somewhat fuddled, but I had come to this drastic decision and was just getting ready to throw the blighter out – when they began again. He started rodgering her once more, for all he was worth, and she of course responded straightaway, putting her back into it, grinding and groaning as gladly as before. She was in luck. I doubt if anyone, in all her rich and varied experience, had ever screwed her so thoroughly. She was beside herself. For a girl who disapproved of blas-

A Gallery of Nudes

phemy in bed – as I remember she had told me – some of the obscenities which she uttered now were, to say the least, appalling. I was shocked and revolted. Filthy endearments mingled in her mouth with invocations of the Almighty, animal noises, and muttered insults. Her scarlet nails, like talons, clawed at the ruffian's hairy back, scratching the humped, muscular neck, digging with bestial passion into his neat, bobbing buttocks. He growled, but manfully bore the sharp pain for a time, then – suddenly infuriated – he grabbed her by the throat, as if to throttle her, and raising himself, struck her savagely across the face, a stinging blow, with the flat of his hand.

Her mad, agonised grimace did not alter. But to me it was an outrage that was intolerable, a typical example of caddish violence that called for instant, chivalrous, condign retribution. I must avenge this maltreatment of a woman, if not the honour she herself had trampled or the respect which Casilda no longer merited. In attempting to do so, however, I tripped – or the young brute hit me, I'm not sure which – and I fell heavily against the fender, knocking my head. Before I could pick myself up – perhaps I was too slow, being somewhat dazed – that scoundrel of a Spaniard pounded upon me, as I lay there defenceless among the fire irons, unable to move. Quicker than lightning, he had ripped off my tie and fastened my hands with it securely beneath me. I aimed a kick at his midriff, but a dressing-gown cord was knotted tightly about my ankles. I was trussed like a goose! He had no difficulty in hauling me onto my knees and toppling me backwards into the chair.

Limp and dishevelled, Casilda sat watching us from the bed. Her chin cupped in both palms, she looked listless and remote, a picture of dejection. I noticed that she did not raise a finger to help me, nor did she say a word, she was too haggard and cowed. When he turned to her again, she dropped meekly back to receive him in the same supine posture as before, with broad smooth thighs lifted above her navel ... I remember nothing else from that moment on, except an aching glare behind the eyes. ...

When I came to, a long time later, the pain was still there but the Spaniard had gone. Casilda was bending over me, her naked bosom in my face, as she untied my wrists, having already freed my feet. Somewhat belatedly she showed intense concern for my condition, and fussed over me like a devoted nurse who arrives on the scene of a childish accident after the harm was been done. I eyed her with derision and distaste. True to the innate, uncaring harlotry of all her sex, she gave not the slightest indication of remorse, regret or even consciousness of the enormity of her offence. She had been having a damned good time; it was over now, and that was that. Surely (her manner implied) I could not be so unreasonable and churlish as to begrudge her a little fun once in a while? After all, I had not stepped in and prevented it. Quite to the contrary, I had allowed her a free hand, for which she was prepared to be duly grateful, so long as I did not go and spoil everything by electing to grumble about a mere peccadillo that was best forgotten. How could I be so tiresome as not to realise that *our* relationship was far more important, whereas this business with the lecherous Spaniard was just a passing fling?

I believe in the sincerity of her innocent attitude towards what had taken place. She did not give it a further thought. Such honesty, even in a flaming whore, should be accounted a virtue. But I could not look on it in that light. My love and loyalty, my every emotion, my own manhood had been spurned, insulted, trodden in the dust. Jealousy flooded my brain like a raging torrent. Casilda was calmly putting on her clothes. She drank a sip of brandy out of my glass, and offered me the dregs.

'I'm so sorry, darling,' she said – but I could not tell exactly what she meant by the remark: she might have been apologising for the mere dribble she had left me.

'How many times?' I asked, through my fatigue, in a voice that may have sounded either casual or surly. She cast a glance at me and understood the question.

'Five in all, I think,' she answered. 'But I lost count.'

Half dressed, she came and sat cross-legged on the rug at my feet before the dying fire, which she dutifully replenished with a shovelful of coal. She braced herself for a postmortem – the errant schoolgirl or the housemaid expecting to be rebuked for breaking some valued knicknack.

'Do you know,' she said sadly, 'he only came twice? I always thought it was less easy for a man who is not circumcised to last out so long. One lives and learns.'

She had got into her stride. 'I must say he amazed me,' she added. 'But there it is. Phew! Give me an uncircumcised cock every time.'

I slapped her hard across the mouth, as he had done. The suddenness rather than the force of the blow sent her sprawling to the floor. She sprang up and faced me, spitting fury.

'You swine!' she snarled. 'You shit! How dare you? You filthy, drooling, dirty, impotent, goddam son of a bitch!'

There have been a few occasions in my life when I have lost my temper with some stupid woman – but never can I recall having been so shamelessly provoked, so wholly justified in the use of violence, as I then was by this crowing trollop. I will not deny that I enjoy a bout of playful flagellation now and again. I have spanked or whipped most of my mistresses at one time or another, for the fun of it. But this was different. I saw red. Her screeching abuse was more than I had bargained for. Strangling would have been too lenient, too quick a punishment for her, I felt. I snatched hold of her by the wrist and by the hair, I dragged her over to the bed, I clouted her again across the face and boxed her ears. She went on cursing me, pouring out a stream of shrill, inept invective against my righteous wrath when I left her there and rummaged through a chest of drawers downstairs for what was needed.

When I returned with a bamboo cane, she had not moved, but she fought like a wildcat to break away from my clutches, until I succeeded in turning her over by wrenching her arm round behind her back, while I knelt on her neck and other wrist, so that she was pinned face down upon the bed, the furious tirade muffled by the pillows, and able only to retaliate with kicking heels because I rolled the elastic knickers into a sort of rope or hobble binding the thighs tightly together, some little way below the bouncing buttocks. They leaped and shuddered and swung from side to side as I thrashed her with all my might, until the sound of her screams, muted as it was, could be heard above the whistling of the cane and the loud thud which signalled each stroke as if to count the crimson weals that marked the wonderful wide expanse of her arse in next to no time. I flogged her blindly at first, as I might have beaten a carpet – but the pattern of punishment, as it deepened and darkened in crisscross streaks, began to fascinate me, and soon I was drawing hieroglyphics in a methodical manner, with more art than sadism, on the taught, quivery canvas that bloomed like a peony. I decorated both cheeks equally with a design in purple, black and blue. When they opened with a supplicating, subconscious jerk, wincing apart as though split by a cruel swipe of my wand, I aimed a lengthwise cut along the smooth ravine itself, which shrank and shut again at once like the big, bulbous jaws of some strange, flustered sea monster. From her nape to her knees Casilda's back heaved, flinched, rippled and shook. It was a windswept yellow cornfield, poppy bright: bowed, tossed, flurried by the gale. It was an ice rink scarred by a thousand skaters' trails, a seething, swollen river lashed to livid turmoil at the storm's mercy. . . .

Mercy? She howled for mercy, but I gave her none. She could not escape; she must only endure. She should smart and bleed and faint, cringing and grovelling, while my wrath lasted. I flogged her till my arm grew tired. I relished her struggles, I joyed in her suffering, I got acute pleasure from inflicting extreme humiliation – where she would feel it most – on the incontinent flesh which she had yielded so readily, so wickedly, to another man in my presence.

I wish to emphasise again, however, that this pleasure for my part was physical perhaps, but not sexual. Her tail excited me: I trounced it for precisely that reason, in reverse – to cure myself of its attraction, not because I was jealous of the promiscuous slut, but simply to break her hold over me, to settle our account, to call it quits, and to teach her a lesson. I would do no permanent damage to her naughty, burning backside; but if it ever forgot itself in the future, it must never forget me – the one lover who had missed his share of the lady's favours, yet had enjoyed her charms to his heart's content, by caressing them in his own special way. . . .

I let her go as soon as I was through – when I had lost interest in her wriggling, and felt she had been chastised enough. For me it was a sweet relief. I discovered that I no longer bore her any great grudge. It had simply had to be, and now it was done; I could rest easy, with the whole load of Casilda Vandersluys, a worthless burden, off my mind. It would be some time before she would care to flaunt her sorely bruised bum under Helen's nose or waggle it at any casual bedfellow, I reckoned – unless dignity mattered as little to her as decency. If she chose to make herself cheap, at least for a week or so, I'd turned her into a laughing-stock, highly coloured and comic; she could only indulge in intimacy at the risk of causing hilarity or actual ribaldry – and of providing me with a private joke in compensation. I flung the cane away across the room and fell asleep.

I do not know whether I awoke after a few minutes or an hour later, but the discomfort of wearing clothes prevented peaceful slumber. Casilda was still lying next to me, huddled on her side. I allowed her to doze on without interruption. She opened her eyes when I pulled the blankets over her and tucked her up for the night, but she did not speak or move, and her absent expression told me nothing of her feelings towards me. I undressed, tumbled into bed, and dropped off to sleep again instantly.

Daylight and the louder sound of traffic, or maybe the clatter of Mrs Howarth, the charwoman, barging about downstairs, gradually impinged on my consciousness and dragged me back to the realities of life which mankind coops for preference within four walls. But there was something else as well that I must have brought with me from the dreamless purlieus of a different, remote, forgetful world – a sense of serenity. I was awake, tranquil, refreshed – still drowsy, but peculiarly cheerful. Casilda lay curled in my arms, her head, a soft, fragrant nosegay of tousled chestnut tresses, on my shoulder. Assuming that she slept, I refrained with the utmost care from the slightest movement that might disturb her, even attuning every breath I drew to the tempo of her deep breathing. I conquered my intense desire to stroke and fondle the warm, firm, delicate flesh of the girl, lest my touch, however light, should rob her of the restful remedy that nature alone provides for rash extravagance.

So we remained, quietly locked in a tender embrace, for some time. But she, too, was feigning sleep, I

A Gallery of Nudes

realised, for when she stirred after a while, her hands glided with gentle stealth about my belly, caressing, fingering and finally clasping the emblems of power, the orb and sceptre of manhood, which she wielded silently but insistently until she was sure of me and satisfied with the result of her research, like the witch who knows that the love philter she has brewed is infallible in its effects. Then she spoke. In a murmuring voice that was low but distinct I heard her say:

'You're a fool, Tony, you know. You were wrong. But – never mind. I don't care. I love you. I really do. Not only now. Before. Only, it'll be still better now . . . you'll see. I'll show you. I had to make you wait . . . this is going to be the real time. . . .'

From nowhere her mouth burst out at me, engulfing mine, pressed to my lips like a hot, ripe fruit that is cool, thirst-quenching, sweet to the taste. In the next instant her body, an uncoiled spring, slid under me, beneath me, length for length, limb against limb. Her arms and legs were entwined about my body like ivy around a tree. . . .

'There, my love,' she said. 'Fuck me. D'you hear? I'm telling you now – fuck me.'

I plunged into her and dug my nails deeply into her belaboured buttocks.

'Go on,' she repeated, 'Fuck me!'

I had the incentive, and her command – and her. From that morning Casilda was my mistress. For both of us the long delay was over – and, as we had known in our hearts all along, the prize was worth it.

V

Eve must have taken an enormous bite out of that apple, to keep us all munching away so happily on the fruity facts of life ever since. From the moment of our somewhat boisterous if belated entrance together into the Serpent's paradise, Casilda and I never looked back. We were both of us habitués of the place, in other company – but that rather enhanced than spoiled our mutual pleasure on revisiting those bright, vast, crowded though private domains where (as Casilda once observed of an amusement park) common-or-garden-of-Eden couples litter the lawns like nudists, literally two a penis.

The prolonged disquiet of the weeks spent in what I might wryly call my courtship of Casilda was forgotten. Sexually and in every way our idyll now seemed a marvellous thing to both of us. We made love like a pair of romantic youngsters or seasoned, vicious, veteran debauchees. We indulged in as many varied embraces as our few hours together allowed. It was still pretty difficult for us to meet, but whenever we got the chance we fell into each other's arms, however hastily and hurriedly – yet always with immense success. So regular and resounding was Casilda's appreciation that sometimes, satisfied (not to say satiated) as I was, a tiny suspicion lurked at the back of my mind that she might perhaps be exaggerating a bit, out of a wish to flatter my ego. Luckily I am not easy to deceive in such matters.

The approach of Christmas was fortunate – a favourable circumstance, abetting our designs. Helen shopped feverishly. Her daughter Cécile would be coming over for the holidays from her finishing school at St Cloud – and Casilda insisted on giving up her room to the girl. This tactful, tactical move to a different floor under the same roof would leave her more often to her own devices – and to mine. At heart Casilda's attitude towards her bosom friend had not changed, but Helen had been quick to detect the shining light of a new love in Cassy's eye, and if suspicion were not to become certainty she must dodge those intimate episodes that were naturally fraught with the danger of discovery, since any sign of diminished ardour on her part would blow the gaff as surely as an open confession. So long as she could avoid getting to grips, Casilda might be able to bamboozle the Baroness, whom she was anxious to hoodwink – for her own sake – while our affair lasted.

Not that either of us had the slightest inclination to end an absorbing experiment which we were only now starting to conduct in earnest. We were ideally suited to each other by temperament. I had not suspected the existence of a masochistic streak in Casilda until I hit upon it, so to speak, purely by accident; hitherto, in the course of all her confidential chatter, she had never so much as hinted at this pleasing kink which added, for me, to her attraction. I freely acknowledge that it appealed to an answering though latent impulse of sadism in myself that I had always done my best to restrain, lest it develop from an innocuous whim into a positive obsession which I should find both troublesome and difficult to gratify. Not since the first careless raptures of my salad days had I enjoyed sexual intercourse so blithely, so intensely as now, on the brink of fifty, with a partner so adept, versatile and willing as Casilda. This was unquestionably as rewarding and splendid a liaison as any rake could wish to preserve among a stock of comforting memories laid by for his old age. Casilda had and did everything it would ever enter my head to demand of a mistress. To my way of thinking, she was frankly perfect.

But perfection, we know, is not of this world. There must always be a 'but' – for true love ends swiftly in boredom if its course runs smooth, and you do not need to be a cynic to realise that this in fact is what the tellers of fairy tales mean when they say the bridal pair 'lived happily ever after.' It's a catchphrase with a catch in it. Matrimony, monogamy and monotony are synonymous, marked by the most melancholy of initial letters. No such morbid menace hung over us, of course; the risk of marriage did not arise. Yet there was a fly in the ointment, I was dismayed to find. The thought of Helen's lasting hold upon Casilda haunted me even now that I had made the grade and won a temporary victory over our wardress. It was an altogether ludicrous situation – but I was horribly jealous of Helen. My charming affair with Casilda was developing right from the start into a sharp-angled triangle.

It did not take Helen long to smell a rat, though she had not guessed that the rat was myself, Anthony Grey. Her intuition warned her something was afoot – and amiss – but she still had no clue to her rival's identity, although I believe she was shrewd enough to read the signs of Casilda's deep-seated contentment as the handiwork of a member of the opposite sex. Puzzled and worried as she was, she put a brave front on her misery and went out of her way to conceal it from Casilda, on whom she now lavished affection and sweetness, presumably in the hope of shaming her into making a clean breast of this latest infidelity, which she knew to be more serious than usual.

'I've no doubt she's being extra nice and kind to you at present,' I sneered, when Casilda stood up for her soul mate. 'But just wait till she discovers who is cuckolding her. She'll scratch your eyes out straightaway – and I shall be made to suffer for it too, you may be sure, even if it takes her the rest of her life to get even with me. Helen can be horribly spiteful. She's going to have to forgive you in the long run, but she'll see me in hell first. She hates my guts, as it is.'

'What utter nonsense you talk! You really couldn't be more wrong,' Casilda testified heatedly. 'As a matter of fact she has quite a soft spot for you, although you always do your best to provoke and annoy her. Besides which, you must understand that Helen would only need to be jealous of you if you were half your age. At twenty-five or thirty she would recognise you as an appalling threat to my virtue – and to her sacred right of ownership – as either suitor or seducer. You might wrest me away to the altar or carry me off as your plaything, if we were blinded by youthful passion. At our time of life the odds are against either of us being so rash or so irresistible. However desperately they may fall for one another, she argues, they are certain to get over it before long. She regards you as a professional philanderer – extremely presentable, but on his last legs where women are concerned. She told me so herself, quite recently.'

'How good of her! But she only said that to test your reaction.'

'Not in the least, I promise you. She's neither such a simpleton nor so complicated and hypocritical as you like to think, but a mixture – like most of us. You shocked her profoundly that night at dinner by your insinuation of untold vice – but you intrigued her too, of course. You repel and attract her at the same time, just as Lucien used to in the old days. There's nothing extraordinary about that, to a woman's turn of mind. You're her type.'

'Well, I'll be damned! You don't suppose I'm tickled

pink to hear that the Baroness has this weakness for me, do you? Or to be compared to a fat and filthy old wreck like Lucien? Let them stew in their own juice, blast them! I would rather not pursue the subject.'

We were lying snugly in bed together on a foggy evening in December. A few minutes before this wrangling conversation began, we had been locked in each other's arms, giddy and choking with delight like swimmers battling happily in the surf of a tumultuous, exultant passion. The strong tide of our desire had receded, leaving us limp but thankfully at rest on a tranquil, firm and sunny shore. In a moment it would be time to get up, to dress and refresh ourselves, to sally out into the raw night for dinner. I lay at ease, sipping my whisky, as I watched Casilda stretch, like a great sleek marmalade cat, and bound in a couple of strides through the door to the bathroom. She would return, I knew, to warm her radiant body before the fire and then, with leisurely gestures, while she discussed where we should sup or prattled about trivial topics, she would don an enticing array of flimsy little garments, allowing me plenty of time to appreciate each frill and flounce, every clinging curve, rotundity and crease, as though performing a striptease act in reverse for my delectation.

It was one of those good occasions which Casilda called her 'Cinderella sprees,' as distinct from the quick, birdlike encounters in mid flight that most often had to suffice us by way of love-making, now that Casilda had exchanged her previous strategy of insufferable delays for a direct approach of uncompromising speed. Tonight was an exception: she could easily get home ahead of the Delavignes, who would be late back from some pompous party. She was aware of my special penchant for dainty lingerie, which did indeed amount almost to a fetish in my case and she indulged it to the fullest, out of the kindness of her heart, whenever there was an opportunity to stage the sort of peep show that I can happily feast my eyes on for hour after hour. I don't believe I ever saw her parade the same scanties twice; she must have owned a vast wardrobe of these ravishing pieces of intimate finery that lend additional temptation to the naked truth, forming a gay disguise to deck out the bare facts, as it were, with an ethereal smile, a trace of mystery which is not meant to fool the onlooker but only to enhance the beauty of each succulent morsel, like the sugar coating on crystallised fruits. In her dressing and undressing Casilda was about as spectacular as a Parisian revue. From the simplest and sheerest to the most fanciful and elaborate, from naughtiest nylon to softest wool, all the decorative variety of feminine underwear in every shape and shade, from the amply old-fashioned, starched and rustling, to the tightly stretched, close-fitting modern style of millinery, my delicious mistress had the whole wanton lot – a galaxy of bows, lace, ribbons, tucks and folds adorning every kind of froufrou, from bloomers to briefs, from petticoats and knickers to panties and slips, cat's-cradle bras and girdles, garters and *guepières*. . . .

I was watching the display no less avidly than usual when a dark suspicion fell like a chill, deep shadow across my mind, as though on a bright summer afternoon a cloud out of the blue sky had suddenly obscured the sun. Jealousy's first stab strikes often in this way, by stealth, like some dread disease. It was then, at a careless moment, while Casilda moved in silhouette against the playful glow of the firelight, that I was struck by a new doubt and recognised the symptoms of further and worse pain to come. Why are we by nature so perverse that our profound pleasure in a woman's sexual experience is undermined at once and blighted by the mere thought of how she must have acquired it? What fools men are to resent the bygone joys that have possessed this body which they now love, and to cavil at those other unknown males who moulded and instructed in the service of Venus! Innocence and chastity appeal only temporarily to an aggressive masculine instinct that derives acute personal satisfaction but no permanent solace from destroying them, and though the seducer himself rejoices at their loss on that unique occasion, it will be mourned and regretted thereafter by not a few of his successors. Blazing the trail, this favoured pioneer stakes his triumphant claim to scalped virginity, for he snatches that invaluable first prize, at one swoop, from all who follow in his wake, yet he will reap nothing in due course but their recurrent envy and hatred. Nevertheless he has served a useful purpose; we must be grateful to him at least for saving us a fair amount of trouble. It is our many other predecessors, down the long line of bedfellows, who incur our maledictions. Who were they to tamper with our chosen property, which ought to have kept intact, fresh and unspoiled, for us? By what right did they dare lay their foul, interfering paws on these objects of delight, which we were destined someday to want? Yet, after all, their crime is understandable: we would have done – and in fact have done – the same thing ourselves, giving not so much as a fleeting thought to those who afterwards will tarry, seeking shelter in this selfsame cosy spot. But she, the woman in the case – ah, there is the horror and the shame of it! – how could she? What vanity, what crazy aberration, rendered her always so prompt, so ready to yield without demur to such an innumerable procession of gross, unworthy lovers? Here is the guilt, the villainous offence, the insult heaped upon frolics with Tom, Dick and Harry. They were quite right to take advantage of the opening she offered, the randy slut, to all and sundry, like a bitch in heat, mounted by every dirty dog in turn, with lolling tongue, at the street corner.

Lucien! The name struck me like a knife between the ribs. Of course! How could I have been such a fool as not to realise it before? His ugly face, with its moles or warts, its sallow, heavy jowl and brilliant beady eyes, loomed in my memory, and I pictured his gesture of stroking his Roman emperor's nose with a crooked forefinger as he talked, smiling sardonically. Ugh, yes – he must have had her too. Repulsive creature! The very idea made me feel sick. He was the perfect storybook ogre, complete with a wife of wondrous beauty – who had inspired more than her due of passionate jealousy in me, as I now saw. I was beginning to commiserate and side with her, for no doubt she, poor woman, had suffered as much as I when she discovered who had been her chief rival in Casilda's arms. Possibly I had less cause for complaint than Helen, since Lucien's fling with the girl must date back a goodish while. Then why on earth could Casilda not have told me, with her usual honesty, that she was involved with both the Baron and the Baroness, instead of only one of them, far the more handsome of the pair? Perhaps that explained Helen's reported friendliness towards me. There was a bond between us, even though she might not know it – a fellow-feeling, subconscious probably, if she were truly ignorant of my connection with Casilda, but telepathic, genuine and valid nonetheless . . . maybe, after all, she was not so impervious to consolation as Cassy made out. Helen and I already had something in common, it seemed. You can never tell with emotional entanglements of this sort. In time she might wish to shift her position and ally herself with me, if only to share my vengeance upon her faithless husband and the deceitful hussy who had wronged us both. Who would have thought it? Casilda, who claimed to keep no secrets from me, had let me down here badly by slyly, deliberately omitting to confide that she had slept with Lucien, of all people, who was the central and certainly the most important figure in our scheme of things.

'A penny for them, darling,' Casilda's cheerful challenge broke in, from a distance, on my grim meditations.

'I was wondering how you could bear to live under the same roof as Lucien – even for Helen's sake,' I answered.

'Oh, Lucien is not much trouble,' Casilda remarked indifferently, adjusting a shoulder strap. 'Everyone agrees that he's extremely witty and amusing. What has he done to put you against him? You used to say you admired the old rascal.'

'He's astute and altogether unscrupulous, that's all. I consider his flair for art impressive – but we've never been close friends. And I don't like the sentimental tone in which you refer to him, as though he was your favourite uncle or your elder brother – the black sheep of the family but an absolute dear who means no harm by it really.'

Casilda laughed. 'Oh, pooh!' she said. 'Lucien has his faults . . . but he's not a prig. Just a bit of a scamp.'

There was a long pause that bristled with conjecture, while I glared at the half-clothed, taunting figure by the fire. She seemed disposed to prevaricate indefinitely. Her raised eyebrows and the quizzical, mischievous smile mocked me until I was forced to blurt out the direct question:

'Do you deny having gone to bed with Lucien?'

'Of course not, Tony. But it was ages ago – five or six years at least. You knew that, surely.'

'How should I have known? Damn you,' I said, 'you never told me.'

'Well – it's such an obvious thing to happen. I assumed you must have guessed,' Casilda blandly declared.

'So jolly simple for Lucien, you mean,' I jeered.

'Trust your benefactor, such a sportsman, not to miss the sitting bird. And you made it nice and easy for him. I expect – out of gratitude for his hospitality.'

Leaning with one elbow on the mantlepiece, Casilda eyed me calmly but said nothing.

'Exactly what took place?' I asked, finally. 'When, and how? I insist on hearing the whole nasty story.'

Casilda laughed aloud again at the sight of my distress.

'Darling!' she cried. 'If only you could see yourself! There's no need to despair – you can relax. It wasn't serious, I promise you. I'll tell all – if I can remember the details. It's so long ago. But please take that suicidal look off your face. I was rather naughty – we both were, I admit – but not half so appallingly wicked as you seem to imagine. Actually the first time was quite funny. . . .'

'Go on,' I snapped. 'I'm sure it was – great fun. Both of you have a highly developed sense of humour. But I wonder if Helen saw the joke.'

'She mightn't have,' Casilda agreed. 'Tell her, and you'll find out – if she believes you. We went to bed with her, you see – all three of us together – but she never noticed what happened.'

'I warn you: don't lie to me.'

'I'm not lying. Cross my heart – it was soon after I first went to spend a few weeks with them one winter, and they had asked me to stay on. They lived in Hampstead then. I had been in the house about six months. I was just over eighteen. They treated me like a daughter, and encouraged me to regard the place as my own home, because it was the only one I had. Sometimes, especially on Sundays, I would carry my tray into their room and have breakfast with them. That morning we were recovering from a very late night before. It was the Season, and we had been dancing until the early hours. We were all still practically asleep, and when I complained of feeling chilly Helen suggested I should get into their big bed for warmth. She was reading through a pile of Sunday papers, while Lucien dozed. I got in on his side of the bed and curled up with a novel. Lucien lay with his back to me, next to Helen, who sat propped up against pillows and buried in the *Observer*. I was only half awake when, after a bit, Lucien turned over to face the same way as me. He snored intermittently but scarcely stirred – until a hand beneath the bedclothes unfastened my bathrobe and moved gently about my body. Its touch was deft and exciting; soon I was having the greatest difficulty keeping still and not giving the game away. At such close quarters the least little wriggle, the faintest gasp would catch Helen's attention at once; she couldn't fail to recognise signs which, however slight, are all too unmistakable. . . . Lucien by now had edged up behind me, pressing hot and hard against my tail end, which he bared very gradually and surreptitiously, an inch at a time. . . . I did not help him at first, while he pulled my robe and nightie up at the back and tucked them out of the way, around my waist – but the next stage was the trickiest part of the proceedings, it took a good deal of care, patience and self-control for us to manoeuvre safely into the right position. Lucien had the beginnings of a paunch on him, even in those days, and I was obliged to bend far forward – with the utmost caution, holding my breath – before there was any hope of achieving our aim. When we managed it at last, and he started to slide into me – at a snail's pace, and just as silently – I nearly had to lean out of bed, though we still didn't dare betray the steady progress of our increasingly lively sensations by so much as a sign or a shudder . . . the strain was devilish. I don't know if you've ever undergone any similar experience – but think what it's like, not being able to risk a single brusque movement, far less let yourselves go, either of you, even when deep down inside you're coming closer and closer, faster and faster, to the absolute core of hectic mutual pleasure. We had to stay dead quiet – as innocent on the surface as babes in the wood, while below, under the sheets, we were joined and welded by a raging fire that knotted us tightly together at the hub of a rigid figure K – which became an X finally, as we reached our secret spasm. And that didn't take long, I can tell you – the double effort of motionless energy was overwhelming, it heightened the tension somehow by concentrating every ounce of feeling at the centre, the focal point. . . .'

'The fulcrum – that is the correct term,' I appended. 'And then what?'

Casilda had dressed while she was talking. She came and planted an affectionate kiss on the top of my head.

'Nothing much else, honey,' she assured me. 'There were a few other episodes, at intervals over the next couple of years, but none of them important. Always at some unguarded moment, though, when you least expected it, in the mot peculiar circumstances. Lucien liked it better that way. He was pretty near impotent already. I suppose he needed the spice of variety – but there's no question about it, he certainly has the dirtiest instincts. He's not just lewd but downright obscene. I don't remember his ever satisfying me entirely except that first time, when I was young and eager and felt we were being frightfully wicked. The next incident, I think, was in the bathroom, before a big dinner party they were giving. He sometimes walked in and chatted to me while I was taking a bath – even with Helen in the offing. But it meant nothing to him; what he wanted was to watch me on the can. This gave him a terrific kick – he adores seeing girls pee, especially in the open, squatting down to it, with skirts up and knickers round their ankles, in a ditch or a field. Widdling on the loo was tame by comparison, but he often begged one to indulge his 'silly fad' by doing that – or the other thing. I drew the line at that. I don't mind making water in front of anybody, if it amuses them – but I'm not prepared to go further. Scatological foibles revolt me, I'm afraid. Lucien's particular whim was to urinate between one's legs, aiming the stream at one's clitoris. He tried it on me that evening, and then insisted on playing "sweet little Cassy's nurse" who scrubs her in the bath. He soaped me all over and attempted to take me, slippery as an eel, under the shower. It wasn't a great success – so in the end he sat on the stool and got me to straddle his lap as widely as possible while he rubbed himself off against me. The trouble was we had to hurry – Helen would be along in a jiffy – and gambols of this kind depend on trial and error. Still, he got what he was after, and it didn't really bother me.'

'Evidently not. You appear to have enjoyed yourself considerably.'

'Well, yes, I suppose so – but I couldn't raise a shindy and refuse him, could I? Besides, it did sometimes suit a passing mood . . . he's excessively ardent when roused, but not in the least maudlin. I like sex on those terms. He understood me. We always got on well together.'

'Is that so? Then why did you give up sleeping with him, may I ask?'

'I'm telling you – it wasn't exactly an affair. I mean, we only actually went to bed that once. He didn't want me in the normal way. He infinitely preferred the sneaking, hole-in-the-corner business of sudden odd grabs at you every so often. Except for an occasional savage pinch or some leering remark, he didn't pester me again for months after the bathroom scene. But embarrassing situations were meat and drink to him. One day, for instance, he slipped a hand up under the skirt of an extremely pretty little thing in the drawing room – she was a guest who had arrived early for lunch at the house – and he went on playing with her while I poured the drinks and rearranged the flowers. "Keep a lookout at the window for Helen," he told me. The child was blushing like a beetroot, though she was a forward young piece, the daughter of a peer, and as vicious as a monkey. Lucien talked the whole time without stopping – a spate of the most outrageous remarks in the manner of a running commentary, comparing the two of us and excusing himself to the girl for not pleasuring her properly, he said, because I had exhausted him in my room just before she turned up. She should take lessons from me, he explained, I was incredibly gifted, a world-famous authority, second to none in such matters. He described our relative anatomical advantages and suggested the correct use for them in such lurid detail that we both burst out laughing. She slapped him for his impertinence at one moment, and stuffed her fingers in her ears, but she was giggling so helplessly I was afraid she might have hysterics. Helen was quite mystified when she came in to find us all sniggering like idiots.

'Another time I went into Lucien's study and there he was, necking Helen's French maid on the sofa. He sprawled back, pretending not to notice my presence, and pushed Suzette down on the floor between his knees. But she shook him off and darted out of the room like a scalded cat as soon as she saw me. "Pity," Lucien grumbled. "She has just the mouth for it. . . . Never mind, dear, you'll do nicely instead – it was your fault, barging in and disturbing us." Like a sultan or some randy old raja he looked, lying among the cushions, languidly waving his tool at me – or maybe more like a snake-charming Eastern beggar, flapping that long, limp thing around, though it was I who had to toot the tune and do his ropetrick for him. . . .'

'You of course consented out of sheer kindness?'

'Uh-huh – after a bit of persuasion, to avoid a fuss.'

'I hope he was duly grateful. How often were you called upon to perform these trifling favours? Presumably he repaid them?'

'I'd gladly have overlooked the debt, given the option. But he did go down to me, as a matter of fact, on at least two occasions – though I fought to prevent it one evening, waiting in the car outside a nursing home, while Helen visited a sick friend. It was a fairly dark street, but she would be with us again in a minute, we were hideously uncomfortable, needless to say, and I was as nervous as a nun – it seemed we'd never finish! Lucien simply refused to stop or listen to reason, and my futile pretence at an orgasm he ignored as pure trickery – which it was. What a nightmare!'

'Who won?'

'Well, really he did, more or less – in the very nick of time. He always got away with it, Lord knows why. But what is the good of resisting, if one is going to have to give in eventually? He damn nearly strangled me on a country stroll once, behind a haystack, because I did my best to fob him off with a frigging when he demanded a gamahouche. . . . He had the whip hand over me. It wasn't so terrible, after all – was it?'

There was a pause. Casilda hovered at my side, inquiringly.

'It is rather a scabrous story, I admit,' she said. 'But I wasn't quite as awful as you thought, was I? Are you going to forgive me?'

'Your effrontery is colossal – and your attitude as indecent as it could be, if you want my opinion. Utterly deplorable, even for you – and in such bad taste! The blame is yours, more than Lucien's, I'm convinced.'

Casilda smiled. 'You know what I'm like, Tony darling,' she murmured, and then, after gazing at me fondly in silence: 'Shall I fetch the stick, my lord? I realise I deserve it.'

At my nod, she went to the chest of drawers, remarking lightly: 'The bottom drawer, I assume?' and a hint of anxiety crept into her voice as she added 'this one?' handing me the long, fine, flexible malacca cane.

I pointed to the armchair by the fire. 'Bend over,' I ordered sharply. An anticipatory thrill of harsh excitement mingled with the dull ache of my jealous indignation and disgust. Casilda knelt in the chair, resting her elbows on the back, and waited. 'Not too hard – please, darling,' she entreated quietly, as I rolled her dress up above her waist and gently, deliberately undid her full, frilly panties, which stayed in place and had to be pulled down, inch by inch, over her hips. I took my time about these preparations – for me more enjoyable and satisfying than the subsequent infliction of corporal punishment, whereas for the victim herself perhaps enduring the ordeal may prove pleasanter by far than the preliminary suspense attached to it. Thus I toyed with the intention of removing her frail satin girdle, but left it to form a saucy frame, like a flowered border, around the rich, broad, beautiful view of her buttocks.

'I shan't whip you,' I volunteered, 'if you regret your decision. Only say so now, before it's too late. Cry off at once, if you feel so inclined – but don't give me instructions. You'll get what's coming to you.'

Casilda shook her head, and buried her face in her arms. 'I can take it,' she asserted, 'if you'll promise to drop the subject after this. That's the bargain – a solemn tabu on all further recriminations about Lucien.'

'Kiss the rod,' I commanded.

'Curse you,' she said, complying. 'You mean, miserable bully!'

She glanced at me over her shoulder with a steely-grey, inimical glint in her big hazel eyes. So it was not bravado, she was not putting it on. Her face was deathly pale, but I would not have liked to swear that she was frightened, despite the trace of a tremor on her lips and a certain glassy look belying her defiant tone. After the first half-dozen strokes, however, there was no longer any doubt . . . they landed with a loud swish and thwack across her ruddy rump, each echoed by a piercing yelp. Gnawing her knuckles, biting her own sleeve as a gag to muffle a series of pitiful howls and strident shrieks, she soon shed all hypocrisy and implored me to lay off.

'That'll do! Stop, stop! Tony! Oh! Ah! Ow! Ow-uuh!'

Her hands now had broken loose – fluttering, clutching, clawing the air, snatching spasmodically behind her back in timid attempts to parry the blows; they flinched, recoiled, were whisked away yet returned in self-defence as I gradually increased the vigour of the thrashing, which even so was far less severe than the flogging she got on that impudent Spaniard's account the time before. Lucien was no stranger, after all, but an old, evil acquaintance of mine.

I lammed into her, but she shielded her bottom and swung around in sobbing supplication on the chair. There was nothing else for it: I had to seize her by the middle and lug her down over my knee. I slid my hand beneath her then, and thrust it between her thighs. To some extent my touch was soothing . . . my fingers were instrumental in assuaging the wretched girl's pain . . . they were buried and burned in a fiery furnace, seeking an antidote, a balm to compensate for the heat of the hiding. In a few moments the cure was almost complete. Casilda spread her legs and stuck her arse out eagerly, clamouring for more of the treatment in stronger doses, like a wonder drug. . . .

'Harder!' she shouted. 'Yes, yes – that's it, harder! Beat me – oh – darling – harder. . . . No . . . Aah! As hard as you like . . .!'

VI

'Opera, yes, opera – at Covent Garden,' Casilda patiently repeated, on the telephone next morning, as though to a backward child. 'I forgot to mention it last night, with all the fuss . . . a treat for Cécile – she's off to Paris again on Saturday. You're to meet us in the foyér, if you don't mind . . . because they'll have an awful rush getting up from Sussex in time. Wasn't there a note in the post for you from Helen?'

'No – and I shan't accept, anyway,' I answered shortly.

'Why not? Darling, don't be so stuffy! You swore to bury that little old hatchet, for one thing – and for another, you shouldn't miss this *Aida*. Or Cécile, either – however much it bores you to sit through an opera. She's quite a dish, our Cécile, at sixteen. I assure you. The picture of innocent youth, as fresh as a peach – really lovely. You won't be able to take your eyes off her – I can't.'

'Who else has been asked?'

'There'll just be the five of us. I suggested including you. Sorry, darling.'

'What for? It sounds a swell party – almost a royal flush of your dearest friends. I suppose you fixed it like that as a joke – the queen with her court of four lovers, all in a row.'

'No, not in a row, stupid – Luceien's taken a box. Honestly, Tony, you're worse than incorrigible. That's an idiotic crack, quite uncalled-for and you know it.

How dare you imply that I've meddled with Cécile in any way, or even thought of such a thing? Poor kid, she's angelic! Nobody but a fiend would lay a finger on her. Your mind is an absolute sink!'

'Oh, I don't know. Someone will, before long – if they haven't already. You'll see. Most maidens of Cécile's age look purer than snow, but a lot goes on under that icy exterior. Still waters run deep, I've discovered.'

'Well, there's nothing doing, get that straight – I forbid *you* to take the plunge in this case.'

'I won't – you needn't worry. I leave the whole of that family to you, my sweet. They're your pigeons. But it would be the nicest possible revenge for me, don't you think, if I succeeded in seducing Lucien's only daughter? I might be tempted to try my hand at it for that reason, as a matter of elementary justice. Somebody's got to do the job, Cassy darling: it would be a bit tricky, I fear, in a box at the opera. And she's leaving London next day. . . .'

Casilda had hung up on me. She was out when I telephoned later to accept Helen's invitation. It amused me that she, bless her heart, should affect to be so shocked, when I had only meant to tease her. The cheek of the girl! Imagine such an incontinent hussy cavorting on her high horse, as priggish as you please, because I chose to jest about her precious little protégée's virginity! Women are wonderful. Obviously she must be harbouring fell designs of her own on the virtue of Mlle Delavigne . . . one might almost conclude that the charming adolescent stood in need of my gentlemanly protection. . . .

I was weary of these constant quarrels, however, and determined to enjoy my affair with Casilda. It was too profitable and pleasant a setup to ruin by rash outbursts of temper or disagreement over trifles. If Casilda's attitude to certain emotional issues seemed niggling and petty, I must not allow myself to be drawn into a battle of wits which I should only win to my own cost. I wasn't going to let a silly schoolgirl come between us – even if Casilda really was interested in her sexually, which on sober reflection seemed extremely improbable. She had enough on her plate, as it was, and anybody further removed from the hungering, hard-bitten, predatory type of lesbian would be difficult to imagine. It ought to be possible to enlist her aid, once she calmed down and emerged from her huff – if I tackled the problem in the right way. From Casilda's description of little Miss Delavigne, vengeance in this particular case would taste sweeter than usual . . . surely the best plan would be to join forces, when the time came, and launch a combined attack. . . .

She was a peach, all right – with a liberal portion of clotted cream to soften the vivid colouring she inherited from both her parents. She had their raven-black hair and big velvety eyes, Lucien's dark skin rather than Helen's pallor, but the contrasting glow of Helen's red lips and a rosy bloom of health on her young cheeks in lieu of Lucien's sallow tint and somewhat oily complexion. Impeccably fashioned on the simplest lines, like its wearer, her modest evening dress of girlish pink encased the slight, slim figure from bosom to shin and showed it off for precisely what it was worth, without any vain attempt to hide or to improve it. Her demeanour matched her dress, lending her an air of elegance without sophistication, for she was as beautiful and as smart in appearance as her mother, but neither shy nor precious – a dignified and distinguished child, reserved and serene in manner, yet endowed, as one gathered from her few but intelligent remarks, with the makings of Lucien's mundane wit and artistic taste in replica. Paris, too, had done wonders for her. I did not recognise the bashful brat I sometimes came across in Regent's Park only a couple of years previously. Here was a full-fledged junior miss, typical in many ways, but exceptionally pretty – a ravishing specimen of girlhood, if the truth be told – and possessed of the great gift that such creatures normally lack: individuality.

Despite all this – or perhaps just because it was such a very highly polished product – I did not greatly take to Cécile. She made the same effect on me at first as her mother always had, until quite recently. My opinion of Helen had gained considerably in warmth since I had started to trick her with Casilda. Her daughter, I was grieved to see, left me as cold as frozen lamb. I admired Cécile's delicate profile, her regular features, her straight back and the low, melodious tone of her voice, as I sat leaning forward in the box at Covent Garden between her and Helen – but it was the latter who attracted me and stole my attention entirely. We were in W formation, with the three women in front. Lucien, beside me, had closed his eyes and slumped in his chair, listening to the music as soon as the lights were dimmed; halfway through Act I, he was snoozing. Casilda, on my right, had greeted me most curtly on arrival and now turned a bare cold shoulder on me with such studied insolence that I could have slapped her, although inwardly amused by this meaningless display of dudgeon, which did not perturb me in the slightest. I envisaged no serious risk of our breaking off the affair so soon, we were both still much too keen on each other; this nonsense on her part was only a lovers' tiff, engineered as the prelude to a passionate reconciliation. But I wasn't having any, thank you. I didn't need the tonic she was trying to prescribe for added ardour. It surprised me, on the contrary, as I would have thought she'd had all the spanking she could want for the time being. . . .

Helen, by contrast, was exceedingly amiable. I had never known her in a friendlier mood. She apologised profusely for not inviting me to dinner, and her attitude throughout our whispered conversation was singularly forthcoming. It struck me that her nonchalance towards Casilda was equally marked. Why so gay and gushing? I asked myself. What was her object in singling me out tonight particularly, under Cécile's very nose, as such a special favourite? She was as merry as a cricket and – one would almost suspect – positively flirtatious. I could only assume she was jealous and that she acted in this way to spite the faithless Casilda. Granting for the sake of argument that she was indeed as well disposed towards me as Casilda made out, would she have chosen this unpropitious occasion to reveal a weakness which could scarcely be acknowledged, let alone requited in public? She must merely be trying it on, I decided. Her idea was to provoke Casilda into a tantrum that would give the game away, by setting her cap at me while the going was good, in absolute safety. . . .

I saw that I was being used as a decoy. Helen had rather a fancy for me, and she welcomed this opportunity to indulge it, at Casilda's expense, in order to flick her on the raw and find out for certain if Anthony Grey was the nigger in the woodpile. Casilda wasn't saying a word . . . very well then: she would take this potshot in the dark to see how much I meant to her chum. Whether Casilda reacted with tell-tale annoyance or not, she was sure to be deeply riled by the experiment – and that suited Helen down to the ground, even if it left her still in doubt as to which of us, herself or I, was the chief cause of Casilda's irritation and jealousy. It was a gambit, Helen must have felt, by which she had absolutely nothing to lose.

No more had I, come to that. There was hay to be made, since the sun shone so brightly. Maybe I was emboldened to take advantage of this totally unforeseen situation by the number of whiskies I had consumed, in place of food, to fortify myself for the ordeal of an evening at the opera. Certainly I have no precise recollection of how it all began, and only the haziest memories of what was happening on the stage at any turn of the drama which I privately produced and played out, with a limited cast of two, before an oblivious or somnolent audience in our plush box above the footlights. The first I knew was that my hand came casually in contact with the beautiful bare back of the dear Baroness, that it rested there awhile before starting to stroke the firm flesh, from the nape of the slender neck to the pronounced curvature of the waist, and afterwards lingered soothingly between the shoulder blades, on the plausible pretext of plucking idly at the fur that hung over the chair upon which I leaned, supporting my elbow in rapt attention to Verdi's true lovers singing their sweet duet. Helen's vermillion satin dress was wonderfully naked, except for the huge spray of white orchids that sprouted from her bust in such profusion that its purpose as a corsage might have seemed more practical than ornamental, to cover her bosom for the sake of decency rather than merely to embellish it as flamboyantly as possible.

She sat stock-still, without moving a muscle, I was happy to note, when my cautious fingers slid forwards to nestle in the soft underarm, and thence by slow degrees crept around in front to brush, to fondle, and finally to cup her proud right breast – the one farther from Cécile and away from me, next to Casilda. There my hand lay for a time, warmly ensconced, as though gloved in velvet, holding its treasured prize while Helen held her breath; and from that point of vantage, which stiffened under my palm, it sallied forth on brief excursions about her torso, pressing gently against the ribs, reconnoitering along the flank, delving down the smooth valley between her superbly hard, ripe, arrogant bubs, but returning home at intervals, beneath the loose folds of her scant Grecian tunic, to fasten with tender insistence on the alert, small nipple that stood up rigidly on guard, like a sentinel at his post.

Helen's quiet response, her admirable discretion and self-control, encouraged my inquisitive, errant fingers to probe her defences in search of a chink, a crack in the armour although even now, despite my keen enjoyment of a highly diverting situation, I was aware of its intrinsic dangers and conscious of my cruelty in subjecting my mistress's mistress to such a titillating trial of strength. Physically, so far as one could tell from her unruffled manner, she appeared not to be suffering undue hardship; but her mental torment, I could only assume, must be acute enough in all conscience. Surely she was startled and embarrassed to get much livelier cooperation from me than she had bargained for; she had meant merely to lead me on a little, with a view of teasing Casilda, as it were, at second hand. I was to be given the blame for making a pass at her, but she counted on my not daring to go so far as to risk letting either Cécile or Lucien twig what I was up to – whereas Casilda, of course, would be quick to notice, since she was really the guilty party and therefore more vulnerably sensitive. Casilda evidently was spoiling for a fight, she was on the lookout for trouble. But it was Helen herself who was in trouble. I had turned the tables on her. My unexpectedly wholehearted entry into the spirit of the game spoiled everything. How was she going to deny indignantly, when taxed with it by Casilda after the show, that she had been responsible in any way for my scandalous behaviour? No doubt her line, as planned, was a sharp retort that would leave her girlfriend guessing. Casilda could then believe what she liked on the subject – and the worse the conclusions she reached, the better would Helen be pleased. Alas for the Baroness, she was the biter bit; I was proving rather more of a cad than she anticipated.

She was saved by the bell – that is, by the lights going up at the interval. Stoically she had maintained her poise during the past twenty minutes, keeping her eyes fixed on the stage, with her face turned slightly way from Cécile and screened to some extent by resting her left elbow on the ledge and her chin on her knuckles. It was a graceful pose that served a dual purpose in that the line of her cheek and shoulder, smothered in orchids, formed a blinker on one side to direct her daughter's innocent gaze towards the strutting singers below, while by bending forward from the hips she unobtrusively gave freer play to my caressing hand under the loosened folds of the bodice – if indeed so modest a term was applicable to the barely adequate top of her backless evening gown which plunged in a charmingly vacant V from her neck to her navel. Over wide areas of the trail my explorations had been conducted perforce without benefit of cover; to stray off the point for an instant was to venture heroically into the open. Now the first round ended with a burst of applause: I dutifully withdrew my hand to join in the clapping.

'I enjoyed that immensely – didn't you?' I asked Helen.

She gave me a long searching stare, and shook her head slowly, dreamily, as though at a loss for words.

'I thought it divine, my dear Helen,' I insisted. 'Not a single false note – it really was quite remarkable. Not a sound that was discordant, not a quaver – from anyone.'

'Good God, Grey, what did you expect?' Lucien put in. 'A correct performance, naturally – faultless, above reproach, acceptable. But no great shakes – nothing exciting. Don't listen to him, Cécile, he'll only mislead you.'

I laughed, and gazed steadily at Helen, as we went outside to stretch our legs at the bar. 'Champagne for

Cécile,' I ordered. 'And for what comes after. Have it your own way, *mon cher* Lucien – but I find this Aida wonderful, a complete revelation. She's my choice for the part from now on – the ideal slave-girl, docile, romantic, passionate and obedient: utterly enchanting. And such restraint! Amazing! You *feel* the latent power, the fiery temperament under that lovely outward calm . . . a grand performance. I don't know when I've enjoyed myself more, in some respects. The subtlety of it! Honestly, I can't wait for the finale . . . I'm dying to share her gallant death, the climax of her last panting sigh in her lover's arms.'

Helen's enigmatic look had not altered at all – unless it was not purely a mirage, that faint glint of a forgiving, secretive smile of connivance that I caught in her dark eyes. My own pleaded for a clear signal, but there was none to be had – which in itself I interpreted as a favourable sign. Encouragement would have been too much to ask. Still, she did say offhandedly:

'I'm so glad you're having a good time, Tony, at any rate. But one has to lose oneself entirely at the theatre, as I always tell Cécile. You miss the whole meaning and value of it if you allow anything to distract you, even for a moment. Every ounce of concentration is necessary to forget one's wordly cares. . . .'

'Distractions are Tony's chief aim in life,' Casilda cryptically announced. 'They are all he ever worries about.'

Helen made Cécile change places with her when we returned to the box, but I could not guess whether she hoped to keep me at arm's length this time or was effacing herself at the end of the row for greater privacy. The stratagem did not bother me, anyhow; I am ambidextrous. I drew my chair close up behind her, tilting it against the wall, so that I could keep watch on the others, while my left arm surreptitiously circled Helen's waist. I moulded her hip and explored her lap, spanning her belly and stroking her thigh. With a quick flick at my wrist, she tried to dislodge my hand, to push it away. Taken aback, I retired momentarily and then returned, with a definite gesture, to pursue my advance. Thrusting thumb and forefinger under her leg, just clear of the seat, I punished the flighty, wayward fool with a hefty pinch. That made her sit up all right; she jumped and let out a yelp that brought sharp inquiring looks from Cécile and Casilda, who peered at her suspiciously in the semidarkness.

'I've just remembered something.' Helen muttered lamely as an excuse.

I left her to simmer for a while – with excellent results. When I recommenced my stealthy encroachment along her left flank, the lesson had sunk in. She stayed quiet, and I could feel that she was braced in every nerve to undergo a further session of this enervating test, which troubled but assuredly did not displease her. She had allowed and induced me to take these liberties in the first place; now, it seemed to me, their effect on Casilda was no longer the whole object of the exercise, which she was beginning to assess, personally and directly, on its own merits. From every angle this was a most gratifying development; it was a highly flattering tribute to my talent for persuasion, a just reward attained by dint of subtle skill and patient effort. Nor was that all: to my delight I saw that I was killing two birds with one throw, for I became aware of a change of attitude in Casilda. I sensed this volte-face by instinct – there was little to convey it outwardly, save a vague air of greater friendliness on her part. I kept an eye on her, and smiled ingratiatingly when she turned her head, as she frequently did, to glance in our direction. I was operating in utter silence, of course, and the ample satin folds of Helen's dress covered and muffled my advance around her hip towards the promised land below the waist, but I could tell that Casilda

A Gallery of Nudes

had tumbled to what was going on. As soon as she made certain that her surmise was correct, though she could not follow my progress with any accuracy, it struck me that she was both relieved and amused to observe her friend's peculiar predicament. Cécile, at any rate, was safe, which apparently was the main consideration. Helen she must have regarded as fair game, for far from continuing to sulk; she now almost beamed on me. Things were looking up – though I could only conclude that the girl was plumb crazy.

Casilda's unfathomable motives at this point did not concern me. I had other good fresh fish to fry. It was a slow process, but I was doing nicely. The time came when, at a firm hint from me, Helen rose rapidly from her chair and rearranged her spreading skirts so that, to suit our mutual convenience, I was able to slip my open palm under her left buttock. There for a moment it lay imprisoned under the smooth, warm weight of her naked flesh – since she was stripped, beneath her heavy evening gown, for all emergencies – until I persuaded her to shift again, granting free passage between her legs to my probing fingers. At long last I had reached my goal, I could now caress her intimately, to my heart's content – and also, I hoped, to hers. Try as she might, she could not sit still; she was the dignified *grande dame* only down to the navel – below that, amid all the sumptuous decoration of the crowded theatre, the sparkling jewels and elegant bearing of the audience, the air filled with magnificent music, there was nothing but her open, eager, hot wet twat, a sensitive, sucking sea anemone hidden beneath the surface calm, yearning and squirming in answer to my touch, like some soft, warm furry beastie crouching in its moist, narrow trench under a thick pile of tangled leaves. True, every woman in the dimly lit auditorium guarded the same rich, scented female secret, nesting in repose between her cheeks on the padded seat, like a priceless heirloom set in a velvet case, to be produced and admired on special occasions. I agree, naturally, that the groove into which my fingers pried was one of many, in no way unique, not a particular or notable exception to the generous general rule of life. Or was it? Did it not differ in fact from all the rest in one respect, which was by far the most important? Of the myriad oysters in that vast oyster bed, young and old, fair or dark, pure and sweet or sick and rotten, did it not alone contain at this precise moment the fine, the incomparable, the only pearl of pleasure? There was none other in that shimmering swell, I'll warrant, that could boast of being at this very instant in the same condition. What single cunt in the whole collection could hold a candle now to Helen's? Her cup of happiness was well-nigh full to overflowing, as I played and toyed with it at will, rubbing, tickling, squeezing, coaxing the tender button that protruded from her parted lips, like a little pointed tongue, with delicate impudence, taunting as a flame, yet hard and anxious as a sentry's challenge at the gateway to a defenceless stronghold.

In the end I had to lift the siege, when the fortress was trembling on the brink of unconditional surrender. Helen's sexual excitement, bottled up inside the shapely urn of her cool, classical beauty, rose to a steaming degree of heat, almost on the bubble, like mulled resinous wine, as though about to splutter forth in a gurgle of sound from her dry throat, while the dwindling notes of the tragic duet from the condemned pair on the stage told us that Aida's strength, too, was ebbing away under the breathless strain of her martyrdom. It was a race between the four of us to see who would finish first, which couple – Verdi's *dramatis personae* or ourselves, so very much alive and nearly kicking – would consummate their fate before the other.

Harassed as she was, torn between the onrush of

delight and her fear of discovery, desperate both from desire and with disappointment, Helen was denied all outlet for her feelings, which she could neither relieve nor restrain. Even if she had wanted to break off the engagement just as the culmination of her crisis seemed tantalisingly near there was nothing she could do about it, short of rising to her feet immediately, before the lights went up – an abrupt gesture which she dared not risk and did not trust herself to make without undue commotion. Besides, it was only a question of seconds. She hesitated, as well she might. Seated, her position placed her at my mercy. However tightly she strove to close her legs, she could not hope to dislodge my hand or protect the wide gap in her reargurd. By crushing her thighs together she might have warded off the boldest frontal attack; but I had broken through. I was already in full command of the situation, I had penetrated her bunker to its innermost depths, looting all that it had to offer, and her buttocks, outspread on the chair seat, were powerless now to bar my way or repulse my thrusting fingers, which held her fast on actual tenterhooks. . . .

Regretfully I was obliged to drop the unfinished business.

Lucien held forth so knowledgeably about this rendering of *Aida* when the final curtain came down and we were wrapping ourselves up to face the damp outside world that I was seized with panic at the thought that, perhaps, he kept one eye open during a fair amount of the performance, after all. I convinced myself, however, that he was simply forestalling the sharp conjugal reprimand which such a lowbrow lapse on his part was liable to bring from the high-principled Helen. The joke, in fact, was on him. But anyway, to give the dirty old beast his due, would he be so uncivilised as to cut up rough if he had seen more than he ought of what had transpired between me and his stuck-up spouse, to whom clearly he was as much wedded as an ox to its yoke? He appeared tickled pink – probably, with the show over, at the prospect of getting off quickly to bed. At any rate he would not hear of going on somewhere for supper. Helen assured everyone that I must be famished – but of course Cécile would have to bundle home at once, she had an early start to make on the morrow and, as they had been in the country all day, she hadn't even packed. Poor Cécile! Her eager acceptance of my invitation, when I suggested I be allowed to escort the three ladies to a nightclub, was firmly quashed by her mother, whose nerves were evidently on edge.

Not only was the Baroness extremely agitated but it struck me that she was more than a trifle tipsy. She chattered like a magpie most of the way, as I drove them all back in the car to Regent's Park, but at times fell into deep, dreamy silences which she would break with a sudden fresh spate of verbosity, quite out of context. She made no move to join us on their doorstep when we arrived and Lucien asked me in for a nightcap, so I was grateful to Casilda for taking charge of the situation at once with natural ease and diplomacy: she kissed Cécile goodbye 'in case I don't see you again in the morning' and told Lucien 'I suppose I must help Helen toy with the expensive supper Tony seems set on buying us – *à demain*, then, and thank you for a most enjoyable evening.'

'You don't mind if I join you?' she enquired as we went back to the car. I shook my head.

'Of course not. But I'm going to lure Helen straight to my place if I can. Don't interfere.'

'Whatever for? Hadn't I better make myself scarce then? You don't want me there.'

'I do indeed. And Helen may, anyway. I suspect it's you she's after, really. We shall see. . . .'

'Well I'll be damned!' Casilda laughed. 'OK, try your

luck,' she added, climbing in beside me.

'Wouldn't it be a good idea to skip the stuffy *boîte* and go back home with you, Tony?' she asked, as we started down Baker Street. 'Helen, what do you think? Personally I could do with a bit of rest from crowds and music. . . .'

'I wanted to talk to Tony,' Helen objected, 'and I thought at a nightclub – '

'My God, yes – impossible,' Casilda cut in, deliberately misunderstanding her. 'Too distracting – all the wrong atmosphere. I couldn't agree more.'

'But isn't he ravenous? He must get something to eat,' Helen argued.

'Oh, there's plenty of food in the house. I'll fix us up something, don't worry.' Casilda's tone was bland, friendly, and definite. We veered towards Chelsea.

'Suits me,' I said. 'I have a little caviar up my sleeve. How about that? And a magnum of Mumm. You've never been there, have you, Helen? I'd like you to see my humble abode.'

'I'm sure I shall enjoy your pictures,' Helen replied, but the inflection of her voice gave me no clue whether she was being polite or ironical. Did she mean me to infer that she was proof against so transparent a subterfuge, or that we must resign ourselves to Casilda's tiresome intrusion? What was in her mind? She seemed puzzled, in a fuddled way, that our chaperon should know so much about my domestic arrangements. Had she really only wanted to be alone with me for a cosy *tête-à-tête* over dinner in a discreet, ill-lit corner of some classy dive? To discuss Casilda perhaps? Vain I may be at times (as which of us isn't, in such matters?) yet even so I hesitated to believe, on the strength of our recent slap-and-tickle, that she was all set to go through with it and aching to tuck up with me right away. I was perfectly prepared to take pity on her, since I had worked her up to this lecherous pitch – but what came next must remain to be seen. We had sauntered off down a side alley, the adventure was on a new tack . . . let her take the helm for a bit. I had every excuse to indulge my male conceit. I might have claimed a just dividend. If the lesbian leopard had changed its spots, and was starting to purr, whose doing was that? It was I, not Casilda, whom she should call upon to quench the fire which my sympathetic intervention had so charitably kindled for her in the weeds of her deserted back-garden. For my part, however, I was determined to proceed with caution, modesty and candour. I preferred to discount the glow of alcoholic optimism and not to rush things, but wait for the clear green light. So far, so good. A most entertaining party might develop, with the pair of them in tow. But neither Cassy or I must rub Helen up the wrong way or bungle it at all. She was in heat and in her randy condition could go sour on us as easy as winking, for I still thought it was Casilda she craved at this point – Casilda, who had been so standoffish of late, and whom she probably aimed to win back tonight, come what may, at any cost, under my roof if necessary . . . in a mood of sensual, sentimental intoxication – not unlike my own – she was ready, I felt, to risk a showdown with her loved one which was unthinkable at home in her own house, where Lucien or Cécile might hear them if she staged a flaming row, or maybe, too, if it went well and a passionate, tiddly reconciliation took place. . . .

On the other hand it hadn't been her idea certainly that Casilda should join us, nor had she exactly jumped for joy at the prospect of our all whisking out to Chelsea. What possible hope was there of fun and games with me, though, since we were not alone and hadn't a chance to get rid of the tactless Casilda? Most likely she could not have said herself what she desired so intensely, with such deep, troubled longing in her crotch that she shut her eyes to nurse the turmoil and the ache inside her. . . .

Anyhow, here was my lemon-yellow door; we had arrived.

VII

Now Helen was lucky: fate played right into her lap. No sooner had we crossed the threshold than Casilda announced, decisively, that she would take over the commissariat and did not wish to have anyone else barging into the kitchen. 'I know where everything is,' she said. 'Just tell me what it's to be – bacon and eggs or cold chicken with salad?'

'Both, darling,' I answered, but Helen asked for 'only the caviar, please, if I may.'

Leaning against the mantlepiece she watched me uncork and ice the champagne, but almost before the menial duty was done she had melted into my arms. With hers about my neck, reaching upwards on her toes, she clung to my mouth in a burning, greedy kiss that seemed to have no end, until my roving hands had almost had their fill of feeling firm flesh under the slithering, soft satin of her dress – a subtle, exquisitely thrilling contrast of textures and temperatures, between cold and warm, crinkly and smooth, limp and solid, yet both combined, her naked body with its sumptuously sleek covering, the single source of mixed and most marvellous tactile sensations. Eventually, without dissolving our joined lips, I put off the yoke of her giddy embrace and tenderly unwrapped this alabaster statue from its protective folds, which I unfastened and removed, disclosing its ideal purity of form, as one would eagerly but cautiously extract a Ming vase out of a straw and paper parcel. First I unpinned the clump of orchids – and the contamination of their over-ornate, sickly exoticism – from a crevasse between bare shoulder and boiled shirt; then off came the long, plain, full expensive garment, from which she nimbly stepped, as though escaping through its deep, vermillion ring of fire on the floor about her feet, while I, released at last, knelt and took off her tiny, high-heeled shoes.

Once more, as she stood in the light of the blazing new logs, my hands ran over every inch of this slim little Aphrodite, whose bosom was there, staring me in the face, at point-blank range a prey to my lips, which absorbed the stiff defiance of its twin gun turrets, smothering any faint signs of a token resistance that might still be met elsewhere on a wide front. Here was an opportunity denied to me, naturally, at the theatre. I was following the logical, correct, classic sequence, progressing along the regular route from one erotic zone to the next, well-nigh automatically, for there is nothing in the world that varies so little, yet is always so novel, so freshly inspiring, as this same old unalterable strategy of the senses, which is particularly delightful on the very account of its unfailing simplicity, that miraculous blessing born anew in each case from primordial instinct, universal experience, mutual agreement and constant practice. I moulded her breasts, her hips, her navel, buttocks, thighs and mount of Venus with my palms and thumbs as a sculptor would shape the planes and masses of cold clay to recreate the beauty of his model – but it was not from the life that I worked out Helen's figure; the reality, the palpitating splendour of life itself was the divine material that, on my knees as though praying, I now held and pressed ecstatically in my hands.

Her body, magnificently a woman's, was as light as a child's. Rising to my feet, I lifted her off hers, carried her to the sofa and laid her down on it like a doll. But half the charm of a doll is its fancy frills, whereas Helen's reclining pale nudity among the cushions lent her the appearance of a cut flower herself – like one of those wicked, waxen-white blooms of her corsage which I ostentatiously shut away in a drawer as a keepsake, before returning to carry on where I had left off: bending down again, in other words, to dally with her dear wee tits, which I nibbled, sucked and nuzzled for a while until I judged the moment had come to lower my sights and dive more deeply into the dark, narrow, salty creek between her sheltering thighs . . . ah, the cool, chic, imperturbable hostess Helen, with her lofty airs of intellectual superiority, her overweening culture and meticulous judgements, where was all that snobbish highfalutin nonsense now? Here we had the same good old, useful bag of tricks as ever, opened up for inspection at the customs, under my prying nose. What had she got to declare? Her rare spiritual values? Her precious taste? Nothing exceptional about this paraphernalia; it was just as one expected it would be – familiar enough, yet somehow easier to recall than to define from memory, its precise flavour pungent but swift to dissolve, fading upon the tongue. No luxury at any rate, but quite the reverse – by far the most ordinary, least costly of perfumes, not dutiable and (maybe for this reason also) that which many men prefer.

I had seen Helen in these straits before, though she was not aware of it. Nevertheless, her total transformation came as an enchanting stock to me. The difference between watching and doing, of course, was incalculable: I was most actively involved in the transports that now sent shivers vibrating through Helen's fragile frame; I held her in my power, I was responsible for what was happening to her, for the destruction of her poise, her fainting condition, her loss of any semblance of serenity in a dizzy swirl of desire which I stirred with every ounce of skill and energy that I could muster.

Absorbed by my task of demolition, I proceeded steadily to undermine her facade, and all that mattered to either of us at this juncture was my mastery over her emotions. We were both, I think, quite oblivious of our surroundings. I did not care if Casilda were suddenly to appear from the kitchen with our supper, which Helen no doubt had utterly forgotten – or she may have imagined that it would be served properly, in formal fashion, elsewhere. How could the Baroness conceive that I seldom make use of the dining room next door, except to show pictures in the best light? Her body was brimful and oozing with sensuality, her brain was emptied of coherent thought. At times a low groan escaped through her contorted lips, but for the most part she seemed bereft of speech and only gasped occasionally: 'Aah, it's so good . . . so good . . .'

For her, this was wild enthusiasm. She was all over me, you might say, in more senses than one. We had no time to spare, and indeed it was ripe, as I could tell, for immediate action. Further preliminaries were obviously unwanted and unnecessary. The goose had been plucked and cooked in readiness for the feast. It was clear that my guest required to be served soon without delay. Even the most finicky operator could have found no excuse to procrastinate any longer. She had slid down flat on her back on the sofa, raising her knees in evident anticipation of open warfare. Zero hour had struck. It only remained for me to go over the top, the invasion was planned, I was to carry the day with fire and the sword.

I sprang up and whipped my weapon from its sheath – my alas not-so-trusty blade, which this time appeared swollen with confidence, like its owner, as it stood at the salute with the proud, menacing mien of the hardened duellist who has laid many an adversary full length upon the field of honour. But Helen showed no interest in the sight whatsoever. Her eyes were shut, her head turned away. I was a trifle chagrined, I confess, by her abstracted air, her inattention to the point I wished to put to her, clinching our long and heated argument. After all, in the nature of things she could not have been offered such weighty, ocular proof of male devotion for a number of years now. You'd have thought it must be a matter of relative importance to her at least; normally it is not a question that any of her sex can regard with complete indifference.

Still, there it was. Let her have it her own way. She was eaten up with impatience, for all that. And I could not afford to wait about, we hadn't a moment to spare – not even for me to shed the encumbrance of my stiff shirt, white tie and tails. I propped her trim little rump on to a fat cushion, and gave her what she had coming to her with a straight, strenuous uppercut that took the slack out of her rigging. Ha'ah, yes – there, that brought her round, snap back to life, as though touched, tapped, struck by a magic wand! Up came her face, open-mouthed, with staring eyes, startled and frowning in an anguish of delight below me, as I raised myself on my arms, pressing her shoulders down hard into the soft, deep mound of cushions on the sofa. She was with me now, and no mistake. At the first flick of the conductor's baton, the music crashed out, the orchestra blared, *vivace, bravo, fortissimo!* Away we went, at breakneck speed, like the wind blowing a full gale – on, on! – for all we were jolly well worth, racing ahead in double time together.

But it went wrong, the excitement petered out – I couldn't tell you why. It was one of those things . . . we were doing fine – but after that flying start, the sweet, ineffable fervour of the first few moments which, packed with the wonder of rediscovery, are the best of all, the best for both, the most divine because, paradoxically, the climax, better yet, is still to come . . . gradually, imperceptibly we began to droop, to wilt,

A Gallery of Nudes

the flame commenced to dwindle, slowly to sink, unaccountably we lost our grip . . . there was no outward sign of failure that anyone watching could have detected, I feel sure – and maybe it was not Helen's fault nor was it mine; that much I know. Yet our eager illusions were dashed, the promise of an imminent mutual cataclysm was denied, our dazzling inward glimpse of paradise faded like a mirage . . .

I gritted my teeth and strained every nerve, but pleasure gave place to resentment as I laboured on, getting nowhere. It was a bad dream . . . I had leaped into the saddle and galloped off into the night, since we must flee to safety in a distant land, my willing mare and I – dear life depended on it – yet, spur her as I would, the rolling, endless desert sands refused to move beneath her pounding hooves, which shook the earth with ever more desperate and jerky strides, exhaustion claimed us both, as I lay prostrate across the pommel, and her staggering gait hammered into my mind the dreadful realisation that there was no escape, dawn would not break on these eternal wastes. How well I knew the galling misery of such defeats! I loathed the thought of letting Helen down – but with the best will in the world I could not entirely absolve her from her share of the blame. I had embarked on this inconclusive struggle radiant with hope and bursting with desire. Here I was, caught in a trap of chugging drudgery – but if we were both deluded, why should she have more right than I to complain of frustration? There had been no collapse as yet on my part: my member was still on the job, hard at it, although his original zeal had diminished somewhat now, as was only natural. He had done manful work, in all conscience, and it would be maligning him to describe his present effort as half-hearted. I was giving her the regulation six inches, confound it, and as many twists and turns as she was entitled to expect at her age. Most likely we had had too much to drink, she and I –

that might well be the answer. At least it explained the debacle in my case, I was convinced. The symptoms were recognisable, leaving little room for doubt . . . but could she make the same excuse? Any full-blooded, normal woman would have come by now, releasing me from the wearisome obligation of expending my remaining strength on this futile enterprise. I had sworn to myself that I would ring the bell with this damned, lecherous lesbian bitch before giving in, if I died in the attempt. But it was not to be. What ignominy, that she should cheat me twice over, robbing me of both my orgasm and hers! Not that I could accuse her of failing to meet me more than half-way. Her timing, the movements of her pelvis and the shifts of her whole body, her muscular contractions, lascivious ingenuity and vigour in response to my dull thrusts were a credit, frankly, to one so frail and so long out of practice in the act of coitus. We clung together with dogged determination to squeeze the final, assuaging spasm from our agonised embrace – it seemed so near – when suddenly Casilda entered and crossed the room with a loaded tray, which she set down on the table next door, merely glancing at our entangled mass on the sofa as she passed.

'Don't mind me, you two – carry on,' she remarked in a casual, quiet tone of voice. 'Supper isn't quite ready yet.'

Stopping as though shot, Helen let out a little shriek of shame and embarrassment. She flung an arm across her face to hide its expression of pathetic misery, not realising that as she lay beneath me, almost obliterated, it was shielded from Casilda's view by my black-coated shoulder.

Casilda's attitude, on the other hand, evinced merely amiable and sympathetic curiosity. She emerged from the dining room, gnawing a chicken's leg, and hovered behind the sofa for a moment or two, reflectively biting shreds of meat off the bone as she observed our antics – or rather mine – with as much interest as the school coach takes in a training bout between a couple of fifth-form boxers.

'Hold it a minute,' she advised with unconscious irony, which I mistook for heavy sarcasm. 'Don't come yet, either of you – I'll be back in one second.'

The instant she was out of the room, Helen, who had been lying flat and still under me, like a corpse, began struggling wildly, trying to break away.

'Quick, quick – get off me, let me go, please, Tony, get off, let me go!' she clamoured, pushing at my chest and at my chin in a violent, vain endeavour to lift my oppressive weight.

She had gone crazy. What? Stop now? When Casilda was taking it so well? She must be out of her mind. On me Casilda's entry had produced exactly the opposite effect – it had immediately revived my flagging spirits and administered a sharp stimulant to my lost appetite, which brightened under her scrutiny like a rusty old lamp polished anew: Aladdin's lamp, no less, whose genie at a twinkle sprang to life in Helen's guts, prepared to do my bidding. I was another man now, armed with redoubled courage. I started in at once to rodger that silly, grizzling fool as furiously as an angry rooster treads a cackling hen.

Nevertheless, it did no good. I gripped Helen by the buttocks, pulling them fiercely down and apart in each hand, to nail and stretch the slit for deeper penetration, while bracing my feet against the arm of the sofa; but I could strike no answering spark in her. She was not even hostile – simply inert. This lack of antagonism was worse than any mere absence of cooperation. My fresh spurt waned. Resuscitation had been momentary, as briefly invigorating as a pinch of snuff up the nostrils. By the time Casilda returned from the kitchen and poured the champagne, I had run down like a clock.

The game was up, psychologically doomed. I gave in, and withdrew.

I sat back, clasping my forehead. Casilda held out glasses to each of us, but Helen had rolled over on her side. She buried her face in the cushions, and her shoulders shook. There was no sound in the room, though she was sobbing.

Casilda looked from one to the other of us with a puzzled, inquiring smile.

'A drawn match,' I told her. 'Even after extra time.'

'Really?' Casilda laughed. 'You don't mean it! Helen, I'm surprised at you,' she said.

During the long pause that followed, Casilda warmed herself by the fire. Helen had not touched the glass on the floor beside her. She did not speak. I wondered if she had fallen asleep from exhaustion, both bodily and emotional. Casilda appeared lost in thought.

'Supper is ready, you know,' she announced. There were no takers.

She shrugged, and stared with amusement at the pair of us, but when she came over and sat next to me, away from Helen, who lay curled up in a ball, it was with a comically reluctant gesture, as of one bestowing alms on a beggar. Pressing her lips to mine, she settled herself comfortably and treated me to a long, voluptuous searching kiss that sent hot shivers down my spine, while her hand dragged my battered tool once more out of my fly into the limelight, and frigged it firmly, expertly, with her long, slow, gentle strokes, at the same time subtly massaging my flaccid nuts, until in a short while I had a horn on me that any sultan might have envied.

Stars danced before my eyes as, head back, gagged by her darting tongue, I relaxed – except at the focal point – in surrender to her skilled manipulations, which vaguely I sought to repay in kind with groping fingers.

She allowed my hand to reach its goal, accepting its somewhat automatic tribute to her sex with proper and ladylike complaisance; but when my other hand strayed to the neck of her Prussian-blue taffeta evening gown, she pushed it away and nodded in Helen's direction. I obeyed the order – only to have Helen sit up like a jack-in-the-box the moment I slid a caressing palm between her thighs.

'Don't touch me!' she almost screamed.

We gazed at her in astonishment.

'Helen – for heaven's sake, what's come over you?' I expostulated.

She did not look at me. Glaring murderously at Casilda, she cowered at the end of the sofa, trembling from head to foot, as though fighting to find words in some dark inner whirlpool of rage.

'Casilda,' she pronounced at last, in a voice colder than a mortuary slab: 'This man is your lover. You have been lying to me. Your life with me was a lie. Oh my God, the whole situation is too repulsive, too loathsome! You have hurt me terribly. I did not deserve this of you. I shall never recover from your deceit. I will leave you now – with him. I am going home.'

'There, there, Helen darling,' Casilda said. 'Calm down, now, take it easy. We've shared so many secrets in the past . . . look, this isn't a secret. It's just exactly what you need. You're a tiny bit hysterical, my sweet. Don't be so rude to Tony. He can't stand up for himself. But he's all right now. I fixed it for you. Come on, honey – let him give you a damn good lay. It won't go wrong this time. Listen. I'll go out of the room, if you'd rather . . .'

I thought Helen would fly at her. She leaned forward, hugging herself, taut as a coiled spring. She was a porcupine, a miniature atomic rocket. There was a mad, homicidal glint in her eyes.

'I'm going home,' she repeated. 'Where's my wrap? Let me out of here.'

Casilda only laughed. 'Well, you're missing a swell opportunity,' she said. 'It's a lot better, this, than that beastly old dildo of yours – take my word for it. Don't be so stupid, Helen. You're wasting all my beautiful handiwork. Go on, Tony – fuck her, why don't you? What are you waiting for? She doesn't know what she wants. That's what's the matter with her, poor poppet. She can have *me* any time. But one does like a little variety . . .'

I turned towards the blazing bare bundle of outraged womanhood, as she backed away on the sofa, with some trepidation. It was an exciting idea, all the same. I was attracted and frightened. If only Casilda would help, maybe . . . You would have to get someone to hold her down – at any rate for a start. It would be like taking liberties with a small black panther.

'Helen,' I pleaded. 'You really can't leave me in this state, you know. Don't go home yet – stick around. I've shown already how much I wanted you – and I still do. It was wonderful, Helen – you are quite marvellous. Such a lovely, lovely body . . . but first let me get all these hampering clothes off. I'll take you home later, both of you.'

At one bound, before I could lay a finger on her – I approached rather gingerly – she was across the room and had squatted down facing us, in front of the fire. She snatched up her dress from a chair, where Casilda had placed it, and tucked its vermillion folds modestly about her knees. Casilda bubbled with mirth like a fountain.

'A ladybug to the life,' she said, 'And, oh dear, what an awful rebuff! Must you fly away?'

She still held my cock in her hand; even when she shoved me over towards Helen she had not relinquished it. Now, in full view of our audience, she bent down and stiffened my prick again to her liking with a few careful kisses. So far as I was concerned, she could have gone on forever, licking and tickling the tip of it with her tongue – but apparently she had other plans. For the second time that night my phallus was enveloped in a narrow, hot, tender prison that kept it for a while confined and captive. Which fleshly dungeon was the happier burial place – Casilda's mouth or Helen's nice tight twat? Before I could decide that delicate point, she set him free, jumped to her feet, and standing over me, with her back turned on Helen, she picked up the hem of her dress and pulled it over her hips, where with both hands she rolled it in a bunch about her waist. It was a lewd and slightly ludicrous figure she cut, towering above me on her high heels and long, straight legs, so temptingly naked all the way up, except for a simple black lace triangle, like a bull's-eye, that merely added provocation to the ensemble, but with the top half of the body more than decently covered – too much, too grandly clad, hindered and overdecked in an accumulation of glistening taffeta and jewels. It was a lovely sight, as festive, touching, brilliant as a Christmas tree. I studied it in detail gladly, with leisurely appreciation, and gently tugging the dainty patch of her lace down to her ankles, unmasked the gorgeous thicket of brown curls that sprouted out at me, demanding my instant homage, at eye level.

'No, that's enough – hurry, lean back!' Casilda said.

Not till then, as she stepped forward, straddling my legs with her fork widely separated, and lowered herself without haste onto the turgid prong which I guided and aimed into the open slot that softly descended to close down upon it, to meet its match, its fitting mate, the richest gift from heaven, was I suddenly chilled by the alarming thought of Helen's ferocious jealousy. From where she sat, huddled near the fire, she must have witnessed the whole operation from just that low angle that was calculated to spare her nothing. I could picture what she saw – the gaping rear view under Casilda's out-thrust tail, as it hung suspended in midair, with the tangled tuft parted by her spreading thighs to show the scarlet gash of her vagina that slowly swallowed up my penis inch by inch and dropped to rest in contact with my scrotum, sealing it across the entrance to the pit, as with a boulder to stop a secret passage. And this was all only the beginning of the film – suppose the spectacle proved more than she could bear? The sequel, with Casilda riding a cock-horse hell for leather, might end disastrously. What could I do, in my helpless position, if Helen were to attack her girlfriend from behind? At one blow – with the poker, for instance – she could kill her. I would be lucky indeed if they only scratched their eyes out. Was I to sit back and let these two harpies fight over me? A gentleman was bound to intervene. Brawling was one thing; insults did no lasting harm. But at all costs I must avoid bloodshed on the premises . . . Casilda was the stronger, no doubt – but we were at a frightful disadvantage. The spectre of imminent murder loomed over me in the rocking, plunging, writhing shape of the victim as, swaying to and fro, and tossing her mane – thought I was the mount and she the rider – Casilda bore down on top of me until, our roles reversed, with all her weight on my belly, she seemed to be screwing us further and further into each other . . .

With head thrown back – an easy target – while clutching the crumpled dress across her tits, she was as bare as Godiva around the middle, whereas Helen now, I could see, had got her clothes on. Peering anxiously under a sawing elbow, I kept an eye on her to prevent any surprise move . . . she was making ready, as I guessed, for a quick getaway after the deed. There was no means of defence within my reach, not even the bottle. Helen had collected all her things . . . I spoke to her urgently. I begged her to stay, to have a drink, or a bite to eat. I promised again to take her home – if she could wait just a moment . . . I offered her coffee – there was some in the kitchen, I said.

She did not deign to reply. She found the orchids and threw them into the fire. Then, with her face averted, she delivered herself of a valedictory address to Casilda, who took no notice. It was a curt and definite farewell, but not particularly abusive. She would never consent to see the immoral, faithless slut again so long as she lived. She ran to the door, and was gone.

We came, I recall, as she went.

VIII

Calm reigned over the cabbage patch. Now that we had each other to ourselves, with Helen out of the way, I presume some sentiment oddly akin to love must have accounted for the agreeable fact that our life together showed no signs of palling on either of us, although in every respect save one – except in the eyes of the law, that is – we were as bad as married. I never could have guessed that I might take to a virtual state of wedlock so meekly, with such benign resignation and tolerance. Casilda fetched her belongings next day from Regent's Park, timing the visit so as to avoid her former hostess of many years, who would be seeing Cécile off at the airport, and immediately took up residence with me. My spare room was certainly not large enough to billet a lady in the style to which Casilda was accustomed, but by unpacking only about a third of her wardrobe and stowing a dozen pieces of luggage in the basement she was able to settle in fairly comfortably as my guest for a couple of months or so. That, I believe, was what I suggested. Casilda put it differently: 'for the duration,' she said. I liked the arrangement: it suited me to a T, and the problem of how to get rid of her eventually, when I'd had enough of a good thing and my bachelor character reasserted itself, was a bridge I felt I could cross when we came to it.

The charm of the situation, its saving grace, was that we were free to play at matrimony in make-believe, like children keeping house, and the kick we got from this perverse parlour game was due to the knowledge that our honeymoon romp would entail no dreary aftermath of domesticity, deception, debt or doubts. The great final bust-up with Helen had cleared the air, and our predominantly sexual liaison took on a new lease of life, since we no longer suffered the constraints attached to what is generally – and graphically – described as a hole-in-the-corner affair. Indeed we now went to the other extreme, seldom caring to be parted from one another, but neglecting our many friends entirely, once we had set up a home. If two such socially minded types as ourselves did not consider this abstention any sacrifice, but found adequate companionship in their own company, then, as somebody remarked about us wryly, 'it must cover a multitude of sins.' True, we spent long hours in bed together – withdrawn into our private shell, if you like – but most of that time we slept. Sensual delight had not gone stale on us already, after a few short weeks; it was scored to a slower, easier beat. The conjugal state, however temporary and really blissful, takes every couple that way, by an immutable decree of nature. The swiftest racer goes farthest if he sometimes rests on his oar.

Casilda denied indignantly that she might miss the habit of her homosexual gambols with Helen, and I was content to have exchanged a measure of variety and freedom for a unique asset in the regular services of the only female of my acquaintance who never failed to ring the bell with me. We were, quite simply, in clover.

It was at an exhibition of paintings by a young Austrian artist, one wintry February evening, that we ran into Janet, whom Casilda had not met before, though I, needless to say, had related to her many memorable incidents from the annals of our tempestuous, jauntyblithe, dingdong engagement, which had lasted on and off for nearly seven years and broke up in final disorder, to our immense mutual relief, on the way in her car to the registry. I have a weak ankle still as a result of that thousand-and-first fracas, while Janet wears two wedding rings, a false front tooth, and a big white streak in her dark mane as reminders of what she calls 'the public wars' or 'my grim Grey period.' We were now fond friends, sharing the curious jocular charm that passions spent acquire as a patina with age, but I had not seen her, either, nor her inoffensive Scottish husband, Andrew, since 'the evening you vamoosed halfway through dinner,' as Janet reminded me rather tartly. She shrugged off my apologies. 'I only hope she was worth it,' she said, 'I assume so, as we haven't heard from you since.'

We were standing under the shadows of an elongated Battersea Bridge at sunset, and Casilda drifted in from the next room at that moment, catalogue in hand, looking for me.

'I rather like that,' Janet declared, waving a glove at some bathers on a canal bank and narrowly missing Casilda's nose as she approached.

'Me too,' I said. I introduced them. 'This was the reason why I owe you and Andrew an especially good dinner,' I explained, 'to make up, Janet dear, for my rudeness in leaving you that night a trifle abruptly.'

'Janet, the famous Janet!' Casilda exclaimed. 'Knowing Tony as we do, I needn't tell you how often he drags your name into the conversation. It's a household word with us, if you'll forgive me saying so.'

'Oh, my God, yes, I'm sorry for you,' Janet laughed. 'He's such a tireless reminiscer, isn't he? You must know all – but everything – about me in the most lurid detail, I'm sure. How dismal of you, Tony!'

'Let me give you the lowdown on Casilda in return,' I offered. 'When can you have a quiet, gossipy lunch with me?'

'I insist on getting my word in first,' Casilda stated. 'We girls have a lot in common. What do you say,

Janet? Unless we let him come along as well – just to eat, shut up, and listen.'

We took a stroll round the gallery, discussing Klaus Ritter's quite commendable stuff, and gave Janet a few drinks at the pub on the corner before she dived into the Underground for Hampstead, where we were to dine with them the following Thursday. My two darlings, past and present, had taken to each other in a big way, and I was completely ignored in the frowzy saloon bar while they got on like a row of houses on fire, chattering and giggling so gaily that I noticed several staid customers regarding them with greater interest and more frankly amused admiration than any freak or foreigner can normally count on arousing among the British at home. They made a striking pair of beauties, even for the West End, I will admit, in that dowdy setting, though there was nothing bizarre about Janet's lean English looks and Casilda was so un-American an expatriate that she could happily refer to herself as a crossbred mongrel, instead of just taking it for granted.

'I'm nuts about that Janet of yours,' Casilda informed me as the station swallowed my ex-fiancée down its fetid gullet. 'She's loads of fun – and madly attractive, in a famished style of looks. Not much of her, is there?'

'If Janet were ever to shed an ounce of weight off her spare frame, skinny would be the only word for her. But that isn't feasible because there ain't no flesh on her anywhere that she could lose, as I used to tell her, without the light showing through. You'd have to scoop to hollow out even a sliver of Janet. My cronies used to describe her as scrawny, but dressmakers call it "slenderly built." She's a sylph – irremediably thin, or, as she says herself, "thin with knobs on." That's more accurate. The knobs are all there, and the curves – long and slight and sinewy as a greyhound's, but perfectly in proportion and finely drawn, like a streamlined, sensitive piece of machinery, a shiny steel instrument of some sort. Janet, stripped, presents a far less gaunt appearance than the fashionable self you saw in her clothes. A bit lanky, of course, but a damned sight more human in shape when she's naked.'

'So I would imagine,' Casilda commented with a smile. 'You and your nudes! You analyse and compare every woman's body you come across. Wouldn't you do better to photograph us all for the record, instead of trying to remember a whole jumbled mass of mental notes?'

Where Janet was concerned, if I wished to be critical, I would set against her undoubted good points two anatomical flaws that are often found in this tall breed of Englishwomen. Her tits were appealing, firm and excellent, although of course too small – but they also were placed too low and rather too far apart, pointing outwards, which gave her a flat chest at first sight, and yet, almost as a pleasant afterthought, a distinctly feminine bosom. This was charming enough in itself, once discovered; but it seemed to have little, if any, connection with the strongly marked, splendid pectoral muscles that could scarcely be needed to lift those sweet, prancing, miniature breasts. Secondly, under her fork, at the top of her long, lean shanks, though she was not bow-legged, there was an empty space, an unsightly, inverted triangular gap between the thighs, which were devoid of any fat, so that, here, at the vital intersection itself, you got more room for manoeuvre than is usually provided for a man's comfort or the woman's ease in accommodating a visitor's retinue, however bulky. It always struck me that this fault – I would hardly call it a drawback – detracted from the obvious merits of Janet's smooth, pretty concave belly and proud, very prominent mount of Venus, which were among her best features, to my taste.

The Mackenzies lived on the far side of Hampstead.

Andrew wore glasses, an incipient paunch, and a canny, good-natured expression, as though all three attributes were as congenial to him as the pink complexion which was a shade darker, if anything, than his now greying carroty hair. Physically he was not prepossessing, but he had the proverbial Scottish traits of dry humour and reserved gravity, though he carried neither to that excess which amounts, in many of his race, to unwarranted conceit and taciturn boorishness. The martinis, after a hard day's work at his printing office, loosened his tongue before we sat down to the delicious, unorthodox sort of meal in which both our host, and hostess, as butler and cook, were right to take great pride, for its succession of exotic specialities was typical of the house. Casilda could not conceal her admiring envy and thereby won Andrew's heart, so that no stranger joining us at table would have been able to guess who among the assembled company were intimate friends or had never met before in their lives.

Andrew assured me, when I complimented him on the choice variety of his food and wines, that above all else he had a passion for his trade as a typographer, which took up every moment of his time, he said, apart from weekend golf, because he had allowed it to become his hobby as well. He too was a collector – of books. 'I have a very small library,' he told me, 'but most of the items in it are prize specimens, and some are unique. You'll see – though they may not be much up your street. I only go in for fine bindings and perfect examples of print.'

Andrew kept his cigars also in the cosy little room off the hall, where we retreated with a decanter and plenty of coffee to inspect the shelves that glowed, like a tapestry, with rich tones of leather and gilt. He showed me a wealth of magnificent volumes, among them half a dozen that I had not merely seen before in booksellers' lists or behind glass, and though I did not doubt his word it occurred to me that sometimes perhaps he let the merits of subject matter outweigh the intrinsic value of the production. There was a priceless Aretion, the *Decameron*, Crebillon's *Sofa* and other curious works that may have owed their presence there to outward beauty, but, rubbing shoulders with them, I found a tome or two – a smudgy, tattered copy of Rochester's *Sodom*, for example – whose rarity alone would rate them worthy of inclusion, whereas the few modern editions, maybe a score, in a separate section, belonged to the same single class of illustrated masterpieces intended solely for perusal by adult and discriminating readers.

I was poring over the pages of Sade's *Justine* when the telephone pealed out beside me, and the bookworm Andrew answered it. An agitated voice spluttered at length into his ear, eliciting no more than an occasional gruff query or dour affirmative in reply. Finally he snapped: 'Well, all right then – I'll have to go down and cope with it myself, I shan't be long.'

He turned to me. 'I'm sorry,' he said. 'A call from that fool of a head printer. Apologise to the girls on my behalf. I might get back, with luck, before you go.'

He started to ring for a taxi, but I insisted on driving him at least as far as the station. It was a dirty night, and I was glad to let myself into the warmth with his latchkey. *En passant* I picked up another cigar and some brandy from the study before joining the ladies.

There they were, on the sofa together, in front of the drawing-room fire, but I could not say that I caught them in a compromising situation, because they showed no sign of heeding my intrusion in the least. Janet was almost lost to view in Casilda's arms, but both were still fully clothed. Casilda was kissing and fondling my former love, who very evidently relished her attentions, for her head was thrown back, her eyes were shut, and she was sighing and squirming in that abandoned way she had, which I remembered so well. This went on for some time, until Casilda, becoming aware of my diffident presence, looked up and gave me a wink of the most entrancing vulgarity. If she did not wave in recognition, it was because both her hands were deeply engaged, at first on a roving mission and then in a definite pincer movement that appeared to rouse our hostess from uneasy slumbers to a vocal and increasingly active share in the proceedings. Janet's staring peepers opened like a doll's, she suddenly found a great deal to say – all of it highly flattering to her newly acquired friend – and her arms, linked about Casilda's neck, dragged the happy, wide, scarlet mouth down to her own, silencing them both, to some extent, for neither one of the excited pair could speak again for a while in coherent terms, though the language they used was an expressive universal *lingua franca* sound beyond the limits of speech, as they kissed, mumbled, panted, gasped and sighed. . . .

I was sitting back in a large armchair, quietly puffing at my mellow Larriñaga, as utterly at ease as a millionaire impresario watching a deliriously popular stage turn from the wings. The success of the act did not exactly surprise me, though it had never crossed my mind, earlier in the evening, that the girls would fall for each other in such startling earnest, practically on first sight, or that their mutual attraction could produce this happy harvest, before one could say Tallulah Bankhead. Casilda, I realised, might perhaps have been feeling a trifle starved for this special form of love, which no doubt meant more to her than she was prepared to admit. Bless her wicked heart, I couldn't blame her for getting up to her old tricks again so soon, at the drop of an eyelid! But, casting my mind back over Janet's case history, I did not recall that she ever showed much liking or aptitude but rather, on the contrary, a natural distaste for any hint of these naughty digressions, which

I would, I confess, have been only too ready to encourage and approve. It was obvious that Casilda had taken the initiative tonight, and was calling the tune, but I was equally fascinated to see that Janet must have welcomed her overtures without the faintest hesitation of demur, judging by their present harmonious pitch of enthusiasm. There had not been time, after all, for any lengthy process of persuasion, and Casilda, with her unfailing sixth sense in sexual matters, had clearly neither delayed nor rushed the pace unduly. They seemed meant for one another – and both were bent on proving it.

I crossed over and sat on the arm of the sofa. Casilda's black jersey dress was off one shoulder. She had undone Janet's shirt and removed her bra. Between them they struggled to get her out of her tight tartan trews. Casilda signalled to me for aid. She had slithered on to the floor and delved deep into Janet's lap at once, leaving the upper half of the long, slim body in my care. Janet's rosy limbs were flung wide across the cushions, like a starfish stranded helpless on the shore. Hers was the emaciated, abandoned carcass, we the plundering crows that swooped on her in unison to gnaw her vitals. Neither of them at last could bear the strain another moment. Leaping to her feet, Casilda wrenched off her sombre plumage, quickly cast the layer of downy silk beneath, and, launching the full force of all her naked weight into the saddle, bestrode the eager mount that bucked, quivered, reared, bounced hard up to meet her with a wild, savage will of its own. I was thrown off my perch and was forced to relinquish the tiny, tender, dancing tits to Casilda's strong grip, as she seized them for reins and clung to them also for support while she rode the cleft of Janet's crotch, hitching it fiercely to her own, twisting and writhing against it, plunging, pressing, thrusting more and more closely, more deeply into the devil's dripping mouth, the open breach, the entrance to the loins' dark, leafy-locked, mysterious cave, to dig within its folds on a hot quest for hidden treasure. . . .

I could have sworn that the violence of this encounter made the roughest moments of the frenzied frolic I had witnessed between Helen and Casilda seem like child's play. Among several reasons for this distinct impression were the fact that here was a new and unexpected challenge, that it was largely a novel thrill for Janet, whose physique was particularly well constructed to ensure that she should get the utmost enjoyment out of such an awkward method of fornication, that both girls were conscious of their appreciative audience, so may have been tempted to play up accordingly, and not only had Casilda lately been deprived of this pleasurable outlet but probably she felt that, given the chance to cuckold me a little into the bargain, she must trespass on an ancient light-o'-love of mine with an extra vengeance. She did not stint herself, certainly, nor pull her punches. But Janet was never one to take things lying down – at least not in any metaphorical sense. She gave as good as she got, on principle – and in this case she put up such a gallant show that she succeeded, with all her wiry might and by a swift, wrestling eel-like motion, in turning the tables completely on her more solid opponent. I did not see how it was done, but in a tangled flash, after a brief upheaval of flailing legs and humped muscle, the lightweight came out on top, like a bantam in the cockpit, amid a triumphant flutter of wings, spurs and waving crests. It now seemed better so. She held Casilda in the scissor grasp, and their joint movement, fast and furious, grew, rose, galloped, pounded, swelled to Valkyrian speed . . . when the door behind me opened, and Andrew walked in.

He must have used the back way. He stopped dead in his tracks and stared at the scene that confronted him, but said nothing. I handed him a drink off the mantelpiece, which one of our women had sipped and left. We stood side by side in front of the fire, watching with all eyes. Still he did not speak. I was glad. Only brute force could have separated them. It would not take long . . . suddenly there was a single loud, sharp cry from both their throats – followed, seconds later, by a choking, breathless rattle of joy that fell away in the lost, heavy silence. Languidly Janet withdrew, as a man does, quitting the flattened body that has received the gift of his sperm. She staggered slightly and dropped into a chair. I passed her the rest of my cognac. We gazed at Casilda, lying motionless and spent, lax and spread-eagled on the sofa, as uncovered and starkly indecent as a corpse. When she moved at last, and looked at us, it was to clutch at her fork, her throbbing parts, with a quick shiver and a broad, quiet smile; but not to shield the wound or hide her trembling flesh from view. Her playful fingers parted it in fact, lightly toying with the matted curls, stroking the flushed red rim all round, as though applying an oily balm to soothe a gently tickling sore, and skimming down its blatantly bare, gaping length, as in a quick canoe between bushy banks, she sighed, arched her back lazily, with yearning, and rolled her tousled head upon the cushions. We knew what she wanted – a different, immediate and deeper solace. She had made that plain enough.

'Take pity on her,' I said to Andrew, 'since she's asking for it. You have my permission.'

He glanced at Janet, who nodded. 'And mine,' she said.

'No – that won't quite do.' It was Casilda who spoke, to our surprise, as though she could not yet have revived sufficiently to communicate with us directly by word of mouth, but must continue to employ her more expressive sign language.

'Both men – I'll have you both,' she said, sitting up.

'That's it, that's what I want – and always did. Hurry, can't you – get undressed! One in front and one behind. We can manage that if we try. . . .'

It took some managing. Andrew had already torn off his clothes, before I could work out what Casilda meant or how she proposed to set about it. She sat huddled demurely on her tail now, a caricature of modesty, waiting. She studied us carefully although of course she didn't need to examine me, it all depended on Andrew. He was enormous. The tool he carried was a long, gnarled, hefty great club – a bludgeon. I was astonished. Casilda's eyes opened wide. She wet her lips. For such a little fellow, upon my soul, you would scarcely believe it possible – the most lavish endowment, and considering that it did not show up to advantage, under that bulging stomach, frankly excessive, an outsized monstrosity. How women can contemplate such repulsive objects without flinching in horror at the sight, they alone know! It had a curve on it like a rhinoceros horn or a hockey stick – and no less vast were the balls, slung in a hideous, wrinkled sack, as big as a cantaloupe. The corona itself was a dark, bursting ripe red plum, stuck on at the end of a thick, knotted bare branch – nothing short of grotesque. There we were, standing to attention, with weapons at the ready, presenting arms for Casilda's inspection. She leaned forward, putting out a hand to each of us, in an unconscious, ribald parody of a royal command soiree, assessing our offers – medium and immoderate – with judicious concentration on the big problem that faced or otherwise intimately concerned her.

In point of fact the choice was obvious; but she anointed us both for her own ends, when Janet's sisterly perception had sent her post-haste from the room, to the medicine chest, on an errand of mercy. The sofa looked a bit cramped, I thought, for the three of us, but Casilda shook her head when I beckoned her to the wide, woolly hearthrug, and, firmly drawing the two members of her party towards the couch, she lay down on her side, without letting go of us, as we loomed above her, wondering what to do next. There was only one solution, which Janet, the idle spectator, promptly advised, though it probably dawned on us all simultaneously. We turned Casilda on to her back. Andrew got up into position with some effort and misguided vigour, yet not so precipitately as the pawing stallion who needs assistance to put him into a proper fix, oddly enough, rather than to pull him out of a hole – and they settled down to it straightaway, going great guns, hard on the job with everything they had.

It was a sight to see, and thrilling to overhear, for they made the deuce of a noise, rootling like stoats, though neither of them said a word. None of us had a stitch on. A lurid light shone in Janet's eyes, as she hovered and circled around the inebriate pair, like a referee. I hopped, in sheer torture, from foot to foot, torn between fiendish impatience and jealousy. My turn would come to repay this lewd, hot-slotted nympho in kind, and I hoped it would hurt the crazy, cock-struck whore – hell take her grinding guts, I'd give it to the bitch till she laughed on the wrong side of her foul, fat fanny, damn it. I'd shoot some decent good sense up her leching, bawdy bum and fill my lovely lady with a jolt from a prick every bit as rich and randy as his . . . but when? Would they never stop? She was carried away completely, curse her, she had forgotten all about me. He'd spend, and spoil half our fun in a minute, if she didn't watch out . . . ought I to take the risk and cut in? Where was Janet? She'd serve, at a pinch. It was then, praise be, that Casilda rolled over, pushing the chap with her, jabbing him in the ribs, shoving them around, both of them, to lie, still copulating like monkeys, on their sides, with him facing out towards the fireplace, his back against the sofa, and she, in reverse, showing me her buttocks, the white, milky full moon of her bottom turned to me. There it was at last, beaming, big, broad and beautiful, in all its innocence or insolence, bland or crass, according to how one looked on it, delivered into my power as a hostage, meat indeed for the slaughter, rakish and docile, the sinful flesh. . . .

It was worth a further fleeting delay, a moment's scrutiny. I bent over the two-backed beast, ran my hand along the steep ravine between the smooth, cool cheeks, which jounced about distractingly under stern orders from in front, though Casilda thrust her tail outwards as far as she dared, while I probed the pursed little brown buttonhole, like the bud of a tiny wildflower, with my fingertip at first, and then, flinging myself on the sofa behind her, and prising the massive mounds apart, with an inch or so of the old codger himself. Easy does it, in he goes – just as slippery and sweet as you please . . . no trouble at all – for a couple of split seconds, that is, until we got the warhead in place, truly embedded, streaking up her fundament like a dentist's drill through a temporary stopping, an express train roaring full-on into a tunnel, a bulldozer boring a trench in a stiffly packed squelch of clay. But then, ye gods, what a to-do! What shrill yelps and yells, what wriggling, tugging and dodging, what tearful entreaties, elbowings, fisticuffs, and ghastly oaths! I held on to her grimly by one hip, with the other arm round her neck, and ploughed on, regardless of the cloudburst, which passed and was gone in a few more shakes at the crucial base of the triangle. . . .

The last of this trio, however, was the first to quit. It wasn't my fault. I had shot my bolt a little while before the others finished – which apparently they did, bringing it off very adroitly, together. I might have lasted out, too, if Janet had not seen fit to chip in as an auxiliary to our already somewhat overcrowded act by prodding me from the rear and swiping at my backside with her open palm, just when we were all approaching the terrific climax of our intricate threefold exercise. It's true that I was teetering on the sofa's edge the whole time, and nearly got butted off on to the floor once or twice, because there simply wasn't room for three on it: Casilda had her arms and legs coiled around Andrew in a ferocious hug to keep him in place, the cough was far too short, we stuck out in every direction like a cactus patch. But Janet's well meant intervention hastened my undoing.

I started to dress, and Andrew was about to follow suit, but his wife would not hear of it. She had snuggled up next to Casilda, cooing affectionately, but her hackles rose on the instant when she saw what was afoot.

'Hey, no you don't!' she cried with comic indignation, although quite seriously. 'That's all jolly fine – but what about me? You two stay right where you are, until I'm given just the same treatment as Casilda here. How frightfully ungallant of you, Tony, to try to sneak out on me, again! Really you're both absolute bounders, I do think. But I shan't allow it! I won't have you make such cads of yourselves. Come here!'

'Janet, honey,' I pleaded, 'have a heart! With the best will in the world . . .' I pointed to my cock. It was shrivelled and limp.

Andrew's, as she could see for herself, was in an even more pitiful plight – shrunk to a third of its former size, it hung down only a quarter of the way to his knees, like a discarded old rope end, frayed and soggy. Ugly enough at the peak of its rampant grandeur, now, in this tatty, slack, bedraggled state, it was simply revolting.

'I'd be no lousy use to you, my sweet,' he protested mildly. 'Another day – '

'Come here!' she repeated. 'We'll look into this. . . .'

A Gallery of Nudes

We were leaning against the mantelpiece, side by side, warming our backs at the fire. We did not budge – so Janet dropped on her haunches between us on the hearthrug. She refused to lose faith. She was not going to take no for an answer. We swayed, drooping before her very eyes, our crinkled, deflated organs dangling under her nose. She set to, an ardent revivalist, tackling the desperate, double task with both hands. I got the left, her better one – and she took us to task with both hands at once. She was making a lovely job of it, quite like old times . . . soon it was better still: I got her undivided attention, when Casilda flopped down beside her, and took over half the work. Now Janet could devote herself wholeheartedly to doing one thing at a time – too beautiful for words . . . her undivided attention was nothing if not widespread . . . she flag-wagged signals to Casilda, reporting progress, while simultaneously she massaged my scrotum and slid a hand between my legs, to visit warmer regions, where a venturesome middle finger went on an expedition to explore the interior . . . Janet was never so rash and clumsy as to frig a fellow at all strenuously until it was required of her. In my present condition, any but the most gradual first aid would have proved fatal. She rubbed and kneaded my testicles, pinching and playing with them, while merely brushing and stroking my phallus, as though to chafe and polish it, with a certain curious maternal fondness, for its own dear sake. Comparing by results – which are, after all, what counts – I'd have said she ran rings round Casilda; but I may have been biased by gratitude in her favour – especially when she went the whole hog and adopted heroic measures, with her tongue at first, then her lips, and finally her mouth, that other vulva, a cavity as scorching-hot and spongy but twice as clever. . . .

We were the more advanced; Casilda was finding it an uphill, gruelling chore to strike a spark into that dormant, mouldy member, so she consulted me with an air of punctilious servility. 'May I?' she asked. I gestured dumb assent. She clapped her kisser like a leech to his gross organ, which had begun to swell and stretch by infinitely small degrees, like some slow-waking giant. There, she had something to be going on with! Personally, my cure was almost complete . . . we looked like queer bookends, the four of us, like heraldic supporters on carved figures, flanking the chimney piece, although the caryatids knelt, shoulder to shoulder, while the quaking male pillars could barely stand upright, but had to be propped and girded, fore and aft by sustained, intimate pressures from below. We were lifted and wired underneath, Andrew and I, to make a peculiar nude frieze with our two ministering angels, the fairer and the darker, identical in their position yet so different in built, the one full-bodied and shapely, the other spare and lithe. With heads bent over their labours, noses to the grindstone, their agitated mops of hair were hoisted on our joysticks at half-mast, as though luxuriant, extra fleece had sprouted from his protruding paunch and my pale belly. Casilda linked the circuit by lending a hand to fiddle with Janet's pussy – a bonus which Janet promptly requited in kind. Andrew's arm lay, lightly touching mine, along the mantelshelf.

Casilda took command as mistress of ceremonies, but Janet jibbed at the sofa, like a horse at a hedge, so our tricky threesome was accomplished this time, in the end and with equal or even greater difficulty, after various vain attempts on the rug, when Andrew was shored up with pillows on the edge of a large armchair, Janet impaled herself upon his prong, to sprawl face down on top of him, crushing him against the springs and hitching herself high up into the air for me eventually to perforate at my leisure, though not without some jabbing and incitements from Casilda, who skipped around the simmering stewpot like a witch doctor. My orgasm was the last – a feather in my cap, I thought – and for a few moments after we were through with the smothered underdog, Janet and I shunted to and fro in ecstasy, a toppling pile of flesh, like a three-decker sandwich, that sagged to rest where it lay, until Casilda called us to get a bite to eat in the kitchen, which Andrew aptly compared to a nudist's canteen.

'Whenever you feel like a return match,' said Casilda brightly as we left, 'just let us know.'

IX

Until she reminded me, I had forgotten that Casilda's three-months' 'probationary period,' as she slyly called it, was nearly up. One evening I told her that I would have to go over to Paris soon on business. She was soaking in her bath, like a delicious archipelago gleaming in an ocean of foam.

'I see,' she said, rising Venuslike while I talked about the trip. 'Hand me my towel, honey . . . I've been here long enough, I guess. It was time I got out, anyway,' she added, turning around to hunch her wet shoulders into the big bath towel, which gave her the air of a bather getting undressed with elaborate modesty on a beach.

'You've boiled yourself a fashionable pink, as usual,' I remarked. 'Luminous but painful to look at. How you stand it, God knows.'

'Easy,' said Casilda, drying herself in a sequence of unconsciously alluring poses that would have earned a photographer his month's meals. 'I'm in my element when I get into hot water. You should know that, Tony darling. But it's not what I meant, of course . . . oh, well, never mind.'

'What the devil did you mean then?' I was slow on the uptake.

Casilda sifted a white cloud of French Fern over certain parts of her rose-flushed, tawny, yellow-brown self, and eyed me with a half-pitying frown.

'Just that I count on you to bring me back something

pretty from Paris. How long will you be away? Can I hang on here for a bit, until you let me know?'

'Do you want to?' I asked, much amused. It had never occurred to me that she might misinterpret my words as a tactful farewell. 'As you like,' I continued, grudgingly acquiescent. 'I only felt that – '

'No, all right then,' she snapped. 'Let's call it a day.'

'I thought you wouldn't care to be left here on your own. I don't need to stay very long in Paris, it's true – but that small attic I share in Montparnasse will be empty for the next couple of months. Margot has gone to the States, as I told you. So I might as well camp there awhile – why not? We could have a good deal of fun in Paris, one way and the other. I was sure you would jump at the chance. Still, if you'd rather – '

'You mean I'd go too? Why in hell didn't you say so, Tony?'

'It went without saying, damn it all! What made you think otherwise? Maybe taking coals to Newcastle, I agree – but I assumed you'd expect to come along.'

'You're a lousy bastard, my good sir,' said Casilda, adjusting the loose toils of a frail suspender belt that dangled from her middle like the feelers of a dead octopus, framing her belly in elastic brackets about the thick, silken splodge of her powdered short hairs.

'You led me up that garden path very neatly,' she admitted. 'But the great thing in life for a floozy is to know when she's wanted – or not any more. I'm only here on appro, after all. How long have I had to prove my worth? Three months, nearly. I was expecting my congé any time now . . . not that I deserve to be thrown away yet. You've got yourself a bargain here, if you ask me.'

Hands clasped behind her neck, she swung her ripe breasts and revolved her ample hips in a brief, fetching parody of a Turkish tummy dance. I held out my arms, from close range on the bathroom stool.

'Your contract is extended indefinitely, Miss Vandersluys – until we get a colossal bid for you from an oil king or some rival studio who can afford to compensate us decently for taking you off our hands,' I assured her.

With reptilian fingers weaving before her face and an odalisque's hypnotic eyes darting shafts of amorous enticement over her *yashmak* – a chiffon slip draped across her nose – Casilda gyrated onto my lap and sat astride my knees, swaying, wriggling and twirling her arms. She was her master's suppliant slave, but, as such, she took the lead with astute anticipation of my every wish – which in fact she herself created. Needless to say, I was already aroused and equipped to deal with the insinuating houri in summary, straightforward fashion. She would not, however, permit me to do so. A properly instructed harem vamp has more respect for the union rules of her craft. Men are clumsy, ungrateful brutes – but they are capable, if subtly inspired, cajoled and guided, of dispensing to the top of nature's bent the lavish bounties of their wondrous godhead. That is what a girl wants most in all the world, and can have at any time, if she goes about it wisely. Casilda had more recondite uses for my impressive erection than that which had occurred to me ipso facto. The whole thing was taken out of my hands there and then. Bemused and contented, I lent her my tool, and she – humbly, solicitously, with a pretty fair imitation of the resourceful wiles of oriental lovemaking – did the job. I accepted her blandishments as my lordly due . . . the result was that we staggered out to dinner very late.

Lifting a corner of her flimsy makeshift veil, she engulfed my mouth in a lascivious, liquid kiss that pushed me into an almost horizontal position with my neck propped against the wall. At the same time she reached over into an open drawer of the medicine chest for an electric vibrator which I had quite forgotten I owned. Trust Casilda in her leisure moments to unearth so pleasant a toy! She plugged it in, and employed it with stirring effect on us both, before springing up to swivel me around on the stool as a pivot, so that my elbows rested, firmly supporting our joint weight, on the edge of the bath – for she surged back immediately on top of me, with a supple movement, to perch and lie down full length upon my prick. I lay pinned, like a butterfly, underneath her though my role was rather that of a guinea pig in the laboratory or of the heftier partner in an acrobatic act at the circus. Continuous evolutions were performed upon my supine torso by this undulating, improvised nautchgirl, whose gymnastic talents I had hitherto never suspected.

From a swimming posture on my chest Casilda raised herself, curling her legs beneath me, and then, leaning backwards, she lifted them both, one after the other, until her knees were pushed up under her chin, almost touching it, as she huddled herself with a sort of sinuous concentration, clasping her ankles, so that her feet rested in the hollow of my stomach and her heels were pressed against the stretched expanse of her squatting thighs. Motionless she remained at this angle for a moment, gripping and distending the strong inner muscles that held my shackled member within her burning, slippery sheath as in a vase. She had me on the rack, splayed out, recumbent in a levitated luxury of mingled pain and pleasure, a raging contrast of sensations, acute and dazed which she contrived, with a tormentor's dexterous cruelty, to check, reduce, renew or aggravate at will.

Casilda changed her position three or four times, as one chooses a different combination to the lock of a safe. Leaning on my thighs, she uncoiled her long legs and stuck them straight out in front of her, so that my head was flanked to left and right of her shins. She made me hike myself nearly upright, slid us across the floor and hooked her knees over my shoulders to draw me still closer down towards her by crossing her feet again tightly behind my back. My trunk was bent forward, hers leaned away from me as far as possible: we were a couple of oarsmen wildly rowing opposite ways in the same boat. It was not easy skulling – but Casilda increased the strain wilfully, very slowly, with scientific precision, when she undid the knot, pointing her toes into the air above my head, and gingerly worked herself right around on her pelvis – and mine – to end up facing outwards, with her back to me.

It was not until we had completed these elaborate exercises and got ourselves at last into a comparatively simple fix that Casilda consented to discard all caution and gallop through to a passionate finish – yet, even then, she scorned to lean out frontwards in the normal manner, but on the contrary lay back against my chest thrusting me down flat once more until only my nape and bottom were squarely supported on the edge of the bath and the towel-topped wooden stool.

I had investigated all these various clinches before – most of them with Casilda herself as well as with my other concubines in the past – but I cannot recall having sampled the whole gamut at one sitting on any previous occasion, nor ever in such highly precarious circumstances. One is willing to try everything once, of course, or more often – and so are two, I've found, half the time – but really bed is the only place for gallant conjuring feats or sinewy tests of endurance. Casilda's flights of fancy had wafted us through a dizzy, dazzling firmament of stars – but I begged her, when we returned to earth, never more to drag me from the safe anchorage of a mattress planted squarely on terra firma.

Soon after Easter we were installed in my dear old flame Margot's dusty, ramshackled studio off the Rue Lepic, with spring in the air and just enough money to scrape by on for the time being. If we were to have a summer holiday, I had to buckle down to work.

'D'you know what?' Casilda remarked at breakfast one morning. 'I should have a kid sister in this city, some place – if she's still knocking around. I lost track of her a year or two ago. By way of studying art in Paris, she was. Wonder if I can contact her through the old address – or we would certainly meet up with her if we settled at the Deux Magots for a while . . . you'd take to Anne, I think. Very easy on the eye – unless she has managed to ruin her looks by now. She's six years younger than me – a half sister, actually. Her father was a crooner from St Louis. If you consider me a minx, wait till you see Anne. . . .'

'Barely twenty-one,' I mused. 'An attractive age – but maybe a shade unfledged for me still. . . .'

'Gosh, no, not on your life!' Casilda snorted. 'Besides, you're already headed for the pinafore stage, *mon vieux*. Haven't you noticed? A criminal taste for the sweet young things is developing fast, I'd say. How about Cécile, for example?'

'Well, yes, all right, now that you mention it, what about her; oughtn't we call on the little chit at school, or take her out or something, since we're over here? It would be only polite.'

Casilda raised her eyebrows but made no comment. Nor did I. What was there to say? We exchanged looks that might either mean nothing at all or else were pregnant with intentions too iniquitous to be expressed between us in words. I had a sort of inkling that Casilda had come round quite a way recently from her idiotically priggish attitude on the subject of the little Delavigne lass. I would not put anything past her in that line. She was vicious, my darling Cassy, but also and above all she was unaccountable. She had an exceedingly soft spot for Cécile – and now, in addition, there was a keen desire on her part to be revenged on Helen.

In fact, she was quite serious about that, unlike me – which wasn't unfunny. She had taken her dismissal by the Baroness with a far more ill grace than I ever expected. Personally, though, I did not feel much inclined to egg her on in her nefarious schemes. The thought of Anne attracted me, but I wasn't particularly interested in the snooty little schoolgirl, who would no doubt yell blue murder and run to Mummy if Casilda or I even looked like touching her. . . .

Or would she? Had I not hit the nail on the head that time when I taunted Casilda about the deceptive quality of maidenly innocence? For all I knew, Cécile might turn out to be a slim little chip off the old block – in which case she would surely take to any necking games we might propose to play, like a duck to water.

That was certainly the opinion I formed one evening when I came home to the studio and found Cécile closeted there with Casilda – in an atmosphere that struck me as charged with strong, peculiar currents of feminine conspiracy, though it was obvious that they had merely been having tea together, Cécile and her mother's best friend, whom any impressionable damsel might look up to with affectionate admiration and envy. In Cécile's adolescent eyes Casilda must have appeared as a glamorous film-star, an elegant lady of fashion, a worldly-wise companion and a sweetly condescending older girl, all rolled into one.

Our pretty visitor was just about to leave when I arrived. Her manners, as always, were perfect; she thanked us both for the lovely time she had had and looked forward to coming to this picturesque pied-à-terre again, if asked. I could see that Casilda had not glossed over but rather stressed the carnal nature of our relationship, which stood out a mile, anyhow, in the restricted lebensraum of the studio, so that, without overdoing it, she had been able to give the teenager a discreet object lesson in the happy art of living in sin –

not by a sordid display or crumpled bed linen, but by a bohemian profusion of laundered underclothes strewn about the place to betoken an easygoing state of conjugal intimacy. Casilda hastened to explain this gaudy disarray.

'It looks like a naval occasion, I know,' she said. 'We're dressed overall with bunting – but that was done for Cécile's benefit. She was crazy about my "mass of nice things." I'm afraid I encouraged her. I've been modelling this whole pile of nonsense for hours – and sent her off with a couple of my naughtiest numbers as a gift. Her eyes were popping out of her head. I wished you'd been here – you'd have adored it. She's really an absolute honey. I shut the bedside table drawer and pretended to hide one or two whatnots which it would be good for her to see. She was desperate with curiosity, of course – and she blushes most becomingly! I was itching to kiss her – but it was better to go slow and win her confidence. I've made tremendous progress . . . by the time tea was ready – or rather, port and pastries – we had broken the ice to a powder, I can tell you, and began to let our hair down in earnest. We are as thick as thieves now. For a well-brought-up kid, primed by her mother not to unbend an inch in any direction. I must say she's amazing. I gave her a few shocks, which were a big treat for her, I guess – but they helped to draw her out beautifully. She knows it's ill-bred to appear inquisitive – and she would die, as you can imagine, at her age, rather than let on that any aspect of sex might still hold some mystery for her, except from actual experience and practice. She thinks she has the whole thing taped, theoretically speaking. I dropped several veiled references that properly foxed her, but she never made a slip or shot a line or balled up her understanding manner in any way. It was a delicious conversation. She is no faker and no fool. She's terribly eager to learn – though there isn't much fruit left on the tree, to be honest, that she hasn't already spotted, if not nibbled. . . .'

'What did I tell you?'

'You're dead wrong. As her mother confessor I can pass on her confidences to prove to you how pure she is, poor pet, in spite of having been exposed for months to an appallingly corrupt influence out of St Cloud, my dear . . . that's a smart finishing establishment, all right. Cécile is having the whale of an affair, as adult and romantic as you please, with the daughter of a Tunisian sheik. It's a positive hotbed of vice, that high-classed joint. But she is only on the fringe of the ring – probably because she's too scared to join the really fast set. The trouble is that Leila, the Tunisian, is a lot younger, but she makes the running. She's stuck on Cécile with a true schoolgirl pash – imagine that, on top of a sultry temperament, the seraglio background, a colour complex, what a bonfire! She's Cécile's abject slave and meek, "pi" handmaiden, of course, but an importunate, brow-beating bully into the bargain. If it weren't that she keeps threatening to poison her, I gather Cécile would have cut adrift long ago. She's a good deal more frightened than fond of her dusky chum, and but for that she would probably have achieved her heart's desire, which is to tuck up with an older girl, a Greek named Marina, who sounds to me like the only genuine lez of the lot. She's their Queen-Empress, and her word is law on matters of sex. She cashes in on being a compatriot – if not a direct descendant, naturally – of Sappho herself, and all but the dumbest other moppets stand in awe of her because she was raped, she claims, at fourteen and had several men before she set foot in the place. There's a court of three favourite rosebuds in constant attendance on her. "My vestals," she calls them – a Dane, a Chinese and a Belgian. I reckon she has had her eye on Cécile for some time, but is biding the moment . . . she had sampled and cast off the Tunisian, and takes it out on the Dane, whom the others – I mean the lesser lights – envy terribly, because she too is no longer a virgin. She was seduced more or less in the nursery, and can't see anything wrong with that. Nor can Cécile. The obliging Dane likes it both ways, and makes no bones about it. She is known to have kicked up her heels for the music master and the gardener at St Cloud – so of course she has the jolly reputation of doing any chap a good turn at the drop of a hat. The upshot of it all is that Cécile is the classic *demi-vierge* – mentally, though she has had no leadings with the opposite sex. She simply can't wait to leave school and launch out on a roaring affair with the first comer – that is, if he tackles it right. She is moderately attracted to Leila, *faute de mieux*. But she is yearning to play a truly female role under a man's rod of iron. Subconsciously it's a lover she wants – and needs. Failing that, for the present – since she's timid and unsure – her great ambition is to make the grade with the Chinese or the Greek. Socially, in her world, that would be tops. She cordially dislikes the Belgian, who pokes fun at her innocence and accuses her of being so terrified of masturbating that she wears rubber gloves whenever she goes to spend a penny.'

In point of fact, the conquest – or, if you will, the violation – of Cécile Delavigne was not such plain sailing as Casilda had led me to expect. For Casilda, of course, it was easy enough – a simple problem of seduction – but I had to use force. I didn't mind that especially – it added a bit of incentive, in a way, to an otherwise fairly dull adventure – only the thing was I hadn't envisaged any difficulty, and it came as rather a nasty shock to me. I do not look back on the episode now with any pleasure. Doubtless the silly fool couldn't help it at the time – but she hurt my feelings considerably, blast her, so nobody really enjoyed the incident, except Cassy.

It was a fortnight later that she fetched the girl from St Cloud to spend the day with us – her main idea being to catch a glimpse of the famous Marina, I surmised, and some of her young ladies-in-waiting. I was out to a business lunch – with a book at a bistro round the corner. I let myself in as noiselessly as possible, and neither of them heard me, though I recognised the sounds all right, from outside the door – the low, sweet, unmistakable rumble of lovemaking. I tiptoed across to the curtained alcove and leaned against the wall to listen. What soft music of delight in the ear, not only heavenly and divine but of this world of earth, the battle hymn of the flesh – starry music of the spheres the deep, rich, endless melody of sex – ah, harken to its strains once more, how blissful a duet to sing, how good to hear it sung! I scarcely could capture what was said – a word, a phrase at most, amid the muted, whispered murmurings, between the strange, long intervals of pregnant silence, broken now and then by a faint quiet sigh, a louder, sudden, sharp intake of breath or the hurried, urgent, glad confusion of speech that bursts like a torrent, like a hot shower, upon the excited eavesdropper's brain, fretted by the mysterious, intermittent, barely audible tune of rustling bedclothes, creaking springs, bodily movements or by an occasional brief sequence of muffled, plaintive, incoherent groans, which ends abruptly, as though the torturer had gagged the victim with a kiss.

The sound track was familiar – a transient, lovely recording which I knew by heart but never could hear too often, nor carry in my head, because this is an intricate ditty, a part-song calling for two voices, and always, to strike a fresh, gleeful harmony, they must be new. Casilda's gentler tones, with their slow, clear American cadence slurred to a more husky yet caressing pitch, were dominant most of the time that I waited and trembled, holding myself in check, for a cue to release me from purgatory. When I peeped round the curtain, they were locked still in each other's arms, with heads on the pillow, almost motionless, while lower down, at the centre of activity under the blankets, their intertwined, cuddling limbs sent now and again a dense volcanic tremor rippling and heaving up to the surface. There was little to be observed at this initial stage of the proceedings – but the slightest disturbance would, I knew, prove fatal. I retired and contained my impatience with a *fine à l'eau*, and then undressed without a sound, donned pyjamas, and gazed out of the window at the view, while keeping both ears cocked towards the ladies' annexe.

Curiosity at last got the better of me – yet my entrance was perfectly timed. Casilda's twisted features greeted me with a grimace of only partial, pent-up recognition, for the writhing, naked, top half of her body was largely obscured by the coverlet which rose and fell in a flurried, scrambling hump across her middle. The hump, roughly female in shape, was her invisible companion, who was dragged up from the depths after a while by Casilda, to reappear – somewhat reluctantly, I thought – like a diver. Blushing scarlet and flushed from her exertions, she looked, I have to admit, unspeakably bewitching. Casilda embraced her fondly, stroking her hair, her nose and brow, and as they lay back in bed, the pair of them, exhausted, stretched out like half-waked cats, glossy brown and gleaming black, their slight or ample curves outlined beneath the sheet pulled up to their chins, they formed a picture of such beauty that it would vanquish the heaviest sorrow. . . .

I stood there smiling at the sight, at my own good fortune, at both the girls so snugly abed together, and at each in turn. But the instant Cécile's drowsy, faraway eyes focused on me, they went wide with alarm and were filled with embarrassment and shame. She gave a little gasp – 'Mr Grey! Oh! Oh dear?' – and buried her face against Casilda's shoulder, under the blankets, as though she were still an innocent child, and even butter wouldn't melt in her tender young mouth, let alone the honeydew briny tang of sex.

'Why is he here?' she bleated feebly. 'You promised me . . . it was us two alone – our secret. He was never going to know – you promised me that. You did, you did!'

I sat down at their feet on the divan, thoroughly nonplussed and crestfallen. Casilda tried hard to soothe her little pal – she talked, she argued, pleaded and cajoled. She besought her to see reason, just to be sensible and calm. Everything was fine, it would be all right, she'd see, if only she wouldn't take on so. Now, really, what was this stupid fuss about? Why could she not be gay again, and kind and sweet, as she was before? At first Cécile's misery seemed to grow worse, but in the end it looked as if she was persuaded. Enough, at least, for me to slip between the sheets by her side. She even cheered up sufficiently to sketch a nice, meek, rueful smile. I attempted to make light of the whole thing as a merely silly, trivial misunderstanding. For a time I did not touch her. I chatted airily, affably, quite aimlessly about this and that . . . it was best to leave the next move to Casilda – whose capable hands began, very gradually, to work wonders. Cécile stirred – uneasily at the start, imperceptibly almost, it was the tiniest wee twitch, she was determined not to squirm. The flesh was weak, although far from willing. I smoked a cigarette, got up to fetch us all a drink – just coffee for Cécile, she said, which I laced with brandy, dawdling over it, while I could hear them whispering to each other. . . .

'I've explained to this darling, foolish poppet of mine that you simply want to watch us, that's all,' Casilda reported, 'when we're like we are now, so close and cosy together . . . she's adorable, Tony. You mustn't be angry with her. It's such a cute, wonderful – oh, heavens, *umph*! – delish person. And, honestly, what a body it has – bless it! You never saw . . . I'm going to make love to her a little . . . she's my own good, dear, marvellous sweetie-pie. Look – take a load of that!'

She flung the clothes off for me to see, and I caught a glimpse – a miserly fleeting glimpse – of girlish nakedness, before the crazy, cringing little nincompoop grabbed them and covered herself up again to the neck.

'Oh, no, please! He mustn't!' she squealed, 'really he mustn't!'

I might have lost my temper there and then – but at a warning glance from Casilda I managed, with an effort, to control it for the present. I got back in beside them, but refrained with the utmost stoicism from all physical contact with either the nitwit pupil or her admirably industrious teacher. I sulked, in fact, while Cécile bristled with nervous hostility or suspicious caution, and Cassy did her stuff. She did it well, as I had foreseen – superlatively. It was not long before she had stoked the fire to a white heat. She had the hypocritical young hussy tossing and thrashing on the five-yard line in next to no time . . . Cécile gurgled and spluttered like a burst pipe. She did not know what she was saying or doing – or whom exactly she had to thank for what she was feeling. She moaned, she cried, she frankly howled for more – more! She entreated us not to stop, never ever stop. I took her at her word, now that she had changed her mind. I was devouring her tits. Glorious they were – hard, round, small, juicy and pink, like apples. I can't say, of their type, when I've tasted better. I was in love with my work – deliriously happy. Casilda wasn't letting up either. She was down there, guzzling away, gulping like a pig in a trough, feasting on the girl's slimy-spiced innards, hammer-and-tongs, putting her heart and soul into it, the gluttonous bitch, with all the gallant tenacity of a bulldog. I had the corner of one eye on her the whole time, it was fun watching her. Even then, with the three of us wallowing in our excitement like lunatics, my sense of humour nudged me, mentally jogged my elbow, to point out a ludicrous detail: she was a film star advertising some common brand of soap or cosmetics, her priceless, ideal countenance defaced by a guttersnipe's jest with the inappropriate addition of a thickly scrawled, twirling black moustache. In the circumstances I considered, all the same, that Cécile's lustrous fungus suited Casilda's style of beauty, for, as a silken, hirsute, androgynous adornment of her mannish upper lip, it was perhaps not entirely out of place. . . .

Her thoughts, it seemed ran parallel to mine. She wanted more definite offensive action on that cracked front that even she could offer. Cécile's clinging arms were linked about my neck and shoulders, to prevent me from abandoning her bosom. Casilda's free hand was frantically engaged in stiffening my morale for the assault. She knew, only too well, my sudden limitations, my maddening aptitude at the last moment for turning tail . . . this was no easy hurdle. I must be whipped past the sticking point, but yet not overshoot the mark. Disaster loomed ahead, if we failed through faulty timing . . . we were coming up to it now – a trifle too fast? She gave me the high sign, sending me off with a slap on the bottom. It's all yours . . . I got what she meant, I sprang up, as she rolled out of my way. She sat back on her haunches and in one quick movement pulled a pillow down under the girl's arse, lifting her squarely onto it and tugging the legs to either side, wide open, completely apart, as far as they would go. . . .

What screams! What an unholy hullabaloo! I was chilled, panic-stricken by the noise. I thought she was having a fit. I couldn't say when or how, but I let her go, eventually. It was beyond me. I did my best. I fell flat out with all my weight on the struggling, shrill, raucous bitch. I pressed and thrust and butted and pushed. I pinned her claws back out of my eyes, I muzzled her with my mouth. I did what I could to wind her, to keep her quiet – and Casilda helped. Casilda was a tower of strength. But there was nothing for it. I had to give up. I had pierced her slightly, the merest fraction. She wasn't even bleeding, though. Anyone would have sworn, I had deflowered her with a carving knife, to judge by the shindy she raised, the cowardly, snivelling, prudish little clot.

She sobbed and shuddered, she wept and whined and implored me to let her dress and go away. She used her tears – most unfairly – to retaliate and choke me off when I endeavoured to reason with her. Well, there it was. We sat around, the three of us, dejected, upset, baffled. Alternately she kept up a stony silence or babbled excuses and apologies in a repetitive rigmarole: she was sorry, it had been too much for her all at once; no man had ever seen her stripped, even, until I'd been so rough and cruel and horrid to her just now; she couldn't help it but I must be kind and have patience; why wouldn't I wait a little longer, because bit by bit, maybe, later on she might, after a time, in a different way, only not yet, not straight off like that; she was a virgin, and it had hurt terribly, dreadfully, she hadn't realised, she had no idea, though, of course she did know it would; so if I'd promise to be more gentle, when I asked her again, but now, please. . . .

'No, no, please no,' she droned. 'I can't – and you simply mustn't. I won't. Please not. . . .'

Did I have to lecture a grown girl on the harsher facts of life? I was too tired . . . in the rare previous cases when I'd come up against this minor but irksome chore of domestic surgery, the patient had the decency not to involve us in a distressing scene of futile tears and recriminations.

'It was for your own good,' I warned her, 'and you would be well-advised to take a hold on yourself and get it over, pretty soon – unless you want to end up a pathetic, desperate old lesbian like your mother.'

I suppose I should not have said that, although it was true: I wasn't thinking.

She blew up, sizzling with fury.

'What d'you mean? How dare you? Filthy, dirty beast! Anyway, you're far older than she is – old enough to be my grandfather, you evil lying brute!'

She clobbered me like a wildcat, scratching and screeching. I was too taken aback to defend myself. My lip was cut very painfully, and I could hardly see out of one eye. In a flash she leaped out through the curtains.

She had got most of her clothes on already when I caught up with her and hauled her back into the alcove. That was all right by me – it meant tugging her skirt off and fighting to pull her knickers down. Or were they Casilda's? No, they fitted those twin perky young pumpkins too smoothly and neatly, dotting them simply with embroidered specks and enhancing the general presentation with the sweetest blue bows at the side. It seemed a shame to remove so dainty a dish cover . . . but Casilda held her flat while I bared the rotund, cute, plump, childish bum of the Mademoiselle. Damn the rampageous, highborn little savage – she had whetted my appetite by her antics, she needed correction, she had it coming to her, she was in for it, to spare her would be to desist from my obvious duty. I did not weaken, I took a long-handled clothes brush to her. Severe chastisement, I grant – but it had the most salutary effect, in opposite ways, on the pair of us. Scarred and softened, roused and rampant, we were more attuned now to each other, properly equipped and receptive – or at any rate acquiescent. The rest was comparatively easy. We rolled her over, and Casilda rained kisses on her face and throat while I drew her down into position, half off the edge of the bed, lifted her knees towards the ceiling, and splayed them out at convenient angles, as the executioner steadies the block or widens the noose for his victim.

Cécile uttered a single piercing howl then she fainted clean away – which perhaps was fortunate.

Casilda brought her round, and nursed her, I'm sure, with the utmost solicitude, when I mooched off. To fill in time, I went to a movie.

X

Neither of us bothered any more about it, until the letter from Helen arrived, bearing a Paris postmark. I thought after the event that I had maligned Cécile, but here were my previous fears all too grimly confirmed. She had squawked to her mother straightaway, the shoddy little sneak. Helen needed to see Casilda urgently, at once, the letter said. Cécile had written to her in terrible distress and 'has told me all!'

We were glumly pondering on this pretty kettle of fish when the depraved young so-and-so herself rang up, in a dreadful state of penitence and confusion. No, she couldn't talk right now – but she had to explain, they simply must meet 'before you talk to Mummy.'

'I've already heard from her,' Casilda replied. 'She wants me to call immediately at an address in the Rue' – she glanced at the writing – 'Passy . . . oh, you're there too, are you? She has taken you away from school? No, I shall get in touch with her tomorrow sometime . . . yes, that's what she suggests. I gather you spilt the beans, and told her everything . . . all right, come around here, any time . . . yes, but I can send him out . . . oh, very well, but what's the use? Do you know? Then it wasn't awfully fair or sensible of you to give your mother the wrong ideas about us . . . you didn't? Are you sure? How much does she know in that case? I don't follow. Cécile! Listen – Cécile!'

'She hung up,' said Casilda. 'Helen even talks of putting her into a convent – imagine! But it seems she kept quiet about us – me and her at least – in her SOS to Mamma. You got the rap all to yourself, my boy – not me! Our little fling is our own precious, safely guarded secret – though I'll bet Helen guessed it, knowing her. I wish I could figure just what the story was – I'll have to get hold of the girl and find out.'

Casilda did not telephone Helen the next day – which was lucky, for two reasons: we got word from Janet, and Cécile hung up again, charily. Janet's news was very disturbing: she felt she ought to warn us without delay of the evil gossip she had picked up casually, from mutual friends, over cocktails. It appeared that for weeks now Helen had been spreading the most fantastic and atrocious slanders about us in London. She had assured anyone would would pass on the titbit that I fled the country with Casilda because I was wanted by the police for criminal assaults but of course Casilda had left me, for a Negro pianist, as soon as she discovered I was impotent and only got any pleasure from being unmercifully flogged – a whim which she was willing to indulge, at a price, until she got bored with such repellent, insane habits when I tried to turn pimp and live on her immoral earnings in Hamburg.

Janet's report made Casilda spit with fury. 'Helen is off her head,' she decided. 'How could she invent such foul crap about me? I'll get her guts for this! Malice is one thing, when old chums fall out – but this is downright calumny, and it stinks. She'll be sore and sorry after I've rubbed her nose in the shit! You're going to help me, too.'

Cécile's call was timely. She pressed again with quavering anxiety for an interview. 'I've dropped Helen a line to say I'll go round there about six o'clock, Sunday,' said Casilda. Oh, then couldn't she make it a wee bit earlier, Cécile begged, because Mother would not be back until that time from a visit to the elder Delavignes, and she wasn't keen on taking her along 'in the circumstances,' so Cécile would plead a headache or something and stay at home to wait for Casilda, who coldly agreed. 'That'll be lovely!' Casilda described their meeting to me afterwards. Cécile received her with tears of contrition, a gush of excuses, and open arms. She had a lot to say that was muddled and unimportant, but her mind was made up. 'I was as stern and ungracious as possible,' Casilda declared, 'but she led me straight through to her room, babbling fifteen to the dozen all the way and trying to kiss me, like some slick, hulking she-wolf, and before I knew it, there I was, flat as a pancake on her maidenly couch, with my skirts over my head and that young trollop was sucking me off, fit to beat the band, as if this was just what the doctor ordered. OK, my child, I thought, get your snub little snootful, now that you're at it, while the going's good. There was no stopping her, anyway – so I did my level best to last out long enough for Helen to come in and catch us red-handed. Can't you picture the scene? Wouldn't that have been perfect? As it was, the smart kid covered up all tell-tale traces before Mamma arrived – but I strolled out of the love nest, tidying my hair and purposefully plying a lipstick. . . . Helen wasn't going to be drawn, though. She ignored the ugly hint completely. It didn't suit her to quarrel with me, apparently – she had other ideas. The conversation started quite calmly, on the most normal note. I let her take the lead. She didn't expect to be taxed with her lies about us, I could see it rather shook her – but she denied them flatly. That is when we began to get a trifle heated. "Don't shout so!" she kept saying. I had cottoned on to the game by then – she really and truly hoped to win me round! We assumed she would be full of fire and breathing threats like a dragon, didn't we. Not at all! She never came out with it in so many words – but, believe it or not, she was ready to forgive me! She would take me back, and let bygones be bygones, if

I'd throw you away at once and return with her to London! Oh, yes, and Cécile, too, I suppose. Think of it – how extraordinary! – I lost my temper, I'm afraid, at this point – so she sent our innocent witness out of the room. To spare her blushes! "Go and lie down, Cécile – Cassy and I have to talk things over. Don't interrupt us till I call you – in a little while. . . ." Of course after that I led her on. I changed my tactics – slightly, not too, blatantly. I lit a cigarette and took a drink. "Very well then, Helen," I said, "let's have it out, heart to heart. Why do you hate me? Because I like sleeping with Tony, or because I won't go to bed with you any more, since you've taken against him? It's your own stupid fault, you have to admit. We gave you the chance – remember? – that night when he fucked you – " She sprang at me then. I had gone too far. I had used a rude word – and mentioned your name, in the same connection. I made to defend myself, all the time I'd been waiting for this attack . . . but I was wrong. Murder was not – obviously not – her intention. I struck her quite hard in the face as she leaped upon me – but her arms were round my waist, and as I was knocked off balance by this cannonball in the midriff, and fell backwards into a chair, she smothered me with kisses. She always was a passionate bitch, but now she was starved, incensed and crazy . . . I repulsed her as roughly as I could, with a slap that sat her down sobbing on the floor at my feet. We remained like that for a while . . . she had gone all to pieces. I looked at my watch. You were due to arrive any minute now, the way we'd timed it. So I spoke to her – just to see what she would do – a little less gruffly. "Off you go," I said. "If you want me that badly, get undressed." "Why? Don't make fun at me," she sniffled. "You don't love me . . ." "I'll show you how much," I told her. "But only this once – and no more, ever again; it'll be the end between us." Of course she couldn't understand or believe such a drastic ultimatum. "What about Cécile," she asked. I dared to taunt her – "Afraid she'll be jealous?" I sneered. It was too easy. I waved her out of the room. Helen, of all people! No shred of pride, no comeback, nothing. . . . She swallowed even that indignity. "Shoo!" I said. "Cécile won't mind – but we'll lock ourselves in. . . ." I waited a few minutes, left the front door ajar for you in the hall, went through to Helen, who was there naked on the bed – and the rest you know.'

The rest was a cannibal picnic, with Helen as the pièce de résistance. Casilda as high priestess of the cult, myself – the chief slave-trader – presiding, and Cécile served up as a tender green salad on the side. We did not invite her to the party, although she was mainly responsible for cooking up this whole mess. She nosed her way in, during the second course, when it got pretty rowdy – so she had to take the consequences of her spitefulness, curiosity, impertinence and deceit. She'd have raised the alarm, and made trouble if we had let her go. Casilda kept her promise. She allowed Helen a thorough good innings – without a murmur, as if inert submission to the labours of love was not the response Helen expected, at least it gave her a candid, bitter reply to her question, as well as the opportunity she so desperately desired. Cut to the quick, she rebounded her frantic efforts, cherishing without stint the flesh of the beloved, only to beat her brow against a blank wall of relaxed, almost comatose indifference, which drove her so nearly out of her wits that I arrived to find her digging her nails into Cassy's flanks and pummelling them with her clenched fists.

My entry broke up the sensual farce with the melodramatic denouement of a veritable deus ex machina. There was no need for a word to be spoken. Helen could have died on the spot from surprise. She gazed at me as though I were a ghost – a ghost with a horsewhip

– and at the bedroom key clutched in Casilda's hand, which showed her that she had been bamboozled. Like a rat she was trapped – and like a snake in the grass she tried to slither into cover next door. But Casilda seized the slender small body, slung it back struggling onto the springs, and grappled with it fiercely, lashing and twining in naked warfare as silent and sinister as the mere hiss, thud and cracking of twigs in a fight between a python and a cobra on film.

It was an exciting parody, in reversed positions, of their previous embrace; they shifted and tumbled through varying holds and poses, and as a carnal display of the female physique from all angles, one could not have wished for a finer spectacle. I sat entranced at the end of the bed, poring over this album of bawdy snapshots which was being shown to me like an illustrated catalogue of strength and beauty, a rare production that would have warmed Andrew's heart, I reflected, as much as mine. Not for the world would I have interfered to call down the curtain on such a lively and lovely ballet. I had come to this place as Casilda's ally. I was there to help her, with the allowed purpose of seeing that justice was done, that it did not miscarry. But Casilda herself was the avenger, the actual executioner; I was the solemn judge. It was she who felt so strongly about Helen's outrageous affronts to our honour. I meant merely to ensure fair play – and to take a hand in it perhaps, at some later stage of the proceedings, if the spirit moved me to act. At this point, I swear, I was content, as the onlooker, just to watch. . . .

It was a foregone conclusion: the odds against Helen were too heavily weighted, she did not stand a chance. I was almost glad, from the sporting point of view, when reinforcements turned up for her in the wild shape of Cécile – a flying column in a flowered cotton housecoat – who burst upon us, alerted now by her mother's cries, as if to rescue her in the nick of time. Casilda had forced her disloyal friend flat down on her face, I had tossed her the riding crop, since she was clearly the victor, and holding the slim bare back securely in place, with a knee on the nape of Helen's neck, she was about to thrash the living daylights out of her. The first couple of whams had landed at whistling speed with a dull thump that was instantly drowned by a shrill scream, which would echo too loudly through a respectable neighbourhood; though it was music to my ears, I cast around for some gag to stifle so strident a sound, or mute it at least to a more refined note that might pass for enjoyable revelry in the 16th arrondissement since Helen's own was evidently beyond protection . . . it was then that Cécile popped up – and flew at me! At me, the linesman, minding my own business! I shoved her off into the melee, where she belonged, the silly twat. She only upset everything, got buffetted about, all mussed, torn, scratched and womanhandled – and came bouncing back to me out of the scrum, straight in the pit of the fly-half's stomach. I spun her around and held her fast, with her elbows pinioned behind me so that, bent up close against her, I had the willowy little body with its jutting, pneumatic buttocks pressed to me tightly, moulded on my codpiece like a fruity plum pudding. But the meddling brat had knocked Casilda arse over tit, Helen slipped through her fingers, cutting loose in a flash of greased lightning across the room – and when she turned, glaring at us from the corner next to a chest of drawers, there was a revolver glinting in her hand.

It was a tense moment. Luckily Cécile happened to shield me in front to some extent – but she was woefully slight, there was scarcely anything of her. I was much the taller of the two, and had it not been for Casilda's mad, foolhardy impulse to fling herself forward in a headlong angry rush on Helen, wrestling the gun from

A Gallery of Nudes

her grasp, I might not have lived to tell the tale. As it was, Cassy emptied the pistol and we breathed again – but Helen wasn't joking, there was no damn doubt about it, that was certainly a very narrow shave.

Helen only had herself to blame. My blood was up now, the ugly fright she had just given us made me see red. I cheered and shouted encouragement to Casilda when she bundled the dazed Helen back onto the pillows, stuffed a nightdress into her mouth, and laid it on thicker than mustard, larruping the hide off her until her arm grew tired. I pushed Cécile nearer from the other side of the bed, to get a better look, and could not resist tipping her down over the edge, crossing her wrists across her shoulder blades, so that I had it all just where I wanted it and in two twos, with a mere flick of the hand, prettily exposed. This time there was no difficulty – at least I noticed none, or next to none. I backscuttled the girl at my ease, as she lay across the downy, facing Helen – and a glorious pair of martyrs they made, mewling, quivering and sprawling together like blind kittens in a basket, while we both exerted ourselves to the utmost, determined, while we were at it, that the lesson should sink in.

Yet it seemed to me that Cassy's vengeful rage soon burned itself out, for after roughly a score of strokes her whip hand wilted. Then she was struck by a brilliant idea. She rummaged in a drawer. 'I thought so!' she said. 'Always totes this around with her – our darling gadget. Never say die!' – and she produced a realistic rubber replica of the male organ, the hugest, toughest-looking dildo you ever saw, with leather straps dangling from it, which she affixed in a trice, changing sex automatically, with the great threat erected between her hips, like a flagpole or an ack-ack gun planted on a mound of golden gorse.

'Ladies and gentlemen,' Casilda proclaimed 'I am pleased, nay, honoured to inaugurate this splendid and expensive subway, which I hereby declare open for public use.'

Without further ceremony she rammed the monstrous contraption home in Helen's cunt almost jolting her upright on that hefty lever in the process. I had my work cut out to prevent her raising the roof and to keep her, like a captive balloon, from snapping her guide ropes and sailing away into space. This exciting tussle made a new man of me, though – and once I had quieted her down a bit. I managed to deal with Cécile in similar, simultaneous but much milder fashion, vying with Casilda in an orgy that reduced us all to mincemeat before we had done.

'Well, we put them through their paces,' said Casilda. 'Let's go.'

It was safe to leave them now: they would not, be getting up to any serious mischief again for a while. So we scrammed. The sullen, damp drizzle chilled us in the Rue Passy.

XI

There was method in our badness. Operation Vineyard had been planned beforehand in detail: it covered one hour of reckoning with the Delavignes, our prompt departure from Paris, and the sunny southward trip to start our summer holiday. I was in funds again, we were taking Sister Anne with us, Casilda had been loaned a villa by the sea in Spain on a generously indefinite lease, everything in the garden was lovely. To hit the road in the Citroën was like riding the crest of a wave.

The hideout we were headed for was a film star's weekend residence that belonged to her director-husband (number three) a former pal of Casilda's and a sweeter sugar daddy than most. Her rollick with him during her first marriage probably owed its success to her having played, for once in her life, hard to get. It was among her least humdrum experiments, and when we ran into him at Maxim's with his wife, the exquisite, dumb, pampered Gloria Gilmour, he recognised his old split with genuine relief and gratitude. That single sentimental reunion may have sufficed to work the oracle (as Casilda always doggedly maintained). I don't rightly know, but in view of how much talk there was, when we joined them at dinner, about 'this Spanish bungalow of Gloria's that's just going begging,' I prudently made myself scarce the next couple of nights, because if Paris was worth a Mass, it seemed to me Putonas was a fair swap for the trifling loan of a temporary poacher's licence. Schminsk himself ('call me Milt') had picked the place up for a song, he explained, but would be filming in Italy till August, though Gloria might drop over to relax between contracts maybe ('she's off my hands, on Sid Cleanfart's payroll'), which should suit us all OK, he guessed, as the cottage was plenty big enough – it had everything and was kind of cute – so they would both be very, very happy to have us utilise it, anytime. 'Rope in a few houseguests,' he advised; 'I'd sure hate those lazy dago servants not to earn their keep.'

Anne naturally headed the list. Later, as there were six bedrooms at El Delirio, we hoped the Mackenzies would come to stay with us awhile. But for the present, after the trying, long winter, the prospect of two or three months of utter idleness in the heat, under clear blue skies on the beach or in the scented shade of the pines, had us cavorting and chortling from sheer joy all the way. We had shaken the city's dust off our heels, which soon would sink into pure sand, a load of worry had slipped like a halter from our necks, and for full measure, to top perfection, there was Anne – life was beginning anew.

No problem at all, our little sister, but a fascinating, bright fresh page, one that I had not turned to date . . . it made my mouth water to think of the journey ahead, the moonlit nights and drowsy, sun-filled days, the torrid siesta, the naked, baked prostration, gasping with the gorgeous sweat of sex, that alone stirring, burning, full-blooded, wine-fortified, real and rampant within the dark secrecy of shuttered rooms. We had run Sister Anne to earth only the week before – and here we were now, launched on the wings of adventure, with a ravishing, romantic idyll in the bag, bound for a treasure trove on distant shores that stretched away in vistas of delight. The moment I met Anne I had said:

'She must come with us – we'll take her too.'

'We will, too,' Casilda agreed. 'Sure thing. We two will take her – no?'

Then, after a thoughtful pause, she added: 'I never have . . . but I don't mind the idea – of being half-incestuous. She's only my half sister. There can't be much wrong with that.'

She read my unspoken query.

'Oh, her – she won't care,' Casilda said.

Nor did she – not in the least. Casilda was right, as usual. Anne made a heavenly change from some other stuffy punks I could mention. There was nothing of the tough swell dame about her, either. In every way, down to the last and most personal particulars, she was no Gloria, and she had nothing, so as you would notice, in common with Helen or Cécile – or even Janet. A wholesome trollop – gay, good-natured, and vastly entertaining. As unspoiled as a spring flower plucked in a woodland glade, as refreshing as a gin fizz or the brine-laden breeze, as plump as a partridge, sweet as a pigeon – and promiscuous as only the devil or she herself could be. She had beauty, youth, health and high spirits, with the humour and the unconscious charm that goes with them – the amoral animal quality which even Casilda's gay temperament, lacked, or had lost with the years. Here was the milk of human kindness in purest form, on the counter, nourishing, creamy and curiously good – in limitless supply. She was admirable as well as adorable; no man could help liking her.

Anatomically, for my taste, she was perhaps just a shade too buxom, and I preferred Casilda's less vivid, more subtle colouring – but with her poster curves and her brilliant vitality (a 'vulgar appeal,' Helen might say, as distinct from 'sensual allure') it was clear that Anne, like her sister, would look better for artist-friends as a model – and at Putonas we both intended to paint. Anne was a corn-yellow blonde, where Casilda was merely fair-skinned, and the fur of her pussy was deep orange, like some cats' – or marmalade thickly spread in a triangle on buttered toast.

That breakfast relish I discovered betimes – on our first stop for the night. We dined superbly, and on our cheerful return to the hotel, Casilda slid an arm round her sister's waist, as we climbed the stairs, asking point-blank: 'So which is it to be, toots – cock or cunt?'

Anne actually had the grace to blush – but she found the choice altogether too hard, as one might have known, and plumped in the end for both. A born good lay in her own right, she erred if anything on the side of excessive zeal and impatience – a fault in the right direction, as nobody will deny – and showed herself never averse to learning a few special, invaluable extra tricks of the trade from her sister's wider experience. The teacher-to-pupil relationship was a source of happy amusement to me during our Spanish journey – and it may have saved my bacon, what's more, because Casilda's tuition gave me a much-needed rest now and again, whereas without such peaceful intervals I might not have survived the first carefree month of our tri-angular exertions. Anne – bless her warm heart and even hotter you-know-what – soon became something of a handful which, single-handed, would have floored me for the count.

I hit on a grand solution, however. Jeremy, my son at Oxford, would be the answer to a maiden's prayer and a middle-aged man's problem. He would leap at the chance of such a stunning vacation, little knowing what he was in for. It was arranged by cable that we should collect him off the train at Jodete. I hardly recognised the lanky, solemn yet engaging youth, with his good clean looks, his slight shy stammer and his sedate air, as my own small bastard whom I had not seen for years. Nobody would have said that his mother was the sass-iest Irish barmaid I ever met. We tried to liven him up over a healthy lunch at an inn on the way back, with

A Gallery of Nudes

lashings of rough red wine. Jeremy had a strong head, but I despaired of his ingrained diffidence. We drove off into the sweltering afternoon, with the sun overhead like a blowtorch. Casilda was dozing, barelegged, on the rear seat. Anne, for some reason best known to herself, had elected to squeeze up in front between Jeremy and myself when we set out again, though she would have been more comfortable, as before, sitting at the back with her sister.

'She wants to snooze,' Anne explained to me confidentially, and at once dropped off into an oblivious, somnolent state of digestion, herself, with head lolling, crucified arms stretched out behind us, east and west. After a while, with one hand on the wheel, I laid the other on her knee, starting to stroke the left thigh, slid gently tapping, probing, skating fingers under her pleated grey linen skirt, and dipped them into the thicket of soft brambles that guards the hidden, brackish well of love's delight, the spring of life itself. Anne's adoration of the sacred mysteries was not by any means a secret or a selfish cult. Opening her legs, she welcomed the intrusion with as glib a grace as if no tourist had been admitted past the turnpike to visit this famed grotto during the recent 'off' season. That I knew to be untrue. But I was not alone on the excursion. Pretending at first not to notice, eyes fixed straight ahead into the glare, Jeremy hovered. He fidgeted, gulped, his mouth was dry. Anne stretched and mumbled, settling herself at ease, but did not wake. Emboldened faintly by her tact and a broad wink from me, eventually his hand started up the smooth path in gingerly pursuit, on the opposite side of the gulch, timidly following the beaten track, yet venturing after my lead no further than about halfway. We each had a leg to ourselves, but I was already waiting, though not idly, at the crossroads, where, if only he would join me, we could divide the spoils to everyone's greater satisfaction, including

Anne's. He did not want to gatecrash, to go too far. He stopped dead, or lingered and kicked his heels, then crept forward again, testing the terrain as cautiously as an advance patrol, not a mere forage party. He was a very raw recruit indeed, new to this front, evidently, but guided by an old scout he did his duty like a man and ended the campaign a credit to his instructor. Meeting me up there at last, entrenched athwart the tiny milestone, he pushed along the low road while I took the high road, dividing our labours in a combined, two-fisted operation, for as he vigorously frigged her quim, I tossed her off, lightly rubbing her clitoris with my most gentle touch. We blended our endeavours to perfection – basso profundo, pizzicato – and were rewarded by so delirious an ovation that Casilda awoke in alarm, crying: 'Look out! Careful – damn you, Tony, pull up!'

Anne was already madly vociferous over her enjoyments; you could hear her coming for miles around. She copulated altogether like a jungle cat. I braked in a patch of shade, and she was gone almost before the car halted, tumbling out at once with Jeremy into the sparse, dusty clump of trees by the roadside. Casilda smiled. 'Quick off the mark,' she commented.

'It's amazing,' I said, 'but, d'you know, I think the boy is a ruddy virgin . . . at nineteen!'

'No! Well, for Heaven's sakes! Ought we to supervise?'

'It would probably put him off his stroke. Anne can cope. He'll be all right.'

But we went in the end. Curiosity got the better of us. And he was far from all right. They seemed to be making an awful mess of it. Even through a thick carpet of pine needles, the ground was baked hard. He had cleared some away, but the place was littered with rocks and thorns. 'Maybe scorpions, too,' Casilda remarked cheerfully, in a hollow tone, squatting beside them. Anne, flushed and grimly silent, was near to tears. He was sprawling awkwardly on top of her, his shirttails fluttering, but otherwise there was little movement. It was a sad picture. Both were half clothed, looking dirty and crumpled. His face was distraught, and pouring with sweat. Anne's head was turned to show a scowling profile as she stared at some insects scurrying among the stones. He must have wasted a great deal of time to reach this piteous stalemate before we got there, without apparently having progressed at all. It was a plain case of premature ejaculation, one could tell that at a glance. Poor chap, the excitement she had provoked in him by the novelty of such yielding, unabashed sexual contact in the car had burned his fingers, yet when confronted with the gaudy flower of the open female flesh, known to him solely by its sticky touch, his blood ran hot and cold in waves of sharp desire, sick shame, fear and nervous haste. By waiving the romantic preliminaries of a delayed approach to what Swinburne calls the 'foliage-hidden fountainhead' itself, the crazy, cocksure tart had unmanned him with the unadorned revelation of a tremendous gift that took his breath away. No doubt he strove to tarry awhile before entering the haven that was both a refuge and a whirlpool in one, as he well realised – only to foul the shallows, a buffeted and broken wreck on his maiden voyage. He had blurted out his brief, pretty speech too soon, and now remained there, quaking, a piteous victim of stage fright, unable to withdraw. . . .

Casilda went to the rescue, without demur. She rolled Jeremy's loose-limbed, doleful corpse, like a shot rabbit's, to one side, and flopped down next to him, after folding his trousers as a bolster which she wedged beneath Anne's bottom. For me, in my frisky condition at that propitious moment, it was an opportunity not to be missed. While Casilda fiddled with the young fellow's pathetic, conked-out periscope, seeking to repair it to the point where he would get a less glossy view of life, I ripped off my pants, and also Anne's sports shirt and bra, which robbed me of the view and feel of her exuberant bosom, whetted her appetite again by knocking at the door very formally for admittance, then shut it tight behind the visitor by crushing her fat thighs together on my ballocks – like lackeys huddling outside on the porch – and topped her soundly in that position: the double nutcracker.

Casilda was making up to Jeremy for his sorry debacle with solicitous care, and the lucky blighter profited most emphatically from both her frank hand-to-mouth treatment and the object lesson that Anne and I laid on for him, with several interesting variations, at close range. Casilda allowed the callow youth to reciprocate her kindness to some extent – chiefly for his own sake, as an indirect means of spending his renascence and bringing him up to scratch. He watched us deep in coition, goggling with envy, and gesticulated to convey his readiness to require the services that had pulled him around, hand over fist, by pleasuring Cassy there and then. He would have wallowed all afternoon in that dingy copse, which was an oven, thinking to stuff Casilda first and have enough spunk on tap for Anne when I got through with her. A boy's bravado! Why weep over spilled milk if there's plenty more to be had for the asking? His effrontery infuriated me, such fantastic assurance was unbearable! Yet I was to discover during those next few weeks something I had forgotten since I myself was his age – that Jeremy's ever-readiness to tumble a dame at any time and just as often as he chose (once he caught the knack of it) was no empty boast or flight of ambitious fancy. What he lacked in finesse (he had none) as a lover, he could supply without stint in activity between the sheets; call it mere manpower, rather than stamina – it produced much the same result in the long run. The short, sharp bash was his speciality, and his stock of such fleeting favours appeared inexhaustible, which suited Anne, and others like her, truly down to the ground. His impudent pounce on Casilda was not rebuffed but eluded; he was fobbed off by her uncommon talent for masturbation. 'Not now, thank you, Jeremy dear,' she smiled, as a long, thin thread of his seed spurted, like a rope of scattering pearls, over the stubbly soil. 'That will do to go on with. Between us all, we'll make a man of you tonight. . . .'

There was a wire from Janet at the house: Andrew could not get away, but she could come out alone for a bit next month. Anne was in a somewhat disgruntled mood still, which was extremely unlike her, and she complained morosely that we needed a couple more men, maybe – he-men – but certainly not another skirt around the place. An argument started between the two sisters, whose nerves twanged like guitar strings, and was kept up as bitchily as possible through evening drinks and dinner. I was deeply flattered, for it was plain to be seen where the trouble lay; now that I had lassoed Jeremy into the party, Casilda and I obviously would be tucking up on our own again, leaving Anne to do as best she might with this almost beardless boy of mine. She rebelled against the arrangement, which struck her as grossly unfair. She couldn't expect Cassy to give me up or consent to take Jeremy on in part exchange, and the thought that our gay little threesomes were already over, almost before they had begun, sent her round the bend with disappointment and wounded pride. She felt she'd been tricked, and claimed we were lousy, inconsiderate heels, guilty of deceitful discrimination in palming her off on a stranger. Misguided as it was, her attitude showed she was nuts about me, and Casilda bore out this highly complimentary conclusion when, strolling down to the sea, behind the other couple, for a midnight dip, she assured me that I was more than a match for any young puppy she had ever encountered in the lists of love. 'There's no pro like an old pro, darling,' she said. 'It doesn't take much to deflate one of these boisterous whippersnappers, soon as look at him. Jeremy is sweet. Give him time. But cheer up – if I ever go in for baby-snatching, I'll loiter around the pink cots, I expect, not the blue. Maturity is my motto – in men and wine.'

This touching testimonial lifted a load off my mind. Jealous pangs had assailed me already, at this early stage of our happy holidays at El Delirio, and I cursed myself for overlooking the potential dangers of a tricky situation when I summoned Jeremy so blithely to my aid, I had thought only of securing a measure of relief from Anne's exhausting demands, but stupidity did not envisage the likelihood of the boy wanting to sample Casilda's charms as well – which doubtless he might prefer, after tasting and comparing the two lays. It would be devilishly awkward if he pressed for a swap-over, snaffling my girl and landing me for keeps in that other promiscuous floozy's arms – or even if, more reasonably, he insisted on the general family principle of share and share alike. Four might turn out to be a lot worse company than three. On the very first day that the kid showed up – until Casilda quelled my fears – I got a nasty feeling that I had put my foot in it.

I need not have fussed at all, as it turned out. Everything went swimmingly. I mean that we swam, Casilda and I, to the raft moored in the middle of the bay – and there, glistening in the moonlight like fish awash on a slab, we came upon the youthful pair still swimming, as you might have said, in different styles, back stroke and breast stroke, on the sodden matting-covered planks. She had broken him in – that was abundantly clear. They paid no heed to us, though afterwards we all struck out for the shore together, chatting easily, when they were through with their thumping, noisy, rather less hurried poke, and there, lying naked in the sand dunes, they elected to stay a little longer under the stars, while Casilda and I trailed off home.

Later, Anne made a pretty gesture of amends, looking into our room to kiss us goodnight. She yawned and, as she stretched, her bathrobe swung open, like curtains, to reveal that flaming orange patch that now shone lighter in shade against her beautifully bronzed, toasted body, smooth and gleaming like a freshly painted hull, with the two dark scarlet beacons topping the summits of the hard, high, rounded hills, the small speck of her navel – and here and there a deeper stain traced by someone's bruising bites at her throat, abdomen and thighs.

'Know what?' she said. 'I'm – hmm! – as happy as those sand-girls you read about, folks. Oh boy, have I had a coupla grand fucks since we all went for that lil' swim!'

I did not object to Casilda exciting the boy on occasion: it amused her as a pastime, and I saw no harm in it, if he craved any extra solace or the added spice of variety. So long as she stopped short of actually getting herself screwed by him, I let them monkey around to their hearts' content. We frequently joined forces, so to speak, or hopped back and forth between beds. It was ideal for me: I had Anne whenever I wanted her – not often, but sometimes during the siesta hour, on a walk through the woods, at night by the water's edge, and once standing in the sea, with her back pressed against a rock and the waves lapping up to our chins. . . . We had just finished a quickie before lunch, I remember, the day Gloria arrived. That was on a bench in the hall, because the maid, Conchita, was laying the table, Gloria narrowly missed stumbling over us. She had not announced her visit.

I paraded my party straightaway, while she was changing, and read them a lecture on seemly behaviour now that the lady of the house was our guest. 'Lovemaking will be strictly confined to our bedrooms,' I ordered, 'and grinds outdoors must take place beyond earshot.' We lived model lives from then on – which was just as well, for I soon discovered that the famous film-star's icy temperament utterly belied her luscious, captivating looks. Gloria Gilmour was as cold, glossy and blank as a coloured picture postcard of some exotic beauty spot. By repute among her fans she was one of priceless wonders of the modern world. The figure (36–24–36) was perfect, and she displayed it freely, all too generously, with innate cruelty and practised grace. Every pose was studied, sensually intoxicating, obnoxiously refined – but if one could tear one's eyes away from the tantalising, scantily clad marvel of her physique, the divine, unearthly radiance of that pure and lovely face was still more blinding to behold. In the sultry seclusion of her palatial home at Putonas this sacred goddess, the idol of a million male moviegoers, walked about in next to nothing but her make-up. Yet, incredible as it seemed to me – and also, as I subsequently learned, to Jeremy – she was frigid. She gazed right through you with a huge, uncomprehending, cowlike stare if you so much as tried, by any possible means of approach, however devious, to mention or even hint at the subject of sex. The very fact of the mating urge did not exist for her. The mind within that platinum dome was two-dimensional – like her bright image on the screen. The gorgeous, natural, palpable shape which she inhabited was merely the mocking, transient reality of a dream. I made several earnest passes at it – totally in vain. She never noticed. She moved away and talked of something else, or left the room.

I was so puzzled that I took Casilda into my confidence on the matter. She had reminded me that Janet was due the next day. 'I can't see those two hitting it off,' said Casilda. 'Not for five seconds. It's a pity we mustn't let ourselves go at all, with Gloria in the house. I was looking forward to quite a bit of fun with Janet. We could have had a hell of a fine old orgy . . . listen – I have an idea. There's a big bullfight on tomorrow for the fair at Jodete. Why don't you take Gloria to it? Tell her it'll be good publicity for her to be seen ogling a matador, like all the other Hollywood hoodlums.'

'Jeremy's going,' I said. 'That's better still – he can escort her. Though, as a matter of fact, she an absolute iceberg. I'm positive that the only portion of her anatomy that we haven't been shown just isn't there. Between the legs she is made the same way as a statue. She's not normal in the least. I believe she is not a woman at all.'

When I had finished telling Casilda my woeful tale of failure, she burst out laughing.

'Tony, how funny you are!' she gurgled. 'I had never given it a thought – but I guarantee you're wrong. Maybe she is undersexed – but if you passed her over to me, I'd seduce her for you. I don't suppose she has ever tried it with a woman – but she detests men. You can tell at a glance she has never fallen for anybody. She's not a virgin, of course – except perhaps where us girls are concerned. And even so, I wouldn't be too sure . . . she'd need a lot of rousing, and someone to make love to her, getting nothing in return. I might have a shot one of these days. Is it a bet?'

Jeremy got Gloria off to a fairly early start, and we three plodded up from the beach for a late Spanish luncheon in time to save a famished, waiting Janet from collapse. Before dusk, between the afternoon sleep and the drinking hour at sunset, we showed Janet around and bathed. Casilda was overjoyed to see her again and quite shameless in selling the pair of potential lovebirds to each other, as though licking her lips at the prospect of piloting them both into bed with us at truly indecent speed. I felt obliged to chide her for pestering Janet.

'Sure, I'm slavering at the mouth,' she replied. 'I can't sit still. You don't mind how frank I am about it, do you, Janet precious? Since Jeremy has been with us, we've been as hetero as the dickens, of course, and – oh, come on, let's skip dinner. Tony, tell Conchita the ladies are too tired to eat. . . .'

In fact we had an excellent supper, but did not linger over it, though Anne and I took our coffee without undue haste. I lit a cigar.

'So long,' Anne suddenly said, and vanished.

I allowed her five or six minutes by my watch before going in from the terrace. The two great tawny cats had Janet's lean carcass stretched out across the broad, bare expanse of sheet, and were gobbling her up alive; her whole body shuddered slightly, or at times shook with a deeper spasm, the knuckles of one fist were rapping on the clenched teeth between the grimacing, twisted lips of a tragic mask, a mask of exquisite pain, while the other hand clutched now at arm's length the empty air, now at her own or someone else's tresses. The staring eyes in a head that rolled from side to side were fixed on space, and the faint, continual sound that issued from her throat was the soft, dying, querulous bleat of some exhausted animal. I drank in every detail of the scene with an avidity to equal that of the pair of officiating sisters, whose cleft behinds, like lunar landscapes, vast, glowing, smooth save for that one dark central furrow, presented themselves both to my caressing fingers conveniently enough in their kneeling posture, if I spread my arms wide . . . Anne's turn came next, and I was making free with Janet's boyish rump when the headlights of a fast-moving car swept round a bend on the coast road and shone in through the window. The others were back! Fortunately I had not yet undressed, but only had to do up my fly.

Gloria was alone. Jeremy had met some friends, who would drop him off on their way home, they did not know when – but later. She had left them to their own devices. I could guess what had transpired. Gloria, for her, was almost ruffled – while looking outwardly as cool as ever.

'These Spaniards!' she snapped. 'That bullfighter attempted to paw me! Where are the girls?'

'In bed.'

'What, already? It's not eleven yet. . . .'

'Our friend Janet has arrived, you know.'

'Does that explain it? I'd have thought, on the contrary, you would all have stayed up later perhaps than usual. . . .'

'Well, no. . . .' I edged along the terrace. The noise in our room echoed in my ears. She would not be listening for it, of course, but any time now, I was afraid, the sonorous Anne (what rotten luck – wouldn't you know it'd be Anne on the rack at this moment?) might raise the roof with one of her blood-curdling shrieks of pleasure. I must muffle her somehow, before that happened. I turned to dive indoors. 'Goodnight,' I said.

Gloria followed me. 'Don't go,' she almost pleaded. 'Stay here awhile – if they're all asleep, at this hour.' Her tone was petulant. 'Listen, I know he'll be along, I couldn't shake him off, he's after me – that awful bullfighter, Jeremy's soul mate. I refused to dine with them. But he is bringing Jeremy back to serenade me. He swore he would, and that I couldn't resist him. They mustn't find me here alone. I'm frightened.'

'But that's ridiculous!' I scoffed. 'If Jeremy picked up this matador fellow, and made a chum of him, and they got drunk together – well, all right, what of it? We will send the Spaniard about his business pretty quick – and I'll deal with Master Jeremy in the morning.'

'You don't understand. There are dozens of them – his troupe or something.'

'Well, then look here – let's wake the servants.'

'Conchita and the old couple? They're no damn use.

No, the only thing would be safety in numbers. A bunch of us – foreigners, aloof and superior, a group of aristocratic foreign ladies. That'd keep them in their place. I must get those girls up. They'll have to help me.'

Before I could stop her, deaf to my entreaties – and deaf also to the fully audible psalm of Anne's raving pleasure, Gloria strode along the passage, knocked at two doors, opened them, and found both rooms empty. She turned to me accusingly, with an incredulous, perplexed look, biting the ripe cherry of her lower lip. I jerked my head towards the sounds emanating from farther down the corridor, and led her gently to them by the hand.

Probably I was as surprised as Gloria to see the trio lying there in a row, as good as gold, with a sheet drawn up to their chins. They may have heard our footsteps outside, and evidently they were resting between rounds, but in any case the sight of the three innocent heads on the pillows, if one ignored the tousled, matted hair, the flushed, smeared faces, the feverish light in the eyes, made a quaint, comical, appealing impression of a somewhat salacious fairy tale or into the senior girls' dormitory. Gloria's impeccable features, that oval countenance resembling beauty's permanent image in a mirror, reflected only sheer bewilderment as she and I gazed down in silence at the three prone, shrouded figures laid out on the bed, as it were for our inspection. We were surveying the snowy mountain scene, with its high peaks, soft slopes and hollows, from an aircraft on a night flight thousands of feet above those mysterious, lofty ranges in the stillness of the moon-filled room. No one spoke. An introduction seemed called for. I ought to say:

'You have not met Janet Mackenzie. This is the famous Gloria Gilmour.'

Instead, on the impish spur of the moment, with the

sudden speed of a conjuring trick I whipped back the sheet to uncover the three naked graces, and swiftly rounded off their sleight of hand by hoisting a whole forest of waving legs in the air, like the circus trainer who puts his team of prancing horses through their act. Hey-presto! There – I had shown her the very gist of the matter. She could take her pick. What more could anyone ask than this ravishing choice of targets? Like a barker at the fair, I was inviting Gloria to view the special attractions of my private, astounding, magnificent booth, the original, the authentic Aunt Sally. I catered to all tastes. Where was the gourmet who would turn up his nose at such an array of ripe red fruit so prettily set in charming nests of dark and light and yellow moss?

Helen's dainty black and white – perfect of its type – was absent, out of the running; but Gloria's palest golden loveliness would complete my colour scheme most admirably. All these bodies were brown, with no discordant note among them: only in shade and shape did they vary with that bounteous natural variety which the connoisseur of the nude seeks, appraises and values, as the salt of the earth, in his collection of masterpieces. Visually, Gloria's stunning contribution would make the four-in-hand a marvel beyond price, a bouquet beggaring all description. She would top the bill, wiping the floor – I hoped – even with these notable rivals. Here Venus stood at my elbow – *hors concours* – while Juno, Minerva and Psyche lounged on the bed, awaiting the judgement of Paris.

There was an unbearable interval. Gloria hesitated. I was tongue-tied. The others did nothing. It was better for me to efface myself – but somebody must put a stop to this appalling impasse of coyness and confusion.

'You're safe here from any visitors, Gloria,' I said. 'The girls will protect you. But you should be naked, too, like them. They want to see you as you really are.'

The call to duty before an audience worked like a spell. Automatically, calmly, the complaisant Gloria threw off her voluminous lime-green stole, unfastened the low-necked raw silk dress that matched her tan, and emerged from wisps of lingerie, as a snake sheds its skin, more dazzling than a candle flame, and as bare – except for a cache-sexe the size and colour of a fig leaf. This object, in the expectant pause that followed, she made no move to discard. Uncoiling with insolent languor from the bed, Casilda knelt up, plucked at it inquiringly, and drawled:

'What happens under that thing? Are you shaved?'

The fat was in the fire now, in every sense, and the fur flew. Not that the baffled, bullied Gloria put up much resistance. Morally and physically she was overwhelmed. Casilda snapped her G-string and pushed her, struggling wildly, into the scrum. She went down like a ninepin, and though for a time she tried to escape, protesting and wriggling, shouting and straining. I noticed that she fought cleanly, gamely, without resorting to violence. Not once did she kick, scratch or bite the milling bodies that enveloped her in the fleshy toils of their fiercely lascivious embrace. Janet took the least active part in the scrimmage; hers was mainly, like mine, a watching brief, though she weighed the scales in the two sisters' favour by helping at times to curb, quiet or comfort the progressively less reluctant victim of their unsparing ardour. Gloria's strength of will was sapped, it began to weaken, ebbing away under the ubiquitous pressure of the attack, which drained from her all sensation save that of intimate, increasing surrender. Casilda's persuasive tongue was licking her into shape. The odds were with the big battalions. Gloria's soothing defeat was inevitable, and she accepted it, when it came, in the spirit of a deliverance to be celebrated with a thankful, almost victorious clamour.

The truce did not last long, however. I, at least, if not

Casilda, had misjudged the peculiar sexual proclivities and foibles of our hostess at El Delirio. Hers was a split personality. Chilly and unwilling undoubtedly she was – but Casilda had found the only way to her heart. Once roused, there was no holding her. She was a lesbian masochist. Women she loved, but she wanted them rough. It was seldom that she got what she wanted: they were all too kind. In her calling she dared not risk disfigurement – but she longed to be hurt or at any rate mauled, dominated, overpowered. Men's brutality disgusted her, and everything else about them; she spurned and despised the swine. I was kept at arm's length that night. I scarcely managed to lay a finger on her – except in the thick of the fray. For it was a white night with a vengeance that continued until dawn – an untrammelled orgy whose vivid succession of separate episodes would fill a book. Yet how could one separate them? My wearied member loses the thread of events in a tangled skein, a topsy-turvy, rough-and-tumble heap of twitching bodies and jerking limbs, in a crazy, flashlit sequence of clinches, as those four insatiable females tussled together, grunting, gasping, cursing, groaning, and always changing sides, with first one, then another gaining the upper leg. No sooner were Janet and I making love to Anne, after that first bout of theirs with Gloria, I remember, than Gloria fell upon Casilda, athirst for revenge . . . that is how it started – and it ended, long hours later, in a five-flowered daisy chain, a ring-around-a-rosy that ran, I think, head to tail, like this: Casilda – Gloria – Anne – Janet, and me. . . .

Yes, that indeed was the end, little as I guessed it at the time. We fell asleep where we lay, on the bed or the floor. But there wasn't much room for us all – not for comfort. It was too much for me. I am not as young as I was . . . I went and tossed down somewhere else, undisturbed. Conchita woke me the next afternoon.

There was nobody in the house. They had all gone, she said. The villa El Delirio was empty. Only my car in the garage – they had not taken that. Casilda and Gloria had left together, and Jeremy had eloped with Anne – in Janet's Sunbeam. And Janet? I asked. Oh, the new senorita had departed with my great namesake, Antonio Carajo, the matador, the Lad from Jodete.

That was seven months ago. I am alone now – still alone. But it can't last. I did have a sort of little affair with Conchita – quite a pretty girl, though simple. She stripped well . . . of course it won't last. How could it? Casilda will come back to me. I know she will.

The Town Bull

Preface

When I, Bob Stirling, was born, Venus was just risen from the bed of Mars and filled with amorous satisfaction, and she may have looked down as I uttered my first weak cry, and, as a return for the joys with which she was still panting, gone onto the altar and as grateful offering prayed:

Sweet Priapus, may this child born at the climax of my happiness with Mars be richly endowed by thee, that the earthly woman may know and taste the sweets of his godlike image of thy scepter.

I say something like this must have happened, for when I was adolescent I developed manly qualities that my lady friends vow they have never seen equaled; and although I am modest, I am too polite to contradict them, and I therefore write you a 'Tale of my Tail.'

I

At twenty-one I was a clerk at a good salary in New York, spending money freely on wine and women, until one of the Wall Street panics shook the whole business community and I found myself stranded with only a few dollars left in my pocket. I paid my landlady and asked her to keep my trunk for a few days. I strolled out to seek some cheaper lodgings and to try to find some new employment.

As I wandered through the fashionable promenades, the brilliant electric lights shone on a scene that I knew full well, and on many a free and easy woman into whose good graces my pocketbook had been an open sesame. But now, what had I to do with them?

They were earning their living – so why harbor ugly thoughts of them, if they passed me by; rather, leave this brilliant scene and go into the byways, where pocketbooks were as slim as my own.

As I wandered through the dingy streets of the East Side, I was thirsty. No half-bottle of Roederer now – a glass of beer must suffice me, and I went into one of those small German saloons that abound in that quarter – a few bottles of cheap wine, a keg of beer, and a woman fair, fat, and forty, were the entire table of contents.

The buxom proprietress served me a foamy mug and chatted pleasantly while she quaffed one herself. She seemed to take a deep interest in me, and thinking that she might by some chance know of a suitable lodging, I asked her.

'Why,' she said, 'I am alone here, and back of the shop there are two bedrooms; if you like, I'll show you one of them.'

'I would like to look at it.'

'Well, we will have to shut up the shop first, it is getting late; you just lock the door and pull down the shades while I wash the glasses.'

And as I turned the key in the lock, I looked back to see her leaning over the low sink, busily washing. By jove! What an expanse of buttocks I beheld, what a magnificent pair of legs! The Town Bull was ready to serve!

'Ah, my dear, your splendid bum and legs have made me as stiff as a poker!'

'Go away!' she said, and then, changing her tone, she continued: 'You haven't seen them yet; would you like to?' and before I could answer, the lively woman, still leaning away from me, pulled her skirt up to the middle of her back and I was handling buttocks as luxurious and rosy as any that Rubens ever painted, and my fine erection was poking them in a jiffy.

'Wait a moment, this ain't comfortable!' And straightening up, the now eager woman lifted her clothes to her waist and threw herself back on the table. As my prick entered her, she exclaimed: 'Lord, what a big prick you have!'

As I worked my spigot hard and fast in her bunghole, she sighed and wriggled and called me a splendid diddler, and her juicy spendings oozed all around my prick, just as the foamy beer does round the spigot as it is driven.

Her heaving belly quickened; then as I left her it began to quiet. I sat opposite to her, gazing at her richly developed charms, and she continued to praise the way I fucked her and jumping up, said: 'Come, let's go to bed.' In a twinkling she showed me into the small room, and both stark naked, we mounted the bed.

She was not bad, a mountain of fruity, firm flesh, not too heavy yet, but lively as a young girl who is just beginning to know the fun of tickling.

'Oh, but what a whopper he is!' and her plump hands grasped my fast-stiffening prick. 'What a fine comforter for a woman every night in the year! And he is raising himself so quickly too. Lord, how big he is getting! Oh, it is splendid, my dear boy, put it in me again!' And once more her buxom belly shook with the pleasure of a good hard diddle, till she squirmed again and vowed that I fucked like a 'bull.'

As I rested after this play, she caressed my fallen pintle, and I asked: 'Won't you kiss him to make him stand for you again?'

'No, I won't. I have never kissed a man's cock and I won't! You may fuck me as much as you like but I never will suck it, it's nasty!'

Here was a new kink in lechery. Many a lady, dainty and supposedly virtuous, have I had kiss and suck my cock and even call it my ruby-headed spear. From experience I know that the higher in society and the higher the tone of the woman, the farther she will go in debauchery, and my story of experiences proves it.

For a week, my German Venus boarded me and kept me in trim. I had only to serve as a stallion to her and I took her adoration pleasantly. She even went so far as to rope in a young married woman who lived over the shop, for whom I had expressed an admiration, having seen her in the privy with her skirts up to her waist, making water.

The woman's husband was at work and as we saw her go up to her room, my mistress, seeing how agitated I was, said: 'Ah, my lusty plugger, I will see if I cannot get that pretty piece of virtue to take a piece of this.'

She drew out a good ten inches of rosy stiffness from my breeches. 'Go into the small room and strip naked!' was her command. As I obeyed her and lay on my back on the bed with a perpendicular prick, she said: 'I am generous to give another cunt a taste of that, but I will!' and off she started.

I soon heard their voices in the shop: 'What, you never have tasted brandy?'

'No, never!'

'Why, it is good! It warms your insides so, it makes your blood boil!' and as I peeped into the room, I saw my hostess was pouring two big bumpers of cognac, each enough to go to a man's head, let alone a woman's.

Mrs Virtue from upstairs seemed to like it, sipped it at first, then took a big gulp.

'Oh, it makes me feel real good!' she said.

'There is no trade during the middle of the day. I will lock the door and we can spend a little time in jollification,' and the two glasses were again filled and emptied.

'Oh, how lively it makes me feel,' said Mrs Virtue. 'I feel as if I could dance like those girls at the theater, who throw their heels as high as their head.'

'Well, let's both strip and try it!' said the older one and in a second her clothes were in a heap on the floor.

'Oh, what a fine woman you are!' cried Mrs Virtue. 'Why don't you get married? Any man would like such a plump piece of flesh in bed with him.'

'That's all right, my dear, but I don't want to tie myself to one man, for if I meet a nice fellow, it is so much finer, you know. I can take a fuck out of him without any fear of a jealous husband raising hell about it. But hurry and get out of your clothes.' And with the help so readily offered, Mrs Virtue was soon arrayed only in two pink stockings.

'What a pity to keep such a pretty shape for one cock

only!' cried my hostess. 'Why don't you steal a diddle once in a while when your husband is at work? Lot of men would pay you well to get into you.'

'Oh, stop talking about men, let's dance!' And the half-tipsy Mrs Virtue began to kick her heels in the air. She was limber and light of foot, and in complete abandonment she whirled around and around her heavier seducer, who managed it so that the lively girl gave me, peeping through the door crack, the fullest possible view of her.

'Now I would like to see you dancing up and down on a good stiff prick,' cried the older one.

'Well if I had one, I would do it!' answered the girl. 'I have often dreamed of doing it with other men, but have never dared to venture it. If now you had only a good stiff cock growing out of your fat belly, I would make you fuck me this minute.'

This was enough. Grabbing the girl, she pulled her into the bedroom, where I had hastily thrown myself upon the bed and pretended to be asleep.

The girl saw me and gave a little scream.

'Hush, you will wake him. Ain't he a fine fellow? He is lazy and I keep him just to have his big prick handy. Just feel of it, ain't it a beauty?' And the elder one carried the younger one's hand to the ten inches of perpendicular that stood out from my belly. As the pink hand grasped it, I could stand it no longer and, springing up, grabbed Mrs Virtue and laid her flat on her back, kneeling between her thighs.

'Fuck her! Fuck her!' cried out hostess. 'Let her feel how much better are stolen sweets than always diddling with the same old cock.'

'Well, my dear,' said I, 'would you like a few shakes of this?' I held its hulky length out to her, the skin drawn from its head to show its red readiness.

The girl squirmed and cried out: 'You shall! I'm drunk; my slit is on fire, quick, fuck me, the very sight of your big prick makes me want to spend.'

And I was on and in her, my big prick fleshed in Mrs Virtue's hot and eager cunt.

'Give it to her!' cried our hostess. 'Show that a husband's fucking is not worth a fart compared to a lover's!' And the girl seemed to be of the same opinion, for I was no sooner stretching her sheath with my enormous erection, than fright forgotten, the true nature of the girl came out, and in a spasm of lechery she seized me with arms and legs, fired her kisses on every part of me that she could reach, and heaved her bum and wriggled till her belly was as lively a bit of flesh as I had ever got under me.

And as my prick began to swell and spend, she cried: 'Oh, it's heavenly – quicker – give it to – to – me, diddle me harder – there – there – there! I'm off! Oh, how I feel it getting into me, oh you darling fellow! Give it to me – all of it!' And squirming and panting, I ran my prick to a grand but gradual standstill in her and lay panting on her belly.

As I rolled over and lay beside her, leaning on my elbow, she flung her arms about me and kissed me, soon taking the fallen hero in her hand. 'Stolen sweets are the best,' she said; then throwing herself in the arms of my hostess, she continued: 'Oh, my dear, dear woman, I am so glad that you made me do this. It was splendid, but how you must feel. Let me rub it for you.'

And so excited was our hostess that she spent in agony on the frigging hand of Mrs Virtue while her own hands were playing with my prick and balls, until she had dropped off and I was near heaven.

But my prick was not allowed to waste its rosy invitation on the desert air for I made the nimble Mrs Virtue get up and give us a continuance of her dancing. This, of course, exposed all her person to me; we made her turn head over heels, stand close to the bed and put one leg on the headboard, and then our hostess, springing up, made the girl stand on her head on the bed, her legs wide open in the air.

Then, between them, they handled cock robin, told him what a fine fellow he was, till they really had a good stiff erection to gloat over. And now, throwing Mrs Virtue flat on her belly, I got behind her and plunged into her body with a good rousing probe that sent her buttocks bounding in a delicious spasm of jerks that made her scream with delight. And if her husband did not find her well stretched that night, it was not my fault.

II

For a month or two, my hostess and Mrs Virtue continued to consume all the sperm that I brewed in my large cream jug, and two better oiled cracks could not be found in the great city of New York. I did not get tired of them, but a man hates to go round without any money in his pocket and one day while reading a newspaper, I noticed in the personals:

'A widow of thirty-five, with means, wants a man's services in the house – must be young and strong.'

As it gave initials and a post office box address, I thought perhaps this was an opportunity – what kind of services did the widow want? At any rate I answered it, describing myself, and the next day received a letter:

'Walk past – Hotel at twelve o'clock exactly, wearing a flower in your hatband.'

I laughed as I read, thinking, Well, that will identify me well enough. And at twelve o'clock I walked past the hotel several times, wearing two violets in my hat. Nothing happened, except that as I was walking away, a messenger came up and handed me a note.

'I have seen you; if you are discreet, call at 10 Broad Ave and ask for Miss Belle Strate – but an indiscreet word will get us both in trouble.'

At three o'clock a colored woman opened the door of the house and, leading me silently to the parlor, left me alone. It was an assignation house, where frisky wives wiggle in livelier beds than their own.

A voice said: 'Your correspondent is here but will

not disclose herself till she knows that you will suit. She is a respectable married woman of thirty, her husband is a cold-blooded business man who is traveling a good two-thirds of the year; she lives in good style in a flat with a Creole servant; she wants a man who will pretend to be a servant but who will have as his chief work the keeping of her amorous feelings in check.

'You look as if you could be trusted. Will you let me, and also her, see you as you would appear at her bedside, imagining her to be laid out naked before you?'

I could hear whispers that I felt proceeded from the correspondent herself and they were such as to prove her a woman of refinement.

I quickly rose from the sofa, where I had been seated, and in a moment's time I stood ready for her inspection, a new Adam awaiting his Eve, and with a pego that the thought of a possible new slit to raid had lifted to a giant hard.

Out from the curtained door of the alcove stepped a nude woman, as lovely a bit of gentlewoman's flesh as I had ever seen, small of stature, but beautifully made and rounded. One glance told me she was no less than a Venus – naked but for the black silk stockings that made her white skin still more dazzling, and a small black mask, hiding the upper part of her face, except her sparkling eyes.

I stepped forward, but she held out her hand, stopping me:

'One word. I want a lover who will forget my respectability, who will appeal to my lascivious longings, and who will treat me just as he would a loose woman in a brothel. I want to give and take with him lewdness in every form!'

I could now wait no longer. I sprang at her with a lecherous cry. I kissed her mouth, her shoulders, her breasts, her belly, and, opening her thighs, her hairy cunt. I threw her on the bed, and putting a pillow under her head and kneeling over her, I held out my prick, now ready to burst:

'Will that suit you?'

'Oh, it is superb – it is beautiful!' And taking it for a minute in her hand, with a sudden movement she kissed its swollen head with open lips.

This was too much. I seized her beautiful hips with my hands, crying: 'If you want it, put it in,' and I shoved down till her soft hand grabbed the stanchion and pointed it between the lips of her slit.

'Fuck me – diddle me – think I am a common whore!'

'Well, my fine harlot, how do you like that and that?' And I thrust into her hot cunt, shove after shove of as vigorous stroking as man ever gave.

She yelled with delight: 'Oh you darling! Go on! Go on – go just as fast and as hot as you can. I have a belly full of hot stuff to bathe your splendid prick with, and it – it – it – is com-i-n-g!' Throwing her plump legs high up, she crossed them round my waist, and with a lightning lunging, burning plunge, I gave her a shower of sperm that sent her into a wild frenzy of lustful heaves and satisfied pantings.

Snatching off her mask, she cried: 'See, see a sensual slave to all the lust you can pour into her – he has kept my cunt starving all these years and now I am going to fill it full with that splendid prick of yours – talk bawdy, talk vulgarly, talk wildly, teach me all you know of lustful pleasures, even of the outer sort. Order me around as you would a common strumpet.'

I now lifted her up and as I lay on my back, let her rest on my belly, her bum rising and falling, while her lovely breasts were on mine.

'I am rich and I will give you plenty of money, and you will give me that lovely life-giving sperm of yours.' Rising up, she broke away from me and knelt on the floor between my legs, covering with hot kisses the fallen god of her desires.

'That is all one-sided!' I cried, lifting her up again and pulling her onto the bed, feet first, till my hand was opposite the hairy home of lust, and my fallen prick close to her face.

Her hands fondled it, her eager kisses covered it, and the red purse below she now held in her dainty fingers, saying: 'Oh, you darling!' and her open mouth received my pork, and with lecherous lips she rolled it like a sweet morsel, while I, with out-pursed lips and thrusting licking tongue, soon made her work her lovely buttocks with amorous wiggles.

'See how stiff he is again!' she cried. 'I would love to suck its lovely head some more, but not this time, my belly wants it too badly!'

And her belly got it; flat on the bed, belly to belly, wound close and tight, clinging legs and arms, while tongue and cock were pushing into the two places destined for places that few women have to the same perfection.

'Let me bathe you off?' I said as soon as I could get my breath.

'No, you shall not, not until the end. I like the sticky stuff to be plastered all over – see, I am not a dainty.' She took my sperm-covered pintle in her mouth. 'Let's look at each other in the mirror!'

And standing there naked, we gloried in each other's shiny bodies. Starting at the forehead, I kissed her mouth, titties, belly, slit, buttocks, thighs, till she squirmed, and as I rose, she threw herself onto me and with her luscious lips paid me back kiss for kiss. On her knees before me, I had the delicious picture in the mirror of this lovely, dainty woman kneeling before me as I stood there, pouring hot, impassioned kisses on my prick and balls, taking the humbled giant into her mouth and with fond lips and rosy tongue recalling again and again its robust stature.

The Town Bull

'Oh, it is a big mouthful now!' she cried eagerly. 'Shall we suck each other?' she asked.

'No, that is too quick, let us prolong the delight – let me see you rolling on the floor – put yourself into every lustful pose you can think of.' Throwing myself into a chair, I watched the beautiful, lewd, nude body, so white, roll over and over on the crimson carpet.

Now flat on her back; now with open legs; then standing, jutting out her belly, with her fingers pulling wide open the lips of her slit, the portal of heaven for my prick; then with a leg high in the air on the end of the bed, the other on the floor; now flat on her back again till she almost split herself in two; then standing – her limber body bent forward and her head touching her feet, her beautiful slit plainly open before me right under those beautiful, broad buttocks – till unable to restrain myself further, I rushed up behind her and stuck my prick into its rosy depths.

'No! No!' she cried. 'Our mouths are to enjoy this one.' And rolling on her back on the floor, she continued: 'Come – come – my lips are eager to eat that spending mouthful!' And she quickly had it while I in my turn opened her slit with my lips and plunged my tongue in.

Oh, what a delicious duet of sucking it was. Never did an epicure mouth and taste and roll his tongue over a dainty morsel with greater gusto than we did the quick live flesh of each other's cock and cunt. Finally, with working thighs, the electric signal of the coming flood was struck and I found that my mouth sucked from her cunt the rich stores of a delicious flow of lust, while her lips bulged with the swollen, bursting flesh, and the hot sperm flew into her eager mouth and nearly choked her. Then as she retired a little, it flew in a generous shower over her face and breasts, till catching her breath with an ardent cry, she again engulfed it and sucked till the very last drop of heavenly agony was swallowed and she lay quivering and sighing: 'Oh, you darling!'

And as she lay half on me, one arm stole round my neck, the other playing with my prick: 'Oh, you darling lover – will you be all mine? Will you come and live with me while my husband is away? He won't be back for two months now and there is no one in the flat but Mollie, the servant, and she is a pretty little virgin Creole of sixteen. She is hot too, and we often frig and suck each other. Won't it be lovely with you between us, both of us playing with your love-stick? Won't we make you spend, and won't you make us spend also!

'I cannot talk about money while I am naked in your arms, but I have enough, and when that husband of mine telegraphs me that he has started for New York and you have to leave me, you shall be well paid for all the sperm that you have spent for me out of this lovely purse!' And she squeezed my balls with her plump and caressing hand.

So it was decided that I should report for duty, ostensibly as a servant, the second day after this glorious tête-à-tête.

III

As I walked home, the fresh air brightened me up. I felt that I was going to leave my good hostess and Mrs Virtue, and I must picture to them that I had received an offer of employment in a distant city and bid them goodbye forever.

I told my hostess that I was tired and went right to bed and slept the sleep of the just till nightfall – when I awoke, the buxom landlady was seated beside me.

'Oh, I have not touched it, and see how it looks!' I saw and felt that my prick was standing at a great rate with lustful rigidity, for she had pulled off all the clothes and was already gloating over the prospect of a hot diddle.

'For we must get all we can tonight,' I cried, throwing her on her back and exposing her anxious belly, 'as tomorrow I have got to go away and will not be able to return for some time.'

She burst into tears at this, saying:

'Oh, how cruel that is!' But I pacified her and proposed to give the night up to revel and smuttiness, when a knock came and Mrs Virtue entered.

'Why, you were just getting to work, were you? Wait, I have something to tell you. My conscience has been troubling me about deceiving my husband and so last night as we lay in bed, I confessed all to him. I did not know how he would take it, whether he would kill me or not – instead of that, however, he was excited by the thought, called me a prostitute and a whore. But I did not mind that, for at the same time he rolled over on top of me and gave me the hottest fuck he ever gave me in his life. I told him all the details of our meetings here and he would like to come in.'

'Well, we will now have a night of lechery and lust and all four will get drunk with both wine and lust!' cried our hostess.

Kissing my prick, Mrs Virtue ran out. Then my hostess and I, still naked, went about lighting the gas brightly in the larger room and carried my bed into the center of it. A knock came and the couple from upstairs entered.

Mrs Virtue rushed up to me, saying: 'Gee, hubby, are you jealous?' She was dangling my prick in her hand.

'Jealousy be damned!' he cried, and he and our hostess were handling each other. Then stopping, Mr Virtue grasped his wife, saying: 'I'll show you how jealous I am,' and he forced her down on her knees and made her take my prick in her mouth. Then, throwing her over onto the edge of the bed, he cried: 'Whore her!' And he and our hostess frigged us, till I gave her a fresh fuck that made the wildly happy wife yell in an agony of spending.

'I want to be a whore, oh, whoring is heavenly! Hubby, I love you, but I love to be whored best!' And as we quitted, the buxom mistress threw herself down beside us and the excited Mr Virtue vented his lust in a hot race in her belly, and in a minute, all four of us lay panting.

'It is our last night. Let us all get tipsy!' said our hostess and she brought each one a tumbler of whiskey. 'Now, each is to drink without stopping.'

It was fiery stuff but we were reckless and drained every drop. Its fire made us tipsy. Leaving me, Mrs Virtue ran over to her husband.

'Hubby, I've never kissed your prick.' In a second

The Town Bull

she was nearly swallowing it.

'Stop, you whore, or I shall be going off in your mouth!' he shouted.

'No, you shall not!' And rushing over to me, she grasped my staff in her hand and pulled me to the bed. 'Whore me!' she cried, as I plunged my prick into her reeking cunt clear to the hilt, and the excited hostess knelt over Mrs Virtue's face, while the wife guided her husband's cock into the other's reeking cunt, so randy for it. The two women were beside themselves with lust.

If there was any preeminence among us four for lechery, the modest Mrs Virtue took the cake. The liquor had turned her head from quiet respectability into a chamber of bacchanalia, as you would have acknowledged if you had seen her when the hostess rolled over on the bed, squirming with a good, full belly. She seized her husband's limp prick in her mouth so as to completely hide it and she would not let either of us men leave that place till we were completely empty.

As Mrs Virtue lay resting her head in my lap, kissing and squeezing my cock and holding it close to her face, her lewd fancy hit upon another new idea: 'I've got a new one!'

'A new what?' we asked in chorus.

'A new cock to fuck me and one that will always be stiff!' And jumping up, she went over to where a barrel of beer lay with its big bright spigot, and said: 'I am going to let a beer keg fuck me!' And seating herself on a stool, she tried to make connections between the spigot and her slit but could not.

I quickly went to her assistance and, straddling across the barrel, I made her lie on the floor in front of it. Lifting her legs up, I grasped her by the ankles, bum first, until the spigot was just in the opening of her slit and she was resting on her arms and shoulders.

Another pull and the fat brass nozzle was imbedded

in her cunt. I turned on the faucet, and the lively, foaming beer rushed into her with wild velocity, fizzing and frothing, till gorged with the continued flow, the lascivious wife's belly swelled almost to the bursting point. Her whole body was in a wild frenzy, and she shrieked with her delightful lustfulness.

Then, as her cunt could hold no more, I turned off the beer, lifted her onto the top of the barrel, and, with my mouth glued to her slit, sucked a pint or more of the female-flavored beer into my belly, and although she still dripped with beer, my prick called my attention and I cried:

'Wet it!' Pushing her down on her belly on the side of the bed, I presented it all wet with her spittle at the small entrance between her bum's fat cheeks.

'Where are you putting it? Can't you feel what you are doing? Oh, it's going into my arse – ah, oh dear! It is too big!' She wriggled her beautiful bum from one side to the other until I grabbed her with my hands, held her tight, and with one frantic lunge, was in complete possession of the narrow defile, marching in double-time up and down its tight alley.

'My cunt – my cunt – quick, hubby – do something for me!' Her husband, crawling under us, soon had his mouth fixed upon its red, hot lips, and with his tongue in her slit and my cock in her cul, she yelled as we worked in unison, and we all shouted as we spent. Our hostess had brought her cunt to Mrs Virtue's lips and that somewhat smothered her screams and I could see from the older woman's heaving belly that the smut-gutted one was fucking it well with her tongue.

As we finished, Mr Virtue grabbed the broad buttocks of our hostess and fingered her slit; she in her turn had her arsehole watered with his boiling sperm while her own hot emission wetted his fingers in her cunt.

IV

The next morning, desiring to avoid a farewell scene with my kind friend and landlady, I slipped out with my few possessions, determined to rest that day in some lodging house, and the following day I would become the body servant of the aristocratic Mrs Strate.

I took a long walk in the park, then went to a cheap bath, and when I left it I was so invigorated that I thought as night came on that I would, after a hasty dinner, go to my new mistress's house; waiting till nine o'clock, so that any visitors she might happen to have would be gone, I was at her door on the third floor of the apartment house where she lived.

On my ringing, the door was opened a little and a fresh, young, olive-colored face peeped out, while I asked:

'Is Mrs Belle Strate in?'

'Yes!' answered the girl.

'Tell her – ' But I got no further, for my new mistress had recognized my voice, rushed to the door, opened it, and pulled me in. The door closed, and I found myself in the naked arms of Mrs Belle while the pretty little brown Rose looked on, clad only in a shawl thrown about her shoulders.

Belle said: 'You darling fellow, I wished for you so hard that you came. I could not wait for tomorrow. My passions were too much for me, and Rose and I were just going to have a thumb tilting match with each other.' During this speech, I was led by the amorous woman into a lovely large room, furnished with luxuriant riches. The center of the room was empty; on one side was an inviting sofa and on the other side a bed fit for Venus and Adonis to make love on.

'Rose,' said Mrs Belle, and the pretty, dusky handmaiden came into the room a few steps, trying to hide her virgin slit with her small shawl. 'Bring in two quarts of champagne.' As the plump girl turned her back, we had a full view of a fat little chocolate bottom and of her straight, well-rounded legs.

'Oh, you have got your eye on her, have you?' cried Mrs Belle. 'Well, you shall have her any way you want, except that you shall not rupture her virginity with this!' And the lustful woman grasped my stiff rod in my breeches. 'Oh, you are ready for the fray, are you! Well, come, strip naked!' And on her knees before me, she unbuttoned my trousers, pulled them down to my heels, and as I pulled my shirt over my head, she clasped my naked thighs in her arms and kissed the object of her desire.

I raised her up and threw her on the side of the bed.

'Wait a minute. Hurry, Rose, if you want to see me take the first fuck out of this splendid prick!' And the pretty girl came running in, a bottle under one arm and another in her hand, while the other hand carried three glasses.

As she ran, her shawl fell off, and putting her load down, the naked hussy stood close behind her mistress.

'Put this prick into my cunt' was the order of the excited woman, and Rose's plump little hand grasped my swelling penis and guided it till she aimed it deep into her mistress's slit. As I plunged it in still deeper, the black ringlets of her hair curled in with mine, and I had her fat arse firmly clutched, while mine began to work with all the engines of my lust urging it back and forth; the delighted Mrs Belle, working her buttocks in lustful harmony, cried:

'See, whoever want to – I would not care if the whole world were looking on! I am a whore from mouth to cunt. I live only to be whored. I cannot get on without it; my cunt is made to have a prick in it all the time and yours, my dear fellow, fits me exactly.

'Each thrust, makes me squirm. Don't it look lovely, Rose, pushing in and out? Oh, I cannot hold out any longer!' Her handsome thighs were thrown around my waist and her legs joined foot to foot on my back, the heels kicking my arse, while the voluptuous woman screamed:

'Give it to me now. Fuck me with all your might. Oh, those lightning thrusts, that swelling prick – squeeze his balls, Rose, and kiss his lovely shaft!' Rose, on her knees, with excited lips and hands, obeyed her mistress's order, till the mad woman cried: 'There – there – there, oh-ah-a-h-h, there goes the first shot! Oh, I feel his hot sperm hit me way up in my belly – my womb! Oh, it's so hot, it burns me! Splendid – keep on – pump it into me – splendid! Now – oh-ah-now I am going again!'

The wild wanton held me as in a vise while our bellies thumped together and my enormous prick, swollen even bigger than before, flooded and deluged the hottest cunt that I had ever entered, and meeting a downfall of her hot spendings, we both cried out and continued our heavings till, almost breathless with happiness, she murmured: 'Oh, you darling ravisher, you splendid diddler, my cunt can never be happy without you again. I am your slave, your harlot, ready to be whored out in the public street even, if you want to, and I live only to be whored by you. I will die for you!'

And she had indeed seemed to be dying as the reaction set in, but Rose filled the goblets with life-giving champagne, which soon revived us both, as we lay so happily side by side.

'Oh, Mrs Belle,' said Rose, wriggling her pretty

thighs, her hands pressed on her slit.

'Poor girl, she wants it too.' Seizing the pretty young virgin, she placed her astraddle over my face as I leaned back against the pillow. Grasping her plump little bum, I pressed her lightly shaded cunt against my mouth and tickled her clitty with my tongue, sliding nimbly in and out of the lips.

'Oh! Oh! Oh!' said the burning virgin, and with frantic heaves of her thighs, rapid throbbing of her belly, and quickening thrusts of my tongue, the lovely lass spent in my mouth and fell back on my belly, her gaping slit close to my eyes.

Now Mrs Belle and I gloated over the pretty panting picture; then, with a sudden rousing of herself, the wench turned completely over and kissed the big prick again and again, and as her pretty backside stared up at me, I spread the cheeks with my hands.

The lecherous Mrs Belle caught my thought and said 'Yes, some day you shall put that monstrous cock of yours in there, but now I want it all. I am on fire again!' and pushing Rose off me, she cried, 'More wine.' The virgin tottered over to the table, still panting, while Mrs Belle was fondly but gently caressing the now-awakening priapus. From the goblet we took a drink; then she said: 'Rose, bring me the bottle.'

Taking the bottle from Rose, I put it under my testicles and made the neck of the bottle a glass prick aside of my own, and the two eyes were looking Mrs Belle right in the face and caused her to exclaim: 'What a mouthful and do you want me to take all that in at once? I could swallow them both together!' Her wide-stretched lips took in the quick flesh of my staff and the mouth of the bottle, which I tipped up; the voluptuous woman had the wine pouring into her, while her tongue was rolling it round my wet prick, bathed in the sparkling liquor, and she gulped it down till at last, breathless, she threw her head back on the pillow.

Jumping to my feet on the bed, I pulled her back on the pillow, her head on the bed, and hung her legs over the headboard, so that her body was standing almost on her head; and kneeling over her face, I took the half-emptied bottle, and covering the mouth of it so that it would not spill, I inserted the neck of it into her wide-stretched slit and let the wine flow, gurgling down into her excited abdomen.

'Oh, that's fine! I'm drinking wine with my cunt!' And her upright body still had it stored in there, so I glued my lips to her grotto and sucked it out, allowing her to gradually fall back with me as I continued to drink the wine out of her slit till my head reached the bed. She, having turned a complete somersault, was kneeling over my face, which was pressed tight to her belly, my mouth continuing to suck the flow of the wine, which her now-upright position caused to flow out in a goodly stream.

When the last, bubbling drop was in my stomach, I grasped her broad buttocks in my arms, buried my face still deeper in her slit, and fucked it hotly with my tongue. With a lecherous cry, she threw herself forward on my belly, took my cock bursting with sperm into her eager mouth, and we both sucked and tickled till our swollen parts gave up the fight, and the rich overflowing of our sensual secretions were swallowed with lustful ravenousness, hers by me and mine by her.

V

When company was in the house I was a servant, if it was necessary for me to appear at all, but generally I was able to keep out of sight in my own room. Most of the time, however, Mrs Belle, Rose, and I were alone in the house, and I was master – at least, my prick ruled the place.

One day a niece of Mrs Belle's, living in a distant city, called up, and they were soon chatting in the parlor. Presently Mrs Belle made an excuse to leave her and, coming to me, said:

'Maggie has been married a month to a rich old chap, and as we know each other's voluptuous natures, she will probably tell me her nuptial bed experiences.'

So, when she returned to Maggie, I hid myself behind the curtained doorway and listened.

'Well, Mag, how do you like being married?'

'Oh, don't ask me. He is kind and good to me, but Aunt Belle, you know how warm I am and he has seen his best days and – and . . .'

'Well, will you go on?' said the aunt.

'I believe I am still as much a virgin as I ever was. I know he has not broken it – he just goes in a little ways and goes right off – just you see, Aunt Belle, if he has even ruptured the virgin veil, as they call it.'

Peeping in, I had a fine view of the handsome bride as, lifting her skirts and dropping her dainty drawers to her heels, she exposed her belly and thighs to her aunt's eager eyes, and in an instant those limber fingers I knew so well were thrust into a bride's slit. It did not take long for the experienced touches to decide.

'Oh, you poor girl! Married and yet a virgin. I cannot understand it!'

'Oh, I knew it, and I have made up my mind to let the very first man that wants to finish the job. It is a shame, I know, but I am resolved, and once open, perhaps the old prick will go in farther and thus give me more fun. Oh, Aunt Belle, let's have a razzle-dazzle, just as we used to, with fingers and tongues!' And the two were clasped in each other's arms with nothing left for clothing but pink and blue stockings and those did not hide their naked charms from me.

'I want your tongue in my slit!' cried the eager niece.

'Wait a minute, Mag. You know I am somewhat in the same box that you are. My husband is away most of the time and yours is incapable. Do you know what I do? I have got a splendid, strong lover who fills the gap royally and I am not ashamed of it!'

'You mean that you keep a man with you that fucks you every day?' cried the bride in excitement.

'That's it exactly.'

'Oh, how splendid,' said Maggie.

Hearing all this conversation, I instinctively knew what was coming, so hastily stripped myself naked.

'And, oh Mag, he has the finest prick that I ever saw. It is so firm and juicy. Let me call him in. He will carry away your hateful virgin gate and then perhaps your husband will find it clear sailing. Shall I?'

'Oh, no!' cried Maggie, frightened at the thought, but Aunt Belle knew that even if one mouth did say no, the other must be saying yes.

'Bob.' I instantly stood naked before that dear whore of mine and her virgin niece.

One quick glance and the bashful young matron hid her face on the naked breast of her aunt, exposing beautifully her naked bottom.

'Come, show it to her, Bob!' And the aunt, seizing the bride's hand, placed it on my rampant prick. 'There. Do you think that could knock a hole into you, dear?'

I could see the girl's feelings were on a rampage. Her aunt called out for proper food, and it was there handy. With a sudden resolve she turned on her back across her aunt's lap and, opening her legs, offered her virginity on that lustful altar. I quickly seized her bottom, bringing my raging prick close to her belly.

'Put it in yourself!' cried the aunt.

'I will!' answered the virgin wife. 'I vowed that I would give my maidenhead to the first man who wanted it.' Quickly taking my weapon in her hand, she guided it into her hot cunt, waiting for the overflow that was trembling on the threshold.

What Mrs Maggie learned of man that day – how he can be used and abused, and also how a woman can be used and abused, if she is willing! With what avidity she worked her charms to raise again the flame of lust upon its firm standard.

Five times I diddled her dizzy, and between times my ponderous prick pierced every opening she had. She was an apt scholar, prone to lechery, as the sparks flew upward. The generous aunt would not rob her niece of an opportunity to enjoy a manly feast, but contented herself with the fingers and tongue, assisting in Maggie's initiation into the inner courts of lasciviousness.

And when the bride returned with virtuous mien to her legitimate couch with her ancient husband . . . but let me give you the letter she wrote Aunt Belle:

Dear Aunt Belle:
  Last night my kind old husband did it to me. I managed at table to make him drink twice as much as usual, and when he rose, he was half-tipsy and commenced groping and hugging me.

'Let's have another quart of wine, Mag?' And we did. He pulled me onto his lap and felt me all over till he came to my cunt, and I snatched his hand away, fearing he might notice that someone had done his work for him.

'This is not the place for that — if you want to fool with me, why, come to bed!'

Pouring out another big bumper for each of us, I stood facing him, glass in hand, crying:

'What is the toast?'

'I drink to your pretty slit!' he answered. 'Let me see it.'

I grabbed up my skirts, raised them on high, then kicked one leg higher than his head. He started for me. But keeping my clothes high up over my arse, I ran laughing to our room and when he got there I was lying naked on the bed.

He unbuttoned his trousers and wanted to mount me at once, without undressing, but I rolled out of bed on the other side, saying: 'You shall not touch me till you are undressed,' and as he pulled his undershirt over his head, I threw myself at his prick and kissed it, making it stiffer than I had ever seen it.

Quickly I threw myself on my back, my feet in the air, and the dear old fellow stuck it into me, and never for a moment did he guess why it was that it went in so easily, slipping farther than ever. He was wild and at the same time half-drunk, and he did fuck me enjoyably but even then not with the regal strength of Bob Stirling's cock.

So, my dear aunt, you see that this morning I have a happy little cunt down here between my legs, which opens its lips to you in thanks, dear aunt, for making it take what it has so yearned for, from Bob's dear staff.

Tell the dear fellow that I am dreaming of his

colossal cock all the time and that the very first chance I have, I am coming to have another good fucking out of it and more than one, my good aunt, if you can spare the delightful diddler to your –
                              Naughty Niece

VI

Mrs Belle was a Roman Catholic. One day she came in, her face flushed, and, running up to me, her bonnet and cloak still on, she pulled up her dress as far as it would go and I could see her belly heaving with excitement.

'Quick, Bob, fuck me, my slit is on fire!'

I caught the fever of her lust, took out my cock, held it up ready to spike her and she straddled over me, pointing the red rooster into her cunt and we fucked, or rather, she fucked me; she was so excited that her bum worked as lively as mine would if I had been on top.

'Oh!' she exclaimed as she spent. 'What a relief. It is so delicious to know that I have such a pleasant cock at home to ease me when I get hot!'

I took her in my lap and, caressing her belly with my hand, asked: 'What touched you off so?'

'Oh, Bob, I went to a new church this time and, finding it apparently deserted, came to one of the confessional boxes and saw a priest's frock and feet under the front curtain.

'I don't know what possessed me but I knelt down at the little window in the side. He questioned me closely about fornication and adultery. I could not lie to him, so I told him that I had a lover and I couldn't live without a man – that all my pleasure came from diddling.

'At first he pretended to be shocked but as I went on, the father's lust seemed to be aroused.

' "Ah, my dear, but I would like to keep you in order with this!" and as I peeped in through the window, the robust priest had opened his habit and held his monstrous poker pointing straight at me. "How would you like my assistance, my dear?" And standing up, he stuck his cock right through the bars of the window into my face.

' "Oh, my father, how lovely!" And I pressed a loving kiss of desire on its crimson beak, when he lunged forward and plunged it into my mouth till it touched my palate.

' "Suck it, suck it, quick. I am burning up, that's it, my dear girl, oh, you fine young sucker, keep on. Oh, how your tongue tickles. Faster." Reaching an arm through the bars, he held my head closer to the job.

'My mouth, breast, and chin were all bathed in sperm and, Bob, I told him my name and where I lived and he is coming tonight to have a razzle-dazzle with you and me. No, Bob, put it up, save it for tonight!'

Darkness found Mrs Belle in bed, with a black silk negligee the only article of clothing, and that, she said, was in honor of his profession. It was thin and sleeveless and just covered the lovely breasts over the nipples and made her rosy flesh stand out in a luscious shine.

She had dressed me as a Roman vassal, short muslin tunic reaching just above my knees. As she looked me over, she said:

'Lord, but the Roman girl could get at her lover's cock handily. It is no wonder that they were hot-cunted!' And her one hand under my tunic was holding the Roman spear, while the other raised the tunic.

'Well,' I laughed, 'you will have a Roman cock tonight, even if you do not have a Roman!'

'Yes,' she answered, giving my balls a fond squeeze, 'and I will fuck both the Roman master and slave, till both are so dry, they will crack!'

Venus brought darkness quickly, knowing her votaries were awaiting her coming. My Venus, flushed with venereal thoughts, lay on the sofa while I was busy icing the wine to refresh and renew the lusts of the flesh.

A ring at the door and on my answering it, two black frocks entered instead of the one expected: Father Anthony, who had confessed her, and Father Ambrose.

'Ah, my dear madame,' said the former as Mrs Belle rose to meet them. 'I owe you an apology for bringing Father Ambrose uninvited, but I wanted you to meet him.'

'Don't speak of it, my dear father, any friend of yours is welcome!' She slipped gracefully forward and offered a hand to each.

'Welcome to where?' asked Father Anthony.

'Wherever they may do me the honor to present themselves!' and their hostess bowed long, till before she raised herself, from the light robe her nipples sprang stiff and pink-tipped, and those lovely naked breastworks stood eager to be stormed.

Enough for the abstemious priests; with cries of voluptuous eagerness, they both seized the delighted and delightful woman and, facing a mirror they, with quick hands, tore loose the confining bonds and, Mrs Belle stood boldly bare to their lustful eyes and touches.

How these starved martyrs of clerical superstition gloated over the royal feast of flesh before them, covering with kisses of adoration every spot of my beloved mistress.

'On your knees, both of you,' she ordered. As they obeyed, she threw a naked leg over each neck, and they rose to their feet, while in the glass all three had a magnificent view of her gaping slit between their heads; their fingers quickly invaded it; first one and then the other turned their heads and kissed the inviting cunt with protruding tongue.

'Quick!' cried my dear whore. 'Quick, let me see your pricks!' And each cassock was torn open and two sturdy lords of lust pointed straight up at her wide-open cunt. 'Fuck me! Diddle me quick! Whore me – just as you are, in priestly frock.'

Quickly they laid her on the edge of the bed. Her wide-stretched thighs wrapped round Father Anthony and her eager hand stuck the lordly prick that she had sucked that morning into her fevered slit.

'What a hot cunt – how soft and yet so tight. By Mary Magdalene, but she is a fine stroker.'

'Oh, father, your cock is fucking me splendidly. Work it as fast as you can, and talk smutty. I will be ready for you. I am on fire!' And her panting belly met his blow for blow.

'Now, you lovely harlot, now it is coming, com-ing . . . !' The quivering flesh and the bursting bliss of fruitful fucking brought from her a spending cry.

'That's it, father! I feel it – I feel it – give it all to me. Water your whore with all the sperm that you have got. Oh, how satisfying. Give me every drop. Keep hard at it and squirt it into my very womb. Oh, what delight!' And again the panting thighs and belly ran down to a gentle heave and almost rested.

Father Ambrose, crazy with lust, pulled his brother of the cloth away from the sperm-filled cunt and, wildly lecherous, drove his immense engine into her gaping cunt.

'That's it, blessing on blessing!' cried the excited Mrs Belle. 'I never have had enough and never shall. Go on, dear father, I will be with you at the finish and will wet your prick just as richly as I did Father Anthony's.

'Oh, it is heavenly to be whored over and over again by two such lusty lovers. See, father? My bottom is working again and my slit is clutching your cock. That's it, keep at it as long as possible. It is too delicious to let go. Oh dear, there it goes – oh, ah – dear Venus, look down and see your happy child; and Priapus, frig yourself and let the boiling drops fall from heaven on your loving votary.'

Now radiantly happy, my mistress reclined between her naked priests, a leg over the knee of each, a fall staff in each hand, while her rosy nipples were being sucked by two amorous mouths, and her moist crevice was frigged by their fervid fingers.

My cock was ready to crow and as she glanced up, I thrust it through the opening in the curtain. They were too busy to see it, but the dear whore saw it and said: 'Let us have something.' Then, raising her voice, she continued: 'Bob, serve us, will you?' And grabbing up the waiter that was ready – as the Roman slave – I entered and placed it on the table.

'Don't mind his presence, my fathers, he is only my body servant.'

'And does he serve you here?' asked one, moving his knee to her palpitating notch.

'Yes, indeed he does! Bob, come here and let the fathers see how richly you are gifted.' And as I stood between her legs, she lifted up my tunic and the fathers both cried out in rapture at the sight of the 'prick of pricks' as she often called it.

'Oh, he is all ready to fire it!' said one, taking it in his hand.

'Quick!' I gasped. 'I cannot wait!' And the lecherous priests held on to guide it, till it was engulfed in my dear whore's slippery cunt and we drew from their lips exclamations of vivid pleasure at the sight, while they forced their hands to prepare their ardent pricks to follow. It was a short ride but hot as hell, and the wine came next.

Father Ambrose rolled on the floor and pulled my dear whore onto him, while kisses and caresses were given all over her body; and in good, old-fashioned, belly-to-belly style, they fucked each other royally. As she started to rise and had reached her knees, the insatiable Anthony sprang at her, stuck his firm pego into her from behind and swung her back and forth with powerful thrusts, raising her on her elbows.

'Give me something to kiss,' she cried, and the fallen prick of Father Ambrose was instantly under her face. Holding on to his broad buttocks, she sucked the hero of the last battle.

As she rested on a cushion on the floor after this last skirmish, I took a glass of wine and knelt at her side.

'Oh, fathers, these are lovely playthings!' she said. And she took my pego in her hand and fondly stroked and petted and squeezed it till, firm as a rock, she pressed a kiss on its vermilion head.

Father Ambrose sprang up, his lance stiffly standing, and said:

'Do you know how priests amuse themselves when they are shut out from cunts?'

'No,' I answered, 'show us.' And the libidinous priest threw himself on the floor beside me and in a second had his cock staring me in the face and my prick in his mouth.

'Sodom and Gomorrah!' cried Mrs Belle, maddened by this new lechery. 'You shall. I want to see it!' Holding his prick in one hand, with the other she shoved my head down on it. Never before had I done this, but now, with my passions all aroused by his hot sucking and the atmosphere about me, a flash of lust overcame me. I took it in more willingly than I would have supposed, and our two strong bodies were writhing on the floor, our well-sucked pricks spending in each other's mouths in copious floods.

Mrs Belle was beside herself. 'Oh, what a delicious sight! And I never saw it before. Oh, how delicious it is to learn something new. Teach me more. I mean to run the whole gamut of lecherous experience.'

Father Ambrose stepped up to me and fondled my

fallen prick and empty bag. 'Ah, my fine fellow, you are done for the present. Do you know the surest way to stiffen it again?'

'Let's see your method!' cried the eager Mrs Belle. And as I was always ready for anything with woman, man, or beast, I leaned over at the motion of direction from the priest, and he pointed his prick at my back doorway. The enormous head stuck in the entrance of my cul, but quickly the mad-with-lust woman knelt beside me and, wetting his cock with her tongue, she held it to its work at my very narrow arsehole.

The priest, now beside himself with lust caused by her tonguing and the tight passage that he was entering, seized my thighs with his muscular hands. Holding me tight, with cries of frantic lust, he shoved his great cock in farther and farther, till it was almost in to its full length, in my buttocks.

Its enormity irritated and excited every sensation of lust in my body and his wild thrusts made my prick spring to its full stature at a bound, as it were, and I voluntarily took its robust erection in my hand. But the other sodomite was only waiting his chance, and on his knees before me, Father Anthony took its throbbing head in his mouth.

For me it was the ultimate frenzy of lust. Never did I teem with more lecherous enjoyment than then; Mrs Belle, kneeling beside us, watched the outrageous sight and felt the two throbbing pricks and kissed them as she got the chance while they rushed in and out until, as my sperm flew in a mighty shower into one priest's mouth, the mighty engine in my backside exploded and I was deluged with a flood of sperm behind, to take the place of what I lost in front.

The climax was excruciating and we three men were pictures of the fullest enjoyment of lewdest lechery.

The instant Father Ambrose's cock was withdrawn from my cul, with the cry of a vulture, Mrs Belle seized his buttocks in her arms and his still stiff and oozing cock in her mouth; she sucked and sucked in a wild and shameless agony of unsatisfied lust till she rolled over on the floor, crying:

'Help! Help me – do something for me.'

Quickly, Anthony picked her up bodily and threw her with some violence on the bed in the form of the letter X, her arms above her head, her legs as wide open as they would spread. Then we tied her in that position with bands of cloth and Father Anthony, seizing a big pillow, stuffed it under her bum. Helpless, she lay there, unable to move hand or foot.

Like a flash, Anthony knelt beside her, his tongue pushing with lightning thrusts into her madly hot cunt without stopping; he kept up the friction till, with a scream, she spent!

He now quickly rose and Father Anthony rushed to the breach and his tongue made the second assault, charging in and out till she spent again, screaming: 'One more! One more!' and panting and wriggling, almost crazy: 'Give me something to suck and give it to me quick!'

As I was her last stallion, I mounted over her and, kneeling so that I was over her face, I stuck my prick in her mouth. Lying flat on my belly, I covered her cunt with my mouth, and my tongue frigged it till she for the third time gave down her inexhaustible spending and was in turn half choked with my swollen cock and the plenteous flow of sperm.

As I write this, it is odd enough! The memory of that scene is too much for me. My prick is ready to burst. Ah, dear fellow, you remember that hot, smoking mouth, do you? The oil of happiness is rising in you and there is no girl to take it. Well, if you need it that much, I must do it myself!

You like frigging, I know, and a hand will do in a storm like this. That is it, swell your rosy head. There,

The Town Bull

my dear prick, you feel it coming, good – good, the dance is on, the sperm is near the top – eh – oh – ah! It flies – golly – it struck the wall ten feet away.

'Go on!' you say. You bet I will. There – there's another supply! Eh, how contented you look as I squeeze out the last drop and fall back in languid lassitude.

VII

What a blessed life I led with Mrs Belle and the two priests who helped me manage her. How delightfully the time sped. As for Rose – perhaps you think I have forgotten her – at the time of our theological séance she was away for a few days to stop with her folks.

One evening as my dear whore and I lay on the sofa, softly playing with the fire that would burn more fiercely soon, Rose rushed in.

'Oh, Mrs Belle and Master Bob, I am glad to get back with you again and oh, I want to tell you, I am going to be married – '

Here Mrs Belle interrupted to ask: 'Who to?'

'Oh, a nice boy. I've never seen his cock and he's nearer my cunt than my knees but my cunt does burn. But' – (and the girl's merry face clouded) – 'I don't know what he would say if he knew I had been naked in Master Bob's arms and that I had sucked his prick. Oh dear, I don't dare tell him!'

'But, Rose,' said Mrs Belle, 'take my advice and tell him everything. It will save you a lot of trouble in the future.'

'Oh, I couldn't do it.' And the frightened girl hid her face in her hands and exclaimed: 'Oh, missy, won't you tell him – how smutty I have been. Bob and I will hide behind the curtains and hear you. And, Mrs Belle, if he gets stiff and hard, do let him do you first.'

'You minx, you want your lover to fuck me first before he does you?'

'Yes, I do, missy, and he is in the kitchen now. He would see me home. Master Bob and I will hide behind the curtain. You call Rube in and tell him all.'

'Well,' laughed my delightful whore. 'Do you want me to appear stark naked before your lover, the moment he first sees me?'

'There,' said the girl, putting a big shawl round her naked mistress. 'That makes things decent and you can get rid of it quickly.' And calling 'Ruben, Ruben, come in here!' she and I disappeared behind the curtain as a short, thick-set, light-colored youth came bashfully into the room.

'Ruben, you and I should be good friends. Rose and I are.' She held out her hand in welcome, the movement intentionally displacing the shawl and leaving a lovely bare arm and shoulder so that his eyes flashed as his hand met hers.

She made him sit on the edge of the sofa on which she lay. 'Ruben, you know Rose is a lovely girl. She is a virgin, but, well . . . Ruben I will come right to the point and tell you I am a hot-natured woman and I have a lover. We have been naked in bed and she has been with us and kissed us all over, and we have kissed her – there, are you jealous of that?' I saw the lovely woman's hand slide down into Ruben's lap.

'I am not jealous, for I have not frigged and fucked many wenches before.' He started to rise. 'But I must not stay here any longer.'

'Oh yes, you must, Ruben!' And the amorous fingers opened his trousers and held a new prick in their grasp. 'Oh, I must rob Rose of one little diddle. Come, my dear boy!' And the lovely Mrs Belle threw aside the shawl and lay naked on her back.

The young animal was fully aroused and in an instant was flat on Belle's belly, his fresh cock in her cunt and savage cries coming from both. His bottom worked so fast that in half a minute Belle's legs went up around his waist and her tongue and his were fighting a duel while, her lively bum held tightly in his grasp, he poured a plentiful supply from his lusty balls.

We spectators were excited but contained ourselves while I undressed Rose, knowing that she would soon be wanted.

'Oh, and I have robbed Rose,' said the satisfied mistress. Grabbing the young lover, she pulled him down across her lap and with hand and leg commenced to put starch into him.

'That's right, raise your rosy head! You will do a nice job, just as soon as you get hard. Just think of yourself tearing into that new cunt of Rose's. Ah, it makes it swell, does it?' And calling out, Mrs Belle said: 'Bob, bring in the victim and lay her on the altar.'

I picked her up and the naked, dusky bride was taken in and laid flat on the bed, and my whore, who had just enjoyed him, led Ruben up to Rose, his rooster rampant. He would not wait but fell with a lustful cry on her belly. We could not see his prick pierce, but her cries were milestones of his progress.

'Now he has hit it! Now, pierce her through, dear Ruben!'

'Oh, I don't want it any longer – fuck me, I am mad for it!' And just as Ruben withdrew to get a chance for a final lunge, and just as his prick was piercing through, Mrs Belle gave him a resounding, stinging slap with her hand on his heaving bottom, then another and another; all the time they were squirming and sighing and we knew by the shrieks that we now had a full-blown rose.

And she was blown breathless and battered down, with her firm belly bumping his, but her lover did not spare her in the least. Springing round on the bed, he rested her back on his belly and shoved her bottom onto the edge, crying to me: 'Come on, put that big white prick of yours into her. Fuck her right up to the handle.'

Belle, assisting me by directing my prick deep in the gory cunt of Rose, watched us diddle first fast and furious, then slower and slower, then satisfied and slow.

As we lay together in a satisfied siesta on the bed, my own hot-bellied whore seized her new flame and, sliding down on the rug, pulled him on top of her. The lad learned lewdness quickly for she had not been a moment flat on her back before the ardent Ruben had kissed with rapture every hill and vale of the fair, undulating, fiery landscape. His kisses had started the rills flowing in the hidden cavern and with kisses on his mouth, belly, and proud pintle, the dear whore clutched him in her arms, put his prick in her pussy, and with her legs round her waist was wiggled into heaven by his delightful diddling, made hotter still by Rose's rapid hand-rape on his bottom.

VIII

How happy I would have been to have passed all my life with my dear whore, but along in the third happy month, there came one day a telegram from her husband, saying that he had been badly hurt in a railway accident and asking her to come and nurse him.

With a sad heart, I helped her to make arrangements to let her flat and pack her belongings, until everything was ready for her departure the next day.

'Now, Bob, you go to your room and sleep and I will go to mine and we will then both be fresh for our final fucking.'

And so, late at night, when respectability was seeking its cold couch, she called me, and naked, I stood beside her bed, contemplating half-happy, half-sad, her bare beauty.

'Come, dear Bob, a first fuck flat on top of me.' Lying on her breasts and belly, with encircling arms and legs, and fervent kissing mouths, the god she worshiped was enshrined in her inmost sanctuary and, with rapturous thrusts, was pouring its offering of libations on her altar.

Throwing herself outstretched upon the sofa, she made me bring her a full bottle of champagne and, taking another, I sat in an easy chair facing her. There we rested until my prick put up a perpendicular finger without a touch.

But the dear girl bade me sit still until we had both emptied our bottles. Then, with swimming heads and boiling semen seething in our sexual organs, she rose and threw herself upon me.

Kissing her forehead, I passed to eyes and cheeks; then her open mouth caught my tongue, and hers and mine met, now thrust on one another's like lances in a tournament, then rolling round each other in close embraces, clasping hers as far as it would go while her hot lips squeezed it and tried to drag its full length into her mouth; then in the hollow between her breasts, my hot lips burned her and then seized the tempting nipples and with tickling touch tasted their ripe ruddiness.

Oh, the soft sighs and heaves when my eager lips raided the rounded belly and thighs and ravished the gaping grotto of her cunt.

'Fuck me! Fuck me – fuck your whore once more!' But I held her tight and, turning her buttocks to my face, I stuck my tongue into her cul and worked it in and out.

Drunk with the wine and with my lascivious touches, she sprang up, glued herself to me, and rolled to the floor, taking me with her. My rigid prick pierced her gluttonous slit and worked with lightning lunges till she shrieked in sensual satisfaction; still stiff, I withdrew and, jumping up, gloated over her voluptuous charms writhing in lecherous luxury on the floor.

Then, turning her on her belly, I threw myself on her back and stuck my stiff and slippery cock deep into her arse, while my hand clutched her cunt and frigged it. As the delightful sensations of the two set her to quivering wantonly, she turned her head round so that I could see her wide-open eyes, flushed cheeks, and trembling lips, which soon broke forth with: 'Oh, my dear lover, my dear fucker, your whore is happy to her fingertips, each crease and crevice is teeming with sensual delight, each rounded hillock is throbbing with lust. My cunt is oozing forth its slimy flood and your sweet prick is ravishing my very vitals with its spendings, oh happy, happy, well-whored whore!'

And in the ecstasy of our hot contact, we lay and gently heaved until, jealous of the fleeting hours, we rose and bathed each other with smarting alcohol. We took a bottle of wine, and as we lay side by side on the bed, tasting it, a new thought struck me and, filling my mouth with wine, I fastened my lips to hers and squirted it all into her.

She was quick to return the favor and I drew the nectar from her ruby, ardent lips. Then, holding her breasts close together, she poured some wine between them and I lapped it up below.

Her cunt crevice next received its portion of the bubbling glow and I held my mouth under it until my tongue and lips had drawn every drop; with my teeth I seized the curly hair and pulled it until she almost cried; then turning her over, I poured myself some more wine down the valley of her buttocks and let it flow through the ravine into my mouth.

She was by now so excited that she sprang out of bed and ran around the room, climbed up on the windowsill and stood there with open legs, jutting out her belly; then she ran round to the end of the sofa, flinging herself back over it and raising her legs like banners in the air, and I rushed at her, holding her straight up, standing her on her head, pushing my face down between her legs, and tickling her cunt with my lips.

Together, to the floor we rolled and, grasping her heaving bum in my hands, my tongue was in her slit, my prick deep in her mouth, and a finger of each plunged in the anus of the other. How often that night we reached the summit of spending bliss, I cannot tell – we were drunk with wine and wantonness.

I only know that when her hot lips sucked from my cock the last oblation, the sperm was mixed with blood, and frightened, she drew back, the red and pearly drops mixed, falling together on her ivory bosom, and then we lay in close-clasped, naked contact.

IX

She left the next day, my darling Mrs Belle, and as we were folded in a last fond embrace at the door, she slipped a packet into my hands and told me to open it that night.

I took lodgings nearby and as I sat lonesome in that room that evening, I happened to think of her parting gift. On opening it, I found that my dear whore (how happy she had been always to be called that) had made a deposit of $500 in a savings bank in my name and I then recalled going to the bank with her and affixing my signature to a book, but I had supposed that I was merely witnessing some legal form for her.

As I dropped asleep alone, my last thoughts and later dreams were of my dear whore, my generous, wanton Mrs Belle.

What next? Listless and lonesome, I wandered round aimlessly for about a week, then began looking in the papers among the advertisements for 'Help Wanted.' I kept it up every day for some time, without finding anything that attracted me, till some time later I accidentally ran into:

WANTED
  A small school for young ladies wants a strong man for porter and to be generally useful. Apply from 5 to 7.

  Madame Bovary
  91 Blank Street.

The Town Bull

The address being in a fashionable quarter, I determined to follow the advice of the advertisement and apply. Plainly dressed, I went to seek employment and Madame took me to her study.

I found her a French woman who spoke excellent English – petite but plump, not handsome but vivacious, bright, and active – and saw that her eyes took me in completely.

'I have here a small finishing school,' she said, 'for young ladies, all from distant parts of the country, and you won't have much to do.'

I thought I might find plenty to do with five young girls and a fine woman like her but I said little, as she explained more fully the situation.

Two days later, I was the porter, or janitor, as you might like to call it, at Madame Bovary's select school for young ladies and I was introduced generally to the five scholars – light, dark, plump, slim, blond and brunette – varied, but all sprightly and attractive.

What a harem this would make, my amorous mind suggested, but for a week everything was as tame and respectable as one could wish, spiced lightly it is true with now and then a show of pretty leg going upstairs or a girl in her nightdress as I passed an open door.

The second floor was the dormitory where all the girls slept in separate beds, while Madame's room was on the next floor and I had a small hall bedroom on the same floor.

As I have said, a week passed eventless; on the evening of the eighth day the young ladies had gone to an entertainment at a neighboring school and I was in my room reading when the bell that connected my room with Madame Bovary's rang; knocking on her closed door without opening it, she directed me to bring a bottle of wine.

'Bring me a quart, Bob, as I am very thirsty. And see

that the house is well locked up, the girls will not be in till late.'

When I returned with the wine, her door was wide open, the room brightly lighted, and there, stretched out on the bed with a book in her hand, was the plump figure of Madame, clad in a loose white wrapper, showing fine shoulders and bare arms.

She quickly thrust the book under the pillow and turned on her side; her bubbies rose rounded up like mountains from the valley of her dainty waist, and as she stretched herself luxuriously, one well-rounded leg peeped out below her wrapper and made my tool sharpen itself for work.

'Oh!' I said, to myself, 'you want something, and I have got just the thing that you want.'

Pouring out a glass of wine, I handed it to her and as she sort of sat up in bed to drink it, her legs were opened just enough to let mine get in between them. My prick had now been some time idle and when I filled her glass the second time, the protuberance in front of my abdomen was truly shocking, so I replaced the glass on the table and asked:

'Is there anything more that you would like?'

'Come here!' she said, and I stood facing her close by the bed. 'Your disrespect to me is shocking!' she added.

'Disrespect?' I asked.

'Yes!' she cried. 'Don't you suppose that I can see the condition that you are in.' She fixed her eyes on the part of my breeches that was bulging out with its load of stiffness.

'Well, Madame,' I answered, 'a man is a man, if he is only a servant, and no man could gaze on your voluptuous pose unmoved.'

'Oh, you are a flatterer!' she cried. 'Why, I am forty – but perhaps the best way to cure you is to let you see more,' and the fascinating little Madame daintily unhooked her wrapper and the two plump globes bounded out.

'Lovely! Lovely!' I cried. 'Let me see more – more!' The voluptuous woman let go all her modesty and, squirming down flat on the bed, with eager hands drew her only garment up to her waist.

In an instant my cock was out and, grasping her by the ankles, I pulled her roughly to the edge of the bed; lifting her legs high in the air, I brought my cock down and stood close to her dainty, curly-haired cunt.

'Fuck me!' she cried. 'Put it into me, I have been dying for you to fuck me ever since you came. Oh, what a monster! There, I will put it in myself. Oh, what a splendid prick! I have never had so big a one before. Quick – quick – fuck me – fuck me hard, I can't wait!' Seizing the palpitating thighs, I did fuck – fucked hard, fucked with the freshness of a long rest.

The now unblushing lewdness of her whole body and the tight grasp she had on my cock all woke me to fresh movement.

'Oh, you splendid lover – you royal diddler! Don't keep a thing but give it to me hot and heavy.'

Grasping her bottom, I pressed into her a double of such thrust that she whined and gasped with pleasure.

'Oh, I'm going to spend, my dear boy – oh – oh! The delight of those hot shots – shoot it into me again as soon as you can. It is too much! I never was fucked like this before, oh, how splendid, how lovely, you lusty lover! I will be your slave, anything, just to have such heavenly pleasure, take me in your arms and roll on the bed in mine!' Gasping and panting, she kept me still embedded in her slit and we lay entwined, how long I know not. Hot kisses shot from one to the other, with eager hands ravishing each other, until the wanton made me kneel over her as she lay flat, and handled, frigged, and kissed the whole domain of priapus.

Oh, those vivacious French women, not always

handsome but vivid, graceful, active like busy bees, now here, now there, leaving an amorous stinging touch or kiss wherever they light, till all the tingling spots unite and one's whole body is red-hot with lust.

Now fondling the staff of life and love with a gently frigging hand, then placing it between the bounding titties or hard buttocks, and ending with a dainty kiss on its crimson peak.

'Oh, I love you so, that I must ride you.' Pulling my bottom to the edge of the bed, my feet on the floor, she mounted me man-wise and on her prancing stallion, safely spiked on the proud prick, she galloped, cantered, squirmed, and danced, then seizing my buttocks in her hands, she pumped and pulled with never tiring loins, until she had the last drop of nervous ambrosia shot up in her quivering belly.

Myself up on the pillows, my filly still panting for breath on my belly, she reached for the book I had seen her reading.

'This,' she said, 'stimulates me to be bold with you!' The lewd woman showed me plates in natural colors of all the forms and fashions of lasciviousness, and read to me the hottest portions of the text, till my staff was stiff and throbbing in her belly. Fastening her thighs securely round my loins, I rose from the bed and ran about the room with her impaled on my prick, and right before a mirror, we watched our agile fucking until, with a delightful agony, we both spent to the music of our sighs and the picture of our heaving arses.

I the master, she the servant now – bringing me wine, bathing me off, covering me with carnal caresses till again my blood boiled in the stiffening prick and I pressed her face down on its point.

'Oh, you want a French cunt, do you?'

I laughed at the new name and she went on: 'Did you not know that the French were great for sucking? Why, that was my first experience in lust. Father Anselmo, the confessor in the seminary where I finished my education, found out what a frisky girl I was and twice a week used to smuggle me into his room, and we enjoyed each other "*à la française*." '

X

Madame knew all things of voluptuousness and sexual excitement. Often, as the young ladies went to bed, she took me to a room where the raising of a curtain gave me a full view of the dormitory, with the five young ladies in every form of dishabille, romping and fooling with each other, playing tag and leap frog, naked, until my excited prick screwed the wanton school marm, as we watched their exciting antics.

But my reserve with the girls was complete, although often when I caught one of them eyeing the big place on my trousers, showing the shape underneath, it was all I could do not to show the virgin the naked reality.

But sometimes elders propose and youngsters dispose. One Sunday morning as the five pupils and Madame were finishing breakfast, Madame, as I was waiting on them, said:

'It is time for you to get ready for church. I don't feel very well and shall remain at home this morning.'

I knew, or rather thought that I knew, just what that meant – we had not been together for some days, and now with the girls out of the house, we should have a good chance for a razzle-dazzle.

But as the girls filed out and went upstairs, the last one left a letter for Madame on the table. Alone with me, she opened it –

'My God!' she cried, 'they know it all! and the minxes have seen us together!' She read:

Dear Madame:

    We like you very much but we need something of the same pleasure that you get with Bob. We have watched you twice, naked in his arms, and we are all in an excited condition; if we cannot get what we want, we shall have to seek a solace elsewhere.

    We are not going to church today, and we will all wait in the dormitory.

All had signed the note and for a minute we were silent; then Madame sprang up.

'There is no way out of it if we do not do something for them, they will tell, or worse, go outside and lose their maidenheads to some chance fellow. Swear Bob, that whatever temptation, you will never try to break one of their virginities.'

'I swear!' I replied, and seeing what was ahead, my prick became wildly rampant.

'Come,' she said. 'Stay outside the door; listen and be guided by circumstances.'

So going upstairs, I stationed myself where Madame and I were in the habit of watching the girlish gambols, while Madame walked into the dormitory and threw herself into a chair.

'I am truly repentant, girls, to have been the cause of a note like this. I am a free woman and thought I had the right to a lover if I choose but I did not intend to seduce you girls placed in my care.' And she buried her face in her hands. The girls gathered round and kissed and petted her.

'Oh, Madame,' said one who seemed to lead the others, 'don't take it so to heart. We are bound to face men someday. We are all on fire, hot and eager. Why should we not learn all about man and what he does to woman, here and now, as part of our education?' And as she paused, the other girls all applauded.

'Well, why not?' said Madame, rising flushed and lustful. 'At your age I was a virgin but had tasted bliss with two different priests and knew as much of voluptuousness as any maiden can.' Then, catching up a prayer book, she exclaimed: 'Here, swear on this that while in my charge you will keep your virginity unbroken.'

And the girls, trembling with amorous ardor, kissed the book.

'Now strip!' In a moment, one naked woman, five naked girls, and one naked man constituted a class of five eager pupils and two well-qualified instructors in the new study – that of sex.

In another minute, Madame had pulled one of the beds into the middle of the room and, piling two extra mattresses on it, built an altar that was on a level with the god of all their wishes.

Kissing each girl in turn, she made them draw lots and ranged them in the order drawn at the head of the altar. Then, taking me by my prick, she began a lecture on its way of fulfilling fate and the girls stood silent and half-frightened, but trembling breasts and heaving bellies told of their close attention.

Madame leaned back against the bed and I stood with my prick directly between her legs. I could not wait, and, throwing her back, with a lustful cry I plunged my fevered cock deep into her cunt and fucked her to the music of their excited cries.

They gathered close, throwing themselves on their knees on the bed.

'Feel us both!' Madame cried in agony.

Five pairs of maiden hands felt belly, thighs, balls, prick, breasts, bottom and then cried out: 'Take it out and let us see it shoot!' The generous supply of sperm, floating and spouting in the air, fell on her belly, amidst their lustful shouts of glee; then, plunging it in again, it finished its lustful work, to Madame's satisfaction and the girls' delight, with quivering lunges.

The Town Bull

'Now on your knees in a row.' The five virgins knelt like vestals at the altar and the wriggling Madame made me walk in review before them, the wet but still lustful monarch on a level with their faces. She now told them all about it and each one in turn, as it passed, held and felt the lovely novelty, and in their vivid young passion each one kissed it.

Now, when the last hand released it, they all threw themselves back on the floor panting and sought with their own or their neighbor's hand to put out the fire that burned within them.

'Stop!' cried Madame. 'Don't touch your "things!" ' Jumping on the cot, she sat close up to the pillow. Pulling me between her legs, she made me lie on my back, my head resting on her belly.

'Now, girls, he will fuck you with his tongue – number one, you first.' The trembling but lustful maiden was assisted by the other votaries till she was kneeling over my face.

With her buttocks in my hands, I pressed her down, into her virgin cunt my tongue went glibly till her beautiful belly heaved, the hairy mount pressed close, and the unrestrained cries told the tale of a maiden's first spending when in the company of a naked man.

Each in turn mounted and was sucked and fell back in amorous agony. As I polished off the last, I was ready to spend and Madame cried: 'On your knees, girls.' Leading me to number one, she said: 'Frig him with your hand.' Half a dozen jerks of the soft hand and my discharge flew in the air and landed full in her face; then, moving me down the line, each one of the maidens frigged my prick and had a baptism of sperm, for I was in a constant spouting. Finally, drawing it away from the last dainty hand, with a cry of lechery unappeased, I threw Madame on the edge of the bed and fucked her as they knelt in order to watch us closer, and their wild touches roved all over the field of battle.

XI

Summer was coming and the end of the school, when one day I received a letter from my dear Mrs Belle Strate. Her husband had died soon after she left New York, and she wrote:

> Dear Bob,
> I have been virtuous since I left you but now the thought of the bliss we had from one another forces me to write. Will you marry me and come live on this beautiful plantation with me?
> I won't be jealous of you and will help you to enjoy any pretty woman you may lust for; and if another man wants me, you must not be jealous either, but we will love each other best of all.
> I have money enough. Come and we will enjoy the rest and best of life together.
>
> Your love,
> Belle Strate

Of all the women I had ever met, she was the queen. Therefore, I did not hesitate, but wrote at once that when school ended I would come at once. And I told her of these amours and how her image had always supplanted the passing passion for others.

School closed, and the night after commencement I had my last, longest, and hottest lustful fight with Madame and the five virgins. Then followed a week with my lustful Madame alone.

One day I bethought myself of my buxom hostess and Mrs Virtue and determined to call on them. My kind hostess almost ate me alive. Of course, I had to tell her a lot of lies about having been out of the city and of going again that night.

'Well, you may have been out of the city, but you . . . you left something here to remind Mrs Virtue and me of you.'

'What?' I asked. Leading me into the small room where I had slept when there, I found two pretty girl babies slumbering on the bed.

'They are both yours!' she said. 'Just your color and hair and they were born just nine months after our last razzle-dazzle, and Mrs Virtue's a week later.'

I kissed her warmly and, leading her back into the larger room, I put her in the way of having another one nine months later.

Mrs Virtue came in just then, and with happy ardor she let me plant in her the same horn of plenty, whose fruit was slumbering in the other room.

For an hour or two, we three, in lustful nakedness, recalled the sweet sensual sports we had so often enacted. On my return I recounted to Madame all, and she was compelled to let me rest, and for the day to only take pleasure from my thrusting tongue. But she had had enough this last week of school, as I had devoted myself to her only.

I had made friends with four jolly young fellows, so one night I prevailed upon Madame, for a change, to go with me to a house of pleasure. The minute she and I stood ready, I gave a whistle and the four friends joined us, all stark naked, and the lively Madame had before her, five, stiff-cocked, eager lovers.

She lost her head completely, throwing herself first into the arms of one and then another; she almost squeezed the life out of us each in turn; then, dragging me to the bed, she made me quickly fuck her – then she received one after the other, till the white balsam ran out of her overloaded sheath.

It was a revel such as few women have ever enjoyed. Five fresh and firm cocks and one lively bantam hen. We were all large and muscular, she so small and light, that we carried her round the room spitted on our pricks, without aid from our hands.

She was crazy with lust, not only by nature but by the wine that we gave her. Now each in bubby-bed, now in cunt-bed. Three copious crops of sperm from each branch of coral, she plucked and stored within her and at the end, she was so faint that I had to take her home in a carriage.

A week later, I alighted at a Southern station and there, looking just as I last saw her in New York, was my darling Belle, my darling whore, whose memory had been cherished deeper than all other transient mistresses.

Alone with her, she drove me home in a low basket wagon, and as we left the village I took her in my arms, not lustfully but lovingly, and with the fond affection I cherished for her.

A little country church was on our way and I stopped the horse. Without a word from either of us, we entered the parsonage and asked the aged parson to marry us.

With his wife and daughter as witnesses, we two were made one, not only as in the past by bonds of lust and love, but one in law.

XII

I am in a heavenly haven with my wanton whore, my darling wife, so why write further? I will but add two closing facts.

Our plantation adjoins one other. These aside, there are no habitations for five miles in either direction.

Just previous to our marriage, five couples bought this plantation and lived in separate cottages, while owning and operating the farm in community fashion. Of course, we were all soon acquainted.

One evening, my dear intriguing Belle asked one of the couples to dinner and soon the four of us were jolly with lively talk, wine, and the good eating, till the young wife and Belle retired, that we men might smoke.

My young friend and I were soon confidential and praising each other's wives, when my dear Belle called out: 'Boys, we are lonesome and it is nice and cool up here.'

'We are coming,' I answered.

My bold Belle replied: 'Well, I feel just like making you come!'

My companion jumped up, exclaiming: 'What does she mean?'

'It means that she is ready to take a diddle out of you, if your wife will take one out of this!' I pulled out my redheaded gentleman, ready to be introduced to a new lady.

'Good!' cried the new lady's husband. In less than

three minutes, two naked Adams were bounding into the room where two naked Eves were lying. Each had a new cock pouring sperm into her eagerly excited cunt and when we four parted that night, each had parted with all the amorous ammunition we could bring to the field of battle.

Two days later, another couple, another dinner, another diddle; and so on, till I had fucked five young matrons who had never tasted sperm other than from their husband's spigots, and those brisk spigots had all five fucked my active Belle.

Then came a night at our house, and we had an orgy with six naked women and six naked men. All signed a compact that I had drawn up, forming a community to be perpetuated by our children and such as might be unanimously agreed upon – property, wives, and children, all to be held in common. A natural nation, a scene of sensual society.

No fatherhood or motherhood after a child was weaned, all the products of our prolific pricks in their hot cunts to be brought up in common, children of the community. At maturity the boys and girls should become full-fledged members and compelled to copulate with young and old alike.

Why not? Who could tell who was the father of any child? As I write, one of the pretty little sixteen-year-old daughters of the community enters – my daughter perhaps, but who can tell? Her mother's conception might have come from any one of the six pricks that indiscriminately injected seed into her fertile field.

'Good morning, Bob!' she cries.

'How is Pussy?' I ask. Up goes the light dress covering the plump little belly.

Pussy stroker is up in arms at once. I strip her light gown off and lay her on the bed, gave her a taste of my big prick and still abundant sperm. Then my dear whore comes in, clothes pulled up to her waist and with one of the young men of the community, his staff clutched in her hand.

'Oh, what a shame that we missed yours, you have just had your diddle. Well, you shall see ours!' Dropping her clothes to the floor, my darling whore soon squirms and pants as of old, from the swift, eager strokes of the young cock of her ardent lover.

Belle then says: 'My dear girl, let us make them stiff again and change cocks.' The pretty sixteen-year-old is kissing my old prick, dancing round it, rubbing it here and there and everywhere, until, as her lips leave it at last, the rigid staff is ready to be planted in my dear whore's citadel, and she has worked on the dear boy's pintle till it is on eager stand.

With interlaced arms and frigging hands, we watch the young couple as they, fresh and active, bound on the bed, giving and taking pleasure with their agile loins, till breathless and glued together, they lie and watch us slower and older fuckers as we in turn take up the battle. I give my dear Belle a strong and juicy fuck, as firm and sweet as that of years ago when I first met Mrs Belle Strate, and diddled her in an assignation house in New York.

We soon added a darker shade to the community, for we found so much work to keep the Elysian Fields in order that I went to New Orleans and hired two stalwart young black men and, taking them to my room, told them what kind of people we were and how necessary it was that I should know that both were healthy; they stripped at my request and I went all over them.

As they stood in front of me they became inflamed with lust and as I turned back the foreskin to see whether they were diseased, they both shuddered.

Diseased? They were both magnificent, healthy specimens of the genus cock, and as I involuntarily moved the soft skin back and forth, they lost control of themselves and, seizing each other, were in an instant rolling on the floor, working their bums and sucking each other's sweetness out.

Need I add that I soon garnered a second crop from each! I took them to our dear Elysium, and the very first night that these lusty workers were present at the meeting of the founders, all six women were ploughed by one or another and African seed was sown that later on added a darker shade to the community.

XIII

We worked as well as played and finally found the markets about us too limited to buy the large quantities of supplies needed in such a community, so it came about that twice a year, I, as chief, went to New York to purchase them.

When there, I tried in vain to find my old hostess and Mrs Virtue but they – and even my little lively French Madame – had disappeared; but as I wandered the streets one night, two pretty girls about sixteen years of age 'picked me up' as they say.

'What do you girls want of an old cock like me?' I asked as I groped them.

'Oh, you know, we like nice middle-aged men. We don't live in a house but we have our own room where we pump men dry!' Both girls had their hands on the pump, which had had no work since leaving home.

In a neat little room, a naked man of middle age was soon lying between two plump and pretty prostitutes and quickly both juicy cunts, one after the other, were pumping up his cream.

After this double duty, we were resting and my prick was peaceful. I chanced to examine their faces carefully. They had a similar look but said they were not sisters. I was frankly puzzled, I seemed to be carried back to the old days in the rear of the beer shop.

'Girls, we don't know each other very well, but will you give me your history? Something about you recalls to me my old days in New York.'

'Why not!' said one, as she fondled my old pleasure-giver in her hand. 'We are not ashamed of our history. We don't know who our daddies were and shall not try to make any man father our babies if we have any.

'We are good-hearted but find it pleasant to earn our living by giving ourselves to any nice man who wants us, and we really like it. We are whores by inheritance, for though one of our mothers was married, they told us that we were the children of one man, and he was not the husband of either. They were sure of it by our looks and often used to tell us of their amours.'

A woman knows her child always, a man never! As I gazed on my young harlots, gentle and kind in spite of their trade, I soon had down on my belly first the one who bore a closer resemblance to my dear hostess and then one who was as much patterned after dear Mrs Virtue who lived upstairs.

And as I thought more and questioned further, I knew for sure that these, my last loves, were the daughters of the old and were the two babies that I had seen upon the bed when I had said goodbye to my old friends.

'Come, he's in good condition now. Let's toss up to see who'll be the first to take the stiffness out of him!' The two lively little wantons stood one on each side of me as I lay on the couch naked.

One tossed up a coin, which fell on my belly, and as it should have been, the one who cried 'tails' won the throw and soon had tucked my tail between her legs in her pretty quim. With hard riding she soon pumped my sperm again; she did not entirely empty my spigot but generously dismounted from the stiff staff and pushed me on top of her half sister. I poured out the remaining drops of the flow of sperm with hot thrusts of passion.

Then, with one in each arm, I told my story, which dovetailed with theirs as nicely as my old cock had in their little cunts; now standing before the glass, we were able to trace resemblances that might mark me as their daddy. 'Well, I don't care,' said one, 'if you are my father.'

'Nor I!' echoed the other. 'You have fucked us twice, and a hundred times is not a bit more wicked than once.'

Now on their knees, the lecherous young women kissed and fondled the cock of their possible father, until I laid them down, one on top of the other, their pretty cunts one right over the other. First in one, then in the other, my excited cock plunged deep till, what with the novelty and all that we had talked about, the fountain spurted again and I gave up all.

As I rested, I told them where we lived and all about the community, asking as I finished: 'Girls, would you like to go home with me?'

They were wild with enthusiasm and excitement, I was ravished with hot kisses, head to foot; and spurred on by their fervor, I gave them caresses on breasts, mouths, bellies, and heated cunts.

I drew them, first one and then the other, down on me. As I lay, with my tongue and clinging lips, I titillated their touchy little slits till each in turn wriggled and throbbed and panted as she spent. Then, as I knelt with both hands upon the pillows, my thighs enclosing their forms, my now ponderous prick was wildly seized, tongue tickled, and sucked, first by one and then by the other till I poured in each as much cream as they could swallow; they almost bit off and ate the rare and juicy fruit, until age told and my prick lay withered and wrinkled like an old man, but was even then the object of their never-tiring kisses and touches.

There was a vacant room next to theirs and we made an opening so that, unseen, I could see them entertain their lovers, young and old, sometimes one, sometimes three or four.

It was delicious, this panorama of these half-dressed

or naked votaries of lust, giving each other in every form and on every part of their body voluptuous touches, gropings, kisses, and friggings, fuckings, suckings, till when their companions had disappeared, I often need must rush upon these pretty whores and vent into every hole they had what lust had engendered.

A week thus and my work was ended. I brought them to the South with me but to celebrate had my lively little doxies ask eight of their sprightliest young cocks to hold us company in a revel the last night in New York, for which I hired a luxurious parlor in a house of pleasure.

Lying on a sofa, I held in each arm a nude and lewd companion, and black men servants brought in eight nude youths, who ranged before us, handsome and eager, with pricks at present arms.

My pretty little harlot had on one red garter and one blue, so I put four blue and four red cards marked from one to four in a hat, and then, at my order, each boy took a card and ranged themselves in two rows by matching colors and numbers; the numbers one were fucking the two tight slits as they lay on my arms and I was able to grasp them as they progressed, till with lascivious yells they fired the first shots and numbers two were stiffly in the heated slits and working madly; so followed in turn the others; then my robust prick was the girls' plaything; they kissed and frigged it until I made them, with united hands, jerk the heated sperm in the air while their dainty mouths sucked the few remaining drops as they oozed out.

Then I pushed the girls into the middle of the floor: 'Go for them, boys!' All ten of them were dancing and squirming in a labyrinth of fresh and throbbing flesh, yelling and screaming with delight, till cocks could stand up no more and the cunts and mouths and culs of the two little whores could hold no more sperm.

One of the youths taking hold of my stiff staff, said: 'What shall we do with this?'

One stalwart youth sprang up, jutting out his backstroke to me, and said: 'Well, perhaps he would like to fuck in here. My boss, who is about his age and size, says my arse is better than a woman's cunt.'

'Go on, bugger him!' cried the girls. I laid him over a chair and, pointing my prick at him, worked it frantically into his cul. It was magnificent.

'Do you mind it?' I asked.

'Mind it – it is splendid!' My prick was fast stiffening, so amid the shouts of all the others, I plunged in to the hilt and, too mad with lust to quit, I sent my sperm deep within him.

Still crazed with lechery, I soon drew out and, leaning my head against the couch, pulled him down on his knees before me and handled his stiff prick, while the girls exclaimed: 'Suck it!' I tasted the sweets of Sodom, while my fingers were plunged into his slippery cul, until only a lazy-looking bit of flesh lay on his testicles.

The girls were now crazy with this new lechery: 'He shall suck every one of the boys, one after the other!' they chanted. I grasped the plump buttocks one after the other and sucked the sweetness of their nuts, through fresh firm pricks, until I reached the next to the last. I seized one of the girls and straddled her over his face until the sperm began to squirt, when the dear girl squirmed off his staff to let me suck the last drops from the spouting spigot and the act ended with the last fellow and the other girl in the same manner.

We now rested until I made the boys tell stories of their lewd encounters. After a while I rang the bell and the two in long dominoes came in with wine. I had arranged for their services and told the mistress of the house that I required them with good, long, stiff pricks; and they served us till the roisterers had two stiff bumpers of sparkling wine in their bellies.

I had the glasses filled again and again and the now half-drunk girls that I held in my arms tossed them off quickly. The blacks stood silent in the middle of the room.

'Strip!' I commanded and naked they stood, with monstrous erections reaching clear up to their navels.

Pushing the girls off the couch, I shouted: 'Run girls, or they will fuck you!'

'No, they shall not; I was never diddled by a black man and I won't be now!'

'Run then!' I advised and the two girls, panting, ran as the blacks darted after them; they ran here and there, dodged, squirmed, darted in behind the furniture, rushed to their white lovers, crying to be saved, until the mad excited men sprang upon them, picked them up bodily as if they had been babes and, kissed their wildly panting forms all over. Then, mad with lechery, they threw them on the bed beside me and in an instant those two pretty little white cunts were stretched wider than ever before with the immense length and volume of those tremendous black cocks.

Clutched tight, it did not take more than a half dozen strokes to wiggle the wantons out of their squeamishness. They could not resist the overwhelming pleasure of such vigorous fucking.

First one, then the other joined in the dance of delightful lechery, with gasping mouths, panting breasts, heaving bellies, and wildly working bums.

'I give up,' cried one.

'It is heavenly, give it to me!' the other yelled. 'I'm going off, it's splendid, see – oh, I would like to fuck black men all my life.'

These lately protesting fillies, their legs and arms round their ugly but manly stallions, lay flat, belly to belly and breast to breast, and kissed the bulging black lips.

'Let us see them squirm!' The two blacks broke loose

till the two lust-filled girls were quivering and shaking from another dose. The black giants seized the panting does in their arms, danced round the room with them, rubbed their pricks all over their white bodies, kissed their bottoms, bellies, slits, and put their tongues far into the palpitating cunts. In return, we saw the crazy whores, wound up to a pitch of lewdness, kiss them in return, and we now saw the black cocks in their unprotesting mouths.

This was too much for the blacks, and spiking the white girls on their fierce arrows, they ran around the room in a fierce frenzy, fucking all the time with magnificent stroking as they ran, till they fell all out of breath on the divan by me. The girls continued to pump up their sperm with buttocks that were bounding with speed.

This was not enough for our dainty whores. They sprang up wriggling and threw themselves upon their ravishers, their mouths clutching eagerly at the fallen monsters. Kissing and sucking, the two wild wantons did not cease till once again the princely pricks stood rampant.

I did not stir, but my mouth watered for their succulent richness, till one lechery-laden girl seemed to read my thoughts. Quick as a flash she forced her dusky champion on his knees before my face. I seized his prick, she stood before me and pulled the black's mouth down to her cunt and he tongue-fucked her as I sucked him and both spent together and lay trembling from the emissions. I now seized the other black man and rolled on the floor to a finish, and we fell apart, tired and empty.

Conclusion

And now farewell. Elysium in the sunny South still flourishes, twenty years or more after my dear Belle first held me in her arms after the marriage. Two generations have grown big enough to use the blessed tools of love, for nature ripens quickly here from climate and from undisguised living for lust.

Only last night as I had my dear whore – still a fine mount, stout and large, but just as lewd and just as sweet to me in bed – merry laughter struck our ears and two lovely girls stood stark naked in the cooling stream, and soon we too were nude and in the brook. Old Grandpa Priapus was fondled till ancient ardor unfurled the standard of assault and the two nymphs dragged their old satyr to the warm sands, where they quickly placed my dear whore, as nature intended she should live and die, in the position of open thighs and arms. Spurred on by eager hands and kisses, I fucked her, my still-vigorous probe ravishing her plump and luscious cunt, and she too, tasted with me the sweets of exuding sperm.

Lying there, my head on the breast of the dear whore, and the charming girls pillowed on each thigh, I knew I was in heaven.

Oh, thou respectable man or woman who through all your life till now, with all heaven-given lust held back, submerged, smothered in the sickening artificiality of a world of make-believes, who do not break loose and let errant lewdness guide you here, where purity, prejudice and prudery are unknown; why not with wildly excited cocks and cunts take the next train for *Elysium*?

Blanche

I

This is an important occasion, this beginning of a remarkable Memoir; and Gladys seems to appreciate its full significance. She has a new dress, or rather costume, for the draped confection that does not at all conceal the exquisite curves of her body, undresses rather than dresses her. You must understand what I mean. She would rather have been far less indelicate stark naked, than in this mazy, fluffy cloud which by its half-hearted attempt to conceal anything, accentuates the charms of everything.

Delicious arms and legs has Gladys, and the rosy flesh gleams through the transparent drapery; nipples as carmine as her lips, and a waist rounded cleanly as her throat. The gauze ceases at her knees; thence is a dress of black silk stockings and natty patent leather shoes.

Her little fingers, bedecked with costly rings, (we have had more than one wealthy visitor since the beginning of the book) – hover over the keys of the machine. A brimming glass of champagne stands at the elbow of each of us, cigarettes are to hand; in fact, it only needs the word for 'Blanche La Mare' to start her redoubtable career.

I never expected George Reynolds to come back. I knew I was done, and my chances of seeing him again about as remote as the likelihood of recovering the two five-pound notes he had borrowed. As a matter of fact, I minded losing my husband less than the money; his conduct and letter had shown him up a bit too much. I could only damn my own folly in trusting him at all. I was cold and tired there, and the grey dawn accentuated my loneliness. I had hungered for man's society and protection, a man's arms round me, and a man's breast to nestle against; also I had been more than a bit curious to discover what the absolute act of love really was. Many girls in my position would have done the same. That I should have wished to get married puzzled me, for the thought of a life-long bondage had always terrified me. I suppose in the depths of every woman's heart their is an elemental store of puritanism that leads her at times to covet the plain gold ring that can cover such a multitude of sins. Also there is undoubtedly a fascination in the term of husband; to be able to introduce my husband to a yet unwed friend is a privilege for which I am quite sure many a girl has taken the plunge and risked the cares of a household and the misery of children. Well, I had taken the plunge, and had soused myself beyond any possibility of ever getting dry again. Here I was, wedded and yet unwedded, with the world ahead of me, a big black mark against my name for a start, and no maidenhead.

Meanwhile breakfast made its appearance, and with the warm tea and ham and eggs, confidence came to me, and I began to seriously consider the future and the career I was to adopt. There were very few open to me. I scanned the 'Situations Vacant' columns in the Daily Telegraph, but there wasn't a thing that could possibly suit. That first haven of the homeless girl, governessing, was effectually closed to me.

To begin with I had no references, and secondly, I should have undoubtedly succumbed to the amatory advances of one or other of the male members of whatever family I found myself in, and so taken the mistress's shameful order and the push out. I canvassed the idea of a lady typewriter, but the probable drudgery terrified me; also I should have to learn to type, and very likely buy a machine, which wouldn't have left much of my twenty-five pounds. Besides I had heard a typewriter's position in this great metropolis entailed a good deal of sitting on the knees of elderly employers, what time the trousers of the said employers were not at all in their proper decorum. If I was going to lead an immoral career I judged it better to do it on the stage. I had all the advantages of youth and health and one of the best figures in London, so I presumed there ought not be too much difficulty in obtaining a living wage, and so, by the time I had finished a really excellent breakfast, I had decided for the dramatic profession; there were agents I knew who arranged these matters, and these agents I determined to seek out and impress.

My first business was to cash a cheque and then find a room. I couldn't stay in this hotel as a married lady whose husband had brought her at seven o'clock on a winter's morning and deserted her before the day was five hours older. George had settled the bill, an act of generosity at which, now, I rather wondered. Luckily I had a few shillings in my pocket with which to pay the necessary tips. That done, I put on my hat and set out without further delay for the bank on which Sir Thomas Lothmere, my recent benefactor, had drawn his cheque. It was pretty close by, in Piccadilly, and I walked.

The presentation of that cheque was really, I think, one of the most trying moments of my life. The cashier, a vulgar bourgeois man, looked me over with the most insulting deliberation, and I was made to feel at once that he supposed I had come by the cheque in no respectable fashion. I think old Sir Thomas was fairly good and proper; and even if, in former days, he had had occasion to make money presents to young ladies, I don't suppose he was fool enough to do it by cheque; so, perhaps, the worthy cashier had never before been called upon to hand over a sum of money to a very pretty girl in a smart hat, who presented a cheque signed by a widely respectable and elderly scientist. At last I got it; three crisp fivers and ten bright jingling sovereigns; and feeling much happier and on a sounder footing with the world, I set out on quest number two – lodgings.

Theatrical folk, one of whom I now proposed to be, inhabited principally, I had heard, strange and unknown lands across the water, called Kennington and Camberwell and Brixton. I had never been on the Surrey side of the Thames in my life, and had no intention of going there now. So possibly very extravagantly, I determined to set myself up in the West End. My little costumiere, Eloise's friend, who had so kindly given me credit, lived close by in Jermyn Street, and it occurred to me that I might get a room over her shop.

Madame Karl lived in an old fashioned house in Jermyn Street. On the ground floor was her shop, a tiny *magasin de robes*, and the rest of the house was used for her own living rooms, and one or two sets of apartments, generally let out to bachelors. I found her in the shop, bowing out a plump lady of important mien.

She was genuinely glad to see me, and laughingly enquired how I managed to get my bill settled so soon. I made belief a few kisses had been all the price paid but I could see she thought I lied. With a laugh she pinched my cheek. 'Well, I wish all my customers were pretty girls,' she said. 'Then I should get my accounts settled more regularly. The lady that just went out owes me over a thousand pounds and on top of that she's just left an order to execute which I shall have to set aside all other work, and spend goodness knows how much on material. Yet I dare not offend her for she is the Countess of Alminster, and brings many American ladies here – who do pay. But it is a heavy commission,' and the little woman sighed and shrugged her shoulders.

Madame Karl was not exactly a beauty but she had a figure that sets off to its best advantage by her perfect gowns and set many a man coveting the charms within. And the charms were worth having, as I discovered the first night I slept in the Jermyn Street House. She must have been thirty-eight or nine, but her flesh was firm and white and unwrinkled. I helped to rub her down with a soft towel before bed, and when I noticed how she wriggled under my fingers, I knew there was still a volcano of love in that pretty little body.

Our pact was soon sealed. I was to have one of the rooms upstairs, and Madame was very understanding about my paying rent at present. 'That can begin when you get an engagement,' she said.

In the meantime I was to make myself generally useful to her, and I soon gathered that many ways of making useful existed in that establishment.

'I let my chambers very easily to gentlemen,' she told me. 'It is so convenient, you know, should a lady call, for there to be a dressmaker's establishment on the ground floor; one may suspect a lady who enters a house let in gentlemen's apartments in Jermyn Street, but who shall question the right of a lady, married or single, to visit her dressmaker.'

So it came to pass that I was to be a sort of generally discreet chaperone. Madame used to give her lady clients tea in the upstairs sitting room. When the lady showed signs of being at all timid, I used to be present at the beginning of the tea, and then be suddenly called away, what time the gentleman accomplished his desire. More than a dozen times my errand did not take me further than the keyhole, and from that point of vantage I witnessed some quite amusing performances. I must say that some of Madame's aristocratic lady clients made no bones about haggling over the price of their bodies, just as if they had been ordinary women of the street.

Certainly the profits of the establishment appeared to be considerable; and one day, after a particularly good lunch, Madame Karl surprised me with her tale of the business done for the day.

'You remember the pretty little girl in the blue costume who came in here this morning,' she said, 'the one I left upstairs with you?'

I remembered perfectly well.

'She is Lord Wetlon's daughter. They are not at all well off, but naturally she loves pretty clothes. Well, you recollect the dark little gentleman who came in afterwards, whom you left up there with her. He is Christopher Echsstein, the broker. What she did for it, I don't know, but he ordered two hundred and fifty pounds worth of dresses for her, and, what is more, he gave me a cheque in advance. He's a true businessman, he wanted the discount.'

Madame had four assistants, all pretty girls, and each one of them hot as they make them. She didn't pay them much, but I reckon they had nothing to complain of about the little extra bits they made out of the husbands of some of her customers.

Of course, I attracted the attention, to say nothing of the lustful glances, of more than one of Madame's trouser-clad customers. Little Blanche was not the sort of beauty to go many days through her career without causing some masculine head to turn, or some masculine sexual members to press against the confining trousers in dumb protest. But the fools dared no more than a passing glance for I think they feared offending Madame Karl. Sometimes I was glad of their reticence, yet often again I so boiled over with desire to be made love to that I could have boxed the ears of several nice young men, who when left alone with me, looked their desire, but made no attempt to express it in more forceful, to say nothing of more pleasant, form. I honestly believe they thought me a virgin, I had looked so young, for I was not yet quite out of short frocks. That is to say, I wore a long gown and put up my hair in the evening, but the day time usually found my red-brown tresses gathered into a loose knot at the back of my neck and my ankles delightfully displayed by a short skirt which only journeyed three parts of the way down my calves. In fact, I was still a flapper.

'A little duck' I certainly looked, especially when I sat down and showed my pretty, rounded calves well up to the knees.

But, as I was saying, I occasionally felt almost uncontrollable pangs of naughtiness, and I am afraid that the forefinger of my right hand was sometimes put to most improper uses – how I wished it had been a masculine digit! Once when Madame Karl and I were unusually confident (we were sitting over our tea and cigarettes and the fire), I let drop a hint of this. She was asking me about my seduction, and I told her that, although it was not all roses at the time, I would willingly have another try at fornication to relieve my lascivious feelings.

'And so you shall my dear girl,' she said, coming over to me and kissing me lovingly. 'Why nearly all the men who come here have begged of me to approach you on the subject, but I didn't like to.'

And so it was arranged, I was to go wrong with Lord X —.

'A Lord! Tut! tut!' *this from Gladys.*

'*Oh, I've worked through pretty well and all the grades of the peerage in my time,*' *I answered,* '*once I had a Viscount and a Duke in the same day.*'

'*And that reminds me of a story,*' *says Gladys.* '*It concerns itself, does this little yarn, with a parson's wife, who by no means got all the pleasure she wanted out of her husband, the anaemic incumbent of a swagger West End parish. And it seems that it came to pass that one fine day Lord "So and So" visited her in the absence of her husband. Hearing someone coming she bade the*

Lord conceal himself on the top of the ancient four poster. He did so; but it was not her husband, only Sir C —, who had likewise went under the bed like a rabbit. This time it was her husband, come home randy for once in a way (he had been taking a girl's class) and he wanted it, too; and had it. At the conclusion, he remarked to his better-half, "Ah Mary, I sometimes think you have not always been as good a woman as you should have been, but trust in the Lord above, He will look after you –.'

'Oh, will he?' came a voice from above the canopy. 'Then what about that bugger of a baronet underneath?'

It was arranged very artistically. I was not going to have it given away that I was a previously consenting party to the affair. Madame Karl, in course of a casual conversation with Lord X, mentioned me: he declared his desire; she suggested he should go up to my bedroom, enter as if he had made a mistake (she told him that I would be undressing at the time), and it rested on his own initiative to complete the job.

I *was* undressing, that is to say I was pretty well in Eve's costume. Madame had warned me by speaking tube when he was nearly at the door, and when he entered he found me all stark naked but my chemise, and that fallen to my feet. Of course I uttered the time-honoured scream, covered my face with one hand and my mons veneris with the other, ran hither and thither about the room as if seeking cover and murmured, 'Oh go away; please!'

But he didn't go; he rushed at me, pulled one hand from my face and kissed me on the lips; pulled the other hand from my cunt and felt it, in fact, in about one minute he had got me down on the bed and his prick was well into me, not one single word did he say till I could feel him coming and the first part of the entertainment was over. As I lay back on the bed, panting, while he rather shamefacedly put back his penis into his trousers, I managed to gasp out: 'Well! What a funny way to make love to a girl! Don't you ever say anything?'

He laughed, 'I'm glad you're not furious,' he said, 'but to tell the truth I was awfully nervous.'

'Nervous?' He need not have been, for I don't mind betting I wanted it even more than he that blessed afternoon. 'Nervous!' How many a beautiful chance of exquisite sexual intercourse had been wasted by this wretched nervousness on the part of Mankind. I can call to mind the tale concerning a nervous person who asked another young man how he made small talk at parties, declaring himself always dumb on these occasions. 'Oh, I don't worry much about frills in my conversation,' was the answer, 'I just get the girl in a quiet corner, squeeze her hand and ask her if she likes fucking.'

'But my dear chap,' was the answer, 'what an awful thing to say; I should think you would get yourself badly disliked sometimes and get thrown out of the houses.'

'Well,' admitted the candid one, 'I do get disliked sometimes and I have been thrown out of houses, but I get a hell of a lot of fucking.'

Moral: Oh Mankind, remember that the woman is as often as not, as keen for it as you are – and don't be *nervous*.

After that we got on splendidly. He undressed, was soon stiff and in again, and we had a long, glorious, slow grind, exquisite pleasure the whole time, and always that delightful feeling that there was much more ahead, not just a few more strokes and the business completed. Twice was all I would allow him, though he wanted more. I made him sponge me all over with hot scented water, rub me down till I glowed deliciously, and dress me. He was no novice at the game, and the teasing little kisses with which he would accompany all the business of drawing on my stockings, fastening my drawers, getting me into my corsets, etc., nearly made me fall again. When dressed at last, we went downstairs. I just found time to whisper to Madame Karl that it was satisfactorily done, and we got a cab and went off to have tea at Claridge's room among all the ambassadors.

Madame Karl seemed thoroughly pleased when I got back home. She was all over me, and gave me a hat lately arrived from Paris which I had coveted muchly. And as my lordling friend had bought me a diamond brooch at Streeter's, I did fairly well.

The secret of what I had done did not remain secret – I don't know how it got to the ears of the girls, but after dinner, when we were all together that evening, one of them got me alone in a corner of the drawing room and whispered. 'So you've been with Lord X —, this afternoon?' My blush was sufficient answer.

'Come out with me this evening,' she whispered, tickling my hand, 'I can promise you a lot of fun.'

Her tone, and the gesture with which she accompanied her invitation, gave me full well to understand that something naughty was in the wind. 'Must I ask Madame Karl's permission?' I asked.

'Of course.'

'My dear little Nemmy,' said Madame Karl, when I told her, 'of course you can go, but I warn you that this will be something quite out of the common. Nelly knows more than a bit.'

Now you mustn't run away with the idea that Madame Karl kept a bad house in the sense that her assistants were tarts and nothing else. As far as they were concerned, there was precious little wickedness performed on the premises; but Madame gave them a free hand on their off evenings; just as all the swagger dressmakers' establishments in London and Paris do.

'They all have their latch keys at Gay's, and at

Madame Marie's too,' says Gladys, *'I was at the latter for a bit myself and I know.'*

Nelly was the youngest of Madame Karl's assistants, and only just promoted to the dignity of long skirts. She was a pretty blonde, very well favoured by nature, with a deliciously plump arm and shoulder, and very well developed breasts. Her legs were perfect; she was one of those few girls who could stand upright in an ordinary position, close her legs and keep a threepenny bit between her thighs. She was proud of this and often used to show us the trick.

She was delighted when I said I could come, and insisted on lending me a dress.

'Your own evening frock is delightful, my dear,' she explained, 'but it isn't quite what we want for this evening.'

She put me into a three-quarter length gown, extremely décolleté, but filled in about the shoulders with lace (which as a matter of fact, rather added to the suggestiveness of the confection). It was so low at the back that I had to wear a corset which was little more than a band around the waist, and my nipples almost escaped in front. She, too, put on a three-quarter dress, I began to see that this looked like a flapper party.

To cut a long story short, Nelly took me to a house in Cadogan Gardens, a swagger enough place to look at, and explained that it was kept by a woman of good family who added to her own rather diminished income by running it as a meeting place for men and girls. 'She's quite the best and nicest procuress in London,' Nelly explained, 'she's delightful to all the girls who go there, and you can be perfectly certain of your money.'

That there was money in the air, had never occurred to me when I accepted Nelly's invitation, but I didn't shrink on that account, I could do with a little of the root of all evil just then. Then Nelly told me that the parties varied. On one evening, for instance, our hostess would collect a few married women who were prepared to go astray from their titular lords and masters; sometimes quite young married women, and sometimes ladies who had attained the prime of life without losing their good looks – (these were for men who desired a lot of experience from their bedfellows) – and sometimes young girls.

'That'll be us, this evening,' I said.

I gathered from Nelly also that our hostess was prepared to find anything. She organised coster girl parties, bringing up pretty little East-Enders; and even parties at which very depraved young men could exercise their desire on quite elderly women. 'These parties,' said Nelly, 'are the most paying of all, for she gets money from both sides, since the old women are under the impression that she has to pay the young men – oh, she's very very clever.'

We were taken to Mrs Cowper in a large room which was a cross between a very elaborate boudoir and a hot house. That is to say, it was lighted by skylights like a studio, carpeted with some soft material into which one's feet sank almost to the ankles – I found out later that a thin mattress lay underneath the carpet – and was full of flowers and ferns of every kind. From the roof of an alcove depended a vine covered with luscious grapes. A table bearing a glittering tea equipment stood in one corner, various small tables bore wine and spirit decanters. We were ushered in and Mrs Cowper noticed me at once. 'Good Heavens, Nelly,' she cried, 'I had no idea you'd brought a stranger; whatever must she think of me, my dear?'

I could not do anything but blush, and Mrs Cowper continued: 'After all, I dare say Nelly has told you we're not very proper here,' and she laid her arms on my shoulders, kissing my lovingly on the lips.

Mrs Cowper was I suppose about thirty-five, and uncommonly beautiful. Her figure was perfection, and the dress she wore showed off all its delights. The dress was carried out in a design of ferns. Ferns, quite small at the waist, but gathering size as they fell lower, made the skirt; the bodice was one large bunch of ferns, out of which grew her ivory neck and shoulders; she had ferns in her hair, and two little pearl diamond ferns for earrings.

I sat by her side sipping a liqueur while Nelly briefly told her who and what I was.

'You'll do for me very nicely, dear girl,' she said, 'I think you will just suit a man I've got coming this evening; let me see, are you a virgin?'

I had half framed the word yes, when she suddenly ran her hand up my clothes, and felt my trembling little cunt – 'Oh no, you're not,' she said, with a laugh, 'and you must not pretend to be. I never deceive my patrons *here*.'

'I've only been wrong with two men,' I said pouting.

'Well, your third will be young Mr Robinson, of the Stock Exchange. I shall charge him ten pounds for you and give you five of it; whatever you get out of him on the top of that is of course your own affair. Here is the fiver,' she handed me a note.'

'And me?' said Nelly.

'A Mr Reichardt, likewise of the Stock Exchange, a friend of his, they will be here in a moment.'

But before those worthies arrived, a number of other girls were shown in. Some arrived singly, but more often they came in twos or threes. I reckon there were about fifteen present before a single trousered animal put in an appearance. They were pretty and, beautiful though I knew myself to be, I felt I had plenty of rivals on this occasion. Some were very young – wicked as I was I could help not feeling it rather a shame when I saw girls who could not have been more than sixteen – and I don't suppose one there was more than twenty-one. All were pretty, often very extravagantly dressed, and I have never since, despite all the varied experiences of my life seen such a delightful assemblage of dainty shoulders, plump little girlish arms, well moulded calves, generally displayed to the knee, and slim attractive little waists.

About a dozen men arrived, and we had music – and a good many drinks. Everything was very decorous; Nelly told me that no impropriety went on *coram populo*, and I flirted in an amiable manner with my Mr Robinson. An occasional touch of his hand gave me naughty shivers, to say nothing of the frequent discreet comminglings of his trousers with my stockings, and I had begun to wonder when there was going to be any serious play, when Nelly took me aside.

'Mrs Cowper wants me to ask you a favour, Blanche dear,' she said, 'it seems there are not quite enough men to go around.'

'Shocking mismanagement –!' interrupts Gladys.

'And she doesn't want any of the girls left over.'

'Prudent woman,' the irrepressible typewriter again.

'Wherefore she wants to know whether you and I will go with the same man – it's that old gentleman over there – (pointing to a lean and lanky old sportsman who was doing prodigies with the spirit decanters in a secluded corner, feasting his eyes on the girls at intervals) – 'it'll be another fiver each,' she concluded.

I was rather glad. I liked Nelly, and I hadn't much modesty even then. I felt that I should be much less nervous, with her to aid, than alone, so the bargain was struck. Mrs Cowper, first giving me the extra fiver – she was extremely business-like – sidled us up to our fare; we went with him into another room and had a little stand up supper against a buffet. Then Mrs Cowper led the conversation round to art, told our friend that we were art students, said that we were dying to see the Correggio in the pink boudoir, and left him to take us there – it was so tactful and nice.

Our old friend got us into the boudoir in due course, and all the time I was wondering where I had seen his face before. Then I tumbled to the fact that his beard and moustache were false – (I noted that while he was kissing me) – and got it. He was the senior classical master at Rocton, my father's school. At first, came terror that he was likely to recognise me, but I soon saw that he was oblivious to my identity – in fact I had changed a bit since he could have seen me last. Then it occurred to me to frighten him – not that any idea of blackmail had ever crossed my mind – no.

He fucked Nelly first – to be blunt; not, I trust, because he didn't think me the nicest, but because it appeared that he had had Nelly before, and was less nervous. There wasn't much art about it at all. I just sat on the edge of the couch and smoked a cigarette while he stripped her naked, kissed her in many places and generally messed her about, till he finally produced a giant weapon, and shoved it up her. The consummation was short. Nelly seemed frantically randy, wriggled her arse like a tortured soul, and soon had him spending into her for all he was worth.

By that time I, naturally, was naughty too, but I had to wait a bit; that greedy Nelly had got too much, and we had to aid our friend with much manipulation of his person, tickling his balls, stroking his little stomach, etc., before he had me on the sofa with his lance in me – the rest was easy, and I kept in till the moment I could feel him swelling with rapidly arriving semen when I said, very quietly. 'Whatever would Michael Hunt say if he saw you doing this?'

The man gave one convulsive wriggle, shot about a gallon of fluid into me, then rolled off, pale to the hair roots – 'What do you know about Michael Hunt?' he asked.

'Only that you're his senior master at Rocton. I know you very well by sight, even if you have a false beard and moustache on. I do hope you've enjoyed this better than to teach at the boys school.'

Now anyone but a fool would have seen the fun of the thing and laughed with us. Nelly told me afterwards he must have known that Mrs Cowper's was a safe enough place, and felt no fear of blackmail – but that silly old thing wacked up fifty pounds for us two to divide, so that we should be mum. I don't say that he didn't have a bit more fun for his money – but fifty is a lot, and I daresay he had paid Mrs Cowper quite a tidy sum already.

Still, this is a little bit by the way, and I must get back to that first day of mine at Madame Karl's.

She took me out to dinner on the first evening of my stay, we went to a small but extremely smart restaurant in the very heart of innermost St James's. Madame knew most of them – the men and women – by sight, and told me their names. She might have been reciting Debrett by the page. When I noted the price of the food, and especially the wine, I was astounded. Madame must assuredly be very rich to afford this.

We did ourselves well, and drank only the oldest vintages, but when the bill was brought she simply signed it on the back and gave the waiter half a crown. A light began to dawn upon me.

'It's like reverting to the old system of barter, isn't it?' said madame with a laugh. 'I dress the manager's wife at a reduction and the manager feeds me. I don't suppose his directors know anything about it.'

As soon as we had appeared to have settled our bill several men whom madame knew crossed the room to speak to us; but she got rid of them all, suggesting to me that we should go to a music hall.

We had a box at the music hall without paying for it. 'More barter,' said madame. 'That silly little man's wife would never have reached her present position on the stage without the aid of my frocks.'

I began to think that Madame Karl was an exceeding power in the land, and also to doubt whether there wasn't something in the dressmaking business after all. I determined to make myself useful to her. I think I must have created somewhat of a sensation in that hall, for upon the door of our box beat an endless tattoo, and from the stalls necks were craned upwards, and a variety of male humanity studied me through opera glasses. It must have been me, for Madame Karl sat back in the shadow.

I did not enjoy the performance; few women figured among the turns; it was a carnival of comedians and a hymn of praise to vulgarity. The audience roared at the antics of the various little red-nosed men who occupied the stage, but the humours of the enterprising lodger, the confiding landlady, and their illicit amours, and the ever recurring Bacchanal drink chant palled most terribly, and I was intensely relieved when madame recognised a friend and signalled him to come and see us.

Mr Runthaler was a gentleman of a comfortable person, an expensive fur coat and a deal of jewellery. Madame had forewarned me that he had a great deal of interest in matters theatrical, and I was very nice to him; he was in turn very nice to me, in fact, rather too nice, for the semi-publicity of a box at a music hall. I found an early opportunity of broaching the subject of the stage. 'Well, little girl,' he answered, 'if you want to be an actress, take my advice and don't go to the agents; they'll never get you a London engagement, and I presume you don't want to spend your life tramping the provinces in a second rate musical comedy company. If you want to play at a West End Theatre, you must get at the managers personally, and for a girl like you I don't think it'll be very hard. If you like, I'll give you an introduction to my friend Lewis, of the Duke's Theatre, he'll see any girl I send. I should advise you to try and catch him tonight; besides, that frock suits you.'

He left us directly, after pencilling a few words of introduction on his card, and soon afterwards I persuaded Madame to come with me to the Duke's Theatre.

The hall porter took the card and handed it to a young gentleman in faultless evening dress, who stood in the hall. The latter examined us at some length, enquired which was Miss La Mare, and then said that Mr Lewis was not at present in the theatre, but that if I went round to his flat in the next street he might see me. He wrote something on the card in a language which I took to be Yiddish, and handed it back to me. Word came down that Mr Lewis would see me at once, and, closely followed by Madame Karl, I went up. We were shown into a large apartment extravagantly decorated in the Japanese manner, and so draped about the walls and ceilings with curtains that it had the appearance of a tent. The chief furniture of the place was an enormous divan extending nearly the whole length of the room; a few tables, mostly covered with bottles and glass of rare and antique design, were arranged in deliberate disorder; two large pictures represented classical and, incidentally, indelicate events; and there were a couple of capacious easy chairs; an upright grand piano, and that was all. In the middle of the divan, arrayed in a smoking suit and one that rivalled the storied coat of his ancestor Jacob, squatted, pasha fashion, Mr Lewis.

He was a little round man, with a straight line of curling black hair across his lip, and a head that was entirely bald. As he sat there he looked like a Hebraic Humpty Dumpty. He made no attempt to rise, but welcomed us with a nod and an expression of annoyance, obviously caused by the presence of my companion.

'You are Miss La Mare, I presume,' he said glancing from the card in his hand to me. 'Blanche La Mare – it should look well on a bill. And you want to be an actress. Well, what can you do, Miss La Mare?'

I answered that I could sing and he motioned me to the piano.

'Sing something light,' he said.

I selected a song out of Mirelda which I remembered. After the first verse he stopped me.

'Very nice, very nice indeed,' he said. 'And now, Miss La Mare, I cannot talk business before a third person; would your friend mind leaving us for a while?' Madame made a gesture of dissent, but though I was pretty sure what was coming, I had thought I'd better see it out, so I asked her to go.

When we were alone, Mr Lewis left his divan and came towards me. 'Well, you're a very pretty little lady,' he said. 'I think you may suit me, just take your coat off, and let's see your shoulders. Ah, very nice too,' and he patted my neck affectionately. 'And what pretty lips, may I?' Without waiting for an answer, he kissed me. I made no resistance. I was quite prepared to pay this sort of tribute.

'Very nice,' he said again, smacking his fat lips, 'so far most satisfactory, and now let's see what sort of legs you have got.'

Madame had told me that the usual way adopted by a burlesque manager for making sure of the suitability of a girl's legs was for the girl to draw her legs tight around the members in question, and this I did.

'Ah, yes, but I'm afraid I can hardly tell by that, dear little lady,' he chuckled, 'you know my patrons are very particular about legs. Don't be shy now, pull your clothes up and let me see what they really are like.'

I blushed, for I felt ashamed, but I did it. I lifted my clothes well above my knees, and as I was wearing rather short drawers, the perfect contour of my lower leg and a good deal of the upper part was plainly visible.

He asked me to stretch them apart, and I obeyed, blushing the more. He came quite close and leered at my limbs through his glasses.

'I think you'll do, my little dear,' he said. 'I'll go and get a contract form. You will be undressed when I get back, won't you?'

'I don't know what you mean.'

'Yes, you do, my dear, you understand me perfectly. If you had been a modest girl you wouldn't have shown me your legs. I like you and I should like to engage you, but before I sign the contract I'm going to enjoy you; what's there to make a fuss about in that?'

It was a bit too cold-blooded, and I could not stand it – 'Well, you've made a mistake this time,' I said, 'I may not be a modest girl, as you put it, but there are limits. So Goodbye.'

He did not seem angry; 'Ah, well,' he said. 'you're a little fool, engagements with me are good and comfortable and profitable. I like you because you're more than ordinarily pretty, but I'm not going to relax my rule. I always have my chorus girls, once at least, and I can't begin making exceptions now. Perhaps one of these days you'll think it over and come back to me again.'

'No, that I will never, you dirty old mean beast,' I answered, moving towards the door.

He laughed again; 'Don't go for a minute,' he said. 'I promise you I won't try to force you, but I should like to argue with you. Now, you're not a virgin, I'm certain of that; you do yourself no harm by just lying down on the sofa and letting me have you, and you'll get an engagement. I shall not want to have you any more.' Then, before I realised what he was up to, he had slipped his hand between his legs, flicked open his fly and was holding out an erect penis for my inspection. With his other hand he grabbed my shoulder and slipped his foot between my legs, tripping me up.

I fell heavily, and if it had not been for the softness of the carpet I think I should have hurt myself. In a moment the little beast was on top of me, holding my shoulders down with his two hands while he tried to force his knee between my legs. I had fallen with one leg a little apart from the other, and he succeeded in that part of his fell purpose. He scraped my dress up somehow, and in fact got as far as banging the end of his panting member against my stomach – but that was all. I had no intention of letting the brute conquer me, and at the moment he thought victory was secure, he took one of his hands from my shoulders to help guide his weapon to its grave. I let him have it with my right hand full on the end of his nose. The blow gave him fair hark from the tomb, as my young friend Charley Lothmere would have phrased it in his quaint Pink'un English, and the blood gushed from the damaged proboscis. It only made him think better of his attempt, and he got up, swearing under his breath, bursting into a roar of laughter.

Oddly enough, as soon as I found myself outside, I felt as randy as hell, and somewhat repented my action.

When I was back at Jermyn Street I told Madame what had happened.

She did not exactly applaud my action. 'Well, you know dear, you're not a virgin,' she said, 'and I must say that I don't think it would have done much harm.'

'The harm was in your being a virgin for damned near a whole volume of this immortal work,' breaks in the irrepressible Gladys, 'and I'd have let the old swine fuck me if he was going to give me an engagement.'

'I would have, perhaps, if he hadn't tried to force me,' *I answered.*

'Force you!' says Gladys, with a tinge of scorn in her voice, 'why I'm damned if I don't think it's half the pleasure. Listen – would you like to hear what happened to me?'

The Story of Gladys

It was during my first typewriter's job in London. I was not a virgin, but I was at that time what I should call quite a moral girl, that is to say I stuck to one man. I resisted the daily efforts of my business employer, and used to hurry home in the evenings to my Bloomsbury lodgings. Twice a week I met my lover who took me to dinner, and subsequently to a furnished room in one of the good old flea ravaged hotels in the Euston Road. It was there, after my young man, who knew a bit, had plentifully peppered the bed with good old Keating, we enjoyed ourselves to the top of love's young delight. We could not afford a more frequent connection, for Albert lived with his family and drew but three pounds a week for his lusts and living, while the boarding house inhabited by myself drew a strict line at young men visitors.

Well on one occasion, a dark and dreary winter's evening, just after a happy time with my young man, who at the time I sincerely loved, I was making my way home through foggy bleared streets, when my way was blocked by a tall figure that loomed up through the darkness and grasped me by the arm. 'Forgive me for stopping you,' he said, 'but there is a woman hard by in sore distress, and we cannot find another of her sex to be with her. Will you come?' His voice seemed so naturally affected that I could not find it in my heart to say nay, and I went.

The man treated me with the greatest consideration and deference, apologising for the queer route our journey took us. At last we came to a tall, ugly house. After two flights of creaking stairs, a door opened to admit us into a seemingly very comfortable flat. Another man had opened the door, but he was silent as I and my companion passed him. I began to feel a little nervous, but the sound of a woman's voice calling in tones which seemed shaking with pain, 'Have you got her, John?' – reassured me.

I followed my guide, whom I now saw, in the light of the flat, to be a powerfully built, strong faced, ugly man with penetrating eyes, into a bedroom. Between the sheets lay a woman, whom at first glance I recognised as a singularly beautiful creature. She was quite small and slight, a little thin in the neck perhaps, and pinched great eyes. In those great eyes which seemed to dominate the room, lay her chief cute charm. She did not look particularly ill, and I was surprised to note that she appeared to be quite naked, for the arm which lay on the coverlet was bare, and there was no sign of a garment about her neck and shoulders. Her fingers were covered with rings; it was obviously no poor woman who needed my assistance. In fact I summed her up at once as a well-to-do prostitute.

I was advancing towards the bed about to speak to her, when I felt my waist surrounded by the man's arms. At the same moment, I noticed a smile on the face of the woman. As I tried to struggle from his embrace it struck me that I was trapped, and the woman's words which immediately followed only too well confirmed my suspicion. 'You've collared a pretty one, John,' she purred in a mocking tone. As my glance ran round the room, I saw that now the third man was present, sitting in a chair by the door, smoking a cigar.

'What does this mean?' I cried, in a choking voice.

For answer the big man gripped me again and kissed me violently.

'I implore you, what does it mean?' I said to the woman.

'Only that you must be a good girl and do what you're asked,' she responded with an irritating smile, and at the same time the big man forced me back against the bed.

'Oh, tell me what you do want; is it money?' I

begged, the tears welling into my eyes.

'No, you little fool,' the man answered savagely, 'we want to fuck you!' and he let me go, then continued, 'undress yourself quickly – or else we'll make you.'

I screamed at the top of my voice, but was answered by a general laugh. Then I swung round towards the woman and raised my hand, threatening her. In a second I found my legs twitched from under me and I was sprawled upon the floor. One man held my knees down and the other my elbows.

As I lay there quite helpless, the woman slipped from the bed, a beautiful little devil she was too, in her nakedness, superbly well formed, though on the small scale, with a perfect skin. She pressed my waist down with her two hands and looked into my eyes. 'Will you be undressed quietly, and let these men do what they like?' she cooed.

I made no answer.

Then they tied me down, by my ankles and wrists, to the legs of the bed on one side, and to a couple of rings which were also used for some sort of gymnastic appliance, on the other. My legs were stretched wide apart.

Now perhaps it may seem rather exciting, but at that time, you must remember, I was only eighteen, deeply in love, and had been wrong with two men only.

I was mad with rage. They made no further attempt to cajole me, in fact, had I known as much as I do now, I should have seen that the very fact of forcing me was three parts of the pleasure to these sinister people.

The woman took a razor from the toilet table. I shut my eyes, fearing some horrible outrage, but she only used it to rip my dress and petticoats to my waist. The halves of my costume she turned over, laying bare my drawers and a good deal of the naked lower part of my stomach, for I wore no corsets.

She laid her hand on my little mount of Venus, and

fingered it affectionately, though she did not succeed in producing the least little thrill in me. I was far too angry. But the sight seemed to please the men, for, with a simultaneous action they each produced a large and erect prick and balls from their trousers and stood over me.

The woman completed my undressing, ripping off everything completely and destroying my clothes. When I was left naked on the damned floor, there was some affair of tossing up between the men as to which one should get a nice hot fuck out of me. The big one won, and promptly disembarrassed himself out of his clothes. I was perfectly helpless, and compelled to lie there awaiting the ravishing of this brute, but he hesitated.

'I don't think I want the girl tied down like a log,' he said, 'let her go and I will try to manage it.'

Well, they did let me go, the woman had no hand in this. I fancy she was rather nervous. She perched herself crosswise on the bed, lit a cigarette and waited. I still lay there when I was freed, but found myself jerked up to my feet, and then the big man grappled with me. I just managed to get my teeth well into his shoulder, and with a right hand to grip him savagely by the balls, and I felt a heavy blow behind the ear and remembered no more.

I came to my senses to find a man on top of me, his prick deep into me, and the girl bathing my temples with brandy. I felt far too ill then to struggle more as the man finished without extracting the tiniest drop of reciprocal juice from me.

My ravisher lay heavily upon me, seemingly disinclined to remove himself from so pleasant a position, and the thing within me stayed stiff and unyielding, but the other man jerked my ravisher's shoulders up.

'Easy now, don't flatten the girl,' he said, then I felt the weight of the man's stomach relax, and his mighty cock slip out of my cunt. It was odd, but the moment his penis slid from me I experienced a thrill of pleasure; not pleasure that the thing had been removed, but real sensual joy, then I burst into tears.

They treated me kindly, lifted me gently on to the bed, and smoothed my limbs with their hands. The woman brought me warm water and bathed my thighs. Why I had bled I can't think; for, as you know, Blanche dear, I wasn't a virgin at that time, far from it. I suppose it must have been my wriggling, and the quite exceptional size of the man's member. But they certainly thought I was a virgin.

'Poor little thing,' said the woman cooingly, 'You'll soon get to love it and you will thank us for initiating you in the art of love.'

I did not speak a word, but lay immobile wondering what would happen to me next. The other man's prick was stiff as a ramrod, and I felt certain I was not going to leave that room till he had gratified himself.

Then the woman slipped down on the bed by my side, and folded me in her arms. The delicate softness of her reconciled me to my position. Gently I returned her caress and in another moment our lips met in a loving kiss. She was very, very pretty; her lips were soft, her breath fragrant, and she followed the kiss by a delicate fondling of my clitoris. My position on the bed enabled me to see a mirror on the other side of the room, and the sight of our soft, white bodies thus folded together entranced me. I wriggled in her arms, darted my tongue between her teeth, and coveted that wandering finger of hers. In a flash I realised that for the first time in my life I was consumed with physical desire for the body of another being of my own sex. I abandoned myself entirely to her kisses.

Gladys's words inflamed me. Ever since I had had the pretty girl as an amanuensis, I had known she was delightful to look at, and more than once I had caught myself regarding her with a feeling which had certainly something more than mere friendship and admiration in it. At last I had come to the conclusion that I wanted her, but I dared make no attempt till she herself confessed through her story that she had before been enjoyed by a woman.

I made the getting of a drink a pretext to leave my chair, I poured out stiff glasses of whisky and soda for both of us, and in handing Gladys hers, allowed my hand to stray over her soft shoulder, we were working, as usual, at night, and Gladys still wore her theatre gown, an extremely décolleté confection, that is to say she retained its bodice, but the skirt she had taken off, and sat in her petticoat, a pretty silk thing of dark red colour which allowed her legs to be visible almost to the knees; her lace silk stockings were so very openworked that the little threads seemed traced with a pen on her gleaming white flesh. She was very desirable to look at, and that must be my excuse.

'I don't marvel at the woman, Gladys,' I whispered in her little pink ear.

Then I kissed her just below the ear, and let my free hand wander over her neck down to where the bosom began to swell out of her corsage. She bent her head forward and bit my fingers softly.

We were both nervous, such an affair between us had never been mentioned, perhaps even thought of on her part, and for quite five minutes I remained kissing her cheek softly while she fondled my hand with her lips. Then, emboldened by the mad passion within me, I slipped to my knees, and ran my hand underneath her dress, up, up to her knees, and on, boldly on, to the bare flesh above her stockings, and at last to the opening between her drawers which gave me free ingress to her delicious front door of lust. Her legs were wide apart, and the lips of her vagina seemed red hot. I could feel her kisses covering my neck while my finger penetrated that sweet grotto.

Suddenly she jumped up. 'Blanche, darling,' she panted, 'come to the photograph studio.'

The photograph studio in my house is a large room (only a few yards from the boudoir where I as a rule dictate this thrilling romance) which we are in the habit of using for taking naked pictures of each one of us.

I followed Gladys and closed the door behind us. In almost less time than it takes to write it, she had freed herself from the underclothes and lay naked, entrancing, voluptuous, on the great couch. All my nervousness was gone in an instant, and my undressing was almost as speedy.

Then I buried my head between her thighs.

I seemed to remain there for hours, although the dear girl told me afterwards that it could not have been more than ten minutes before she freed herself. I could not see her face, but her image was clear in my eyes, and each thrill of her thighs, that told me of enjoyment she extracted from my act, urged my tongue to more passionate embraces. At last she pushed my head from between her legs, my face was covered with love juice. She seized my head between her hands, I had not till then known how strong she was, and kissed the spend from it.

'Now!' she cried, when the last kiss was ended, 'it is my turn!'

I lay back on the sofa, opening my legs to their widest extent, and she gently licked. Her tongue seemed like a javelin charged with the electricity of lust. It darted round my clitoris, softly swept up the little space between that excrescence and my gaping cunt, and stabbed strongly into me. I seemed to experience nothing but one long, voluptuous spend. When at last she left me, I lay back exhausted.

We were too tired for more of that vigorous sensuality, but for an hour or more we sprawled on the couch in each other's arms, and our lips were seldom apart.

We got back to work on the immortal memoir very late next morning. Gladys said no word of our overnight frolic, simply giving me a typewritten copy of the rest of her story, which you shall have directly. I had already sent down, by my maid, my notes of our little affair in the photograph boudoir.

Here is the rest of Gladys's tale.

The two men did not suffer me to stay long in the arms of the woman. I was forcibly removed and the second man stretched me on the rug. In three strokes he possessed me, but kept his place and worked hard until he came again. I was dripping with spend when at last he left me, but he was no sooner off, than my first ravisher took his place, fucked me heartily, and deluged my sore and tired vagina with more love juice.

I lay panting on the floor while he wiped his dripping cock on the long hair of the woman, rather a pretty little trick, I thought, and wondered what was likely to befall me next, when there came a ring at the bell. I was about to jump up, but was held down at once, you can imagine that I had very little strength of resistance, and had the mortification of seeing two more men, strangers to me of course, come into the room where I lay naked on the floor. One was a tall, splendidly made young fellow; the other an elderly man. Both were in evening dress. Both seemed to take my presence there rather as a matter of fact, and kissed the woman as if nothing unusual was in the wind. In fact I was rather neglected, for the young man began stroking the woman's legs and suddenly took on a fury of passion, flung up her chemise, stretched her on the bed, and was into her in a tick. It was a short and wanton fuck.

My turn however came next, and I fell to the lot of the old man, who did not even take the trouble to remove any of his clothes; but fucked me rather laboriously, though apparently with a great deal of satisfaction to himself. When at last he did spend, he announced the fact with some pride, and received the plaudits of the rest. As soon as he was off me the woman bent down and examined my thighs: 'It's true,' she cried, 'my congratulations, Sir Richard,' and she fell to licking the sticky stuff from my legs. 'It's not often I get a chance of tasting any of your spend,' she said, as some sort of explanation of her wanton act.

Then commenced an orgy. The young man mounted me; Sir Richard screwed himself into the woman, and I was scandalised to see, by means of the mirror, that the other two proceeded to get into the young man and Sir Richard *'per annus'* as the classics have it. The weight up on me was considerable, but, whether it was the performance going on in his back door, or whether he really was very much inflamed by my charms the young man fucked me beautifully, and, tired as I was, I enjoyed it. We three were finished long before Sir Richard's party, and the entertainment concluded with my squatting above the woman's mouth, so that she employed her tongue in my arse hole, while Sir Richard licked my cunt, what time I took the young man's prick in my mouth. It was somewhat of an elaborate piece.

'I should think it was indeed,' was my comment, when I had read this amazing confession.

'And that,' concluded Gladys, 'is the end of the story. I won't bore you with further details. There was only one other thing of interest about the affair.'

'And what was that?' I asked.

'They gave me ten pounds,' said Gladys, 'a sum of money which I could very well do with at the time.'

II

'I speak in English,' Madame Karl would frequently say, 'I write in English, nowadays I even think a good deal in English, but breakfast in English I never have done, and I never will.'

Wherefore, when in response to a gently graduated series of knocks on my door I woke on the first morning of my stay at Jermyn Street, it was to find Christine the maid, bearing my *café complet* on a silver tray.

Madame, she informed me, would join me presently, then, as she drew aside the curtains, the crisp, clear winter's light ran into the room, and swept what was left of the dustman's sleep from my eyes.

I must say I like breakfasting in bed; the meal is a necessity at the best of it, not a luxury; wherefore it should be consumed with the least inconvenience and the most luxurious surroundings possible. I experienced a delightful feeling of ease that bright morning as I lay in my pretty bed and sipped the coffee. I had to get out of bed for a moment, and went to the window and looked down on the street below. I could see through an open space in the houses opposite to where Piccadilly roared in full flood, the sun glittering on the panels of the carriages and the cabs, bright and cheery and genial and good natured; so it all seemed. One could hardly be otherwise than good tempered on that perfect morning, and in that jolly room.

Presently Madame Karl slid into the room, a dream of a little woman in a sort of breakfast jacket which was more than principally openwork in its style. It was just nicely calculated to make an otherwise fired out man feel it incumbent on him to have a final fuck in the morning. Her little round pink breasts were glowing under the openwork, with the nipples showing quite plainly. The contour of her body and legs was more suggestive than if they had been seen quite naked. Of course she did not look absolutely fresh; but she was quite carefully prepared.

She sat on the edge of my bed, displaying twelve inches of pretty leg swathed in black silk stockings, and yawned. 'The morning sometimes brings regrets to a widow, my dear Blanche,' she sighed.

I kissed her lips, and I am quite sure that at that minute we both of us thought of other kisses presented by beings bearing a distinctive badge of sex between the thighs.

But about breakfast. Even at Lady Exwell's, where we were supposed to be very smart, the meal did not approach anything like geniality.

There the massive table used to be littered with a profusion of indigestible dishes, and the sideboard groaned beneath the weight of the cold viands. The woman came down shirted and collared and tailor-made gowned, and the talk turned inevitably to the slaughter of beasts. I have only one affectionate memory of the early morning habits of that house, and that was when a new footman, mistaking my bedroom for one of the gentlemen's, marched in with a tray bearing a decanter of brandy, a syphon, and a pint of champagne. Seeing his mistake, the worthy fellow would have fled, but I hailed him in no uncertain tones, and put away my small bottle like the best man in the house. I found out afterward that the midshipman had been monkeying with the boots in the passage, and put a pair of old Sir George's easy twelves outside my virgin portal. However, I kept up my habit of the morning bottle till I found out that the liveried idiot had been inventing gallantries on his part to Lady Exwell's maid, whereupon there was a suspicion of a scandal, and the morning pints had to be stopped. At Sir Thomas Lothmere's the breakfasts were of the same solemn and elephantine nature, aggravated by a preface of family prayers, read by the arch scamp, George Reynolds.

Breakfast undoubtedly is a meal that needs to be tackled in private and in bed. You may say what you will about rosy-cheeked, healthy English girls who go on flower picking excursions in the garden on an empty stomach, and you may prate about the mushroom that you have plucked yourself, tasting the best – a statement to which I unhesitatingly give the lie – but girls do not look their best at breakfast, and as it is their duty to conceal themselves during the hours when they do not please, let them break their fast in the seclusion of their chambers. Then think of the comfort of it; no horrid clamorous gong to wake one from delightful morning dreams, no enforced appearance at a fixed hour, to be mechanically pleasant to other people who are just as cross as you are yourself; but when you have decided that the right time has come, just a pressure of the bell, and in a few minutes your breakfast, and your letters, which you can read without the suspicion that your next door neighbour is looking over your shoulder.

We dressed leisurely, each admiring the pretty body of the other. It was strange how firm Madame Karl's skin was, how round her buttocks and her breasts, considering her age and very considerable experience of a gay life. Upon my word, she had nearly as good a figure as I, and at that time I really think that a looking glass seldom reflected more perfect charms than those supplied by Blanche's naked little body. I used to flatter myself, in fact, that if I failed to do any good on the stage, the career of a model in the altogether was always open to me. In fact, once during my stay with Madame, during a period of hard-up-ness and at that time when I was particularly anxious not to touch the dear little Madame for any money, I did put my pride in my pocket and have a round of the studios. After trying about five I found a man who wanted a model for the figure.

He was very blunt about it. I was consigned behind the screen, and came back naked to the world, to pose before a critical eye, now additionally armed with a pair of glasses. He decided I would do, and I got to work there and then as he had a picture on the stocks. I don't quite know where he intended to exhibit the picture; even the French salon, I should have thought, would have shied at it. It represented a pretty girl at her toilet. She was naked, all save her stockings, and she was taking the advice of an elderly man with her, as to which set of underclothes she should select. The flesh tints of the girl were gorgeously done, and the whole thing was full of suggestiveness. The man in the bedroom was fully dressed.

'Still, this is a little apart from the story, isn't it.' interrupted Gladys. *'I have been an artist's model myself, but it isn't one of the episodes in my life that I care to dwell on. Still an artist hadn't any of the negative attributes. He was not a mannikin with crinkly skin over him, but a big, bluff young man, fresh from Slade school, who used to make me pose for an hour or so, then fuck me on the sofa for another hour or so, and finally take me out to a remarkably fine lunch. It was a sweet thing, his penis, a good eight inches long, and perfectly shaped; and the best of it was he knew how to use it so as to give pleasure to the girl as well as to himself. How he could fuck!'*

'Talking of penises,' I break in, 'what do you consider a really large one?'

'Ten inches, of course is Brobdignagian,' answers

Gladys, 'but I must say that I have met a good many which measured quite eight on the foot rule. Still, after all, the size of a man's weapon is only a matter of curiosity; it is a thing which pleases one to look at, but I don't think at all, the actual length or girth makes any difference to the enjoyment of the fornication. It's the way he uses it.'

I remember a Negro who once – but it's an awful story, and I'll spare you telling – still he had a thing on him which must have measured a good foot. George Reynolds, my seducer, though not a very big man, had a pretty plaything to flatter a girl with.

However, to get back once more to the tale . . .

A few days after my disappointing interview with Lewis, Madame told me she thought it quite time an excursion was made to the agents. To gain that end she first proposed to introduce me to a journalist friend of hers who had some little influence in theatrical circles.

Madame showed me the paper with which her friend was connected, a publication bound in an offensively light green colour, and labelled, 'The Moon' in heavy black lettering. I knew the paper, it was one of Charley Lothmere's favourites. It contained weekly stories, under the heading of 'What the Man in the Moon Thinks' that suited Charley's taste exactly. They were very much up to date and frequently improper, wherefore it was with considerable surprise that I subsequently learned that they were all written by an elderly widowed lady, resident in Scotland.

We found the office of the 'Moon' at last in a small street running from the Strand, and Madame sent her card in.

The office boy took her card through an inner door and we heard the sound of his voice, but none answering. Some minutes passed, but dead silence reigned in the room within. Then Madame, who was becoming impatient, signed to me to follow, and herself followed the boy through the door. We found ourselves in a large comfortably furnished room that looked on to a small courtyard and was quite apart from the distracting noises of the outside world. In the centre of the room stood a square table of considerable size, bearing a large variety of newspapers, a whisky bottle, several syphons, and a half dozen glasses or so. In three armchairs in various corners of the room, sat three men all fast asleep. One of them was tall and fair, his face was clean shaven, and he was rather haggard, he was dressed a little elaborately, and wore a large buttonhole in the lapel of his frockcoat. I should have guessed his age to be about twenty-six. A second was of medium size, and might have been any age. His hair fell in thick masses about the sides of his head, his moustache was twisted upwards with an assumption of ferocity, but in his sleep it was easy to see that he was really a very mild man. In the best armchair, and nearest to the fire, sat a little man whom I took to at once. He was short, and of a well-rounded, comfortable figure, but it was in the extreme youthfulness of his appearance, that lay his charm. His hair was long, and fell in carefully disposed ringlets over his forehead into his blue eyes. His whole chubby countenance was wrapped in a seraphic smile, and in his left hand he still grasped a tumbler. He was snoring somewhat and with each snore the smile broadened across his face; doubtless he was dreaming some happy boyish fancy, and his spirit was wandering in some pure noble land, far away from the worldly turmoil of the Strand.

'The long one is Mr Annesley,' said Madame, and advancing towards him she prodded him sharply in the ribs with her umbrella. He uncurled like a coiled spring that is suddenly released, and stood bolt upright, his hands instinctively seeking his hair to see if it was neatly brushed.

'My dear Madame Karl,' he ejaculated, 'a thousand pardons for the condition of the men in the Moon, but it is the day after publishing day, you see, and we are taking a well deserved rest. Will you come with me into the next room?'

I followed them rather reluctantly, for I was anxious to see what the little man was like when awake. We came into a comfortable little room wherein sat a young lady who was doing her hair before a glass, on the table before her lay several envelopes addressed to the editresses of ladies papers.

'This is Lilly,' said Mr Annesley, 'Lilly of the Valley, we call her, because she toils not, etc., but it is not quite fair, because, though she does not toil, and probably, if you set her before a spinning wheel she'd think it was sort of a new bicycle, yet she spins the most excellent yarns to undesirable callers.'

'Oh, Mr Annesley,' said the girl, 'you do tell them,' and finishing the tying of her hair with a determined twist, she left the room. Almost immediately we heard the sound of a smart blow on flesh followed by a short boyish cry.

'That's nothing,' said Mr Annesley, 'that's only Lilly's way of telling the boy to go and stand outside while she sits in his chair. And now, Madame Karl, I am very much at your service, what can I do for you?'

'First of all,' said Madame, 'let me introduce you to Miss Blanche La Mare, a protégée of mine, who wants to go on the stage.'

Mr Annesley squeezed my hand most affectionately, and then answered. 'That is at once a very easy and a very difficult job, as doubtless you know, Madame Karl. Miss La Mare is very pretty and I am sure very clever but unfortunately that is not all that managers want. Has she seen anyone yet?'

I hesitated to speak of Lewis, but Madame took up the tale for me, and moreover told it with some circumstance and just a little exaggeration. The young man did not seem surprised, but he did not on the other hand seem very confident that I should find the agents much more demurely behaved.

It was suggested that we should lunch first; then I might make my visit to an agent Mr Annesley knew. The fat little man, Walker Bird, was awakened to make our party a square one, and we hansomed off to a place called Estlakes.

I had Walker Bird for my cab companion. I think the other man would have very much liked to have looked after me, but Madame captured him at once and he had no choice but go gently.

I expected the fat little man to improve the occasion, and he certainly did not disappoint me. The street was too open and the luncheon place so crowded that kissing was out of the question, but he made no bones about squeezing my hand affectionately.

I was glad when Mr Annesley said after lunch that I should come at once with him to see an agent.

Mr Rufus, the agent, inhabited the first and second floors of a house in the Strand. The doors on either side of his offices opened into bars, and about them were grouped numbers of shabby men whom no one would have any difficulty in recognising as actors. They all wore long coats, in some cases decorated about the collar and cuffs with fur of a very dubious origin, but in most cases extremely thin and bare. Within the bars I could see a number of ladies, whose costumes seemed to have been designed by an enthusiast of the kaleidoscope, and whose hats rivalled in their plumed splendour the paradise birds of the tropical regions. Their talk was loud and shrill, and could easily be heard in the street without.

'Chorus girls,' said Mr Annesley, laconically, 'they get thirty-five a week, and are expected to fill one of two stalls every evening, if they don't they get the sack, so you see they are duty bound to get to know a lot of Johnnies.'

'Now then, Evans,' he said, to the young man in the outer office, 'I've brought a young lady who has to see Mr Rufus at once – at once, do you understand? Cut along in and tell him.'

In a few minutes the clerk returned with the message that Mr Rufus would see us directly. Presently the door swung open, and the excellent Mr Rufus appeared in person. For a moment, I thought that the poor man would be torn to pieces, for the attendant nymphs gathering up their skirts with one simultaneous and mighty rustle, like all the brown paper in the world being rolled up into a ball, bore down upon the devoted agent and besieged him with shrilly phrased interrogations.

As soon as we went into his room, he cordially welcomed Mr Annesley, but of me he took not the slightest notice; he did not even ask me to sit down, though he had comfortably buried himself in a large and well padded armchair. Mr Annesley began to explain the purport of our visit. It was barely finished, when Mr Rufus condescended to turn to me.

'Well, my dear,' he said, 'Mr Annesley speaks very highly of you, and your appearance is decidedly in your favour. You can read music at sight, I suppose?'

I nodded.

'And sing?'

I nodded again.

'Well,' he continued, 'you've just looked in at an opportune time. I've got to fill the chorus of a company that's just going out, and if you care to have the job, you can. Thirty shillings a week you begin on, but a girl like you ought not to stop long at that. Now, I shall expect you here at 11.30 on Monday to meet Mr Restall, the manager. Goodbye, Miss La Mare, you'd better get out this way, and if you like, when you come again, you can come up this back staircase; ring the bell at the bottom, and you'll be let in. Mind you, this is a special favour.'

I accepted the offer of the engagement; as a matter of fact, I had come prepared to accept anything, and left Mr Rufus by his private staircase. And so, in this way, I put my foot on the first rung of the dramatic ladder.

Annesley met me again outside, and asked me to have a drink with him. I wasn't very anxious to go into a public bar, but from what I saw of the ladies who were to be my theatrical companions, I gathered that it was a pretty usual thing to do. What would my reverend father, I wondered, have thought of his little daughter, had he watched her through the threshold of that glittering rendezvous?

We went into a small compartment, which we had to ourselves – in fact there was little room for anyone else there – and after a minute or two Mr Annesley remembered with a start that he had left his notebook in the agent's office. 'God forbid that anyone look into it,' he exclaimed, and then begged me to wait while he went back.

I could scarcely refuse, so sat perched on my high stool, sipping my whisky and soda, and watching as well as I could the flirtations of the pretty barmaids and the customers in the other little boxes. Suddenly I became aware of a low toned conversation in the next compartment to mine, and by reason of a crack in the dividing wall, I could hardly help hearing it.

The men talking were obviously actors, and their conversation dealt with the theatrical tours they had just returned from. I give it just as it came from their lips, bad language and all. It was a revelation to me; I had not supposed before that any class of men could be so utterly mean in giving away the secrets of favours received from the other sex.

Said actor No. 1: 'How did you get on with the girls

in your show? Had a pretty warm time, I suppose?'

'My word, they were hot ones,' was the answer. 'I started out meaning to live alone, but before two weeks, I had keeping house for me little Dolly Tesser.'

'I know her – pretty girl.'

'You're right; and you should see her with her clothes off, old man! A perfect peach, I can assure you. She was a bit shy at first, but I soon taught her all the tricks. My word, she is a bloody fine fuck!'

'Young, isn't she?'

'Oh, quite a kid, about seventeen – over the legal age though – you don't catch me making any mistake of that sort again. She wasn't a virgin, she'd been wrong with a conductor in the Gay Coquette crowd.'

'What, that syphilitic beast?'

'He hasn't got it really, but talking syph, have you heard the tale of Humphreys and his landlady's daughter?'

'No.'

'Well, he struck a place with an uncommonly pretty girl to wait. She was the landlady's daughter, and he hadn't been in the room three days before he was into her. Then on the fourth day, she didn't show up. He asked the old woman what was the matter.'

'Oh, Mary's very bad,' she said, 'we've had to send her to the doctor, he says she's got syphilis.'

'You can bet old Humphreys nipped round to the chemist pretty sharp, bought a bottle of black wash and kept bathing the old man all day. On the next day however, the old girl turns to him as she's taking away his breakfast and says: "Oh, I made a mistake in what I told you about Mary yesterday, it is erysipelas." '

At that moment Annesley returned, so I was spared any more from the actors on the other side of the bar.

Annesley wanted me to go back to the office with him, but I was too excited at the prospect of my engagement and I wanted to hurry home to tell

Madame Karl – but I did not get back.

It happened like this. There was the usual block to the Strand traffic at the bottom corner of the street, and, gazing idly out of my hansom, I saw a long haired poet whom I had met before. He saw me too, and fled recklessly through traffic to gain my side; he asked no invitation, but seating himself murmured: 'This is indeed a direct intervention of providence,' and told the cabman an address which I surmised to be that of his flat – it turned out to be so.

We drove rapidly down the Strand, and went down Arundel Street, in which street the poet said he had a nest that almost touched the sky. It certainly did, and as that particular block of buildings boasted no lift, it was a tired and panting little Blanche that at length gained the sixth floor. The poet apologised for the absence of the elevator, but immediately afterwards congratulated himself on none being there, for having a lift, he said, means also having a porter, and porters are horrid gossipy scandal mongering beings.

The front door passed, we found ourselves in a small hall, almost dark, save for the little light it gained from a heavily shaded electric globe which shed a discreet radiance upon an admirable painting of the Venus. A touch from the poet's fingers caused me to halt before the painting, and, as I gazed on it I felt his arms tighten round my waist, and his lips press gently upon my neck.

Here in this room was decadence indeed; all heavy curtains, little of the light of day, heavy scents again, and soft cushions everywhere. I sank down on a luxurious couch and waited events. He crouched at my side and began to kiss me; very slowly, but very deliciously and lovingly; his breath was scented with some pleasant Oriental flavour, a flavour which soothed my nostrils. Slowly his hand made its way over my calves and over my drawers; at the same time that he was feeling for the bare flesh of my thigh I was beginning to fumble with his buttons, and almost at the same moment that his fingers touched my clitoris, I had the naked flesh of his penis in my hand. It was very large and stout, a legacy of his north country parentage doubtless – and it throbbed amazingly.

For a few moments we felt each other without a word, overcome by our delicious sensations – and I made the next step toward a nearer intimacy by undoing his braces and buttons and sliding the front part of his trousers down till I could let my hand wander underneath his balls. That stung him into action. He freed himself from me, stood up and began to undress rapidly; in about a moment he stood before me stark naked and another moment saw me in the same condition.

We had only one fuck, but we lay there naked for hours, kissing and talking. I wanted more, and hinted for it, but he would not. 'Another time, little girl,' was all he would vouchsafe. At last the falling shadows warned me that I must get back to Madame Karl, and I let him dress me. He gave me a little miniature on ivory of himself, and made an appointment for that day week, the day which coincided with my first rehearsal with the Restall Company. I made him get me a cab, and gave the Jermyn Street address. I felt full of lust as I sat back on the cushions of the hansom, and suddenly as we came into Trafalgar Square, the remembrance of the woman I had met that night of my first arrival at school, her invitation and her address came back to me. I recollected her promise to find me a dress, should I come to see her. Without further thought I pushed the trap and gave the driver her street and number.

III

I was put down before a plain-looking house in the midst of a row of equally plain looking houses. A pretty maidservant answered the bell, and seemed a little doubtful when I asked to see Miss Clarence, the name of my oddly met friend. However, my confident statement that I was expected, coupled, I dare say, with my generally smart appearance, ended in my being shown upstairs. I followed the maid to a large high-ceilinged room and at once recognised Miss Clarence in the lady stretched on an ample sofa.

She was got up in a most calculated negli-outer garment, but even that was cut low in gee. A semi-transparent tea-gown was on her shoulders and short in the arms like an evening frock, her knees were drawn up so that I saw her uncovered legs right up to well above the knee, uncovered that is, save for pretty openwork silk stockings of a greenish colour. She looked very attractive, her hair was obviously just done up by an artist in the coiffuring business, and she was beautifully made up. She had a cigarette in her lips and her left hand held a half emptied champagne glass. There was a thick, intoxicating odour of scent in the room.

'Goodness gracious!' she said, after a prolonged stare. 'My little friend of two years ago; the girl just going to school. Well, it's a wonder I recognised you. Christ, you are altered, child!'

I mumbled that I had always remembered her

invitation, but that this was the first opportunity I had had of accepting it.

'Well, you've come at quite an opportune moment,' she said, after she had extracted my story from me; how I had been cast off, and what had happened to me. 'I can make use of you this afternoon. I remember saying that you should have a dress, you shall have it.'

I didn't know very much of the world at that time, but I knew enough to realise that my hostess was a bad woman; bad, that is, in the sense of a woman who sold her body to a good bidder, and intuition taught me that she wanted me for the same purpose. Curiosity, and natural desire to make a little money, gave me courage. I was ready for pretty well anything.

She went on to tell me that she had arranged to find a virgin for one of her richest clients that very afternoon. The girl she had selected had disappointed her. 'In fact, my little dear,' she informed me, 'I was so much at a loss that I had got myself up as fascinating as possible to see if the old devil couldn't put up with me – now you've come.'

'But –?'

'Exactly; you're not a virgin, but you look like one, and the physical difficulties can be got over. You'll do very well for a first class virgin. First of all, however, that smart frock won't do; my old man expects a poor girl.' A ring at the bell interrupted her talk, and she immediately pressed an electric button at her side. 'Marie,' she said to the maid who entered, 'If that is General Salis, tell him to wait in the dining room. Give him a drink but don't dare to be loving to him or – '

'But the General is so impetuous,' answered the pretty girl.

'Well, don't let him put his impetuosity into you,' laughed Miss Clarence. 'Tell him that I have a little friend waiting for him.'

'Now,' she said when the girl had gone, rising to her feet, and becoming a businesswoman on the instant, 'are you game for this; it'll be ten pounds in your pocket; not a bad afternoon's earnings?'

'I'm game,' I replied. 'Give me a drink though.'

She poured out a glass of champagne, and while I was drinking it, began to undo my bodice. I was soon disembarrassed of everything but my underclothes, and Miss Clarence looked at me critically. 'Your undies are rather too smart,' she said, 'but I'll tell him I gave you these for the occasion. Now for the virginity part of the business.'

She led me into an adjoining room, filled a basin with water and dropped the contents of a paper into the water: 'That's powdered alum,' she remarked, 'that'll dry your little cunt up, my false virgin,' at the same time filling a syringe with the mixture. I obeyed her and injected the alum and water. 'You'll have to bleed,' she added, 'these old men always look for that. I'll show you how. Here's a little bladder of pigeon's blood, put it under the string of your drawers, or anywhere else where you can hide it. When he's having you, you must wriggle about a lot and scream, and you must find a chance of breaking this. Crack it with your nail and manage to let some run over his cock and balls; get it into his hairy part if you can, but above all get your drawers saturated. If I know the General he'll probably want to take those away as a trophy; of course he'll give you extra money for another set for you.'

Then she dressed me up in a very plain three-quarter length dress of common material and made me let my hair down. 'Capital,' was her comment when she surveyed me, 'you don't look more than fourteen; the old man'll think he's got a treasure.'

With my little bladder of blood tucked into my drawers and my poor pussy dried up to the closing point with the alum, I followed her back into the drawing-room. She rang again, and presently the General followed the maid into the room.

It was a desperately business-like proceeding, and it was not till long afterwards that I recognised how all this straightforward bargaining and arranging appealed to the old rip for whom I made the sacrifice. She had instructed me to be extraordinarily coy, and I sat on the couch with my face half-covered with my hands, taking care, however, to let the most attractive part of it be visible, and taking care at the same time to stick out my shapely legs as far as possible from under my frock.

The General was a fat man with a double chin and fierce moustache. He came into the room with a military stride, and kissed Miss Clarence on the cheek.

'Lock the door, Marie, and sit down by it,' said Miss Clarence, 'General – you trust me, and you must trust Marie – this child may be hurt, and I shall want someone to help me look after her.'

The old devil's eyes twinkled as he looked at me; became fiery lamps as I got up in obedience to Miss Clarence's gesture and suffered him to kiss me.

Miss Clarence was very business-like; in fact she was almost like a governess of a class and her manner was strikingly at variance with her alluring appearance, but how well she knew her man. He was boiling with excitement and anticipation.

'Now, General,' she went on, 'this girl is the daughter of a friend of mine. She is doing this for money because she is almost penniless. She has always lived in the country and knows nothing of men. I have told her what you are going to do to her, and it is the first time she has ever heard of any such thing.' The old reprobate, and I recognised him from his pictures in the papers as being a hero of the last war, was sitting on a couch, puffing a cigar and devouring me with his eyes while his ears followed Miss Clarence's introductory lecture. 'She is innocent, and has no idea of the value of her charms to mankind. You are going to pluck a very rare flower and you'll have to pay for it. Thirty pounds in all, General. Ten pounds for me, fifteen pounds for my little friend – you see how generous I am – and five pounds for Marie, who is staying here to help in any way she can. Is it a bargain?'

The old man rose to his feet. 'No, damn you it isn't!' he cried. 'It's a damned shame.'

'Well, why do you come here wasting my time?' snapped Miss Clarence.

'Thirty pounds for you, sixty for the girl, and a tenner for Marie,' blustered the General. 'I've just won an unexpected hundred pounds on a horse this afternoon, and if the little lady wants money, damn she shall have it!'

The bargain, needless to say, was struck at once, and the General laid a roll of five pound notes on the table.

Then came my turn. I had been instructed by Miss Clarence to be perfectly passive and speak as little as possible. At her bidding I had laid myself out on the capacious sofa, and the old man approached. He kissed me lusciously several times, but I gave him no responding lips caress, and then he began feeling my legs. Miss Clarence and the maid were sitting, silent spectators, smoking cigarettes.

I wriggled and crossed my legs as he felt me, and pretended with little pushes, to thrust him away. 'Oh, damn it all, Bella,' I heard him say, 'I must have her clothes off!'

Bella Clarence pretended to whisper to me and gain my consent, and then disembarrassed me of all my outer clothes. I lay on the couch in my drawers and chemise, my long auburn hair flowing over my shoulders and breasts.

'That's enough off, General,' Miss Clarence said, 'you can't expect her to go stark naked the very first time.'

The General was a big, heavily formed man but his

white hairs had led me to expect a very different instrument from the gigantic phallus that he produced. It was indeed a stout and powerful thing and reared up till its head almost knocked against his navel – he had stripped himself quite bare.

I gripped my little bladder of blood in my hand – and waited.

I shall never forget the scene at the commencement of the pseudo seduction. Above me towered the big old military man, and I remembered with a certain pride, as I felt him groping a way for his penis to my cunt, that he really was a very distinguished man. Behind him I saw Miss Clarence and the maid, beautiful women both, the eyes of both brightened with lustful curiosity, and the dainty room was a fitting box for its bawdy contents. I noticed my own pretty legs, and I drew them up to let the General get between them, and at last I felt the head of the General's penis trying to force an entrance.

The alum had dried me up, and the screams I gave were by no means all theatrical. I felt some real pain until he had got well within me. Then joyous sensuality supervened, and it was with an effort that I remembered to slit the bladder with my nail and release the blood over his member, my legs and underclothes. When it was squeezed dry, I managed, introducing an elaborate fling of my arms, to the accompaniment of a frantic screech, to drop it behind the couch.

The General finished as he had begun, strongly; and filled me with a generous outpouring. I took it in with pleasure, and had some difficulty in raising the crocodile tears with which I was to shame him when he arose.

But my theatrical instinct triumphed, and my whole body shook with a spasm of sobbing when at last the old man drew his artificially bloodstained prick from within me and stood up.

'Well,' queried Miss Clarence, while the maid was sponging me between the legs.

'Magnificent!' answered the hero of Cathistan, glaring at his bloody cock and the sea of red fluid on my underclothes.

Miss Clarence gave me the sixty pounds, saying that my performance was worth far more than that to her, inasmuch as the General had been so pleased that he was sure to come again often, and send many friends. 'He was completely deceived,' she told me.

We went for dinner afterwards, and Miss Clarence insisted on taking me to the Majestic music hall.

We had to go through the Promenade at the Majestic to reach our box, and I was astounded at the sight of the women loafing in the place. An atmosphere of lust filled the hall, and seemed especially to descend on the promenade. There was a set of well dressed, handsome girls, all agog to catch the attention of the men who idled, open eyed, calculating the value of the charmers, along the semi-circular Promenade. I knew of the existence of the women of pleasure, and I had heard the Majestic was a place frequented by them, but I had not expected such beauty, or nearly such numbers.

We spent a quiet evening. Only a brace of men came to chat with us in our box, and about eleven o'clock Miss Clarence decided to go home. I was too full of my new environment to wish to quit in a hurry, besides my sixty pounds burned in my pocket, and I was anxious to know more of a life that could offer such rewards for so little sacrifice. I said as much, rather gaily, to Miss Clarence, as the hansom was spinning westwards.

'Sixty pounds don't drop from the clouds often, my little one,' she said.

We had not gone very far on our journey before Miss Clarence volunteered the information to me that her best boy would be waiting for her at home. 'It's a treat I only give myself once a week,' she added, and asked me if I did not mind.

Of course I did not mind, and very soon the hansom brought us back to Mademoiselle Clarence's.

My friend's best boy was there, waiting for us, a handsome young animal of the hooligan type. Villainy lurked in his eyes, and the low throw-back of his simian-like brow; but my hostess was undoubtedly devoted to him, or at any rate to the animal part of him. She embraced him at intervals during supper, and the meal was hardly over before they were at it on the sofa, her costly evening dress thrown up anyhow round her breasts, and his ill cut trousers down to his knees. It was an odd contrast; the silken, scented finery of the smart prostitute mingled with the coarse clothes of the maquereau. Her legs were beautifully shaped, the dear, and her stockings of the finest silk gave their pretty curves every chance to be fascinating. His legs were good, too, what I could see of them, and very white. It appeared that he was a prizefighter by trade, and had to keep himself in the pink of condition. The hard, tense sinews of his thighs swelled up under the skin, and his bottom seemed altogether composed of muscles. As for that important weapon which seemed to give my friend such intense pleasure, it was really a formidable organ, long, large, and mightily stiff. The first fuck did not take long, but by the time Madame had spent, with a long drawn out sigh of satisfaction, I could feel something wet between my own little lily-white thighs.

Then they stripped and my abhorrence of the hooligan face was quite lost in my admiration of the body. He was splendidly made, and they were a beautiful pair; for she, though no longer in her first youth, had lost none of the contour and roundness of a really fine figure. Over and over they rolled on the big couch, first one on top and then the other, exciting each other to madness with every variety of love's tricks, and poor little Blanche grew very excited indeed. How I longed for that splendid prick in me, and I fancy that the young man longed to put it there too, for after the second bout was complete, he came and sat by me and laid a caressing hand on my leg. I offered not the slightest opposition, but Madame thought otherwise. She drew him away; 'No, no, you are only for me tonight, Billy,' she said.

I sighed: 'I think you two'll drive me mad.'

'Oh, you poor little dear, we must do something for you,' and together they undressed me, and laid me on the couch.

But there was no fucking for me – I was allowed to handle that member, feel it against my breasts, but Madame would not let him fuck me. She sucked me off, and so did he, and I rained kisses all over the two while they were fucking, at last sucking his cock while he kissed her pussy. And last of all, Madame sent for the maid to sleep with us. We were given a dildo, and told to make the best of that. It was something, but both the maid and I wanted that prick. Finally we went to the bathroom, conveniently adjacent to the bedroom, and washed out our hot and tired bodies.

We all slept together. Madame's bed was big enough to have accommodated Henry VIII and all his wives, and fell into a deep, utterly fucked, dreamless slumber.

I awoke first, found the boy next to me – we were all stark naked – and passed my hand over his body. His prick stiffened at the touch, and he awoke. He pressed his lips to mine, and despite the overnight orgies and the commonness of the man, his breath was sweet (that's the best of these athletes who don't smoke or drink, for he had had nothing the night before, through all that fucking) – rolled one leg over mine, and I was just preparing for a gorgeous fuck on the sly, when Madame awoke and pulled him from me.

'You must have thought me a selfish little beast,' she said afterwards, 'but he's my only extravagance, and I won't let him fuck another woman, whatever else he may do to them in my presence. I really believe he is absolutely true to me, as a matter of fact I think he has to be. I pay him well, and keep a damned good watch on him, he'd be a fool to lose me, and he knows well enough that if I found him out, his easy living would go.'

Madame made me promise to come and see her again, and insisted on making me a present of such a pretty nightdress, as a *souvenir d'amour*.

Madame Karl was naturally surprised, and not a little hurt, when I turned up in Jermyn Street looking absolutely washed out. I made a clean breast of it, and she ended by laughing and saying that I hadn't done so badly for myself. Madame Karl, it may here be appropriately mentioned, had in her younger days, when an apprentice at a great Parisian atelier, made a good bit of pocket money on her back.

Rehearsals with Restall proceeded smoothly enough, he liked me, and through his favouritism gained me a jealous look or two, the other girls did not dare to be openly hostile; besides, though I say it myself, I was a jolly, unaffected little kid, with no side, and ready enough to make friends.

I used to go out in the waits, to a scrappy lunch, or tea, with different male members of the company, but took care, acting on the advice of one of the girls with whom I had palled up, not to allow any familiarity on the part of the comedians – besides they weren't nice enough. The evenings I spent with Madame Karl, and we generally went to some theatre; I was anxious to see every play I could. As often as not Mr Annesley and little Walker Bird were our cavaliers, and one evening I shall never forget.

We had been, the night before, to a most admirable comedy, beautifully acted, but witnessed by a very meagre house. This night we had attended a popular burlesque, and had had the greatest difficulty in getting seats. We had supper in Jermyn Street and after supper Madame Karl said she would like to go to bed, she did not feel very well – but as she did not want to go to sleep, would we, after she was undressed, come and sit with her and chat.

We did. Madame looked as delightful as usual in bed; beautifully made up, exquisitely night-gowned, and under a becomingly shaded light. Annesley sat by her side, one arm around her dainty little waist, and the other apparently dangling by his side – he was on the blind side of the bed, so we could not see what exactly was employing those fingers, but Madame was wriggling every now and then.

The talk turned upon plays – Annesley held it a disgrace that what was really good in London should not attract. 'As for that trashy burlesque,' he said . . .

'Rot, oh rot, my dear fellow,' answered little Walker Bird, settling himself comfortably into an armchair. 'You may think it trash, though I know you've been at least a dozen times, but the public love it, and the public deserve to be catered to. Take the men in tonight's audience. They had worked hard during the day, and they had dined heavily when their work was over. They didn't want to think, their tummies were much too full. They wanted to laugh easily, and, above all, to see lots of pretty girls, and feel their old jocks stiffen,' – we four always talked very freely – 'and you bet your life they did stiffen tonight. Cunt, my dear Annesley, cunt, and lots of it, is what the greater part of this blessed nation wants. There's a certain proportion of the stalls who can take the cunt they see on the stage out to supper afterwards and block it, and a much larger proportion who wish they could, but who go home and block their wives or mistresses, instead. So everybody is satisfied, see?'

Mr Annesley must have got his finger rather farther than usual up Madame, for she wriggled furiously, then suddenly kissed him all over his face before he could reply – and when he did answer, he agreed with Walker.

Conversation lagged; Annesley was occupied surreptitiously (as he thought) frigging Madame Karl, while I was getting hot as hell watching them, and Walker was getting hotter still, watching me. At last he got up and said he must be going. 'Don't hurry,' urged Madame Karl. 'I must,' answered Walker, but don't let me hurry you, Annesley, old chap.'

Annesley made no pretense of wishing to hurry, so I saw little Walker to the door.

In the hall he grabbed hold of me, thrust his tongue down my throat till I thought I should have choked, then begged me to let him have a piece.

Well, he got me into the shop, and there in the darkness, lit only by the furtive streetlamp's ray or two that stole over the shutters, the little devil fucked me, on the shop table. He was a good long time about it, he had been drinking, but I quite enjoyed the performance. When it was over he kissed me fervently, wiped his cock with his perfumed handkerchief, exacted a promise that I would see him on the morrow, and departed.

I went up to Madame's room, and knocked. No answer. I went in on tip-toe. The bedclothes were thrown back, Annesley's trousers were down, Madame Karl's nightdress was up, and Annesley's prick was half in her cunt but they were both fast asleep. I switched off the light, and tip-toed off again to my own little bedroom, where I undressed, admired my naked little self in the long glass, read a chapter from one of Madame's naughty books, tickled my clitoris a little, though not enough to come, and fell off into the land of dreams.

In the morning I woke up to find Madame by my side. She blushed when my eyes met hers. 'Of course you know what happened last night, I could not help it. He's gone, got out before the servants were up.'

On the Thursday preceding the Monday we were to open at Oxford. Mr Restall, in a fit of sweetness towards me, produced I think by the generous effect of some very old, old brandy, asked me if I would care to go with him to a theatrical dance that same evening at the Harmonic theatre.

You bet I accepted. Dances were foreign to my experience, and the theatrical dances promised such gay and unusual experiences that I literally jumped at the offer. He bade me look my best, and meet him for supper at the Alcazar Restaurant, opposite the Harmonic, at eleven thirty.

I was there at eleven thirty-five and had fifteen minutes in which to admire the frescoes on the wall.

Then Restall sailed in, to the accompaniment of much bowing and scraping on the part of the attendants, and a considerable addition to the civility shown me. I had been taken, I think, for a lady out on the pick up.

Restall, speaking and behaving in his usual restless, jerky manner, hustled me upstairs and found a table on the balcony.

The supper was a good one; but that is no great matter in the present story. What I want to talk about is that theatrical ball, my first.

Restall liked my dress. I think at first, after he had invited me, he had suffered some doubt as to whether I, being only newly engaged, would turn up in a costume sufficiently worthy of him and the occasion.

But I think that the delicious confection presented

me for the ball by Madame Karl not only reassured him, but even astonished him. He kept turning to look at me with obvious pride as we entered the Harmonic theatre.

The Harmonic was delightfully arranged for the occasion. The ballroom was of course the stage, enclosed in a woodland scene. At the back perched on a built up mossy bank, was the orchestra, and the pit usually occupied by the orchestra was filled for this occasion with flowering ferns, forming a hedge between the stage and auditorium. At intervals in the hedge were gaps, through these gaps were gangways leading down into the stairs, much used as sitting out places by the dancers.

There were of course other sitting out places, and capital ones. The boxes for instance, the big ones on the pit and dress circle tier, though they were fairly easy to see into. Above them, much more private were the boxes on a level with the upper circle and still more delightful were the little boxes only designed to hold two, or at the most three, at the back of the dress circle. And you obtained a fair amount of privacy if you sat out in the gloom of the upper circle.

Restall was at once surrounded by a big crowd and after introducing me to one or two men, abandoned me at once. I was not destined however to linger as a wallflower; I attracted the attention with a nice big handsome gentleman and I was dancing to my delight.

Hardly a girl there that was not pretty, and nary a man who hadn't come to the theatre with the manifest purpose of enjoying himself; there was no duty business. All the girls were all well dressed, and none of them was chary of showing the most of their upperwork charms. I marvelled how some of them kept their bubbies within those dangerously décolleté corsages; I know that I myself had more than once to lift a guardian hand to keep my own nipples from overflowing on to the dress coat of my partner. Not that he would have minded, I dare say.

One man managed to knock down my fan, and was clever enough to get his hand just on to my stocking in the act of picking it up, but I kicked his errant fingers away, and the boy – he was one of the youngest guardsmen possible – blushed and apologised. I had to wait for my supper partner for anything serious to happen.

Walker Bird, who arrived precisely at the supper hour, brought him up to me, and so fascinated was I by his eyes, his figure, and his generally distinguished appearance, that I threw over the man I really should have supped with, without a second thought, and accepted unhesitatingly his suggestion that it was about time all of us felt a little hungry. Walker left us with a murmured, 'Keep a brace of pews for me and mine,' and caught us up at the door of the supper room – the big saloon bar transformed for the nonce into a palm embowered eating place – with a cute little chorister from the Harmonic on his arm. I recognised her in a tick, for were not her photographs in every print seller's window, and did not the evening papers keep stock headlines going for her breach of promise cases? She had on a dress worth at least a hundred pounds, and she greeted me simply, after the introduction, with 'Lord, you could at least speak a bit.'

I supped gaily and well; the wine was exhilarating, the food first rate; the surroundings the gayest, and I had my supper partner's leg entwined round my left, and Walker's left leg round my right. It was a round table, and I have no doubt that the little chorister was being endeared in precisely the same manner. We had a quartette of Tsiganes for a separate supper orchestra, and their strains made my little head swim with naughty thoughts. All at once I felt I was sitting on something wet, and I knew that I had come involuntarily, so much so that I welcomed our little friend's suggestion after supper that we should go and put a puff on.

We were alone in the retiring room – 'Gay ain't it old dear?' she said, as she drew a stick of red across her pretty little mouth, and then passed it on to me – 'makes me feel hot as hell,' she passed her hand up her dress, 'I thought as much,' she pursued, 'I've spent – what a bleeding waste.'

In one of the WC's I took the chance of wiping my underclothes as dry as possible, for I was in that stage of full-bloodedness that I was absolutely determined to have a man that evening – even if I had to ask for it. And so much were the faces of the men altered since supper that I didn't think that event at all probable.

Near the door I found my supper partner and he led me at once into a valse, a deliciously suggestive thing, admirably rendered by the band. He too, was mad for a woman. There was no disguising that fact, for through my dress I could feel his swollen prick pressing against me, he had arranged it up his trousers, pointing to the navel – and I should say very nearly touching that spot, in the careful manner of the man wearing evening dress who realises that he is likely to be overcome by the outward and visible sign of his manhood – and I don't deny that my little tummy pressed back.

We both danced well, both recklessly and with abandon, and whether it was that the other couples admired our performance so much that they wanted to witness it, or whether the other girls were nervous of becoming an obstacle to our wild career, at any rate we pretty soon had the floor to our own selves. I heard several complimentary remarks as we whirled by, and once I caught Restall's eye full, it bespoke admiration, and by the motion of his lips as he turned to speak to the man by his side, I had an inkling that he was informing the man of the fact that I was a member of his company, and that he, Restall, intended to sleep with me. He could have had me then and there if he had chosen to come and ask, and provide a place.

The music stopped suddenly, and my partner and I sank exhausted on to the nearest seat. As he fanned me, he whispered: 'This is an uncomfortable sitting out place. I know one much better – shall we go?' and I only nodded my answer.

'This is the place I mean,' he said, when we paused before a curtained door, situated near the stage. He drew the curtain aside, and next minute I found myself in a cozy little room, and heard behind me the unmistakable sound of a key being turned in the lock.

The room was furnished mainly with a large sofa, the sort that has the ends made to flop down, and a number of theatrical photographs. I thought it was some sort of private sitting room, had I known more I should have guessed at once it was a dressing room. The photographs of the celebrities were mostly women, and all signed.

As there was no other place to sit on I flopped on the sofa at once, and a moment later my partner was at my side, his arm tight around my waist, and his lips on my cheek.

I suppose it was the fact of my clerical descent that made me leap to my feet with a little noise of disapproval when I felt his fingers tickle the bare flesh above my petticoats, or was it the fear that someone might come in? – at any rate he took it for the latter, for he hastened to assure me that the door was locked.

'But,' I replied, still rather coy, 'suppose anyone should want to come in and sit out in this room, too?'

'That they're not likely to do,' he said, with a delicious smile, 'for you see this is my dressing room.'

Then I recognised him, he was the tenor of the Harmonic company but the absence of the small pointed beard he affected on the stage altered him, for the better I think.

'I saw you in a box a little time ago,' he said. 'You

looked like a little dream, but you were with society people. How do you come to be here, and brought by Restall?'

I didn't care that evening; I was carried away by surroundings, and the man seemed so nice, so I told him a good deal of the story (always mind you, my readers, suppressing that fact that George Reynolds had actually pierced my little bird's nest – as Walker Bird is in the habit of calling those inner temples of Venus in which he from time to time inserts his chubby little prick) and his embrace was so comforting, and I suppose I wanted it so much, that I made not the slightest demur when once more he placed his hand beneath my clothes, slid up my silk stockings and eventually laid it on my Mons Veneris.

He slid quietly to the ground, pulled me gently forward till my little bottom just balanced on the edge of the sofa, all the time lifting up my clothes with his other hand, and then pressed himself against me.

'Half a mo – ' interrupted Gladys – *she gets shockingly suburban when she's excited – 'Do you mean to tell me, you little simpleton that you actually let the man fuck you with your new ball dress on?'*

And I had to confess to Gladys that in my innocence I actually did do such a silly thing.

'The man ought to have known better – and a well known actor, you say. Actors I've fucked have been most considerate about my clothes, but go on and get to the fucking.'

First fucks with different men are, I suppose, all more or less the same; unless, of course, the man is some old beast, or ugly, or with a dirty beast you are only doing it for money. With a many you want to fuck, the excitement is so great, and you begin to come so soon, that you really haven't any time to notice whether he does it artistically or not; it's seldom, indeed, that you even distinguish any great difference in the size of his penis from the man you had last. At any rate my friend, I did not even know his name, got into me till I could feel his balls hang against my bottom, and spent very quickly. He kept it right in me and fucked me again slowly and deliciously, and I can tell you I was in a bit of a funk of having been put in the family way when at last the sense of joy had passed, and I stood up. He was sitting opposite me in a chair, his penis perfectly limp.

'Well, I suppose we'd better be getting back,' he said, after I had arranged my dress as well as I could, 'people'll be looking for you.'

I thought at first that he was callous; sufficiently pleased to have had a new girl, and wanted to be rid of me. I was angry – but when I suggested leaving him, he would have nothing of it. He took me into one of the first tier boxes, where we sat and watched the other dancers.

Willie Moorfield knew his way about London, and I spent quite an amusing evening while listening to his running comments on the celebrities present.

Miss Marion Storm, the successful comic opera prima donna of two continents, floated by on the arm of a very nice young man, who looked as near to being made up as any young man I had ever seen before. He was, so said Moorfield, a young gentleman who liked being an actor, and with whom audiences put up because it was general knowledge that he had only four or five consumptive and syphilitic cousins between himself and an Earl's coronet. He loved notoriety, and was at the present moment paying assiduous court to Marion of the nut brown hair, tip-tilted nose, and generally fascinating and devil may care expression, because he knew that a lot of other men in London wanted her; that, in fact, she was the fashion.

'They say he really means to marry her – or rather she's quite determined that he shan't get out of it,' said

Moorfield, 'I only hope they won't both fall in love with the same man.' Which rather amazing statement left me with the idea that the Honourable Mr George Danvers, Clarendon, Hope, Travis, Gwyn Iumthait was by way of real inclination – a sod.

'Don't you think you're getting rather vulgar, Blanche?' this from Gladys.

'You mean in my words? Well, I don't agree with you, and anyway, a sod is a much nicer term than bugger, which old Doctor Johnson so delightfully describes in his dictionary as "a term of endearment, common among sailors."'

But I mustn't waste time. Moorfield went on to tell me that Miss Storm had ruined almost as many men as Belero, and was equally proud of the fact. Married originally to a comedian, far, at that time, above her own station, both socially and professionally, she had thrown him over without the slightest compunction when fortune began to smile on her, and a man with a bit of money came her way.

The man with a bit of money took a theatre for her; procured a play for her, and make her in the twinkling of an eye one of the greatest stars of the burlesque stage in England. Her salary went up, she became the rage, but the man with the money lost it over the venture. 'It was only the other day,' said Moorfield, 'that she met him at Ostend, as she was leaving the boat. He was broke to the world, and the opportunity of the custom house business gave him the chance to ask her if she could lend him a tenner or so. She put half a crown on the douane counter, and turned her back. And that night, too, she slept with an actor who hadn't a sou to his name, and who, more than likely as not, borrowed a cool hundred from her.'

'She has money, and she is an artist to the heels of her little shoes,' continued Moorfield. 'But she has the lust of money, and whoever the man may be, provided he can give her any more, she will fuck him for it. She will marry that ennobled descendant of a complacent Stuart prostitute and despite the twenty thousand a year he can give her, she will go on acting, because she likes it, loves it for itself, and likes the fame and applause it brings her, and she will go on fucking, because she likes that too, and because, however much money she has, she glories in earning more by her cunt.'

'I gather,' says Gladys, 'that you and your new friend had become pretty intimate – to judge from your language.'

Well, gentle readers, we had. A sort of affinity seemed to have sprung up between us – and we glided into using dirty words just as if they had been the ordinary talk of polite conversation.

Little Annabel Cupid was the next goal of his spiteful tongue: he hadn't much to say of her save that she wasn't able to suck a man off because she feared that the enamel on her face would crack.

Of Madame Sydney, the operatic star, he told me that she had an absolute passion for loose life, but that she feared so much to find herself enceinte, that she would only play the sucking game with her lovers, or allow them to make an entrance up her stage door.

'The dirt road, as the Americans call it,' interrupts the conscientious one.

'Americans are dirty people,' I say.

'And have you ever – ?' but at that moment we hear the door open, and our dear old Baron comes into the room.

Interlude with the Baron

He enters with that assumption of youth which long experience has taught me to know that the old boy feels

like it, salutes first myself and then Gladys with cheery kisses, hands us each a bunch of rare flowers, and squats down contentedly on my big window seat –
'You're interrupting, as usual, Baron,' I say.

'If I may only make some trifling compensation?'

'I really begin to think that the only punishment we can inflict, is to put him into the book, right name and all,' this from Gladys.

'I have lunched so well and I feel so nice and I know so well that there is not such company in London as can be found here, may not that be an excuse?'

We try for a little to go on with the work, but the old man is always anxious to put his arm round my waist or to look over Gladys's shoulder to see how she is getting on, and the work doesn't go on at all.

'I see you are writing about Sodomites,' he chuckled.

'Yes,' answers Gladys, savagely, 'aren't you one?'

The old dear man wasn't angry, but proceeded there and then to talk volubly about the particular sect of young and old gentlemen who prefer connection with their own sex to the ordinary channels provided in the female kind by wise dispensation of providence.

'You should see the sods as you call them,' he began, 'and the word reminds me of a dear old friend who proposed to insult a gentleman who had behaved in that way with his youngest son, my friend's youngest son, that is. He left a card at the bugger's club, with the inscription, "You are a Sodomite". And it wasn't till a day afterwards that he remembered he had put two "d's" in the middle of sodomite. It upset him terribly.'

'I suppose you know the tale, Baron,' says Gladys, 'of the New York young gentleman of that persuasion who walked delicately, like Agag, into a New York saloon and asked, "Is my friend Sweet Evening Breeze here?"

"No," replied the bartender, "He's locked up."

"Oh dear," said the young man, "what for?"

"Cock sucking."

"Thank God, it's not for theft."

The Baron laughed. 'After all,' he said, 'I suppose it all seems very disgusting to you girls, but sometimes an old roué feels the need of something new.'

'That may be,' says Gladys, 'but as for what you call buggery, I for my part, don't believe it's possible. I know no man could get up me that way.'

'You remind me rather of the eminent CO my dear Gladys,' answers the Baron, 'the CO who said it was practically impossible to obtain a conviction against a prisoner for that particular offence, because, one half of the jury do it themselves, and the other half don't believe it's possible.'

'I am still a female Didymus,' says Gladys.

'Shall I prove it?' asks the Baron.

'If you like,' says Gladys.

'With your permission, Madame Blanche?' queries the Baron.

I nodded, really thinking that the old man was joking, but he immediately produced a fountain pen, and sat down at the writing table. When he had finished a brief note, he asked me if I could have it sent.

'But Baron?' I murmured, hesitatingly.

'It's perfectly right, my dear Blanche. Your friend doubted the existence of sodomy, and I am going to prove it to her that it does exist. This note will bring two chaps, adepts at the game.'

'But,' I interposed again, 'isn't it rather dangerous?'

'Certainly not. The lads are as discreet as the tomb; it pays them to be. They need not know that this is your house; they will probably think that it is a place I have taken.'

'And what sort of people are they?' asks Gladys.

'Singers, both of them.'

'Isn't it bad for the voice?' I asked.

'Actual sodomy perhaps is, but sucking off is wonderful, as I dare say you know, my dear Blanche?'

I did know. Earlier in my career I had the tip from Madame Sydney, the famous soprano. She kept two fine young men for that very purpose, and every night before fulfilling an important engagement, she sucked one or the other, sometimes both, to a finish. She regarded male semen as the finest possible lubricant for the vocal chords. I took her advice with good results. It's much nicer than voice medicines, and I dare say, many of you dear little comic stars and music hall artists who read and get naughty over this immortal work can bear me out. Take my advice, dears, and if, in a pantomime, you get jealous because one of the comedians is going too well, suck him off; his performance will lose, while yours will gain in proportion.

The Baron's men arrived in about half an hour. Gladys and I had discreetly masked our pretty faces, but masked very little else, for we had both begun to feel very randy, and had employed the waiting interval by making the old man lick our pouting pussies. When the boys were shown in by my confidential maid they found two pretty women lying on their backs on the big rug with bare legs, also bare cunts; temptingly displayed.

They were charming young men, both about twenty-two, and sweet and fresh to look at. The Baron kissed them both on the lips, and told them to begin at once.

They undressed stark naked. Such nicely formed white-skinned bodies they had, and firm pricks, no preliminary dalliance being wanted to make them rise. The entertainment began with sucking, first one man sucking the other, and then both playing sixty-nine. But Gladys was anxious for the action, so the first one was bent over the back of the sofa, his arse distended for the reception of the other's weapon.

'We shall want vaseline,' hazarded the second boy.

'Nonsense,' said Gladys, rising to the occasion, 'this will do.'

With that she placed her finger in her cunt, which was overflowing with juice, and anointed them.

It did do, for the prick slid in easily. A few wriggles on the part of the subject, and then the weapon was right inside him and up to the hilt. The subject seemed to enjoy it thoroughly, for his prick grew stiff as a ramrod, so beautifully stiff that Gladys could not resist fondling it. A few frantic strokes, a quiver, and the fellow withdrew his cock, dripping with spend. It was done; Gladys had seen an act accomplished which could have cost either of the two performers imprisonment for life.

The Baron turned to us with the air of a successful showman. 'Ladies,' he said, 'you once or twice laughed at my inability to complete the act of fornication; if one of you will assist me, I will soon show you now that I do it.'

And this is how he did it; Gladys, her legs apart, was stretched on the big rug, the Baron knelt between her thighs, and the chap whose prick still remained stiff got into the old man from behind. At once his withered cock stiffened, and in two shakes of a duck's arse, as the vulgar proverb has it, he had slipped down on to and into Gladys. The boy thrust, the Baron fucked, and Gladys wriggled. All of them very soon came; but the boy withdrew and the Baron got off the panting Gladys with a little grunt of triumph.

All were satisfied; all that is, save poor me, who had had nothing – but eventually I had the best of it. The men washed their cocks in rose-scented water. I took one dear cock in my mouth, and the other up my back (it was not my first experience – but that is another story). I made the Baron suck my cunt but let me explain the position – I knelt and lay forward with the fellow I was sucking underneath me. The Baron was also underneath me. With one hand I fingered the Baron's prick and with the other felt Gladys's cunt. Gladys had her roving commission. One of her dear, soft little hands wandered over my body, and the other tossed off the man I was sucking – thus everybody came in four distinct ways. I had a cock in my mouth which was delightfully stiff, yet not too big. (Big cocks give you cramp in the jaw muscles) I had a cock exactly the right size up my bottom, and any girl who has been had that way knows the joy that is. My cunt was being licked by an expert in the art, and a dear girl was feeling my bosom, likewise I had the pleasure of tickling a cock with one hand and a cunt with the other. It was a pretty group. I could see it all in a mirror, and I only wish we could have had it photographed. We continued for about ten minutes, till everyone concerned had spent, even including the Baron – it took about a pint of old, old brandy to pull him straight afterwards.

Gladys, who had watched the boy doing me, had noticed that I enjoyed it very much, now had the presumption to express her opinion that she could take a prick up her back door. So she knelt on the rug, and one of the men placed his weapon at the entrance. He had a hard time of it, and wasted some little time getting into her virgin rosette, but with the aid of some saliva, at last got all the way into her, and I think she enjoyed it immensely.

One of the last acts in the comedy was a more simple one, savouring indeed somewhat of the diversions of our sailors when far from land. The Baron put up a five pound note as a prize for which fellow could come first. My man, I am pleased to say, won hands down, thus once more exemplifying the old proverb that experience will tell. He spent with a scream of delight, occasioned, no doubt, by the mixed joy of the action and the reflection that his feat had earned him five pounds.

Subsequently we all sat down to a light refreshment of tea, cakes and champagne – all naked as we were.

Gladys and I, to round off the party, had another go at this new sport. She seemed to have taken quite a delight in this form of fornication. While her fellow was working away in her rear parlour, Gladys wriggled her arse like a fairy. The old Baron laughed uproariously at her antics, and twitted her about her previous remark about her tight little arsehole that no man could get into – offering to bet that even he could get into her now.

After a short rest Gladys let him try it, at the expense of a diamond ring, and he soon succeeded in shoving his big joystick up in her pooper, causing her to squeal with rapture.

IV

But to return to the earlier history of Blanche La Mare, so scandalously interrupted by the Baron and his lusty lads.

I will skip all further details of my life in London till the Herbert Restall Company got away on tour. We were to open at Oxford and the 'train call' was for Paddington, 11:30 of one memorable Sunday morning. I turned up early, unaccompanied, for Madame Karl had gone out to supper the night before, and had not returned – perhaps as a little revenge for my absences.

Still, I was not the first on the platform, and I soon got to learn that the habit of theatrical companies was to arrive very early at the station, and exhibit their best frocks. I had my best frock on, and I'm certain it was the best in the company. Herbert Restall cast an admiring glance at me when he arrived. He did not speak to me, and I noted the reason. His wife, an angular lady past fifty, and of a forbidding and non-conformist type of countenance, followed him everywhere.

We had a special train from platform number three, and I was engaged in looking for it, when Annesley appeared.

'Madame Karl is so sorry she couldn't get back,' he apologised, 'but her cousin was ill, and –'

'Never mind the explanations,' I cut him short. 'I hope you both enjoyed yourselves.'

To judge from the lines under his eyes, he had.

He found me the train, and he found me also the

acting manager, who was engaged in gumming labels on the carriage windows; labels indicative of the compartments to be occupied by various members of the company. Thanks to Annesley's introduction, I was not put to travel with the chorus ladies, but with the two 'Sisters Knock', the dancers, to whom also Annesley introduced me, and we all repaired to the bar together in which pleasant spot were assembled the majority of the company, some seventy all told.

To Annesley's introduction I owed a pleasant journey, for the two sisters Knock turned out jolly companions, and very soon threw off any reserve. I produced my cigarette case, and conversation very soon became not only general, but free.

They were neither of them girls who made the slightest pretence of being moral; they took it for granted that I was the same. They were pretty girls, hopelessly uneducated and common, but possessing a certain subtle gaminerie that gave them an odd charm of manner. They were dancers, wherefore it is not necessary to do more than state that their figures were excellent. They were absurdly alike, in face, figure, eyes, hair and everything and by dressing alike, down to the very smallest detail, they made it difficult for anyone but their most intimate friends to tell the difference. Once, when I knew them better, I ventured to remonstrate with them on this point.

'You must at least make a point of helping people to decide between you,' I said.

But the elder Miss Knock, who was generally the spokeswoman of the two, was not at all of my way of thinking. 'My dear stupid little darling,' she opined, 'that's exactly why we keep the deception up. We don't want people to know the difference. Now, barring that Maud's got a bit of a mole on her left hip which I haven't, we're just about as alike as two peas.'

She helped herself out of a generously sized flask,

passed it round, and settled down to be confidential.

Then she went on to tell me how useful it was when either she or her sister had an engagement with a man that they couldn't keep. It appeared that no man could tell them apart, even in bed, and even when quite undressed and in strong light. All that Maud had to do when her sister sent her in her place was to put a bit of gold beater's skin over the tell-tale mole, and things were all Sir Garnet. In fact Maud once went to Paris for a week with a new mash of Mabel's, while Mabel stopped at home to see after a rich American whom she had just picked up. If it hadn't been for that convenient sister she would have had to forego either the American or the other boy, which could have meant a loss of money. Mabel was the best talker of the two, and it was generally she who first attracted the men, but which sister the men got afterwards, when matters had been arranged, was simply a matter of chance. The girls went shares in all they got, and they did very well. Likewise, to mention a very intimate matter, it came in particularly useful when one of the two happened to be incapacitated from love by the presence of her monthly periods. The other simply filled the vacancy. Mabel collared quite a sum of money on one occasion, it appeared, by wagering with a rich young sportsman that she would take fifteen men twice each, during a night of eight hours, and come every time. Now she was game for fifteen, being a girl of exceptionally amorous and capable temperament, but double that amount was naturally beyond her. So the arrangement was made that the tourney was to take place in her own flat, and that she was to be left alone for a while between each insertion.

Of course you can guess that sister Maud, of the existence of whom the men were unaware, stepped into the gap on alternate occasions, and the deed was triumphantly accomplished and the money won, two hundred and fifty pounds, quite a nice little doucer for the two.

I believe it was a delightful ceremony. The young man who made the bet brought fourteen of his friends, and they were Sandhurst boys in the very pink of health and physical strength, and right lustily they accomplished their task.

The whole affair was very well managed, I gathered from Mabel's narrative. The boy who proposed the bet was rich, and he presented the performers with a supper amply calculated to in every way feed their lust. Likewise a sideboard groaned to sustain the men and the greatly daring girl during the night.

The first supper was decorous enough, for Mabel refused any early advances on the part of the men. A few bawdy toasts were drunk and Mabel made to swear a solemn oath that she would not lie about coming. Supper over, the devoted girl retired to her room, which led out of the dining room, and returned stark naked. And a pretty sight she must have been, exciting indeed to the eyes of those randy young men. I have often seen her naked in the dressing room, for she was one of those girls who have no scruples about exposing herself naked to the gaze of others of the same sex, and I always admired her.

The men drew lots for order of performing, the proposer of the bet, however, reserving to himself the third turn, which he reckoned would be the best. That settled, Mabel led the way in to the bedroom, arranged herself on the luxurious bed, and called to the first man to come on and do his damndest. He stripped, a muscular young giant of nineteen, blushing a little at the unaccustomed publicity of his act, and was into her without further ado. He had given but three or four vigorous thrusts when the dear girl cried out that she had come and forced him to get off her. There was no doubt about the coming; the hero of the wager introduced his finger into the well greased aperture, and abundantly satisfied himself. Then arose a difficulty. Mabel asserted that the act of her coming constituted the completion of the fuck, but the only half satisfied young man naturally asserted that he had an equal right to finish his share of the business. After some argument the poor girl had to agree that he had, and, though she offered to suck him instead, he remounted, and finished, making her come once more before it was done.

Then the assembly filed out into the next room, leaving Mabel alone. She was to ring a handbell when next prepared.

Of course Maud, her gold beater's skin concealing the mole, was produced out of a cupboard, whence she had viewed the proceedings and gathered all the conversation, so that she should not be found forgetful of any subject that might have been broached. The men were not a little astonished to hear the bell go almost immediately after their departure, and then were still more astonished to witness the vigorous lust that the psuedo Mabel displayed.

It was only a question of a few frantic strokes and the second hero and Maud united their spending and obviously completed the fuck.

She went back into the dining room with them to take a little refreshment. 'Maud,' so Mabel told me, 'was ever the drinking one of the two.' She then retired, and in five more minutes the bell rang for the third man who quite unexpecting so speedy a gratification of his lusts had not begun to undress.

And so the game went on, first Mabel and then Maud rising to the occasion, till all the men had had their first go within less than two hours from the start.

After that Mabel – she did practically all the talking – bargained for a couple of hours sleep, which was granted her. At the end of the two hours, she was awakened. Maud, poor thing, had had to put up with the narrow limits of an armchair in the cupboard all that time, and the contest began anew. The girls worked so well that there were but two fucks to be completed when there still remained two hours of the alloted time to run. At that juncture Maud nearly failed. Instead of profiting by the time limit to have a good rest, she pronounced herself ready directly after Mabel had taken the twenty-eighth cock.

When her young man had finished, and he was not unreasonably quick about it, he asked her if she had come, in compliance with the regulations. She, being a straightforward girl, was bound to reply that she had not. The question then arose whether the man who just finished, being incapable of immediate continuance, another might take his place. Maud protested that she could do it, if only the man was not in such a hurry. Eventually it took four of them, one after the other, each working their hardest, while Maud herself made herself naughty by imagining the depraved things, before the blessed dew anointed the lips of her cunt.

It was perhaps bad policy, but Mabel could not resist the opportunity for working a considerable surprise. Almost directly after the fatigued Maud had washed herself and retired into the cupboard, she walked out into the sitting room, quaffed a glass of champagne, and announced herself ready for the last man. He mounted her there and then in the room and they came together in about two minutes.

Then the cheque was handed over, and so ended a surprising evening.

When we arrived at Oxford I was undecided where to stay; being quite in ignorance of theatrical tours and living arrangements, I had intended to go to a hotel. Certainly my salary was only thirty-five shillings a week, but I had a little spare cash. The genial sisters

Knock, however, quickly disabused me of that. 'Come and stop with us, old dear,' they said, 'don't go putting up at hotels and making folks think you're a tart before they can prove it,' – and I went.

The rooms were rather a shock. Small and meanly furnished – the mural decorations consisted of a religious tract and lithographs, and the landlady was as dirty as she was familiar. But the sisters seemed to think they were in clover. 'Old Ma Osborne's a bit of all right,' explained one of the sisters, 'doesn't mind who we have in, or what we do, and that's saying something in a place like Oxford.'

When the question of dinner was mooted, old Ma Osborne grinned, 'Well me dears,' she said, 'I haven't worried about getting you any dinners, because knowing you like and your habits, I've took the liberty of telling Lord Hingley of the House, which is Christ Church College, me dear, that he might be at liberty to call. And Lord Hingley, me dears, will see as how you have a better dinner than I might be able to offer you here.'

I was inclined to be annoyed, but held my peace.

Maud Knock (the one with the mole) became business-like at once.

'Many thanks, I'm sure Mrs Osborne,' she said, 'but who's Lord Hingley, he's not on my visiting list?'

'Is he all right?' chipped in the moleless sister, 'none of your courtesy title paupers, eh, what?'

'All right; that I would say he is. Ten thousand a year he has, as I should know, dearies, my husband being his scout for nigh on two years in college, and as generous a gentleman as ever was.'

The sisters Knock nodded assent, and Ma Osborne retired beaming.

The highly recommended Lord Hingley presently made his appearance accompanied by his friend, Mr Charles Latimer; apparently they had only reckoned on two, and I saw breakers ahead, for, without conceit, I knew well enough that neither of the sisters could hold a candle to me in looks, or in any sort of attraction.

We were conveyed in cabs to Mr Latimer's rooms. Mr Latimer was a rich young gentleman, son of the famous brewer of that name, and he occupied the most elegant apartments. He was plain but well groomed, and very well dressed. Despite his origin he was a gentleman. Lord Hingley was nice looking, if rather stupid, and obviously too fond of drink. They were both scrupulously polite to us girls. We had a most admirable dinner, cooked and served in a style which would not have disgraced a smart West End restaurant, and we all of us drank rather too much champagne, to say nothing of subsequent liqueurs. Still nothing happened, and the men made no attempt at love-making. The sisters obliged at the piano, so did I, and after I had done so, Lord Hingley contrived to get me alone in a corner.

'I say,' he stammered, 'you're a lady, aren't you?'

'I'm certainly not a man.'

'But, don't joke; you aren't like the others. How did you come to be living with Maud and Mabel?'

'Because they are my friends.'

The poor boy became very nervous, so I explained.

'I am a lady by birth, but who I am and how I came to be here, I don't care to have anybody know. If I told you my father's name, you would probably know,' that was a good bluff considering the name was the same as my stage name – poor old Pop La Mare – 'so don't ask.'

But he squeezed my hand; not as a man would squeeze the hand of a chorus girl tart, and I knew that he was in love, the first young man or title who had loved me. He likewise made an appointment for the following day, to meet at the Queen's Restaurant for lunch, subsequently a drive, and a hasty little dinner at his own rooms to follow – (he lived out of college).

I went down to the theatre on the following morning – the first time I had entered a theatre as a member of a theatrical company, and early as I was, several of the girls were there before me, and the best places in the dressing room, which was to contain six of us girls, were taken.

There were the twin sisters Knock, Lily Legrand, a show lady of more or less mature age, but undeniable charm of figure, and little Bertha Vere, Restall's mistress, who was not, however, allowed any special privileges in the company because of her relationship to the 'Guvnor'. I had to hang my clothes up in the middle of the room, and do without a looking glass. My brand new make-up box occasioned great joy among the other girls, who all appeared to have come with the tiniest remnants of the necessary powders and pigments.

My first day in Oxford, also my first day on tour, was fairly uneventful, I went out to lunch with my lordling friend, but he treated me with extreme courtesy, to say nothing of a very good lunch. I found out afterwards that Oxford boys, while always delighted to get to know any actress on the road, yet expect little in return for their hospitality. My young man did not even attempt to kiss me, though we sat for a long time in his rooms after lunch – I think that he was even rather shocked that I smoked.

When I got back to my lodgings I found the sisters Knock there, back also from a luncheon party. They had brought on my letters from the theatre. One of them was from the poet, and of a distinctly improper nature. Its pretty indelicate imagery, and a most sensual drawing by an artist friend which was enclosed, brought so much moisture on my legs that I had to get upstairs and wash before I dared face the semi-public undressing of the theatre dressing room.

As the majority of the company had appeared in

'The Drum Major' before, we had no dress rehearsal, and I had not even seen my costumes till I got to the theatre that night. 'The Drum Major' was a tights play and all the girls in our room wore those fascinating garments. I was rather anxious to see how the legs of the other girls looked. Mine I knew, were all right, a little on the small side perhaps, but quite perfectly modelled. I could submit to the difficult task of inserting a three-penny piece between my naked thighs when placed together, and keeping it there. I had also silk tights, a present from Mr Annesley, who had informed me that the management considered cotton good enough for the chorus. He had found out the colour of my dresses, and had these made for me.

The girls in the room displayed little delicacy. Maud undressed stark naked, and walked about the room rubbing herself down with a towel. Her figure was good. Shapely legs, if perhaps a little too muscular to satisfy the artist who takes his ideal from the ancient Greek statues, but that was the fault of her dancing training. A firm, rather brownish skin, but without wrinkles, she wore no corsets, and round breasts with scarlet nipples. Her arms were also muscular, and she had the hair under her armpits shaved off, though a great abundance of dark and luxurious moss curled round the lips of her cunt and blossomed up on to her stomach.

Lily Legrand kept her vest on while putting on her tights, not omitting, however, to show the hair on the lower portion of her body, and the sexual organ underneath. Mabel Knock stripped boldly to the buff and displayed a figure which was almost an exact counterpart of her sister's, but she was more modest, and turned her back on us while she hurriedly slipped into her tights. Little Bertha, Restall's mistress, was far more discreet, and got into her leg attire under cover of other garments. The reason for that was, I afterward discovered, that she padded. I was also as modest as might be, and immediately aroused the suspicion of the eldest Knock girl that I had come to the theatre with my pads on, a common enough practice with some chorus girls who are ashamed of letting their companion tarts know that nature had not been altogether kind to them. She took me by surprise, and ran her hand all over my legs. 'Genuine,' she pronounced, with a laugh, and Bertha looked envious.

It was a military play and I was one of the officers, and I had practically to open the show with five others, headed by our captain, a very dapper little lady who was the principal boy of the play. When I first walked on to the stage, I could hardly see for fear (luckily I was placed last). I felt practically naked and the music surged in my ears and it was only when I heard the other girls break into the surging melody of the song that I regained enough self-possession to join them. However, in half an hour I was all right, and got the brace of lines allotted to me off swimmingly.

The piece went well; Restall was in great form, and was ably backed up by his leading lady, a well known exponent of soubrette parts. In the third act he was at his very best, but I had an awkward moment when he selected me as the other half of an impromptu gag scene. To his great surprise, I answered him back and got a big laugh for myself. When the show was over, and he had taken numerous calls, he stopped me on the stage. 'Clever little girl,' was the comment, 'we'll do that again tomorrow. Come up to my room when you're dressed and we'll have a little drink and a little rehearsal.'

I was naturally elated, but the other girls laughed and more than hinted that I was wanted for something very different from a business chat.

However, he began in a business-like manner enough, complimented me on the way I had made his gag go, and in his quiet, incisive, clever way, suggested the necessary outlines of the working up.

Then he asked me to sit down, gave me a whisky and soda, and I noticed that his eye was devouring my charms with a hungry gleam. He began to let his conversation get rather frisky, and then boldly praised various portions of my body, my legs, my waist, and my breasts even. I finished my drink quickly and got up to go, but as I rose he followed me and clasped me in his arms before I had moved a step. I felt a passionate kiss on my throat, and his hand pressed roughly against the lower part of my stomach. I protested and struggled for I had no wish to make myself cheap in his eyes by an easy surrender. However, nothing was of any avail. He did not prolong the struggle, but calmly locked the door and proceeded to talk the matter over.

His arguments were pretty matter of fact. He was altogether carried away by my beauty he said, and was mad to enjoy me. What harm would be done? he argued, and he added that he could be a very good friend to me.

Of course, in the end I surrendered, and then came a very improper piece of business. Restall's costume necessitated skin tights, without any trunks, and, in case of any untoward swelling, he had his penis bound down to his stomach. So, when he had slipped off his tights, this curious arrangement met my astonished eyes – and he made me undo the wrapping till a fine stalwart member sprang from its bounds. I was surprised at its size, and condition, for Restall was a man of over fifty who had lived every day of his life. His position had brought him into contact with thousands of girls who were only too ready to submit to overtures, and, if rumour was to be trusted, he had availed himself of every opportunity. Also he was a drunkard; I don't suppose he had gone to bed sober any night for the last twenty-five years.

When once we got to business I was randy enough. There was no sofa, and the floor looked rather dirty, so he had me straddle-wise across his knees, forcing me down on him till I had his penis within me right up to its hairy hilt. He grabbed me frightfully tight to him and fucked me quite brutally, but there was something in his savagery which delighted me. When it was over he drained a tremendously stiff whisky and soda and then sat back in the only big chair in the room. 'Well, you'd better be back to your room,' he said after a minute, 'the girls will be suspicious.'

'I thought as much,' I answered rather angrily, 'you've had all you want from me, and want to get rid of me.'

He became quite tender on the instant, and assured me that he meant nothing of the kind, only was nervous lest I should be suspected of over-familiarity with him. In fact he became so tenderly solicitous that he took me in his arms and kissed me – became naughty again, and the dirty beast fucked me again.

Nothing much of great interest happened during our three days' stay at Oxford – we were only allowed half a week by the University authorities, in accordance with the wise regulation that more than three days of the society of any particular set of musical comedy sirens is bad for the peace of mind of the undergraduates. I went out to all meals, some with my lordling, and some with the friends of Miss Sarel, the leading lady, who had graciously deigned to take me up. She was a bright, pretty little thing, quite passably clever, of a naughty temperament, and very much on the make as the theatrical saying goes; she came out of Oxford with one or two valuable presents in the jewellery line.

I was always stared at in the street, but the stare was not the sensual glance of the man about town who feels his cock raised at the appearance of an attractive female, but the simple admiration of a healthy young mind. Not that everything of a sensual nature was absent from our little stay, to say nothing of that already recounted scene in Restall's dressing room, for I experienced the beginning of a love affair.

One night the Sisters Knock brought home the tenor of the company to supper. Jean Messel was a strikingly handsome man, about thirty-five or so, I supposed, whose dark features betrayed a foreign origin. He had often eyed me at the theatre, but we had never spoken till this party. On this occasion, however, he found courage to press my hand, and, later, to snatch a kiss. That kiss set me on fire. I had known well enough before, the delights of a sensual feeling, but never a sensual feeling coupled with love. I dreamed of him all night, and the next morning when we met at the station, and exchanged some commonplace greeting, I experienced the sensation known as blushing all over, and was almost too timid to speak.

I did not continue in lodgings with the Sisters Knock. Some little unpleasantness over my intimacy with the young Lord had arisen, to say nothing of my obvious attraction for Jean Messel; so at our next stop, which was Manchester, I chummed with a Miss Letty Ross, who played third principal part. Miss Ross had many acquaintances among the wealthy manufacturers of the north – fat, jolly, middle-aged men, with any amount of money, which they enjoyed spending, and a great deal of it which found its way into the pockets of the pretty little tarts of the various wandering companies. They wanted very little for their money, and I was glad of it, for my passion for the tenor produced a longing in my heart to remain quite chaste. Still one cannot exactly accept a diamond bangle for nothing, and more than once little Blanche suffered herself to be extended on the sofa of a hotel private room, and her dainty clothes elevated till the exposure of her naked charms caused some great Lancashire cock to crow lustily with anticipation. How hard they fucked, those north country merchants, and what quantities of sperm they spent, but they spent quantities of money, too, bless their enlarged hearts. At that time I grew very frightened of getting in the family way; those lusty devils were just the sort of men to get me caught, and I could not help a reciprocal spend when they came. However, Letty gave me some pills to take before my courses became due, and I escaped.

At Edinburgh, we boldly went to one of the best hotels, trusting to our fortune to find a mug to settle our bills, and sure enough we did find one, in the guise of a well known whisky distiller. He was staying in the same hotel and took on the two of us, first Letty and then myself. I was not jealous, for it gave me a rest, and I was really sweet to him on my nights. He swore his cock had never, never felt such pleasure. He was nearly sixty, but he had never been sucked off, so I cleaned his cock up one night, and taught him that. He nearly went off his head with joy.

On the Saturday night after an uncommonly good supper, and too many liqueurs, the old man falteringly asked if we two would mind his coming to bed with both of us. He had done so well during the week that we had not the heart to say no. We arranged for him to come to our bedroom in half an hour, when we should be undressed, but our door was barely closed behind us when in he slipped blushing like a schoolboy detected in a fault, and begging that he might be allowed to undress us himself.

He went for me first; I was wearing a three-quarter length frock that night, and the dear old gentleman got excited over it. I didn't raise a hand to help him myself, and he stripped me right to the buff. After he got me out of my bodice, and the skirt, his frenzied cock was nearly bursting his trousers, and when he had got me down to my drawers and vest, the poor panting thing had to be released. I gave it just one pat with my hand and the spend flew all over me, covering my body right up to my neck, some of it even struck me in the face. He was disconsolate, and Letty was angry, said it was unfair to start so soon.

But Blanche was equal to the occasion. I sponged my face clean, did the same to his cock, told Letty to tongue his mouth, and we very soon had him stiff. Then he finished my undressing, till I sat in all my naked beauty on the bed before him. He was so randy again that he would have liked to fuck me again, then and there, but Letty naturally interfered. There was such a beautiful fire in the room that we both lay naked on the bed while our old friend tore off his clothes as if he was undressing for a swimming race against time.

Funnily enough though I often slept with Letty, not till that moment had I the least physical desire for her, but the filthiness of the whole scene overpowered me. I rolled over on top of her, feverishly fingered her pretty body and covered her lips with hot kisses which she returned in no half-hearted spirit. In a trice I had a finger up her cunt, so that ingress was barred to the old man. Next moment, however he was up me from behind, his arms gripping both our bodies, and he came in me while my lips were glued to Letty's and all my lust was for her. Still he must have had a good fuck, for I was wriggling my stomach against hers like fury. Even when he had finished I was so filthily randy that I drew my finger, all covered with spend from Letty's cunt and made him lick it clean, an innovation in sin which he thoroughly enjoyed.

Subsequently he fucked Letty and myself once more and that finished him. He shambled back to his bedroom, while Letty and I, after a hot bath together had one delicious bout of mutual cunt sucking, and then fell asleep in each other's arms.

Next morning when the bill was presented, our old friend had something of a shock, but he could not, after the events of the previous night, make any complaint.

I fancy that one hundred and two whiskies and sodas worried him. Of course, we didn't give it away that we had had all our friends in during the day time, while he was at his business, and he thoroughly believed we had slipped all that intolerable deal of liquor down our own fairy throats. He paid us the compliment of remarking that there wasn't a bonnie lassie from Maidenkirk to John of Groats could have done the like.

All this time I barely had an opportunity of seeing my dark-eyed Jean Messel. His wife, who figured in the bills as Miss Henden, became suspicious and never let him out her sight. She wasn't a bad little woman, and on the stage she looked very nice, but what a fake. To begin with, she wore lifters to give her an added inch in height. Then she wore low cut shoes displaying a nice curved pad where her instep should have been. When she went on the stage her legs were entirely encased in shapes, and even in ordinary walking dress, she sported hip pads. As for her bust, well, one night I got wet coming to the theatre and wanted a change of stockings. I found that every available stocking that woman had stuffed into her bodice. She even padded her arms, for she wore tightly-fitting transparent sleeves, and the flesh-coloured pads, that showed through had the appearance of the most fascinating rounded arms. Her neck and shoulders she enamelled. She wore yards of false hair, and what she had of her own was dyed. Her teeth, I need scarcely add, were removable at desire. Some of the girls used to question whether she had a false cunt or not.

One night Jean and I got a chance of a walk home from the theatre together, while she was at home ill. We came by a short cut through a mean street, lit only by an occasional lamp and towered over by gaunt, stark walls. We were quite alone, for it was late and very dark, and the neighbourhood had a dangerous reputation. There was no noise, save a faint flip-flop of water and presently we came to a place where the river was lazily licking a flight of stone steps. It was an eerie place, and I started nervously, brushing my shoulder against my companion. The next moment his arms were gripping me to him, and my lips sought his. I was willing enough to have let him have me, there and then, but presently he pushed me from him.

'Little Darling,' he said, 'next week my wife will not be with us. Shall we live in the same house?'

I said 'Yes,' with a kiss; and he saw me to my hotel door, and we parted.

Madge

Preface

My dear Jack – I have just received your doleful letter and my heart and something else further down yearn to console you. But what can I do for you, way out there in a camp in the Rocky Mountains, with 'not a cunt within a hundred miles' as you say?

Poor Jack, and you so amorous! Would that I had you here, naked in my arms, your ardent kisses covering me from lips to knees, your darling staff resting rigid in my grasp or receiving a caress from parted lips, until ready to burst with its creamy treasures, you would throw me on my back, and breast to breast, belly to belly, tongues hotly thrust into eager, suckling mouths, and arms and legs so interwoven that one could hardly tell – which you, which me – while that stiff staff of yours, that Cyprian sceptre of delight was plunged deeply in my belly. Those soul inspiring thrusts carried such a thrill of ecstasy to my eager cunt, until the acme of all human joy was reached and my thirsty womb drank in the balmy sweets of manly sperm and I bedewed you with my own full measure of ecstatic overflow!

Oh Jack! Dear Jack! would that you were here. But wishes are vain. A thousand miles are between us. But Jack! I remember that the last summer we were together at the seashore you often asked me to tell you of myself, to give you a history of my amorous life; and I put it off until, at last, our pleasure-giving days were rudely cut short by that sudden order from the War

Department to join your regiment.

And now, dear Jack! I've the thought that perhaps, while you're away so far, a few pages from my life might give you pleasure, even if the pleasure had to end like Onan's, in the Bible, and the seed be wasted on the barren, western soil, instead of thrilling this yearning crevice of mine that calls out so eagerly to you as I write.

I

I was born in Louisiana among the palms, pelicans, and bayous, where the soft air has an amorous embrace and the half-tropical sun breeds voluptuousness. When I was fourteen my father received a consular appointment in Europe and it was thought best that I should be left in America to complete my education. I can remember no relations of my parents except a middle-aged uncle of my mother's, Uncle John we called him, who was rich but a recluse; going now and then to New Orleans on business, when he would make a formal call, and burying himself at other times in his large plantation, which was isolated in a part of the state distant from any other town.

My parents finally settled on the Convent of the Sacred Heart, in New York, as the place at which I was to complete my education and, taking me there, left me in charge of the sisters, while they sailed for Europe.

I have read much of the illicit intercourse of priests and sisters and novices; but I can recall nothing in this Convent that would raise a blush, even though perhaps I was too young to understand things that, to my present mind, would be suggestive.

Two years passed quietly and in all innocence. I was daily expecting the return of my parents when, one morning, the New York journals were filled with accounts of a great ocean disaster and, in a few years, I knew that I was alone in the world. Not a living soul on earth to look after me, a girl of sixteen.

The good sisters consoled me and treated me with more kindness than ever; but the uncertainty of my future preyed on me and I knew not where to turn. One day, just before the end of the session, I was summoned to the office, and there, with outstretched hand, was Uncle John.

He always seemed so far apart from the rest of us that I had not thought of him. But now he was all kindness and soon made me understand that he was to be my protector and that, for the present at any rate, I was to go to live with him at his home.

II

'Beauvoir', out of the world as it was, charmed me. A one storey house buried among magnolias; a wide piazza all around it, with hammocks and luxurious couches, for here one lives out of doors.

Uncle John told me that the Negro quarters were an eighth of a mile away and that they were not permitted near the house unless summoned. The household servants were Sam and Meg, husband and wife; light-coloured mulattoes, showing the Caucasian features of some white ancestor and each with a form and bearing that would fascinate a sculptor.

I was made at home in a pretty room and Meg assisted me in changing my travelling clothes and robing me in thin garments that left arms and neck bare; meanwhile the kind girl praised my shape and budding charms and I, in turn, laughingly lauded her well-developed figure; making her lift her plump breasts out of her dress and even raise her skirts so that I might see as much of her as she had of me; and so, half naked, I embraced her. For the first time in my life a new sensation seized me, and I know now that voluptuousness was at that moment born within me.

But supper was ready and I, seated opposite Uncle John, ate ravenously and drank some wine, a new thing for me which seemed to add to that unknown sensation that still lingered from Meg's embrace. After supper Uncle John showed me over the house, even to his luxurious bedroom, which was some distance from mine; and then, as I had had a long trip, he called Meg and said that I had better go to bed.

I kissed him, and again that tingling of unknown desires came to me as he pressed me to him; but I was not so overcome that I did not hear him whisper to Meg to come to him as soon as I was in bed. It did not take long with her help, and, wishing me pleasant dreams, she left. I lay in the dark, nervous unsatisfied; wanting something, I knew not what.

I tried to analyse my feelings; find what it was that ailed me; felt of myself to see where the sensation came from. As my roving hand passed over the rounded belly to the tufted mount below, it touched the swelling sentinel of love and my thrilling nerves told me that *here* is what I sought. Feeling the soft crevice, I found, in my gently moving hand, a giver of unknown pleasures, until, my desires teaching my virgin instincts, I threw off the bedclothes, pulled up my night robe, opened wide my legs and, pressing my finger between my cunt's hot lips, soon learned the exquisite delight of rapid friction and lay dissolved in a gulf of languorous pleasure whose meaning I had not yet fathomed. What could it be? My hand and hairy mount were wet with some sticky exudation; my heart beat queerly and I lay in a delicious languor.

I could not make it out and again sought the mysterious grotto, but it did not feel nice, sticky as it was, and I got up and bathed myself. Refreshed, I was about to step into bed when the closing of a door at the other end of the hall made me pause. I heard Uncle John whisper to Meg to come to his room. What for? Could it be anything connected with the delightful phenomena I had just experienced myself? Instinct – the Devil – or I know not what, put it into my virgin mind that it was.

III

The newborn lust within me drove me on. Opening the door I stepped into the dark corridor and there, from the open ventilators over the closed door, a bright light shone, a beacon guiding me to a new revelation.

Soon I was close to it and could hear Meg and Uncle John talking; words which I hardly knew the meaning of. I was on pins and needles. A high backed chair stood near. Bracing it against the side of the door I climbed up on its back and my head came to a level with the open panel; the whole, brightly lighted room was in full view. Room? Think you I saw aught of it? No! For, there on the sofa, naked as Adam, sat Uncle John, leaning back, one hand holding the cigar he was smoking, the other the erect standard of love. For the first time I saw the maker of us all, the emblem of fertility; the one thing on earth without which a woman would be a useless creation and her teeming, yearning womb a sterile desert.

Oh, how my eyes glued themselves to his darling object! How my itching crevice told my innocence that this was what it yearned for. A column, white as alabaster, long and rigid, crowned as it were, with a jaunty red cap rolling down at the sides like the bars of an arrow; and, at the other end, a great bag as large as my fist and rosy red; while all around this lovely machinery of love, black hair curled in close ringlets, forming a dark background against which the ivory sceptre stood out rampant, the true and only insignia of love.

'Strip, you minx,' he said. 'I've a whole bag full of sperm for you.' And Meg, erect before him, almost with a turn of her hand, stood out in her olive nakedness. Plump arms and legs rounded gracefully; breasts that were veritable tents of love, and swelling belly that seemed to say, 'Come press me.' 'Are you glad to have him back, Meg?' said Uncle John. For all response the darling girl threw herself back on her knees between him, and taking the hairy bag in one hand, with the other she gently grasped the rigid spear moving the white skin up and down, as I could see; for one minute the spry head was covered, the next, exposed and ready to burst. Then the girl sprang to her feet, rushed to the bed, and on her back, her bottom on the edge and with thighs wide open, cried out; 'Come, Master John, come quick! My cunt is on fire! Fuck me! Fuck my cunt!' In an instant I saw the great red head of his cock pressed into the thick curling hair between her legs and, as his hands seized her buttocks, lose itself completely in the fervid crevice.

Lost, yea, for an instant; then out it comes again almost to the head, then in, then out, faster and faster. 'Oh, it's lovely!' cried Meg. 'I'm spending, give it to me!' and, with a quick movement, the panting girl threw her legs around his waist as, with throbbing breasts and heaving belly, I could guess that something, I knew not what, was being shot from his hidden pego – for she cried out to him as she clutched him in the last frantic throes: 'Give me every drop of it!'

I could stand no more; sliding down from the chair I groped my way back to my room and to bed and, in a frenzy of feverish lust, I frigged myself till I fell asleep, languid and exhausted.

IV

With all my lustful yearnings I was frightened at what I had seen and what I had done to myself. For two days I struggled to keep amatory thought out of my head and my hands away from the centre of pleasure. But it was useless. Naked men and women danced before my eyes. I wandered out in the grounds where the poultry were picking their crops full and a stately rooster would make a dive, mount a squawking hen and, with flushed face and puckering slit, I watched their brief spasms of jerks until the cock dismounted and the hen went away shaking her feathers.

One day I was walking along the road and, in the field not fifty feet away from me, a cow was grazing placidly. Suddenly I heard a low bellowing and, across the field, I saw a bull jump the fence and, with a mad rush, make for the cow, who, seeing him coming, turned to run. But it was too late. With a wild rush the lustful animal sprang forward; for an instant I saw him raised on his hind legs, that monstrous instrument of his sticking out like a mast from his belly; then down he came upon the cow's back, his forelegs clutching her sides and his panting flanks working like the piston rods of a steam engine until, the discharge coming, his speed lessened and I felt such that he was experiencing the same languor that I had felt the night I saw Uncle John and Meg together.

The sight fired me: I forgot my good resolutions and, rushing to a little clump of trees, I pulled up my skirts and with eager hand, rubbed the itching of my carnal cavity until the ecstasy of a copious discharge left me limp.

From that day to this I have not checked my amorous desires when a person and place suited, and prudery alone stood in the way.

That night, as Uncle John kissed me goodnight, I saw his eyes sparkle as they looked down upon the blossoming bubbies which my frock but partly hid; the arms around my waist dropped down and, with a spasmodic motion, he pressed my buttocks until we were so close together that I thought that I felt a hard substance in his breeches print itself against my belly. An instant thus, and releasing me he hastened to his room and I to mine.

I was wild; I stripped to my chemise and, barefooted, stole along the hall, mounted my chair and, again, through the fanlight, saw the heaven I yearned for.

With gently frigging hands between my legs, I saw him undress until, naked, he stood there, his lovely cock bolt upright against his belly. He took it in his hand and, the better to see it, I made a movement on my perch and – well – the next thing I knew I was on my back on the floor.

V

There, half stunned, ashamed, I lay a moment and before I could collect myself and fly, the door opened wide, the light streamed full upon my almost naked person and Uncle John stood over me.

I simply covered my face with my hands and lay there panting. In an instant I was lifted in his strong arms, one around my naked waist and the other hand pressed to my hairy nest.

In an instant my chemise was torn away and I lay naked in his lap, his eyes burning into mine, his hands wandering from my firm globes over my swelling belly and nestling between my legs, and his fingers penetrating the lips of love. 'So – so – Miss Madge, you wanted to see what a man looked like, did you? So you shall. Give yourself up to it, dear!'

His hot lips were pressed to mine, his tongue thrust hotly in and then my nipples were his prey and his rapture-giving hand soon brought my heaving thighs to a climax of enjoyment.

'Oh!' I cried, throwing my arms around his neck. 'This is heaven!' 'Yes, my dear girl for you; but I'm in hell! Just see!' Lifting me up and standing by my side, he took my hand and carried it to his overwrought pego. Oh! the first touch of that velvety truncheon! The quick grasp! – and then, his hand guided mine in the rapid, electric moving of the flexible skin upon the fixed flesh beneath – his buttocks working, his arm clutching me closely to him! 'Go on! go on!' he cried. 'Watch it

Madge, watch it shoot!' I felt his prick swell larger and larger in my grasp; his lips poured ravishing kisses on every spot of flesh he could reach and then – high in the air flew great drops of thick milky sperm-drops coming so fast that they seemed to be a stream of love lava.

Slowly the spasm quieted, and seizing me in his arms, he threw me flat on the bed and rolled on top of me, breast to breast, belly to belly, open mouth to open mouth, breathing into each other; tongue sucking, each of his hands grasping a plump cheek of my buttocks and his fallen but lusty prick and balls rubbing against my sensitive cunt until, with a convulsive clutch, with arms and legs around him, I poured down my oblation to the god of love.

As I lay languishing he seized my hand and put his stiffened pego in its grasp, asking me if I did not want to examine it, and, as I held it upright, moving the soft skin gently up and down or weighing in my hand the heavy bag of love elixir, he told me all about it – why it stiffened, how it broke its way into the virgin slit, and sowed the seeds from which we all grow. He told me of the danger of indiscreet commerce in this artificial and conventional world. But he told me also, the many ways that lustful pleasure could be had with perfect safety. His glowing language and gentle but hot caresses re-illuminated the fires within me and I pressed my ardent mount convulsively to his hand. 'You want more do you?' he cried. 'Yes, dear John, give me more. I'm hotter than ever!' Flat on his back, his head and shoulders raised on a pillow, he lifted me up, straddled me across him, and, pulling me towards his face kissed my navel, belly, and thighs. Then his hot lips sought my eager cunt; his tongue gently tickled the sensitive membrane until squirming and wriggling from its embraces, I gave a cry of pleasure. Thrusting his elongated tongue deep into my burning slit, he worked it in and out, holding me tightly to his face, until my whole body seemed to dissolve itself in a blissful overflow and go gushing down to meet his lascivious embraces.

He held me thus for a moment, weltering in my enjoyment, then seizing me, he laid me on my back against the pillows straddled across my chest – 'Make a cunt of your titties,' he cried, and as his proud prick pressed against my breasts, I squeezed my plump globes around it and held it tightly. His buttocks began to work and I had the lovely spectacle, close to my eyes, of his swelling staff, now all in view; then only its ruby head shining between my snowy bubbies – when, ready to spend, he cried: 'Now watch it!' and the great jets of cloudy essence flew high over my head, hit my cheek, fell in a copious shower on shoulder, arm and breast until, seizing my head, he raised me up – 'Suck it!' he cried. 'Make a cunt of your mouth; squeeze my balls! That's it – roll your tongue around it! That's good – suck harder; swallow every drop I've got,' until breathless, I threw myself back and he, springing up, brought my thighs to the edge of the bed. Kneeling, holding my buttocks firmly in his grasp, he brought down again my ever ready balm with lightning working tongue.

He would not let me stay longer, but bathing me with refreshing cologne, took me in his arms and carried me to bed, making me promise not to touch my touchy titbit, but go straight to sleep. But, before he left my bedside I threw my arms around his hips and rained a dozen kisses on the now fallen and flabby idol of my desires.

VI

The next day he told me how debilitating and injurious it was to yield to love too much, especially in one so young; but he promised me that, on the morrow, he would again taste pleasure.

The morrow came. He ordered the horses saddled and we had a bracing gallop through the woods, returning with blood pounding healthfully through our veins and ravenously hungry. We ate heartily and two glasses of old wine made my whole body tingle with voluptuous desires.

'How demure and modest you look in that riding habit,' said he. 'I don't feel so,' I answered and, unbuttoning my waist with both hands, I held up to him my stiff-nippled titties. 'How lovely!' he cried. 'Now let me see the other hill, the shaded mount of Venus.' And, jumping to my feet, I pulled the long, modest, black riding habit up to my waist and exposed to his ardent eyes my palpitating belly. He was on his feet in an instant, and tearing open his trousers pointed his darling dart lustfully at me across the table. 'Fill your glass!' he cried. 'Fill it full. Drink it all; you to this branch of coral – I, to that rosy crevice.' Draining the glasses – the lively wine spread still more ardent fires in our veins.

'Run!' he cried. 'Lift your clothes as high as they will go and run ahead of me to my room.' And, snatching up my skirts I threw them over my shoulder and ran at full speed along the hall; throwing myself, panting, upon the bed and he on me. His stiff cock rubbed against my belly and against my hairy mount; then, turning me upon my stomach, he pressed it against my plump backsides and, as it nestled cosily between the rounded cheeks, he rubbed it there, while his eager hand sought out my raging slit, and cock and hand moving in unison, we both went off together in delightful ecstasy.

Recovering, we stripped and, making me stand on a sofa with one leg lifted on his arm, he washed away the sticky overflow, bathed me with perfume and, giving my mount a parting kiss, I jumped down and he took my place while I, in turn, bathed him and paid him back with kisses on his humble cock.

Going to a bookcase he brought out a volume, and taking me on his lap, he opened it. Oh, such pictures! Naked men and women coupled together in every conceivable way! All the forms and fashions of lust which the lecherous imagination of centuries have invented and practised; what a revelation it was! My hand instinctively sought his prick while, with one arm under my bottom, his fingers stroked my pussy. Each page was new and provocative. We were nearing the need for action, when, skipping a number of pages, he opened to a picture of a lovely girl upon her side and a handsome man in front of her, his head buried between her thighs and her lustful mouth filled with his inflamed pego. 'How splendid!' I cried. 'Both can enjoy it at once,' and springing up, I threw myself prone upon the soft crimson rug on the floor. In a moment he was beside me, his lips covering my burning slit, his tongue tickling and thrusting, while my eager mouth closed tightly on his lovely, ruby headed spear; kissing, tongue-rolling, bag squeezing, buttock clutching – sucking, till the thick sperm bathed our mouths, throats and was gulped down to seethe in lustful satisfaction in our bellies.

We lay ten minutes thus lost in delicious lassitude. Don't say that sucking the carnal parts is disgusting! Why is not a prick or cunt as clean and wholesome to kiss and taste as a mouth? Why, if I will let a cock play tag in my belly, should I be squeamish if he wants to enjoy the contact of lips and tongue? Both openings are lined with the same membrane and one is as wholesome as the other.

Let the prude pucker only with her slit if she chooses; but for me my lover is welcome to all the holes I've got.

John filled a goblet with wine and, as I still lay panting on the floor, handed it to me and, drinking half, he finished it. Then, getting upon the bed, he filled it again and made me bring my buttocks to the edge of the bed, prop myself up on a pillow, stretch my thighs wide-open and round up my belly. He then poured the whole glassful down the crevice of my slit, his mouth catching it below and his lips and tongue licking up the last drops. Then, again filling the goblet, he gave it to me and, kneeling before me, I washed and bathed his fallen cunt tickler in the wine and then drank all of it – ending by kissing away the drops that hung from his staff or glistened on the curly hair or swollen testicles.

Then he went and got the picture book which we had not finished, and reclining against the pillows, he seated me between his thighs, his prick pressed against my bottom and my legs spread out between his.

Smutty pictures are the true arrows of Venus. Half the women in the world are awkward in attempting lust; backward in lewd variety even when they are willing and anxious to please. But they are imitative and a picture from life will give them a carnal wrinkle.

Turning over the leaves of this concupiscent gallery of lecherous attitudes we came to one which I did not understand. A woman lying belly down across the waist high arm of a sofa, her magnificent bum showing its sumptuous and luxurious richness of flesh in bold prominence; behind her a man had his long and slender staff embedded – where? Not in her slit; it's too far back for that. 'What a poor drawing!' I said. 'Her quim is not there, it's further front.' John laughed. 'Don't you know my dear, that every woman has two openings down there? That fellow has his prick in her cul: in plain English, in her ass-hole. It's tight and fits a cock snugly and some men lust for that more than for the regular channel.'

'How funny,' I said. 'I never dreamed of such a thing.' And as I spoke, John's stiffened prick stuck between the broad cheeks of my buttocks.

I looked up into his face. 'Do you want to?' I asked. He did not answer, but, jumping up, thrust his pego into my face. 'Wet it with your mouth,' he cried, 'so that it will slide easier.' And I obeyed, spreading the saliva over end and sides, so that when he took it out, it glistened with moisture. Lifting me up he led me to the sofa and, pushing me over the cushioned arm, had my broad buttocks boldly offered to his attack. Quickly he penetrated my cul; slowly like a new glove the yielding sides made room for its rigid visitor. It smarted, but I did not wince. I clutched the sofa and braced myself to meet his new and bolder storming of my person. What was the smart to the novelty of these new sensations? And when, passing his hand in front, he fingered my clitoris, I cried out: 'Don't mind me; put it in all the way. I don't mind the hurt,' and with feelings wound up to the fullest tension of lustful activity by the novel scabbard in which his sword was sheathed, he urged it boldly in almost to the hilt. Keeping time with fucking cock and frigging hand, I soon felt the swelling forerunner of dissolving bliss and, with wanton, wriggling thighs, spent freely in his hand while my stretched cul received the easing balm of his discharge.

VII

Twice a week our naked bodies worshipped in the temple of Venus and Priapus. On other days we were so simply affectionate, just a man and a woman; avoiding all provocation and storing up the amorous juices and energy that made us fresh and eager for our holiday of lasciviousness.

I often wondered if Meg and Sam knew what was going on. If they did they made no sign – and as John (I had dropped the Uncle after our first bare-bellied bout) said nothing about them, I kept silent.

A rainy Sunday came, John and I had passed the morning in the library, he with a bundle of journals which had just arrived and I with a sentimental novel that made me yawn. Presently it was dinner time and chatting pleasantly, I noticed that John filled my glass with wine more freely than usual. Soon I felt its exciting effects, felt them most acutely down in that touchy little crevice that was palpitating under the tablecloth. But I had promised not to seek pleasure except on the regular days and I kept silent.

'Madge,' he said, 'this is my birthday.'

'Oh! I wish I had known it before, I would have given you a present!' Then, with flushed face, my pouting slit prompting me, I jumped up, ran to his side and pulling my dress up to my waist, cried out: 'Dear John, won't you take this? Take my virginity, I'm dying to give it to you.'

'You darling girl!' he said, kissing my belly and

mount. 'I know that you would give it to me freely; and you know that no pleasure on earth would be as great to me as piercing your virgin womb. But think, Madge! You are so fresh, and some day a handsome lover will come along and you and he will marry; not until then must the dear little slit of yours be opened. No, Madge, not that. But we will celebrate the day with a revel of voluptuousness.'

He filled another glass of wine and, drinking half, made me finish it. Then, ringing the bell, Meg appeared. 'Take her to my room,' he said, and the lively girl, putting her arm around me, danced with me to his room. 'What is it, Meg? What does it mean?' She would not answer, but, leading me into a small room adjoining my uncle's tore off every stitch of clothes she had on and then did the same to me and, naked as we were, dragged me into John's room, which was brilliantly lighted and in the centre of which a narrow couch was standing, a convenient altar for sacrificing to Venus.

Leading me up to a mirror we gazed upon the reflections of our naked forms, one rosy-brown, the other rosy-white. 'I guess that picture will stiffen things,' she said, and, as she spoke, we heard the door open and there, facing us, stood John, naked, his lance at rest, and, beside him, Sam, his brown, muscular body bare and his magnificent pego standing bolt upright against his belly.

'Oh, I'm wild!' I cried, rushing into John's arms. 'Give relief quick!' He seized me, and laid me flat on the altar. 'Give her a tongue fuck, Sam.' And, in an instant, the eager mulatto was on his knees before me pressing my thighs open to their widest extent; and then, with long, pointed tongue, darting thrust on thrust into my widely stretched slit and with thick, lecherous lips, caressed the sensitive convolutions. Oh, the flashes of almost agonising pleasure that shot through me! And when the crisis came I fairly shrieked as I spent. The three of them watched me wriggling and heaving for a moment. Then John, seizing Meg, threw her across me and said: 'Now, Madge, you can see what a real fuck is like!' and for response I seized his cock and guided it into her slit. 'Oh, how delicious that must be!' I shrieked. 'It is,' cried Meg, 'give it to me harder!' and, like a horse in the stretch of a race track, John spurted. 'How I feel it!' she cried, 'squeeze his balls.' And I did, and from a wild dance to heave and thrust, they quieted down to a gentler throbbing.

'Jolly! I can't wait,' yelled Sam, holding up his burning rod. And John, taking his melting poker out of Meg's furnace, seized my hand and made me, myself, guide Sam's enormous cock into Meg's slippery slit. He was wound up and wasted no time on gentle heaves, but clutching her bottom in his hands, made his thrusts so hard and fast that the girl yelled out. 'He'll knock a hole through me.' But he kept on and in a second, cried: 'There, you bitch, you whore, take that!' And, knowing that he was spending, I squeezed his testicles, but, overcome with my emotions, I fell back on the floor and eagerly clutched my slit in my hands. But John snatched it away and cried out: 'Come, you rascal. Come, do what you like with this smutty virgin. Put your tongue in her and make her suck that big cock of yours.' 'You mean it?' cried Sam, drawing his still rampant rod out of Meg's pickling tub. But he did not wait for an answer. Like a wild animal he pounced upon me, stretching my thighs as wide as they would go and stuck his tongue deep into my coral slit; while I, frantic with lust, threw myself on his belly and seizing his still magnificent erection, sucked away every drop of sperm that was still oozing from that great rod that filled my mouth completely, until out of breath, we lay panting, our heads resting on the inside of each other's thighs, our hands gently soothing the exhausted warriors of love.

John threw himself down beside us and watched with gloating eyes, our still heaving flanks. But Meg's lustful emotions were calling loudly for assuagement. With a bound she sprang to the mantelpiece, snatched a large candle from its socket and, coming to where we three lay in a huge jumble together, she planted a foot on each side of our outstretched bodies and, in full view of our eyes, which were fixed upon her extended crevice, she plunged the candle deep into its depths, and with deft and rapid motions of her agile hand diddled herself until, exhausted, she staggered to the bed and threw herself on her back, the candle almost lost to sight.

She put her hand down to remove it, but it was in so far and so slippery that she could not get hold of it. 'Oh dear, I can't get it out!' she cried. 'Wouldn't it be awful if I was plugged up for good.' I ran to help her, but my fingers could gain no purchase on the candle's sperm-bathed sides: so, kneeling down, I bade her open her legs to the utmost and, pressing my jaws close to her slit, I managed to catch the slippery dildo with my teeth and so draw it out.

We all laughed at this episode and Meg and I stood up and gazed down upon our two stalwart stallions still stretched upon the floor, side by side, but heads to feet. 'Oh,' she cried. 'See them feeling at each other,' and so they were, each handling the other's cock. 'Go on!' she cried. 'All's fair in lust; I'm dying to see them suck each other!' 'We will,' said John, 'but go and get those whips on the shelf and birch our buttocks while we taste the sweets of each other's nuts.'

Wrought up, as we were this ultra-exciting if outrageous conjuncture, we each seized a whip and, as those stalwarts rolled upon their sides and with lustful lips seized each other's cocks, Meg let fall her whip upon the broad buttocks of her husband while I rained tinging blows upon John's white backsides, until it turned as rosy as my nipples.

It was disgusting – say you – perhaps it was. But to us, frenzied and drunk with all the lechery that four votaries of wantonness can, when untrammelled by prejudices, pour into each other's souls – it lost its forbidding aspects and seemed but one step further in the drama we so loved to act: *lust a l'outrance*.

VIII

Time passed. Anxious to run no risks with my health, John kept me limited to weekly revels; and I was obliged at other times to recall the pleasures that had passed, or dream of what would happen when next we gave ourselves to the delightful play.

One morning John found a letter which seemed to engross him more than the others. 'Well, Madge, we are going to have a visitor.' 'Oh, I hope not!' I said involuntarily. 'It's too nice now, I hate strangers.' 'It can't be helped. His name is Ralph Brown, the son of my first love. His mother and I, when a little older than you are now, met and in a week we were secretly betrothed. I was summoned away on business. The last night before I left we wandered down to the shore and, seated alone there on the sand in the bright moonlight, we threw off all restraint.

'The dear girl forgot all her former modesty and did not chide me as I strained her to my breast and rained hot kisses upon her lips and shoulders. 'I am all yours,' she cried. But, wiser than to do what would be sorrow to her, I palpitated her sweet breasts and, both urged on by the same desire, I threw myself upon her panting form and, raising her skirts, my eager belly was pressed naked to hers and each, for the first time, tasted the ultimate pleasure of life; but without my penetrating her virgin bower. Again and again did we give ourselves up to these outward libations and all the pleasures that roving, eager hands could yield. I never saw her after that night. She married; but now they are both dead. When I was in Europe and she dying, she wrote me her last message: how she had loved me better than any other; and asking me to watch over her son. It is this son who is coming to see us. I found a good business for him in New York and, whenever he has a vacation he comes to see me. He will be here tomorrow and stay a fortnight.'

He paused, and, looking at me sharply: 'Why Madge, you don't seem to like the idea of his coming!' 'Oh, John!' I cried, throwing my arms around his neck and kissing him, 'if you are pleased, I ought to be, but – ' 'But what?' 'Oh, we seem so happy and now we will have to be – be so very proper.' 'Oh ho, you minx!' he laughed and, thrusting his hand under my clothes took hold of my brush. 'This is what you mean, isn't it?' 'Yes, John, I shall miss it dreadfully. It's awful to be cold and proper after we have passed so many pleasant days, hot and improper.' 'At any rate, let us make hay while the sun shines!'

I was sitting on his knees; stooping, he grasped one of my ankles and, laughing, raised it high in the air, almost, upsetting me, and brought it down on the other side. I found myself straddled across his legs.

'Now, my dear little cock pleaser, strip, and let me have a little hot buff and fur to pump sperm for me.' As he held a plump thigh on each side of him, I tore off my garments and, in a minute, sat there stark naked.

Then he made me first put one leg and then the other on his shoulder. Taking off my shoes and lifting me up, he pressed my hairy mount to his face and thrust his tongue in and out of my slit. Then he sat me on a sofa and, standing between my thighs, made me unbutton his trousers and take them off, while he tore off his coat and shirt. Naked, he stood before me, his lovely pego staring me right in the face. I laid it between my bubbies, fondled its soft coat, squeezed the wrinkled storehouse of love and, beginning at the foot of the tower, kissed with open lips and caressing tongue each inch of its tall stature, until the ruby head slipped boldly into my mouth.

'You're wetting it!' he cried, and, indeed, this big mouthful did cause the saliva to secrete. 'I'll be wet myself between my legs in a minute,' I cried. 'Yes, and your cul will be the wettest of all!' he cried, and, lifting me up, he placed me on my knees on the bed, brought his prick to the tight channel and, regardless of my squirming 'Oh's' drove it in and, tickling my nipples with one hand, he rubbed my fervid slit with the other until the floodgates were opened and I was inundated with the essence of love; his behind, mine in front. Soon he rolled over on his back: 'Come, glue your sticky slit to my mouth.' And mounting across his face, he smothered his head between my thighs, while I, throwing myself forward, seized his sperm-covered pintle in my mouth and sucked it until, breathless, I rolled over on my back and gave a long drawn cry of satisfied lechery.

IX

Several days later I was walking on the road, when a natural need made itself felt: I wanted to make water. Again, why say: 'Make water', why not 'piss', right out? Going to the side of the road, I gathered my clothes up to my waist and, squatting down, a pretty little golden puddle glistened in the sun. Rising erect and still holding my skirts up to my navel, I heard a step crackle on the dry road and, looking up, there before me stood a handsome man, seemingly in his twenties, with flashing eyes surveying my naked charms. I was spellbound, but in an instant he had his arms around my waist and a hand groping my moist mount. 'Oh ho!' said he, 'you're a virgin, are you? Well! you shall have it outside, if not in.' And pushing me back upon a mound of grassy sward, he stood between my legs and, opening his breeches, I had one glimpse of his lovely white pego as he threw himself upon me, raining kisses on my lips, his hot staff and crisp balls delighting with quick friction my hot slit.

Of course I struggled, squirmed, kicked, and called him all sorts of names, until I felt the climax approaching to both and as I spent and could feel his sperm jetting all over my belly, I had to shut my eyes and press tight my lips to keep from showing the pleasure I was enjoying.

Springing up, he stepped back to gloat over the sight of my panting charms. With a bound I was on my feet and gathering up my dress, I sprang away and ran across the field. He followed for a moment, but soon gave it up and, calling to me: 'We'll meet again, you dear,' he resumed his route along the road. I hastened home and was just beginning to tell Uncle John of my adventure when a knock came, and Meg said that a gentleman wanted to see John.

X

Going to my room, a bath and change of dress somewhat quieted my feelings aroused by that bold stranger, and by the time that Meg came into the room to tell me that John and his guest were waiting to go to dinner, I was ready to join them, looking like a modest maiden whom a smutty word would send into convulsions.

'Ralph – this is Madge.' That was the introduction, and as I looked up at him, I beheld the bold ravisher who, an hour before, had stared lustfully into my eyes while his hot sperm shot all over my belly. My heart stood still and I could hardly bow in answer to his salute, and I sank into my chair.

Fortunately, the two men had much to say to each other and I had time to gain my composure, only to have it routed again when I glanced up and found his eyes fixed upon me with the same vivid passion that had kindled my amorous soul when lying on the grass at his lustful mercy.

For three days I had no chance to be confidential with John, nor was I alone with Ralph for a minute. I avoided him. But his image was always before me. On the third day, as I was going to bed, Meg stole into my room. 'Oh, Miss Madge! You ought to have seen him!' 'Seen who?' I asked. 'Our visitor,' she said, 'as I came along the hall the light was bright in his room and I couldn't help peeking through the keyhole. There he was facing the door and pulling his shirt over his head;

all bare, and that lovely fresh cock of his standing stiff against his belly. I must frig myself, Miss!' And the dear girl threw herself back upon the sofa and, with her hand, rubbed the excited slit until, by her motions and glowing face, I saw that nature had come to her relief.

Of course I was on fire and, when she came to the bed and gazing down upon me, said, 'Oh, wouldn't you and he make a lovely couple in bed together doing the double-backed beast in your holiday clothes?' I could stand it no longer. Pushing my naked thighs to the edge of the bed, I cried out to her to give me relief; and the kind wench soon had me thrilled with her nimble tongue and then, tucking me into bed, she left me to dream that I was part of the double-backed beast she spoke of.

I kept in my room as much as possible for I felt so awkward when I caught those bold glances of our visitor, though his manner towards me was always coldly respectful.

On the fourth day John went over to the farmhands' quarters and I thought that Ralph had gone with him. So, going to the library, I threw myself on a sofa with a book when, from the window curtains, stepped Ralph and, standing in the middle of the floor with folded arms, he said: 'Madge, I love you and want to marry you, will you have me?' My heart was in my mouth. 'No, no!' I cried. 'I cannot – never,' and jumping to my feet, I fled to my room and threw myself sobbing, on the bed.

Did I regret the amorous dalliance with Uncle John that now arose as a barrier to the enjoyment of my new flame? No – and yet I only knew that I was miserable. I must have lain there an hour with my heart torn with conflicting emotions when I heard the door of my room pushed open and, starting up, I beheld my new lover standing, naked, with folded arms, in the middle of the room. 'Madge, John has told me all. Tomorrow we will marry. I want you to come and give yourself to me now.'

Oh, the revulsion of feeling! What cared I for weddings! We loved! I sprang up and with trembling hands loosed my few garments and let them drop to the floor, then started towards him with outstretched arms. He eluded me. 'I want to feast my eyes for the last time upon my hot little virgin,' he said. But his eager lust was not to be delayed and, seizing me in his arms, raining kisses on every part of my naked body which I returned with equal fervour, he laid me on the bed and knelt between my open legs.

'What do you want, Madge?' 'I want you to make a woman of me, burst my virginity with that dear spear of yours. I shan't mind the hurt.' And he was on me, his red lance aimed straight between my cunt's hot lips and forcing its way, little by little, till driven reckless by his sensations, 'Brace yourself, Madge!' and, holding my bottom tightly, his iron rod burst into the useless prison and, wriggling, panting, his magnificent cock was buried to the hilt in my slit and, powerless to wait longer, his swift motion soon brought the voluptuous acme and my smarting slit was soothed by his seething sperm.

Oh, the delicious agony of the moment – pain and pleasure mixed, but the pleasure all conquering! Oh, the languid ecstasy of lying there with his dear form pressed on breast and belly!

And, when our breath returned and he had made needed ablutions, we lay reclining side by side, how fervid the sensation of roving kiss and hand; the avidity of each to explore all the charms we had for each other. My hand had not long caressed his dear hymen breaker before its proud head was lifted again.

'Madge,' he cried, lifting me up on my knees, my hairy, gaping slit before his eyes, 'the second erection to enter here will not be mine. Think how your Uncle John must be suffering. Go and give him the only thing you kept from him.' 'No, no, Ralph. I'm yours now!' 'Madge, jealousy is the cause of half the unhappiness in married life. I'll swear on this dear cunt, and you on my stiff prick, that each will love the other more than all else on earth, but that each shall take pleasure at other founts; knowing that we love each other so well that these wanton excursions will serve but as a stimulant to our mutual pleasures. I kiss the book,' he said, as he pressed his lips and tongue against my slit. Then, springing up – 'Now you kiss, too!' and he held the rosy headed rod to receive my ardent lips.

XI

'Come,' he said, and leading me to John's door, Ralph opened it and, pushing me in, closed it softly. I advanced quietly to the head of the bed where I had so often tasted nameless sweets, and gazed down upon John's nude form, stretched there on his back, his mind filled no doubt with vivid pictures of the voluptuous drama being enacted at the other end of the hall, and holding the inflamed arrow of love erect in his hand.

'Ralph sent me, John. He has ravished my virginity and swears that he won't fuck me again until your sperm mixes with his in my belly.' 'You darling girl! Do you mean it?' and wildly seizing me in his arms he threw me flat on my back and, kneeling between my thighs I grasped his dear old cock in my hand and, myself, guided it to my newly opened quiver.

Oh, that rapture giving tongue, fucking my mouth; that stiff strong prick fucking my cunt; that thrilling flood of boiling sperm shooting at last into its proper channel and now, for the first time, sending bliss to my innermost vitals. How we squirmed and twisted in our lustful embrace and how happy and content we lay, regaining our breath, till a voice at our side roused us.

'Did you enjoy it?' and looking up, there stood Ralph in all his naked, manly beauty, his pego up in arms. Quickly raising himself, John held out his hand, which Ralph grasped, while I, seizing them both, pressed them, joined together, to my happy slit. Then I sprang up and with an arm around each manly form I kissed first one, then the other, and exclaimed: 'Oh! how happy I am with two such lovers!' 'Let us look at ourselves,' said John, and, with encircling arms, we ran up to the mirror and gazed with lustful eyes on the splendid picture of our naked charms.

'On your knees and worship Priapus,' said Ralph. As I dropped on my knees, he turned my head to John's pego, which I quickly seized in my mouth, and which quickly stiffened; and then, with eager lips, I turned to kiss the rampant rooster that had just crowed for the first time – in my virgin belly.

Raising me, they made me stand straddled on two chairs and, each in turn, standing under my crotch, thrust his tongue into my quiver. 'This is too much, how I wish I had two cunts, so as to have both fuck me at once!' 'You know you have!' said John, 'didn't I take your "maiden-behind" and Ralph your maidenhead?' 'Let's put both in at once!' cried Ralph and, making me stoop, his rigid rod was soon engulfed in my excited slit, when John, lifting up my legs, crossed them tightly around Ralph's waist and I was suspended there – hung upon a peg, as it were – while John, pointing his spear against my well-stretched bottom, pierced me to the hilt.

Oh! The wild shouts of agonising rapture that deluged me as those two lusty darts of love were driven with simultaneous thrusts into my quivering body, and as the double dose of sperm was shot, like molten lead, into me, I shrieked aloud till Ralph's nimble tongue, with prick-like stiffness, was urged into my cunt-like mouth and I sucked it, as my contracting slit and cul sucked from their pricks the last lovely drops of sperm.

I almost fainted as they laid me on the bed; but a good stiff horn of whisky poured down my throat revived me, and bathed with spirits, I soon lay happy across Ralph's lap on the sofa while John, lighting a cigar, sat naked in an easy chair opposite us and told us smutty incidents in his life.

XII

Meg and Sam kept in the background since Ralph appeared. But I had not forgotten them. One day, after we had rested after the effects of our razzle-dazzle, John was away and Ralph, as we left the table, lit his cigar and, groping me, told me to go to my room and strip and, as soon as he finished smoking, he would come and we would have a nice, quiet little diddle all by ourselves.

I pressed the bulging balls in his breeches and going to my room, threw myself naked on the bed to wait for him. Just then Meg passed the door and I called her in. I had been too busy with my own slit and Ralph's and John's dear cocks to think of her or Sam, but, as she stood by the bed, I sprang up and embraced her. 'Oh Meg, forgive me! We've been so busy with ourselves. Come strip, get into bed with me and when Ralph comes, I'll make him give you a taste of his old gentleman.' 'No, no, Miss Madge, he is all yours!' But I jumped up and commenced tearing off her clothes.

Just as I, standing upon the bed, was pulling her chemise over her head, Ralph entered.

'See how two girls can enjoy each other!' I cried, and I threw the wench on the bed and, with mouths glued to each other's slits, we gave him a lively duet of tongue thrusting. While watching us he stripped and, as we lay languidly, side by side, he approached and examined my dusky bedfellow. 'What a nice, plump little brown Venus it is?' he said, as his hands roved over her.

'Leave me alone,' she said, 'you belong to Miss Madge.'

But I took Ralph's prick in my hand and held it up, rigid and fierce: 'Do you mean to tell me you don't want a taste of this?' I asked. 'Oh, I do, Miss. I do. My slit's hot now!'

'Get on your knees,' I cried, 'so that I can see the whole race up and down your hairy place!' and the lusty wench did as I told her, and, giving Ralph's rooster a parting kiss, I pointed it for her centre of attraction and gave myself up to the delightful spectacle of their lusty working bung and spigot, and, when Meg's well-filled belly rolled, squirming, upon the bed, I clasped Ralph's loins in my hands and took the fallen monarch in my mouth, sucking into me the last drop.

'One of you must tongue tickle me, quick!' I cried. 'Hold on!' said Ralph, snatching away his hand which I had clasped against my slit. 'Where's that robust husband of yours, Meg? Go and fetch him and tell him there's a lady here who wants the use of his cock for a few minutes.' 'Shall I Miss?' cried the delighted wench, springing to her feet. 'Hurry up!' said Ralph, and he gave her plump backside a resounding smack with his hand as the girl sprang naked out of the door.

'Oh, Ralph! do you really want me to let that black man fuck me?' I asked. 'I know you have let him kiss my slit and suck it, and I've kissed him too and twice he went off in my mouth; but, if he fucks me straight, I might have a brown baby.' Ralph laughed aloud. 'Babies or not,' he cried, 'I'm going to see that big muscular fellow fuck you right up to the handle,' and he threw himself on the bed and pulled me down, with my rump on the edge, tickling my nipples and clitoris as I lay across him.

A moment thus and, in the doorway, appeared the sprightly wench, and beside her, the magnificently muscular and manly form of Sam. He was a little bashful at this sudden introduction into such company, but the royal prick that the wench held in her hand showed how excited his passions were.

'See, Miss!' cried she, 'isn't it a whopper?' 'Walk up to the captain's office and settle!' cried Ralph. And, as Sam advanced and stood between my thighs I lost all my fears and took the splendid specimen of virility in my hand. 'What a monster he is!' I cried. 'He's grown bigger than ever!' 'Jolly, Miss,' said Meg, 'he's had lots of exercise since you and Massa John and Massa Ralph have been fucking and sucking each other all over the house. We had to peep in sometimes and see you three fooling with each other, and this rascal when you all came to the going off point, would make me get down on my knees and suck him while he watched you three wriggling.' 'You wicked peeper!' I cried. 'I'll pay you for that! Go and get that whip Meg, and thrash his backsides.' And I guided his immense prick between the lips of my slit and threw myself back, panting, to taste this luscious morsel.

'Fuck her just as you would Meg!' cried Ralph, and seizing my bum the lusty gentleman thrust that soul-satisfying shaft of his plump rod up to the hilt. 'Oh, it's splendid! It's a splitter, don't spare me, it's so lovely! Don't hold back! That's it! Oh, it's so good. Faster! I'll keep time with you! Whip his buttocks harder! Oh, he's swelling! I'm coming! Squeeze his balls, Ralph! Oh! Oh!' and heaving wildly, clutching the bedclothes with my hands, working my bottom, as if dancing on a hot stove, my cunt, chock-full of that rigid robust mountain of hard flesh, I yelled with delight, frantically threw up my legs and, closing them around him, kicked his bottom with my heels, until he cried: 'Now it flies! Take that in your womb, and that, and that' – and the frantic Hercules forgetting all but that we were two animals in lecherous agony, yelled at me: 'You want fucking, do you; you want your belly full? Ain't you getting it?

Take that! Suck every drop out with your puckering cunt, my pretty diddler!'

And I, wriggling, shrieking, and quivering with lust, called to him: 'Oh, it's heaven! My insides are flooded: I feel the sperm drops burn me as they hit my belly! I'm riddled with hot shots! Give me every charge in your gun! My buttocks are going and I can't stop. Whip him some more.'

For he had quieted his rapid motions. 'Yes!' he yelled. 'Flog me harder and I'll give her another dose without coming out!' 'You mean it?' I cried. For all response he seized me in his arms lifted me up still spiked on his prick, and ran around the room with me; squeezing my backsides, putting his finger in my cul, thrusting his tongue in my mouth, and nibbling at my nipples while I sucked his tongue and clasped him tightly with arms and loins while Meg whipped both our bottoms until, at length, I again felt the thrill of his stiffening pego and, laying me again on the bed, he worked his heavenly probe in and out of my slit until I felt the great drops fly once again into me and with a shriek I fainted.

XIII

When I came to myself in bed in my darkened room, Ralph, all dressed, sat by my side while I clasped his neck in my arms.

'Madge, you are still young and new to voluptuous raptures. You've been going at it too hard. We have been selfish in spurring you on so fast. Gradually you will become hardened to amorous play and be able to bear all that we can give and take together. But now you need a rest and you must obey and leave that sensitive slit of yours alone for four days, or until Sunday. And, Madge, you mustn't excite John and I by going around with your lovely bubbies bare, or letting us see your lovely legs. It's pretty hard to swear off even for a few days. But, for the sake of your health, we must all sacrifice ourselves.'

I kissed the dear fellow and promised to obey him; so we passed three highly respectable days, walking, riding and avoiding all temptations until on Saturday night, I went to bed in perfect health and yearning eagerly to again feel that blissful balm in my belly.

When I awoke in the morning my thing quickly reminded me that its itching was again to be solaced and, as I raised myself on my elbow, I gazed with gloating eyes down on that dear handsome lover of mine stretched out in bed on his back, still sleeping.

Gently I raised his nightshirt and feasted my eyes upon his innocent looking love shaft lying softly on the cushion-like testicles. Involuntarily my hand slid down over his belly and gently caressed the wrinkled weapon of lustful warfare.

Taking it in my fingers, with soft, quiet touches along its length, I saw, with flushing eyes and puckering slit, its softness swelled to stiffness, and soon my hand was filled with the rich rotundity of a glorious erection and my gloated eyes feasted on the round, red head, gorged with blood, and the gaping slit on its top, looking ready to spurt forth a shower of sperm.

Getting quickly onto my knees I drew my nightdress over my head and, without touching, straddled across him. Then, taking his prick in my hand, I held it bolt upright and, settling my body down upon it, it was soon piercing my vagina. In an instant a lustful, upward jerk of his buttocks made it disappear in my hole, and, glancing down, I saw that Ralph was awake and, with ardent gaze, watching my performances.

'Oh, you young lecherer! You couldn't wait until I woke up, but must ravish me in my sleep!' he laughed. 'You've kept me on short commons long enough,' I answered, 'and now I'm going to feast my belly full.' 'Well, go ahead!' he cried, 'but you must do all the work yourself. Wait a second until I stuff this pillow under me; it will help give you a longer stroke.'

As I commenced to work my thighs with rapid, ravishing heaves upon his stately prick, he cried out to me: 'Go to it, my pretty wench, my lovely, lusty lecherer, my sweet suction pump, my coral-cunted cock-pleaser, my dear whore, my ever ready sperm churner, wag your tail my lascivious little buttock worker! Push your slit tight on my belly, keep on – faster – faster!' Until, with a sudden spring forward he caught my bum in his hands and, with the burst of ultimate passion, threw me over on my back and, with straining muscles and bursting veins, gave me those sweet, final thrusts with such rapturous rapidity that my long stored juices oozed out around his pubes and wet his balls.

'I heard that hot-bellied cry way out in my room,' said a voice, and looking up, Uncle John stood by the bedside watching us with lustful eyes.

'She's got a fine action in her bum, John,' cried Ralph, 'let her pump up your sperm, herself.' And John, lying down with his buttocks on a settee, held his darling staff straight up in the air. Ralph lifted me astride of him while I put his cock where it would do the most good. I had just commenced working my thighs when Ralph, seeing a riding whip on the table, let it fall in tingling blows on my high lifted bottom until the excitement of the fight made his own cock get a hard-on and, tackling me behind, he stuck it in my cul while John was struggling to his feet. They both stood upright with me between them, lifted on their stiff staffs and having my whole body thrilled by their eager thrusts and copious shots of sperm.

As we rested and I lay there with two birds in my hand and sure of having them both in my bush, also, 'How shall we do it next?' I cried. 'Shall I tell you,' said John, 'how I first took a diddle?' 'That will be splendid!' I cried. And, settling ourselves in each other's way together, their hands gently caressing my slit and I holding in each hand the two pretty nightingales that had sung so often and so sweetly for me, he began.

XIV

'At sixteen I was a virgin. The sexual sensation had never been experienced and, if I had any amorous longings I did not know what they meant and my pintle was simply a piss-passer for me.

'One day I was climbing a smooth cherry tree, about as large around as Madge's waist, and, as I climbed up, with my arms and legs clasped tightly against it and rubbing up and down, my cock stiffened and a new sensation began to steal over me.

'Wondering what it was, I held the tree still tighter, instinctively, and worked my buttocks. Soon a delicious feeling spread all over me and centred itself in my prick, and as I kept on with faster heavings, I felt it stiffen in my breeches and soon it seemed to burst and shoot out something, I knew not what, while I felt that my belly was wet and a delightful languor spread over my whole body. I was astounded and clutched the tree until, too weak to hold on any longer, I slid to the ground. Lying there, I opened my breeches and found myself all covered with some sticky substance I had never seen before.

'I was half frightened, and went home and, stripping, washed myself and got on the bed, resolved to try if I could not recall those delicious feelings.

'As I took my cock in my hand and played with it I soon found that it grew bigger and bigger. It was soon stiff and swollen while the skin, which hid the head, soon yielded in a vigorous downward motion leaving the cap of love rosy and exposed.

'I did not know but what I had injured myself, but, spurred on by the exquisite pleasure I soon found my frigging hand made, I worked the skin up and down, faster and faster, and soon the same sensation which I had experienced on the tree stole over me. I felt something inside giving away and, in a delirium of delight, saw, for the first time, the milky seed fly high in the air and, keeping up the friction, squeezed out the last drop and lay back, panting.

'My eyes were half open. As I thought of this phenomena I wondered what it all meant until, one day, I saw our buxom servant girl leave the kitchen and, looking all around as if to see if she was watched, go into the barn.

'I followed, and gluing my eyes to the wide crack in the boards, saw another crack that made my prick so stiff as to almost split my breeches open. The girl was in heat, had thrown herself, half reclining on her back, upon the hay full front to where I was peeping and had pulled her clothes up to her waist.

'I fastened my eyes on her broad hips and fleshy thighs, her fat, round belly heaving up and down, and the great mass of black, curly hair which was plainly in view between her outstretched thighs. Her face had an eager expression as she fixed her eyes upon her excited centre and, I quickly saw her hide it from view with her hand and, with extended fingers, rub herself up and down, seeming to penetrate into some opening there.

'Instinctively I tore open my trousers and, taking my cock in my hand, kept time with her self-deflowering motions until I heard her give forth a half-suppressed cry of satisfaction, heaving her hips more wildly and working her hand faster, spending, just as my own agile hand pumped out the white sperm that flew high up on the barn toward her.

'After that I kept my eye on her and, whenever I saw

her go off by herself to the barn or bedroom, I quickly followed and gloating over the sight of her naked charms and lewd actions, joined her, unseen, in a revel of masturbation.

'In fact, I jerked myself off so often that I grew thin and weak and my father, not knowing the cause, wrote to a young curate whom he knew and sent me off to his distant parsonage for a change of air and to continue my studies under his care.

'The minister was an athletic young fellow of thirty and lived alone with his wife, a bright, pleasant faced, plump figured girl of twenty-two, overflowing with animal spirits and jolly, but proper and discreet, as became her position.

'For a week or so I left my cock alone. I was bashful as I said, and the novelty of my surroundings kept me thinking of other things.

'But, passing her door one day, when she said she was going to take a bath. I couldn't resist peeping through the keyhole. There she stood, naked and lovely, sponging herself briskly with a towel; lifting one plump leg upon a chair, her naked, wide stretched thighs open to my eager eyes.

'I yielded to the fires that were burning within me and rushing to my room, ran to the open window and shot a full libation of sperm into the glistening sunlight.

'And I kept it up for a week until one day after dinner, when we were all in the library – the young dominie sat on the sofa and his wife on his lap – while I, opposite them at the window, pretended to be reading but was, in fact, furtively gazing with a carnal eye at the trim ankles and plump calves of his wife that her reclining attitude brought into view.

' "John," said the dominie, "I've got something to say to you. I know how I suffered at your age and I see you wrecking your health and want to save you." "What do you mean?" I asked. "You know what I mean," he answered kindly. And my flushed face answered him. "I've suspected that you were playing with yourself for some time, but yesterday, Molly here, saw you jerking yourself off in your room. Now, I've a proposition to make to you. If you will promise me on your honour, never to masturbate again while you are here – once a week, Molly will let you do anything you like with her. In plain English, today is Friday; every Friday you may fuck Molly to your heart's content, but for the rest of the week, you must leave lewdness entirely alone. Do you promise?" "Do you mean it?" I cried, jumping to my feet, my cock stiff in my breeches. "Doesn't this look like I meant it?" he said, and seizing his blushing wife, he drew her across his lap as he lay extended on the sofa and, pulling up her clothes as high as they would go, exposed to my eyes her lovely body, naked from the waist down. "On your knees between her legs and swear to keep your promise," said the dominie. And kneeling there she seized my hand, pushed it down upon her lovely mount. "Kiss the book," she said, I was only a second there, for I was ready to spend, when rising to my feet, the lovely girl quickly unbuttoned my breeches and taking my over excited prick in her hand guided it quickly into her slit. "Fuck me!" she said. "Fuck me! I want it as much as you do!" And, eagerly grasping her bottom, I felt my pego pierce her tight crevice and enter her completely until belly touched belly and her hair curled in mine. I could not speak. I simply uttered an inarticulate cry of joy and commenced working in and out, as I had been taught by my frigging hand.

' "There! You naughty boy, isn't that nicer than playing with yourself?" and, throwing her arms around her husband's neck – "Are you jealous, hubby?" "Jealous?" he cried. "It's delicious! I enjoy the sight as much as you do the act. Give it to her, John!" "It's coming," I cried. "I am too," she answered. "Tickle the top of my slit, hubby." And the dear girl took my virgin offering deep into the recesses of her gaping womb.

'Then, reaching up she threw her arms around my neck and drew me down upon her, as we rained passionate kisses on each other. "Come!" cried the husband. "Let's have a Garden of Eden. Quick, run to your rooms, strip and come back. Hurry up, see in what a state I am!" and he held up his big prick ready to burst.

'In two minutes there were two Adams and one Eve; and at once, Eve, making me lie on the sofa, threw herself across me and, taking the big pego of the original Adam, the handsome couple were soon pumping sperm at each other. Resting from their labours the lovely girl caught sight of my prick, which was sticking up stiff again. "See this wicked young cock, it is ready to crow again!"

'As I rolled off of her, her husband sprang forward. "By Priapus, Molly," he called, "now you have been taken in adultery you shall do what you have refused to do – suck my cock." "Yes, indeed, I will!" she cried. "Sit on the floor, then, between John's legs," he said, and her backsides were soon close to my belly while he, kneeling before her, stuck his great, inflamed cock invitingly into her face. Quickly her open lips closed over the ruby head and slid down the huge column, while one hand clutched his bum, and the other his testicles. "Work your lips just as you do your slit," he cried. What a luscious sight it was, but so short. "There it comes," and the swollen glands told that he was spending. Taking her hand away a minute, the sperm flew over her and over me, and then, seizing it again in her mouth, she did not let go until, with a deep sigh of satisfied emotion, he, himself, withdrew, melted by the fervour of her lips, tongue, and inhaling breath.'

XV

From the time when Ralph first rid me of my burdensome and hateful maidenhead – carried it away on the point of his lance – I had never so much as thought of marriage. Our entwined arms and legs and his dear shaft nailing me down to the couch of pleasure were all the bonds I cared for. But, before long, he had to return to New York. I hardly dared think of it; we had been so full of the present, at least I had been so full of their doings. One day I had been walking alone and, returning, found Ralph and John talking seriously. They seated me on the sofa between them but didn't put their hands in my bosom or under my skirts. I was really frightened; I thought that something had happened and looked anxiously from one to the other.

'Madge, Ralph and I have been talking about the future. I have business that will take me to the Pacific in a few days and Ralph must return to New York and you must go with him.' 'Oh!' I cried, 'I knew we couldn't go on always as we are – but . . .' I got no further, buried my face in my hands, and burst into tears.

To leave John was bitter, but since the night that he first possessed me, I had held Ralph in my heart, as so-called virtuous women do their husbands.

'Yes, Madge, Ralph and I have decided that you and he be legally married and go and live in New York.' 'Oh John, it's like taking half of my life away to leave you.' 'Of course, it seems so,' said Ralph, 'but John can visit us often, and we him.' And it was all settled.

One evening, not long after, I had gone to my room for something when Meg appeared, entirely naked, and said: 'Miss Madge, they want you in the parlour, in the same clothes I have on.' 'Oh Meg,' I said, 'I suppose they want us to take some of the starch out of them.' 'It's more than this, Miss.' And, curious, I stripped and followed her.

The room was brilliantly lighted. At the head of a couch in the centre, stood a priest, book in hand, while behind him, were Ralph, John and Sam, all three as bare as Meg and I.

I stood still with wonder; when John came forward and, leading me to the couch, threw me on my back. Then Ralph came forward and stood between my legs, his arrow aimed at my bull's-eye.

The priest stood at the side and, opening his book, commenced the short marriage service and, as he pronounced the declaration that we were man and wife, he took my hand and, making me grasp my newly-made husband's prick, guided it into my slit. The dear fellow gave me a hard trot and, foundering at the end, invited John to follow him, which he did.

Then Ralph asked the priest to give me his blessing and the holy man, advancing to the altar presented to our view a Priapus of immense size and got between my legs. 'Will you accept my blessing,' he asked, 'and let me anoint you with the holy oils?' 'Oh, Father, pour oil on my troubled waters.' And that stalwart prick of his went plunging into me and kept, pounding away until a profuse scattering of his sanctified sperm sent me off, wriggling, like a fish on a hook.

Then Ralph, turning to Sam, said: 'There is no black or white in heaven and her slit is at present heaven.' The well wound up and richly adorned fellow gave me a diddle that, for size of cock, vigour of action, and copious spending, was as perfect as the lovely grotto of Venus itself could have wished for.

XVI

And now the last night together came, and I suppose that you must anticipate a wholesale razzle-dazzle; but John and I felt the parting too keenly.

Ralph and I were in our room and I had just dropped my chemise and was sitting, naked, pulling off my stockings. 'Madge, go to John's bed and spend the night in his arms.' I kissed him fondly and went. Not forgetful of him, I ran to Meg's room, told her where I was going to pass the night and bade her go down to Ralph and see if he did not want to have a stroking match with her before he went to sleep.

Then I hastened to John, and entering the familiar room found it dark and he in bed. 'What's that?' 'Me, dear John; I've come to spend the night.' And, wrapped in his arms like a child in its father's, or a bride in her husband's, half tearful and half rapturous with our soft pleasures, I fell asleep on his breast.

Morning found us there, inhaling our souls into each other's lips, glued together, bellies throbbing and his dear shaft carrying soft rapture to my inner soul, until, in the ecstasy of our last embrace a knock came, and Sam entered with John's shaving water.

'Sam, you must say goodbye,' and soon his stalwart pego was buried within me and twice shot its elixir into my womb; the second time while I drew from John's dear staff the last libation of love.

Three hours later Ralph and I were on a train for the north.

The express was crowded, but finally the conductor came and told us a director of the railroad was occupying a state-room, and had consented to share it with us.

We found it a pretty apartment, shut off from the rest of the car, with mirrors and carpets, easy chairs and an inviting looking sofa.

The occupant was a handsome man of fifty, and very courteous. 'I fear we shall disturb you,' said Ralph. 'No, I was getting lonesome and you are more than welcome to join me as far as Philadelphia where this car will be switched off.'

I threw myself on the sofa and watched the moving panorama as we passed the morning in pleasant talk. Once I caught my host's eyes, fixed with a gleam on my plump leg, which in changing position I had exposed.

When we stopped for dinner the two gentlemen alighted, brought me a lunch, and then promenaded the platform.

The train started again, when Ralph said: 'Madge, our host and I have been confidential; you ought to have heard the compliments he made of you! Go sit on his lap, and tell him he can have what he wants.' 'Stop your nonsense,' I said. But the laughing rascal took me in his arms and placed me in our host's lap.

'Won't you be kind to an amorous old codger and stay?' 'Yes, I will and I will make Ralph jealous!' I cried. And throwing my arms around my new lover's neck, I gave him a kiss.

I could feel his staff stiffen against my bottom and his hand instinctively pressed my breast. 'There, you naughty fellow! You shall have them at discretion,' and with both hands I lifted my plump titties out of my clothes and, with a cry of pleasure, he covered them with kisses.

'Pull up her petticoats and I will show you the way into her,' said Ralph, and, jumping up, he let loose his prick, fully recovered from Meg's drubbing.

'Bravo!' cried our host, and quickly snatching up all that hid my lovely legs, thighs and belly, as he called them, my bottom, was clasped in Ralph's hands and his staff was knocking at my slit.

'May I put it in?' said our host. 'Of course you may,' and he guided it in. 'You can squeeze his balls too, if you want to,' and he did. Seeing that we were spending he pushed his head down and with clinging lips and tongue, kissed and tickled my hot clitoris and Ralph's lunging shaft until, as it was withdrawn, the sperm still oozing from its gaping nozzle, he, unable to control himself, seized it in his mouth and sucked it. Fired by his emotions, he sprang to his feet, tore open his trousers and showed me a new morsel to be devoured by my hungry slit.

Ralph stretched me on my back on the floor, naked from the waist, and my grey-haired but virile companion was in a moment a prisoner in my belly – a lively one, too – dancing like mad up and down, while I imprisoned his whole body with arms and legs until we both experienced the most delicious novelty of a first diddle between a congenial man and woman.

When we resumed the role of respectable members of society there wasn't a drop of love juice in either of them.

XVII

Reaching New York, we quickly settled down in the plain but cosy little flat that Ralph had, by writing, made ready for us.

A month passed in all the quiet pleasures of the usual newly married couple.

Then our first trouble came. We had spent all our money in fitting up our apartment and seeing the sights. John was too far away to help and we hated to borrow, and could only wait for Ralph's salary to come due.

Our landlord was a man – a muscular little hunchback of forty – who lived in bachelor quarters in the first flat.

He had been pleasant enough; but now, after calling two or three times for the money and receiving only excuses he began to grow angry and made us uncomfortable.

One morning, after Ralph had gone, a note was stuck under the door. He wrote that if he did not receive the rent that day we would have to move. I threw myself on the bed and burst into tears. Our cosy nest torn to pieces perhaps. Something must be done. Arranging myself, I decided to brave the little misformed lion in his den, all by myself.

Trembling, I knocked at his door. He called: 'Come in.' I found him writing at a table.

Standing opposite, I made my plea and begged him to wait a little longer and not break up our new home.

The man was silent, but his bright, piercing eyes seemed to burn as they wandered over my person, which a chemise and a thin wrapper draped, but did not hide, the contour of.

He arose and, going to a window, gazed out with his back to me. Then he broke the silence. 'Madame, I am a man of business; debts are debts and must be paid. But I am also, a pleasure-seeker. If you are offended you can return to your room. Ever since you came into the house I have desired to possess you; watched you as you mounted the stairs, catching glimpses of your trim legs, and twice I have watched you and your husband, like youthful Venus and Mars, give your bodies up to each other's enjoyment, and causing my seed to be spilled on the ground. I am an ugly dwarf I know, more to be loathed than loved, but if you can forget your handsome lover and yield to my ardour, every outpouring will count to you a month's rent paid.'

'Never! I never sold myself, but – ' and I hesitated and threw myself into a great sleepy hollow chair. He stood facing me. 'But what?' 'If you love a man for love's sake, yea, for lust's sake – ' I did not finish, but, stretching out my legs as I reclined, I unbuttoned my wrapper and lay there, a tempting bit of fluff and fur from waist to heels.

'You splendid creature!' he cried, and, throwing himself on his knees between my thighs, kissed belly, legs and mount, but only for a second; then he jumped to his feet, stripped open his breeches and showed me the first circumcised cock I had ever seen. The great head was more freely exposed than a Christian's; it was of a length and thickness that recalled the immense erections of those black lovers of mine in the South.

'It's as big as you are!' I cried. Quickly aiming it at my excited target, he drove it in and, with athletic thrusts soon made me show, with wildly working belly, that

I wasn't being fucked for cold cash, but was as eager as he was to exchange with him the white coinage of concupiscence.

'You're a very priestess of enjoyment,' he cried, and lifting me up in his strong arms he sat where I had been, and I lay straddled across him, his prick still in, his lips sucking my nipples. 'Oh,' I cried, 'that was delicious.' 'What would your husband say if he saw us here?'

'Do you think I would have let you, if he would object?'

And I told him how we were devoid of prejudices and each gladly yielded the mate to the lascivious pleasings of others.

'After my own heart! Why this clap-trap of fidelity, making necessity for brothels and adulteries leading oft to murder? Why shouldn't a man and woman who fancy each other shake cocks and cunts together as well as hands? But come, my Venus, let me see you in true Venus costume.' And, devoured by his lustful gaze, I dropped the last veil and he likewise.

But he had heavy shoulders, muscular arms and legs, great bulging buttocks – and, oh! – that cock, which was already recovering. Pressing me down upon the bed, he fixed his head between my thighs and, with admiring words and enlivening touches, examined the sheath of his pleasures. 'I too, like to know about the tools I use,' I said. He quickly knelt across my chest, and I fondled and caressed his enormous prick until he seized me and, with my weight, resting on my bubby cushions, my bottom raised, he standing behind me, grasped my hips in his hands and, gorged my slit with his giant erection. My body hanging there, as it were, on his firm pego, he swung me to and fro with ever increasing rapidity, my nipples titillated by friction against the bedclothes, until his balls, which knocked against my belly, gave up the fight and let loose their stores of satisfying sperm.

When I was rested I wanted to go back to my room. 'Not yet,' he said. And, as he sat on the edge of the bed, he put his head down to my thing and commenced tickling it with his tongue. His extended abdomen was asking my caresses and, bending over, I paid his kisses back to his cock which responded quickly to circling lips and titillating tongue.

'You naughty boy, you want me to eat it up.' 'Will you?' 'I'll do anything you want, and enjoy it as much as you do.'

He rolled over on his back, holding his prick and said: 'Come.' 'I'll come, and you will too.' And, on my knees over his face, he seized my hips, raised his face to my quim, pressed the edges apart and darted his tongue within.

Rounding up my back so my mouth would reach his prick, and squeezing his balls, I took the red mouthful and sucked – and sucked – we both sucked, until the succulent glands gave up their stores and our breathless bodies lay panting in satisfaction.

XVIII

When I returned to my room I threw myself on the bed and dropped asleep. Waking late in the afternoon I had barely time to dress and get supper ready for Ralph. As I hurried around I noticed some papers stuck under the door and, picking them up, I found receipts for three months' rent; one for each fuck. Oh, how happy I felt. The crisis had passed and I could lift the care that was worrying Ralph.

It was Friday and I was determined to wait until Sunday before telling him. Worried, as he was, he did not touch me and I said to myself: 'Well my fine fellow, that's right, take a rest; store up a good stock of love cream in your testicles. You will want to flood me with it when I relieve your mind with my receipts.'

Sunday morning we lay in bed – just awake – and I turned to him, kissed him and passed my hand along his thighs till I felt his cock stiffening in my grasp. 'Come, Madge, I'm ashamed of myself for worrying so about this cursed rent. We'll forget it for today, at least, and have a good, old fashioned fuck.' And, sitting up in bed he pulled off his nightshirt and lying back, held up his stiffened staff ready to stick into me.

'Wait a moment!' and jumping up I ran naked in the closet, got the receipts, handed them to him and stood by the bedside, radiant. 'How did you get these?' he cried, and with a glib tongue I told him all. Then he seized me. 'You wicked little harlot, you make your room rent by renting your cunt to your landlord, do you?' And, flinging me on the bed he mounted me and plunging his cock full tilt into my ring of love, diddled me until we both lay panting happily.

I was describing my intrigue with the landlord when a knock interrupted me. Opening the door I found our landlord's card – and on the back written: 'Will you both join me for dinner, at one o'clock?' 'How nice,' I cried. 'You want want to get that big prick of his in you again,' said Ralph. 'Of course I do,' I answered, 'and I bet you're dying to see that little dwarf put it in.' 'Right you are. But Madge, bathe this hard-on in cold water, I want to keep it for this afternoon.'

I obeyed, and succeeded in wilting it without losing anything. Then, dressing to avoid temptation, we went and breakfasted at a restaurant, and, taking a brisk walk, returned to the house feeling fine and ready to dine and diddle. We met our landlord at the door. 'I've told him all,' I said, and my tall hubby grasped the hands of the sturdy little new lover.

'Is the dinner to be a full dress affair?' I asked. They both laughed and Ralph answered: 'Let's wear nothing except stockings and nightshirts.' And, going to our rooms we soon looked like two angels ready to ascend, and I guess Ralph was, from the way he stuck out in front.

Slipping downstairs, when no one was around, we found our host ready. I must give him a name; let's call him 'Noah' – and laughing at our funny costumes we sat down, eating, drinking, and telling erotic episodes in our lives until the board lost its charm and we were eager for bed.

Raising his glass Noah said: 'I drink to the sweetest little cunt I ever tasted. May it always have what it wants as handy as now.' Laughing, I arose, slipping the disfiguring gown off my shoulders and standing there nude before them, one knee over the back of my chair – thus opening my slit wide – and, raising my glass: 'I drink to man, to the manliest part of him; and then those two dear images of Priapus so near to me. May they ever be ready, with rigid staff and juicy sperm, to carry rapture to any woman's cunt that is as hot as mine is now!' And I drained my glass to the bottom.

Both sprang to their feet, Noah on his chair, and dropping their shirts which hung a moment suspended on their pegos, they emptied their glasses and I was quickly in their arms.

A lascivious group of three, groping and frigging each other, soon stood beside the bed. 'After you,' said Noah to Ralph. With my dear hubby resting his shoulders on the edge of the bed, his feet on the ground, I straddled over him and could thus shaft him standing upright.

'Let me put it in,' cried Noah, and, pointing the dear yard straight up, I impaled myself on it and, grasping his buttocks in my hands: 'I'll ravish you!' I cried, and commenced to pump up his spermatic treasures with a lubric working bum, while the lustful Noah handled our battling organs and spurred us on with excited speech until my contracting cunny and Noah's frigging fingers drew from Ralph a bellyful of seed. He did not wait to have his pego wilt inside of me, but pulled it out still rosy, rampant, and juicy, and drawing himself up flat on the bed, made me take his darling spending cock in my mouth. While from behind me on the floor, the immense pego of the excited clipyard was thrust into my suspended belly. I made my still lustful slit so tight and hard and deep that, when his mighty cock began to throb and spend, I had to let off my own excited emissions and return drop for drop, his vivifying emissions while my lips continued eagerly giving pleasure to Ralph's rosy rooster.

Lying throbbing on the bed they washed me off, gave me and themselves a reviving bumper of wine while Ralph, lighting a cigar, threw himself on a sofa and bade Noah do what he pleased with me. In two minutes his hands had groped and his lips had kissed every part of me and penetrated every cranny.

'What a delicious morsel of flesh she is!' he cried. 'What a delicious morsel of flesh this is!' I answered, caressing his stiffened shaft. 'It looks ready to inundate my womb again.' 'It is!' he cried. And jumping up, my short but athletic lover seized me in his arms and standing bolt upright, putting his arms between my legs and grasping a cheek of my buttocks in each hand, he lifted me to a level with his face while I thrust my thighs around his neck, holding his head in my hands to steady myself. His nose just rubbing against my slit, his tongue penetrated it until I squirmed vigorously and he slid my body down along his chest till the stiff spear penetrated my gaping and excited slit. Calling to Ralph to whistle a jig, he danced briskly, while his swelling prick also danced lustfully to my insides and I kept time, with heaving belly and wriggling bottom until languor laid us on our backs on the bed.

'Your belly's too full for this,' said Ralph, kneeling over and holding up his prick in my face. I quickly devoured the titbit of raw flesh and washed the draughts of thick cream down with a plenteous flow of saliva. 'Give me a taste,' excitedly exclaimed Noah; and, as I let myself fall back on the pillow the lecherous man with eager lips seized the full foaming spigot and sucked with eagerness the last sperm drops from Ralph's succulent prick.

'Are you disgusted?' asked Noah, as he drank a glass of wine. 'I haven't done such a thing in twenty years. Away back when I had the mining fever, we were snowed in one winter, six of us men, in one house way up in the mountains. We couldn't get out and time went slowly. One day, as we had just finished dining and each of us had three or four drinks of whisky in us, we discovered written in soot over the fireplace: "Boys, let's suck each other's cocks." We all looked at each other – who wrote it? All looked innocent when the rough but jolly leader spoke up: "Boys I didn't write it but, damn it, it's set me thinking. I bet there is not a mother's son of you here who don't jerk himself off on the sly."

'Then opening his breeches he pulled out his stiff prick. "I'll suck any of you who will suck this." Our pretended virtue melted away, and the rest of us eagerly produced our peckers. In a minute we divided into three couples and each of our mouths were full of fine erections and we were swallowing sperm at one end and spitting it at the other.'

This story, though vile according to our education, excited me and I threw myself between Noah's thighs and kissed his prick. Quickly grasping my buttocks he pulled them up to his head and plunging his tongue into my slit we both started on a sucking race, while Ralph, seizing a limber cane, tingled our heaving backsides with a rapid flogging.

XIX

The next morning when I got out of bed, long after Ralph had left, I found three letters under the door. The first was from Noah and contained a hundred dollar bill. 'Don't refuse this, dear girl, fifty thousand dollars wouldn't repay the pleasures I have tasted.'

The second was from my dear John and enclosed an introduction for Ralph to an old friend in New York. John wrote that his friend, Phillip Weston, was wealthy and might find Ralph more lucrative employment. Then he wrote tenderly and amorously about his thinking of me, and turning the page I read, 'Yes, my dear girl, as I sit here the thought of you sends a vigorous thrill through my shaft. I hold it in my hand wishing it in yours, or your plump bubbies, eager mouth, tight cul or sweet and luscious cunt. I lay it against the paper and trace it thus (here an outline of his prick) and now I fold the paper around it and frig into it the sperm your image raises.' All over the inside of the sheet were blotches of brown stuff that had been hot, rich cream, gushing from his dear pego. Opening my thighs I pressed the paper deep into my lustful crevice and, rubbing it and dreaming that his dear form was naked in my arms – I too, wet the paper and laid it aside to dry and send back to him.

The third letter was in a strange hand and, as I opened it, another hundred dollar bill dropped out. 'A slight memento my dear girl, of a delightful day in a parlour car.' No signature, but I knew that it was from that railroad director who let us into his private room and who I took into my private parts.

'Two hundred dollars,' I soliloquised, and, lifting up my thighs in the air I held them wide apart and gazed into the opening of my red crevice – 'Two hundred dollars just because you were nice to two men. Ah, if you were paid at that rate every time you sucked the delightful overflow out of your frisky guests, your owner would be a millionairess by this time.'

A key turned in the lock and Ralph entered. He burst out laughing. 'Don't stir, you're an awful smutty picture.' 'The picture is at your service,' I answered, hugging my legs closely down to the sides of my body, my feet at the side of my head. 'Keep that position,' he cried, pulling my wide-stretched buttocks to the edge of the bed and, placing my shoulders high on the pillows, devoured the lustful attitude for a minute. 'I'm going to suck you first, fuck you second, and then suck you again and, if you get out of that position before I get through, I won't diddle you for a week.' 'Hurry up then, I'm ready to spend now.' And his tongue was thrust into my cunt, stretched wider than ever before and brought down my ready juices almost immediately. 'Don't budge except to heave your ass,' he cried out, into my still lustful slit he drove his excited penis, quickly sending the blissful balm to the inner parts to solace my lecherous agony, and, again on his knees, he kept his tongue working in my cunt and thrust a finger in my cul until I could stand it no longer and cried out that he would kill me if he kept on.

Then throwing himself on the bed, he made me fondle his prick and buttocks while he read the letters. Later, after a smoke with the landlord, he came up and said they were going to a theatre and, as I said goodbye to them at the door, the air seemed so fresh and

Madge

invigorating that, though it was dark, I determined to take a walk.

Sauntering along looking into shop windows, I came into a side street which I afterwards found out was a cruising ground for women of pleasure. Presently a rough grasp on my shoulder startled me, and looking up, I saw it was a big, burly policeman.

'What are you cruising for, don't you get enough cocks staying in the house? Don't you know it's against the law?' I was too frightened to answer. 'By Jove, you're a new girl in these sections,' he continued, 'and a damned nice looking one. Come into the alley and let me see if the rest of you is as nice as your face.' And he dragged me along a dark narrow street. 'Please let me go!' I cried. 'You will either come with me or I will run you into the station,' he said. And, pulling me along the deserted alley we came to where a solitary lamp threw a flood of light down on a wagon. The powerful rascal seized me and threw me on my back on the tail board of a cart, my legs hanging down. 'Pull up your petticoats!' he ordered, 'I've no time to waste. The sergeant will be around shortly and will give me hell if he catches me off my post. See – I've got a good stiff-on.' And I saw his magnificent prick erect against his belly. It's the quickest way to get out of the scrape, I thought, and, pulling my clothes up to the pit of my stomach, I awaited his attack. 'Jolly, you're a daisy,' he said, passing his rough hand over thigh and belly and gave my brush a squeeze that made me wince.

'In it goes,' he cried. 'How's that for a stretcher?' I tried to keep still, but his big prick and splendid stroking made me forget all but the pleasure of his thrusts and I had to work my bottom. 'Oh, you like it, do you? You needn't deny it. I know when a girl shams and when she is tickled in the right spot.' And working harder, I gave myself up to it and cried out: 'It's lovely. Your splendid cock is making me spend.' 'So you shall, my dear,' and his colossal prick, knocking at my womb, shot its flood of lust into my cunt, sweltering in its own overflow.

'I've caught you, have I?' said a voice out of the shadow. 'Fucking a whore in the public streets and off your post.' And the speaker, another big policeman, stood looking down at our exposed lechery.

'Ah, now, Sergeant, what's the harm of diddling a gal? It don't take long. And Sergeant, look at her. She's a new one. See what a fine pair of legs and how her belly heaves; and her slit's as hot as a slut's. She gives a stroke up for every one down. Try her, Sergeant.' And, standing aside, he put his hands under my bottom and lifted me up to give his superior a better view of my venereal attractions.

The Sergeant stepped between my legs. 'Well my dear, I don't want to be hard on your lover, so I'll be hard on you instead.' And, in an instant his splendid cock was plunged into me and another splendid diddle made me squirm. 'Meet us here again tomorrow night,' said the Sergeant, 'and don't come out of the alley till we are out of sight.'

When I did come out I was not long in getting home. I remember to this day the sensations of shame and fear I experienced that evening, but I also remember the uncontrollable pleasure those two police cocks, as big as their clubs, gave me on the wagon in the alley.

XX

It took me an hour to recover from the effects of the unexpected charge of the blue-coated pair of lusty baton wielders. But I could not, despite the ignominy of having myself thus stormed and barbellied in the public street, be unconscious of the full fledged, firm fixed, fine fucking faculties of my last lovers. And my feverish, yes, ferocious fuck funnel forced me to feel the folly of feeling foolish over this fortuitious fornication, and set my brain to work to plan some new devilry; with my cunt as the centre of the celebration.

'I have it. I'll disguise myself and solicit Ralph and Noah on their way home.'

Donning some old clothes which I never wore, I again sallied forth at about the time the theatre was out and walked along the way I knew they would return.

I hadn't gone a block when two young fellows came along. 'Well sweetest,' said one, 'are you looking for a tenant, who'll move in your empty room, stay a while, dance a jig, and then vacate? By Jove, Jack. She ain't bad. Damn the cost. Let's take her to Mother Jones's for a short razzle-dazzle.'

'Go away and leave me alone!' I said. 'Leave you alone and unprotected? Oh, no,' said the youngster. 'Come along,' and each seized an arm. 'Where are you taking me?' I cried. 'To bed,' said one, and around a corner we went and up to a door. 'Here Mother, here's your dollar. Which room?' 'Is it for one jerk, or for the night?' said the buxom landlady. 'Oh, only a lightning thrust,' one answered. 'Then come into my room,' she said, and into a room we went. 'Pay her,' said the Madam, and the youngsters handed me a bill which I put into my pocket, and, in a jiffy, I was on the bed with a nice, young cock working in me. Then, fire, bang, and another was promenading in my Rue-Rogue. 'She'll do,' cried one. 'She's bully,' said the other. 'We'll make it longer next time.' And they were gone.

Fifteen minutes had hardly elapsed from start to finish. 'Well, my dear,' said the woman, 'that's quick work. If all your lovers take so little of your time you'll get rich quick. Clean up and take another stroll and you may land some more fish. The theatres are just letting out and I bet you will be back with a new stiff in an hour.'

I didn't answer. The word 'theatre' brought me back to what I had started for. So I left hastily to look for Ralph and Noah. Several men accosted me but I said that I was engaged.

Presently my old 'long and short of it' hove in sight. 'What a funny pair,' I said, laughing at their faces. 'You'll make fun of us, will you?' said Ralph, and he began groping me. 'There's nothing like novelty,' he continued, 'and my pego was stiff as soon as she hove in sight. Let's take her to your room for a brace of jerks. The other one will be asleep.'

So done, and into Noah's room we went, and when the gas was turned on there was a tableau. I took off my bonnet and they recognised me. I burst with a hearty laugh. 'I'll stop your laughing!' said Ralph, and, throwing me back on the sofa, he stuck his prick in my mouth for a stop cock, while my slit had another, of Noah's flesh.

One evening Ralph came home: 'Madge, I am going to leave for several days; not a word – I can't explain now. Noah will be your guardian meanwhile. Come help me pack.' As I packed I watched him bathe, till finished he turned and said: 'Now for a farewell fuck.' In an instant I was on the bed with his dear form, almost in tears, but teeming with voluptuous rapture. Finished, he dressed and took me to Noah, and explained: 'Noah, you will play protector to her and see she doesn't want for anything. A field not ploughed and watered soon grows stale. Harrow her well; plough her frequently and irrigate her freely. I won't be jealous if you show her the lively sight of the city. Let her see and feel all she can, for it may be that my journey will result in our leaving New York and settling elsewhere.' He clasped me in his arms and was gone. The next day, Noah said that a Turkish bath would be the best thing to rejuvenate us and that he knew a quiet, small one where a man and a woman could take one together.

As he paid the female keeper he was asked which rubber he wanted, and answered that he wanted the strongest.

Soon we were in a room as hot as my disposition, perspiring and naked, then sponged with cold water and plunged in a cool pool. I forgot all the processes which we went through alone. 'Now for the rubbing,' and entering the room, we found our manipulator awaiting us, a naked giant with a girdle around his loins. We had sheets thrown around us and Noah, dropping his, threw himself flat on a leather cot and the Negro commenced working his muscles, limbering his joints and rubbing him all over with the palms of his hands.

'Ah, Madge, that puts new life into me,' said Noah, as I watched the process. 'I should smile,' said the smiling rubber and he held up Noah's prick strutting perpendicularly. 'It feels as if he wanted something sweeter Miss.'

Throwing aside my sheet I told him to lift me up on top of Noah, and I was quickly taking the starch out of him. As I lay with his prick dissolved inside of me: 'Do you want to pump sperm into her?' asked Noah. 'Let's see your cock,' and the lustful attendant stripped off the girdle and Noah and I had the brown and red sceptre in our grasp.

'Run,' said Noah, pushing me off the side. I ran around the room, the giant after me, until, rushing to Noah, he placed me on top of him; my belly over his face. As I took his prick in my mouth, the lustful black cock was guided by Noah into my slit and the God-like thrusts soon carried rapture through me and drowned by vitals in burning sperm while I gratified Noah with a hot-mouthed sucking.

Then we all took a plunge in the bath again and, coming out, 'Put the girdle on,' Noah said, 'so as not to tempt this young filly again.'

'No, no, I must have one more taste of this delicious prick,' and throwing myself on my knees before the giant, I caressed with hands, titties and mouth the already magnificent erection of his God-like cunt plough.

'You'll promise to quit with one more fuck?' 'I swear!' I cried. And, kneeling on the couch, Noah leaned my back against his breast, my bum on the edge of the bed. He bade the giant lift me up by the legs and, grasping them, he pulled them on each side of my shoulders, leaving my slit a gaping furnace with the doors wide open.

'What a fine view,' cried the Negro, dropping to his knees, and he not only viewed, but stuck his tongue into the stretched orifice. 'Stop, you'll make me spend,' I cried. 'So I will, Miss,' and, on his feet, he quickly drove his big prick to the hair in my cunt and fucked me until I squealed.

Two days later I was alone when a lady called. She was about my size and age; except she was a blonde and I was a brunette. She handed me a card – Mrs Philip

Weston. 'Oh, yes, John had sent Ralph an introduction to Philip Weston – but we learned that he was away from the city.'

'Yes, your Uncle John wrote about you, but we have not been here since we received the letter.' She seated herself by my side: 'We'll be friends, shan't we?' I kissed her and she went on: 'Philip is away, but next week we sail south on our yacht. John, knowing that we're to be with him for a visit sent you this letter,' handing it to me.

'Dear Madge – It's no use. I can't live here without you and Ralph. I have written him to give up his position and for you and him to settle here with me, as the sole heirs of all I possess. You can come on with Mr and Mrs Weston.'

'Oh, how splendid,' I cried, gladly. 'And are you and John well acquainted?' I asked. 'That's a pointed question,' she laughed, 'but I know all about your relations with John and he knows as much about me as Philip does. We're both lewd, lustful women, and I'm not ashamed of it! Are you?' 'I live only for sexual enjoyment,' I answered.

'Let's strip and have our first embrace,' she cried. And soon a naked blonde and brunette were admiring, caressing, praising the charms of each other and, quickly on the bed, sought, with experienced tongues to quench the lustful fires for the moment no man's pego was there to put out.

I told her of Noah – 'How funny to have a dwarf for a lover.' 'You'll have one in a minute.' I ran downstairs and, finding him, quickly told him, while I handled his prick: 'Strip here, clothes will only be in the way,' and in five minutes I introduced my lover to Mary.

Putting her on my lap, 'Come, Noah, and examine her,' and my dear lover was on his knees, kissing and tickling her swelling belly and luscious cunt, which she jutted out for him.

'Stop,' she cried, 'let me feel and kiss that big prick before you fuck me.' Kneeling over her, she soon had a mouth full of stiff prick and a handful of red balls.

'Quick, diddle me. I'm consumed with lechery,' she said, throwing herself back with extended thighs, and as he stuck his flaming nozzle to her door I guided it in.

How that woman loved it. How she heaved her belly, threw up her legs, pounded with her hands his bare bum, till on the verge of the precipice. 'Now, shoot it into me, I'm coming.' As I knelt beside the lustful warrior, the big prick swelled larger and larger. 'Ouch! there it comes. It's shooting all through me! Oh your lovely cock! Your delicious fucking! Give me every drop!' In a moment she lay heaving.

My cunt hot? I should say it was. I was flat on my back, by fingers clutching it. 'Stop! give her a taste of your tongue,' and Noah was in a moment sucking my slit, while she stuck her tongue in my mouth till I overflowed.

We did not separate till exhausted. Mary arranged to have me join her and Philip a week later in Philadelphia.

One evening Noah entertained three of his friends.

After they got lively he came and told me his friends were in a mood to appreciate a female friend, which he told them he would furnish if they would appear as Adam.

He led me naked into his room and introduced me to three fine, stalwart clipyards. And, within fifteen minutes I had been well fucked by four cocks, and lay panting with the sperm oozing out of my slit.

Before Noah carried me to my room, twelve shots had been fired into my various holes.

XXI

All my attention was devoted to Noah the last week, and, when I said goodbye to him he talked more like a father than a lover, and gave me a certificate of deposit for two thousand dollars. 'Something for a rainy day,' he said.

Arriving at Philadelphia, I soon had Mary in my arms. 'Come to my room. For one night one room will do for the three of us, won't it?'

After a bath, she put her arms around me. 'Now dear, I'll introduce you to my husband.' Out from behind the window curtains stepped Philip Weston, stark naked, his rosy rooster ready to ravish me. Grabbing my arms she held them behind my back. 'Come examine this new cock cooler.' 'Cock cooler! The mere sight of it burns me up.' And, his hands and kisses covered me, then led me to the bed. His wife pointed his robust cock at my slit and, with a heave, he was in to the hilt.

The first fuck is always nice, and we played with agile loins until drained of our bliss. Two more rounds, then, for the night he slept sandwiched between two warm specimens of woman flesh.

The next afternoon we boarded the yacht and were off for our long sail. The crew consisted of three big Italians and a Chinese cook who kept to the galley unless called for.

After land disappeared, Mary said: 'Come Madge, let's get into our high-sea rig.'

We were stripped to our stockings and were just reaching for our sailor suits when a voice from the doorway said, 'Missy, Captain Phil sent a bottle of wine.' 'Come in, Ah Wing,' and the cook entered in a blue blouse reaching to his knees, and served the wine as we lay stretched naked on the divan. 'Ah Wing, how's this for a pretty tickler?' as she raised one of my legs, showing my fucking facilities.

'Ah Wing, show the lady what a Chinese cock looks like,' and pulling his blouse over his head, stepped naked to the edge of the divan, and I had a Chinese prick in my hand for the first time. Long, and the end of it curved like a finger with the top joint bent, it was smaller around than a white man's, with a crisp little pair of balls, no bigger than a large dog's.

'Let Chinee-man kiss cunny,' and his tongue shot into my slit, when springing up: 'Me allee ready fuckee,' and I pointed his long slim cock at my crevice and its curved end was soon tickling the instrument of joy. 'Ah, I see why you like the heathen fucking! Don't tickle the itching; Ah Wing will make me say ah-ah-ah in a second,' and he did.

Our sea clothes; our red jackets exposed our breasts at every flop, and a pair of pants in two pieces, only connected by the waistband, leaving our mounts exposed when we opened our legs, and when we stooped our bare bottom was exposed fully. 'Come on deck, I bet there is a quartet of stiff pricks ready to sing to us.'

All in line, with Phil in command, the four muscular men were stark naked, with stiff pricks, waiting for us.

'This is your initiation on board the *San Sousiand*, you must take the whole four of these shots into your pretty cunt,' and they threw me on one of the cushioned seats and, opening my legs, my belly and slit lay open to their lust.

I got soundly fucked by four pricks – one after the

Madge

other, either of which would make a girl heave her belly, throw up her legs and spend! My cunt was as full as an ocean of water; I panted, writhed like a worm, and with glad ears drank in their words of appreciation as they shot into me their spermy fluid.

I lay, with legs fallen apart, panting breasts, heaving belly, and gaping slit; Mary hugging, kissing and congratulating me, until she saw the Chinaman leering at us from the galley. Springing up she rolled on her back at my side, opened wide her thighs and, that long slim cane was soon scratching the red and itching interior of her crevice.

A week of this; living around loose, and exchanging with each other every form of licentious lust – to describe it would be endless. I must turn to the last chapter, of our welcome at Beauvoir.

XXII

We sailed up the Mississippi to as near Beauvoir as we could, and Mary, Phil and I rode to the hermitage of my desires. Peering through the window, we beheld John and Ralph reading in the library. I undressed entirely, then ran into the house and stood, eagerly happy, before my darling lovers.

Wild with delight and made to enjoy me, I denied them until, as naked as myself, first Ralph, then John, with firm, fierce, frenzied pricks, fucked me frantically.

I threw myself on their dear fallen spears and with lewd, loving lips and tongue, brought them to life again. Then Mary and Phil came bounding through the window, where they had watched the first shots fired, and faced us, naked.

'Now I'll introduce you to my husband, as you did to yours,' and guiding Ralph's prick into her, we watched these lusty lovers taste for the first time the sweets of cock and cunt.

Then, John quickly sprang into her saddle and her husband into mine and our jockeys, riding gallantly, our bellies were soon inundated at the first finish of frenzied fucking.

Glancing through the window I spied Sam. I darted out and threw myself in his arms. 'Strip, quick, and carry me into the house on your prick.' And, in a minute, his staff was deep in my belly and, running full tilt, he entered the house and fucked me before the whole company. I squirmed off my still stuck up slit-sticker and, turning it to Mary's face: 'Kiss it – suck it – make it firm again, so he can give your slit a creamy womb opener.'

With her labial touches, his prick was stiffened, swelling glands filled her mouth and, grabbing her, he threw her on her back and fucked her into a spasm of spending.

In the doorway appeared my darling Meg, and I led her in, and tearing off her clothes, I turned to Phil: 'Isn't she pretty? Brown Venus!' 'Splendid!' and quickly his hands and lips fired at her every touch. 'My slit's on fire – seething,' she cried, and on the couch he gave her a fervent fuck.

We supped naked, each of us drinking a full bottle of champagne. In a dancing, prancing, devil-may-care stage of intoxication, we seven naked, in a group of writhing bodies close together, staggered and reeled into the parlour. And all in a bunch, topsy-turvy, kneeling, lying down, cocks in cunts, in culs, in titties, mouths and hands, we went off together and were flooded, inside and out, with showers of sperm, faces and forms glistening with the shiny emissions and cocks, cunts and mouths covered with the exuberant overflow.

I was too far gone to watch the others. I know that one of the fellows' whiskered mouths was kissing my bottom, thighs and belly and opening my slit. A languid tongue was licking the ruby interior while a fallen prick was six inches from my face. I took it in my mouth and rolled my tongue over it, pulling the hair with my teeth and, taking the crumpled skin in my mouth feasted upon the pearly drops that still oozed from it. John attempted to go out to make water, but Mary took his flabby prick in her mouth and, I could see by the motions of her throat she was swallowing his come.

Strangling, she jumped up, shouting, 'Oh, it makes me want to come, too.' John putting his head in her slit cried, 'Come, then!'

Jumping to his feet he seized the shameless Mary, holding the big thighs wide open and, putting her cunt on Sam's big prick, wrapped her legs around his waist. Pushing his cock out for me to wet, he took it out of my mouth and pointed it at Mary's bum, entered it, and the delighted girl screamed with pleasure. Fucking briskly, each cock plunged in and out at the same time, then giving out screams of overwrought excitement, she received the streams from both cocks. And, as her stallions fell exhausted on the floor, she threw herself on top of them and seemed to be eating up their fallen pricks.

The other two men rushed to me and, one in my cunt and one in my mouth, flooded me with sperm and rapture.

Sam, stooping down, put his arms between our legs and, lifting us up, forked thus, and off with us to our room, where he bathed us, laid us in bed as each pressed a goodnight kiss on his pego and he on our slits.

XXIII

But, dear Jack, I must stop somewhere, and it shall be with this chapter.

The men arranged a fishing trip and we, poor girls, were left vacant. While lamenting our luck, I heard the gate open, and looking out saw the priest who had married us, coming up the walk.

Laying Mary flat on her back on the sofa I opened the front of her dress to expose her bubbies and, raising, one knee, pulled her skirts up so that, by stooping, he could get a full view of her coral cavity. Then I hid myself behind a curtain.

When no one responded to his knock he walked to the piazza and finding the shutters were opened he walked in.

Mary's form caught his eye and in a minute he was kneeling at her side: 'Holy Virgin, what a pretty prick pleaser,' he muttered, but as he looked closer, 'That isn't the girl I fucked on her wedding night: it might be the other fellow's wife.' He gently lifted her skirts, and, as if moving in her sleep, she let her legs drop wide open and he had the whole kingdom of heaven exposed to him. Jumping up he took out his monster, then knelt between her legs, lifting them up, the true cross which women love to bear was quickly stored away in her innermost sanctuary.

'Oh, I can't play asleep!' cried Mary. 'It's too heavenly! Fuck harder if you'd save me from eternal regrets. Come, Madge, and see this royal priest's relic giving my cunt a sample of the church's creamy charity. As fast as you like, father, I'm ready.'

As I watched the charming cunt and colossal cock charging at each other with such rapidity, I grew dizzy and fell back on the floor.

In a minute the priest's sperm-spouting prick was relieving me of my rich store of oily oblation as Mary knelt beside us and squeezed the balm out of his buttocks.

He did not leave us till all our holes had hotly held his fresh and fecundatious prick. When he left, a pecker pronely pulseless, or testicles more wholly empty, could not be found in the buttock wagging world.

Walking along the brook the next day, we heard, 'Mine's bigger than yours – I bet I can shoot it further than you!' and we looked down on two lads finishing their bath, and playing with their stiff cocks.

'They'll waste it if we don't hurry,' said Mary. 'You naughty boys, aren't you ashamed to play with those things! They don't belong to you at all, but are for the girls.' And pulling me beside her, she dragged my skirts to my waist, and I did the same to her. We soon had they pretty pricks plugging us to the delight of the four. Then we let them examine us and they were soon again deep in our slits.

When we continued our walk we came upon a black man slouching along. He stood still and I saw his lustful eyes on our trim figures, and I knew he was thinking how easy it would be to rape us both.

I walked up to him. 'Do you remember me?' He looked doubtful. 'I've seen you, Miss, but ain't placed you'. Then – 'Hell,' he cried. 'This tells me,' and he pulled out his monstrous cock. 'I fucked you a year ago.' And in two minutes I was fucked again.

'Oh,' cried Mary, 'help' and she grasped her burning slit. But the man, grabbing one of us in each arm, carried us, running to his hut and threw us on the same grassy mound my rump had pressed a year before.

Another black man, naked, appeared at the door. 'Hurry, Bob. I've fucked one and the other wants it bad!' And, as the lust-burned girl opened her legs, the twin of the last erection was plunged, and lunged into a hole hot enough to turn an anchorite into a satyr. And, the dancing belly received a load that made her feel that heaven and earth were in conjunction on the fiery bed of hell. We stripped bare, and I threw the hot bellied girl again on her back and put her lover's prick into her slit. I then knelt with my gaping grotto over her face, and with her late gizzard tickler plunged into it, I felt her licking my well-filled cunt and my stallion's flying shaft, till as he was spending I jerked it out and stuck it in her face, watching her with one giant in her cunt and a sperming spigot in her eager mouth.

One of the men threw himself on the girl, pierced her with his rampant prick, then rolled over on the ground, finally stopped with Mary on top, till, with a lustful cry she sprang up and squatted over his mouth, and seized his fallen monarch reeking with albumen in her mouth.

The other fellow picked me up and, belly to belly started running, forcing his prick in me as we went, and fucked me on the fly until we spent. Then he dropped me on my elbows, seized my legs and spiked as I was turned completely over and continued to fuck me till, exhausted, he fell beside me and licked my lust laden slit as I sucked his giant prick.

Enough! Dear Captain Jack! If this works on you as it does on me, all the squaws on the plains will be giving birth to Little Jack Gardners, Jr.

Still with the bunch; when your next furlough comes we will welcome you.

I will not justify myself for writing frankly, for my voluptuous soul snaps its fingers in the face of respectability.

I am made of flesh and blood, and all it can accomplish, on pleasure bent, I would experience.

Pucker, poor prude! Pinch yourself in the dark, under the bedclothes, run away from a man in his shirt-sleeves – but for me – give him to me flesh to flesh, lips to lips, breast to breast, belly to belly, and his bold, blissful cock carrying rapture to my ever yearning cunt – I live for lust alone!

More Erotic Fiction from Headline:

FOLLIES OF THE FLESH

ANONYMOUS

FOLLIES OF THE FLESH -

drunk on carnal pleasure and inspired by the foolish excitement of their lust, the crazed lovers in these four delightful, naughty, bawdy tales flaunt their passion shamelessly!

Randiana: the scandalous exploits of a witty young rogue whose wanton behaviour is matched only by his barefaced cheek...

The Autobiography of a Flea: the notorious misadventures of sweet young Bella, as chronicled by one who enjoys full knowledge of her most intimate desires...

The Lustful Turk: imprisoned in an Oriental harem, a passionate Victorian miss discovers a world of limitless sensual joy...

Parisian Frolics: in which the men and women of Parisian society cast off propriety and abandon themselves in an orgy of forbidden pleasure ...

Other classic erotic collections from Headline:
**THE COMPLETE EVELINE
LASCIVIOUS LADIES
THE POWER OF LUST**

FICTION/EROTICA   0 7472 3652 6

A selection of bestsellers from Headline

FICTION
RINGS	Ruth Walker	£4.99 ☐
THERE IS A SEASON	Elizabeth Murphy	£4.99 ☐
THE COVENANT OF THE FLAME	David Morrell	£4.99 ☐
THE SUMMER OF THE DANES	Ellis Peters	£6.99 ☐
DIAMOND HARD	Andrew MacAllan	£4.99 ☐
FLOWERS IN THE BLOOD	Gay Courter	£4.99 ☐
A PRIDE OF SISTERS	Evelyn Hood	£4.99 ☐
A PROFESSIONAL WOMAN	Tessa Barclay	£4.99 ☐
ONE RAINY NIGHT	Richard Laymon	£4.99 ☐
SUMMER OF NIGHT	Dan Simmons	£4.99 ☐

NON-FICTION
MEMORIES OF GASCONY	Pierre Koffmann	£6.99 ☐
THE JOY OF SPORT		£4.99 ☐
THE UFO ENCYCLOPEDIA	John Spencer	£6.99 ☐

SCIENCE FICTION AND FANTASY
THE OTHER SINBAD	Craig Shaw Gardner	£4.50 ☐
OTHERSYDE	J Michael Straczynski	£4.99 ☐
THE BOY FROM THE BURREN	Sheila Gilluly	£4.99 ☐
FELIMID'S HOMECOMING: Bard V	Keith Taylor	£3.99 ☐

All Headline books are available at your local bookshop or newsagent, or can be ordered direct from the publisher. Just tick the titles you want and fill in the form below. Prices and availability subject to change without notice.

Headline Book Publishing PLC, Cash Sales Department, PO Box 11, Falmouth, Cornwall, TR10 9EN, England.

Please enclose a cheque or postal order to the value of the cover price and allow the following for postage and packing:
UK & BFPO: £1.00 for the first book, 50p for the second book and 30p for each additional book ordered up to a maximum charge of £3.00
OVERSEAS & EIRE: £2.00 for the first book, £1.00 for the second book and 50p for each additional book.

Name ....

Address ....

....

....